Michael John is a retired Master Mariner. In a full career at sea he commanded a wide range of ships across the world.
Isabella is his second novel of three published books. Much of the historical background has been drawn from family records.
Michael John has a daughter, twin sons and seven grandchildren
He sails his own traditional boat and lives on the river Tamar.

This book is for my grandchildren in the hope that only by examining history they can appreciate the unknown of the future.

Michael John

ISABELLA

AUSTIN MACAULEY PUBLISHERS™

LONDON · CAMBRIDGE · NEW YORK · SHARJAH

A CIP catalogue record for this title is available from the British Library.

ISBN 9781398464421 (Paperback)
ISBN 9781398464438 (ePub e-book)

www.austinmacauley.com

First Published 2022
Austin Macauley Publishers Ltd®
1 Canada Square
Canary Wharf
London
E14 5AA

Isabella or Guns, Dollars, Cotton and Sterling

Sold into slavery to one of the last British ships before it was abolished in 1807, the surgeon of the slaver Eva is besotted by Isabel; bids and wins her at the slave market in Savannah; escaping with her to Boston where he becomes a wealthy doctor.

On his death, Isabel takes her maid Molly to Niagara Falls, Canada, in 1863 on hearing that it is the destination of the underground railway, wishing to help fleeing slaves from the south.

In New York, Agnatha, a well-connected abolitionist lady, persuades her nephew; who is in love with a southern girl returning to her parents plantation; to join the Union navy. Then hearing of Isabel, sets off to Cincinnati to establish a travel agency helping escaping slaves on their way to Lake Erie. In Liverpool, two brothers, the sons of a cotton importer; travel to America with their sister to provide a pathway for guns in and cotton out. The sister, sympathetic to women's liberation and the plight of the slaves, agrees to take a young girl to safety up the Mississippi into Canada. She meets Agnatha and Molly, and discovers the awful truth that her grandfather possibly had a connection with Isabel.

Isabel charters a ship to bring slaves to safety across Lake Erie, and allows Molly to go on the first ship. Molly returns hanging on to the arms of a Canadian doctor working on behalf of the government; as the rescued slaves tumble ashore and kiss the ground in relief, but it is all too much for Isabel.

Chapter 1

The girl stood sullenly on the low stage with a cardboard tag around her neck; alternatively looking skywards and blinking at the midday sun; or rolling her big eyes and staring at her feet. She rubbed one ankle and then the other where the coarse rope had hobbled her since they left the ship. Around her body a tattered calico dress tied roughly at her middle gave her some sense of modicum. Her only possession was a hollowed pipe from which she could produce a sound when she had the energy to blow it. It was tied to her wrist and now lay at her thigh dangling every time she moved.

She was in a line of women and children and indeed babies, as two had been born during the six weeks of the voyage from Africa, all waiting for they knew not what. But almost certainly it was not something that they were looking forward to; but then if the experience of the voyage was anything to go by, it could hardly be worse.

In the distance, she could hear men's voices crying, shouting and wailing in her native tongue, and the occasional crack of a whip and the constant harsh shouting. They had been separated as soon as they were marched, stumbling and dragged off the ship. Although it was peaceful in the stockade surrounded by a wall and buildings, the like of which she had never seen before; it was in complete contrast to the bedlam of the ship and the serenity jarred her body. She shuddered as she remembered the incessant noise, jostling, beating of breasts, tearing of hair and the constant smell of human waste as they lay in the dark hold of the ship; sore from the constant rolling of the ship and the chains that held them down.

For the past week, they had been cajoled and nursed by two aged women who spoke a similar tongue and whose role was to prepare their charges for the coming auction. They were washed, groomed and their sores treated; and then fed until they could eat no more in an effort to fatten them up to produce the best possible price for the Captain and his supernumerary, the son of the ship's owner. Whilst the Captain searched for a cargo home that might take weeks, the supernumerary would be despatched back to England on the fastest available boat when the auction was concluded.

The girl cast her mind back to the memory of the voyage as she waited for the proceedings to begin—a trial for something that she did not commit, as if she were a felon or murderer. If the weather was fine when the ship was at sea, a chink of light would appear above them as a corner of the hatch was lifted and in turn they might be dragged up to the deck, in small numbers, re-secured and washed down. Over mealtimes, three crew would appear down a ladder, that was quickly removed for safety, to feed them from wooden tubs going down the lines of the shackled slaves. For those that refused to eat they would be taken on deck and their mouths forced open by a special tool that wound the jaw apart.

She felt the weal on her left shoulder which had been stamped by the Captain of the Trunk in Africa, weeks before with the initials of the ship. It was healing well, unlike those on the men who were herded onto the ship. The girl shuddered at the thought of the officer on board whose role was to look after the health of her fellow prisoners. It was the same man who had ensured that she and the rest of the women were only lightly marked by the iron, and who had persuaded the Captain to allow the women on deck in the afternoons.

Under an old sail strung out between the rigging he brought out toys for the children and same musical instruments for the adults. Most of the time the instruments lay untouched. Such was the trauma of those on board who had nothing to do; nothing but lay about resting from the bedlam in the hold, but after a week or two curiosity gave way and muted amusement could occasionally be heard.

It was the same man who had found her extra food as the voyage went on, and gave her shelter in his cabin that he shared with the man that controlled the meagre food for all on board.

The girl's hand strayed to the card that hung across her breasts, which were small with upturned nipples and only just concealed by the dress, and turned it round in an effort to see what was written on it. During the latter part of the voyage the surgeon, who had eventually taken her to his bunk and named her Isabel after his sister; who, he said, had died a long way away.

She smiled faintly as she recognised the name, but she did not recognise the numbers and letters beneath it. The card stated her age as possibly sixteen years, skin Negro, light possibly mulatto by birth.

Six days previously, the crew of the slaver *Eva* out of Exeter, Devon, a total of twenty men had manhandled the two hundred and ten males, fifteen females, five children and two babies off the ship at Savannah. Only by diligent attention by the Captain, the Purser, and the surgeon, who was only an apothecary's son just out of his training, had they lost only six slaves.

It was the Captain's third voyage, two of which had been as Captain and the trade sickened him. Now that the 1807 Act had outlawed British shipping in the slave trade, his only wish was to get his cargo safely in port and return home to invest in a trading vessel around Europe. Looking after the welfare of the slaves was a priority for a cargo safely delivered meant a good return for his owners and a satisfactory reward for him.

He counted the deaths on one hand. Four slaves, all men. It was always men, and all from the melancholy depression. He looked around at his crew all younger than himself. And youngest of all was the supernumerary, the son of the owner and far too arrogant, he thought; but that was due to his upbringing more than anything else. The voyage could only be considered a success when the slaves had recovered from their ordeal, been fed, watered, paraded and sold and a letter of credit was in his hands.

A week was considered to be time enough to restore them fit for an auction.

It was no easy task shuffling men joined by chains at the neck down a gangplank four feet wide when for the voyage ended. During the passage their ankles had been shackled permanently, with only an occasional break when they were allowed on deck in small numbers. The sick were carried ashore and laid graciously under the nearest shade.

Almost without exception the fit slaves fell to the ground, wept profusely and had to be dragged away to the nearest secure stockade. Their first night on land—the land of America, that mass of a continent that could accommodate all of the free world, but not those who came by the southern route of Africa. They would be shackled for life to the man or woman who would buy them, use them and probably at some time beat them.

The girl's attention was taken by the sound of the gate being swung open. She looked at the other women in the line and shuddered. Some began to weep and wail sensing that a repeat of what they endured two months earlier was about to happen. The children clung to their mothers legs wrapping their arms about them tenaciously, not daring to look towards the noise as two score of men shouldered each other into the yard, swinging bottles or alcohol, their jaws champed at cigars and swearing profusely at each other.

Whether they were buying or just observing, the sale of African slaves was an event not to be missed. As the courtyard filled up with this motley crowd of overseers and general layabouts; right on time the plantation owners suddenly appeared in their horse and traps. Self-assured men, snappily dressed, stepped down one by one and made their way through the gathering crowd to take centre stage.

It was midday and despite the heat the girl shivered and a tear escaped down her cheek; followed by another and yet another, until she was convulsed with fear of the inevitable. She looked around for a friendly face and recognised three faces from the ship as they stood well back from the surging mass of men gesticulating at the line-up of the unfortunate women. Of the three, only the surgeon, the man who had shown her some kindness; had fed her scraps from the officers table; the man who had shown her the instrument at her side; and the man who had tenderly caressed her body, and finally concluded their union, showed any recognition.

A week earlier, the *Eva* had made its slow approach up the channel to the port, assisted by two rowing boats that would take them up with the tide and anchor the ship to wait for a suitable berth. On either side of the wide river, apart from the quays docks and the town, wide mud banks stretched as far as the eye could see.

A strange calm hung over the slaves now that the motion of the ship had lessened, the cries were more muted, but the foetid smell of waste still prevailed despite the crew washing down the lower deck down with sea water and disinfecting vinegar. The girl quietly twiddled with the instrument, from which she always could make a tune, deep in depression, secured in the cabin listening to the constant babble above her.

Even her lover said little in passing, going about his duties on deck with barely a smile. In a sign language, punctuated with a kiss and a caress, he had indicated that he would be leaving the boat as soon as the slaves were sold, and would be returning to some place afar together with another crew member, the owner's son. The Captain no longer needed them on the ship that was to be loaded with just cotton, tobacco and timber.

From a doorway a sharp faced man with penetrating eyes and a neat moustache and carrying a small box in one hand and a walking cane in the other marched purposefully across the courtyard. Placing his box behind the line of women, he consulted the sheet of paper in his hand and waited for the stragglers in the crowd to settle down to the business in hand; the business of selling the women and children in front of him to the highest bidder.

Wasters and potential bidders jostled each other examining the unfortunate souls in front of them until the auctioneer finally called them to order. The crowd fell silent. Almost camouflaged in the background, the Captain of *Eva*, supernumerary, surgeon and bosun watched mentally calculating the rewards. The sale of the men the previous day had already made the voyage worthwhile.

"Who will bid for this fine specimen," he called out as his assistant turned the unfortunate woman around to show her best attributes.

"Twenty dollars I bid," a voice at the back called waving a paper.

"And another ten," added another.

"Make it forty dollars and she's yours," the auctioneer called teasing out the bidders, who were trying to conceal their identity with nods and twitches.

"Sold for forty five dollars," the man on the rostrum bellowed banging his stick on the box to conclude the deal.

"Next one."

It had taken less than three minutes, and without delay the woman was bundled away by a half drunk clutching her with one hand and his receipt in the other. The auctioneer rattled through the sales with the brusqueness of a man, having done it many times before. Half an hour later, the only one left on the platform was Isabel, for that was the name given to her on the ship, clutching her penny flute and now calmly awaiting her fate.

"Start me off at forty dollars for this fine specimen, a maid for a lady, a mistress for a man," the man shouted urging the crowd to bid.

The crowd laughed, Isabel cowered, holding herself together and crying uncontrollably; understanding the significance of the actions, but not the words.

"Forty-five dollars," offered a voice, confirmed by tipping his hat.

"Come now," the auctioneer called, thinking the interest was tailing off. "Surely one of you would like to bed this girl while your wife is away shopping."

The babble in the yard gesticulated and dissolved into laughter. Isabel looked at the sky, her head shaking, her eyes rolling, sweat pouring down her back.

"Fifty dollars," countered a man at the edge of the crowd.

"Fifty-five," waved the man with a battered hat.

"And another five," came another entering the bidding.

Isabel looked into the crowd trying her best to see who was bidding for her. It was a sea of faces that was a blur in front of her. She turned away involuntarily and put her hands to her face.

"Sixty dollars. For the first time. For the second time."

The auctioneer on the rostrum raised his stick ready to bang it down hard on the timber box.

"Sixty-five dollars "came a voice at the back as the stick thundered down catching the auctioneer slightly off guard.

"Sold," he declared, somewhat surprised that he had brought the matter to a close, when there was possibly another bid in the offing.

"Name?" he questioned the successful bidder, who stepped forward trying to push his way forward.

"James Nugent."

"Whereabouts in his county?"

"Surgeon from the good ship *Eva*. Slaver out of Exeter, England and inward from Africa," the man answered in a clear strong voice.

The crowd, never having never seen such a result at an auction before, gasped and turned round to see the man that had made the final bid. On the platform, Isabel brushed off a lighted cigar with her left hand which had been thrown at her, and was searing her shoulder.

Bottles, papers and spit rained down on the surgeon, thrown by the followers of the plantation owners, whilst the officers of the *Eva* formed a barrier around him, until the auctioneer called for order and declared a fair bid.

James made his way through the still angry crowd.

"Are you sure that you don't want to re-consider?" the auctioneer suggested, noticing the smartest of the men in the crowd raise his hand.

"No," said Nugent, looking the man square in the eye, "Definitely not. I made a fair bid."

"That man over there will give you a good profit," the auctioneer said.

"Absolutely not, she's mine," Nugent replied.

"Then I suggest, Sir," the auctioneer said wrapping up his papers, "in your own interests that you take her and get the hell out of town before nightfall."

The surgeon nodded understanding the implications.

"You realise you've thwarted one of most powerful landlords in the County," the auctioneer reminded him.

"But it was a fair bid."

"It was indeed."

The auctioneer counted out the dollar notes one by one and a promissory note against the ship, which in total made up the sum for the girl; who now looked even more shaken and forlorn from her ordeal on the platform. Surrounded by the senior crew of the *Eva* with a coat slung over shoulders, she could still hear the shouts of the bystanders as they melted away to the bars and the coffee shops, hurling abuse as they went. But it was still better than the terrible rancorous noise that she had heard daily on the ship.

"Just take my word for it and get away fast," the auctioneer continued with his advice.

"I just can't understand it," he added, "How you want to buy a girl here just beats me. Your job was to bring us the slaves, not purchase them."

The surgeon said nothing waiting patiently for the lecture to end.

"What was your name again?" he asked reaching for his pen to complete the sale. "Nugent was it not, from Exeter."

"The ship is from Exeter," the young ship's officer explained, "but I was brought up and indentured in Lincolnshire in the shadow of the Stump, and finally at Edinburgh medical school."

"That's Boston on the Wash flats by the sound of it. Heard of it," the auctioneer questioned as he wrapped up his papers. "An immigrant ship from Boston arrived here some thirty years ago, but most didn't stay around these parts."

"Yes," came the flat reply from Nugent, 'that's the place, a place to get away from if you can."

"Then I suggest that you don't stop until you reach Massachusetts over here," the auctioneer said. "It'll take you three months hard travelling and the country won't be too friendly until you cross the Delaware river. And take your friends with you until you're well out of town."

"Thank you for the advice," the surgeon replied wishing to get away from the place as soon as possible.

After fifteen miles, half riding and half walking the two of them settled down for the night and ate the food scrambled together by the cook. The girl snuggled into his heavy coat and she reached into the pocket and felt the folded sheet which the man had secreted away not realising the significance of it, but understanding that it was a treasured piece like the little instrument that was tucked away in the folds of her dress.

Earlier they had stopped for a break and the man had brought out a book of maps. She had seen the men on the ship looking at something similar on the ship. He gesticulated where she had come from, and where he was born; and where they were going, indicating the journey by putting his hands together on the side of her head and counting. She looked at the map comparing it to the nights on the ship, shivered a little and took his hand. The man's horse hobbled and tethered, snorted and continued munching some fresh grass.

"Will it be warm," she asked with actions wriggling her body.

He smiled and kissed her warmly holding her tight.

"Maybe," he said after a short delay. "Maybe."

She looked puzzled, ruffled his hair and cupped his head in her hands. It really didn't matter where they were going. She snuggled into the warmth of the great coat. Nothing mattered as she was safe, and safe for life.

Chapter 2

A pale morning sun percolated through the trees of Boston common, casting light shadows into second floor drawing room of the town house. It overlooked the pond that scalloped itself around a clump of trees so that, at no time was the water visible from any one position. It was a typical spring morning. Early walkers moved energetically around the paths scattering the birds that were looking for the first breakfast of the day. Ducks squired their brood across the water in a broad veer towards the shelter of the far side, the babies dibbling away at scraps as they tried to keep up with the mother.

Net curtains kept the room cool in the hot summers and heavy drapes kept out the cold in the winters. In winter, Boston could be cold; very cold and then the maid would keep the fire burning in the grate on an almost continuous basis. The room was airy with a high ceiling, decorated with some elegance and filled with quality furniture that the owners had acquired over the years. A popular designed Empire couch richly upholstered in velvet occupied a dark corner in the room and an early Chickering grand piano stood where it would get the afternoon and evening sun. The lady occasionally tinkled with the keys when she was bored, but although she could hold a tune, she had never totally mastered it; and it was reserved for the visiting guests that they regularly entertained.

Every two months the couple would hold a musical soirée inviting the cream of the Boston society. As a doctor of some acclaim, John Nugent and Isabel were never short of guests and entertainment. Two watercolours of the fall at its best and an oil painting of the harbour hung on the two walls that never saw the sun. On the piano lay a well-used flute, the first instrument that the lady of the house had learnt to play. It was scratched and damaged with the original piece of twine holding it together and was now beyond use as an instrument. But it had a much travelled history and possibly a hundred years old and was at one time the only possession of the lady who walked slowly over to the desk where a beam of sunshine focused on the leather scrolled top.

Standing at her late husband's desk, the lady reached into the top drawer and slowly extracted a crumpled piece of parchment. She had seen it before, but not for some years as her doctor husband did not like being reminded of it. The sun fell onto her face, highlighting her once fine features and delicate skin as she scanned the document that she laid on the desk and ironed out the creases.

Her once luxurious hair now thinned and very definitely grey fell over her eyes and she gently brushed it away only for it to fall back again. Taking a deep breath as tears rolled down her cheeks, she read through the few lines her forefinger pausing slightly over the stark words in ink that was barely readable.

She never knew how old she was, but then did it matter. Without doubt as she looked back into her long life she knew that very definitely she had been lucky beyond belief. Her memory of her mother was so dim that it was as if she did not exist.

She thought she had been taken from her well before the forced march from the jungle shackled to another girl of her age by two forked sticks that were secured around their necks so that they had to walk in unison. Neither did she know her father, although her mother had told her as a child that she thought he was a Portuguese trader, who had travelled by canoe up the Niger delta.

She thought she was approaching the age of seventy, knew that she was a mulatto child by birth and was rescued from slavery. Before that her life was buried in a haze of people in close proximity being pushed and shoved; and noise, the constant noise of shouting, weeping and sobbing. Isabel looked at the faded parchment again as her maid came into the room with a tray of tea, and showed it to her servant with whom she had a strong bond developed over the years

As a free servant in the Union, she had little education beyond the basics, but she was bright and intelligent and had worked for her mistress the past ten years. The girl looked blankly at the piece of paper before her. She had never seen it before during all her years of tidying and cleaning her mistress's house. Not surprisingly it had been locked away by the man of the house, the doctor with a secret and a man with a kind heart and an accent that clearly showed he was not an American by birth.

Now though, he had been buried only a few months earlier and her mistress was going through the painful process of sorting out his business, the surgery on the ground floor and the dispensary in the adjacent room. Here he kept a skeleton strung up from the ceiling and rows of large glass bottles, which from time to time she dusted under his strict supervision.

The girl blanched as her mistress handed her the paper and invited her to read the words that seemed to spring out of the faded paper. Usually radiating humour,

Molly turned away as the words struck home and then her composure failed and holding out her arms as tears rolled down her cheek she embraced her mistress, something she had never done before.

The document that the lady held was not a marriage certificate, of which she already had a copy in her own papers, with her signature and that of her husband and a known witness, but was one of an equally binding nature.

In plain and simple language it showed that she was bought and sold as a slave. The date was smudged where the ink had run, but the year could be made out. It was 1808.

Over four hundred miles to the south a tall gaunt faced man sat alone at his desk penning yet another letter outlining the severity of the problem that faced him, asking for all assistance possible. He had been in post only a few months, had been a politician and lawmaker for most of his life, yet the burden of the position was taking its toll on his health; and although only in his early fifties he could well pass for a man ten years older. It was a matter of the utmost urgency.

He scrolled his draft in a flourishing hand underlining the importance of the request pleading that if help did not arrive there was no way of knowing how the country would survive. He signed it, then sealed it and left it on the pile for his secretary in the morning. The last of the wick on his lamp flickered away as he stretched out his cramped limbs, snuffed the light out, and lay down on the couch in the corner of his study pulling a blanket over his tired body. Down the hall a clock struck two o'clock. Sleep would be difficult, he knew. It was likely that he would be awake and back at his desk before his staff were aroused.

Across the Atlantic, another leader was having an equally difficult time holding his party together and keeping Parliament in line when his opposition opponent was snapping at his heels, and rebel members were warning that mill owners in the north of the country were becoming restless. The House of Commons had not been so rowdy since the Crimean War. Such was the tension across the benches that the Speaker was having difficulty calling the House to order, threatening to abandon the proceedings if order was not restored.

In Liverpool an agitated shipowner, business man and cotton trader was scheming with his sons over dinner whilst his rebellious daughter, aided and abetted by a chance meeting with a Presbyterian leader was preparing to attend a meeting of workers in a town just north of Manchester. Her parents had despaired of her ever taking life seriously, and now approaching her mid-twenties her unorthodox statements were both surprising and challenging to the family's conservative views.

Tucked away near South Street Seaport at the southern end of Manhattan, a middle aged lady boiled a kettle on the stove and made a pot of tea for four teenagers gathered around her kitchen. After twenty five years sailing around the trade routes of the world with her husband, she had decided to swallow the anchor, even though he had decided to make another voyage. As a Captain of tea clippers for some of that time, he was now taking a cargo carrying workhorse of a four masted ship to South America.

At sea she had spent much of that time mothering, teaching and educating young apprentices in their chosen career whilst immersed in a tough man's world, and now she was setting up part of her home as a respite for apprentices and young officers when their ships were in New York. If the sea was a wild place to be, then New York could match it by day and by night.

It was certainly not a good place to be after dark when the street corners where the shadows could hide a man prepared to take a life for a dime. A tough lady with a ready smile, but a steely determination when times were tough; she had no hesitation in tending a sick and injured seaman, nor laying out a man with a bottle who was threatening her husband with a knife on her last voyage.

A native of Bristol, which she had left some twenty years earlier, she was expecting her nephew in two weeks' time, coming in on his second voyage from England.

In the North Atlantic, a New York bound passenger ship approached Bermuda on an unscheduled stop, that aroused suspicion from a young British Merchant Navy officer, who was concerned by an unmarked assignment of cargo stowed on the ship late at night. Five years out of his apprenticeship in the tea clipper trade and on a store ship during the Crimean War, and recently in the possession of a Master's licence; his career was progressing slowly, but not quite fast enough for his ambition.

He was now Second officer on a liner registered in Glasgow, but sailing out of Liverpool and he was scanning the low profile of the island from the bridge as they approached the pilot-age station. It was just another voyage apart from two small consignments of boxes at the forward end of number four hold, which had been loaded just before they sailed. They were almost identical, one of them being for discharge at Bermuda, the other continuing to New York itself.

In Scotland, a brilliant but ageing ship's engineer was perfecting the latest design for his steam paddle vessel in the shadow of the big rock at Dumbarton, which would outpace any vessel currently at sea. He was expecting a visit from a ship broker the following morning with three Americans, apparently intent on buying the vessel just coming off the stocks, or indeed any fast vessel that was on the market.

Newly berthed in Queens Dock, Liverpool, one of the latest Leyland passenger ships, the *S.S. Etna* prepared to discharge its cargo. A mixture of humanity from the New World, businessmen, chancers in life, thieves, entertainers and some just disenchanted with the state that America was heading towards. Catering for three classes of passengers and deep holds carrying about two thousand tons of cargo, she could complete the voyage from New York to Liverpool in ten days; taking only a day longer on the outward trip against the prevailing weather. Four Americans, two from first class and two from second class filed down their respective gangways from the ship and stood looking at the dismal surroundings. The man and lady were expecting to be met unlike the two men, who were making their own way with a list of possible contacts on arrival. They were on entirely different Missions, both with unlimited expenses to help them, and they were sworn to secrecy by their principals on the other side of the Atlantic.

In London, an American girl, one of the first university educated women in the south, engaged the previous year as a junior assistant at the American Embassy, looked forward to an interview and a consignment that she had been invited to attend at very short notice. Even after months of living in the Capital, the narrow winding streets and alleyways continued to confuse her; and the rancorous calling of the London street sellers never ceased to entertain her as she walked each day to her work. She was enthralled by the night life, the theatres and the museums, but even so was still homesick; and wondered when leave would allow her to return to her home and family on the banks of the Chesapeake.

In Wilmington, North Carolina, a feisty southern girl leafed through and tidied up piles of brochures at the local theatre, which had welcomed international stars on the stage in the previous decade but was now locked up out of use. The love of the theatre in the town had flourished in the previous century when Lord Cornwallis had made Wilmington his base, trying to keep America under the British Crown.

Nearby, a trusted second generation slave helped his Master lock up the warehouse on the dockside and another, a free man, fished in the waters of the Cape Fear river for the owner of the plantation that he lived on. The warehouse had just taken a delivery of two hundred tons of the finest cotton bales from Georgia by rail, and the building was now full of the crop awaiting shipment to England. But there was not a ship in the port. For the past three months, nothing more than local trading boats tied up at the quay.

The usual riotous humour of seamen in the bars and the brothels had been silenced at a stroke. The dead hand of anticipation lay over the town like a suffocating cloud. Fires could be spied out in the fields. It was not stubble that was being burnt, but crops of low quality cotton that had little value in the current market. The swamps around the whole coast was more suited to growing rice.

Cotton and tobacco that was usually destined for Europe, cotton that paid for the slave owners estates, their life styles, their women and their children. It certainly did not go towards paying the workers who produced the crops that made them the money. It was money that they craved and that went hand in hand with power for them and them alone, because the producers of the wealth were slaves; men, women and children who worked for nothing and were enslaved for life.

They reasoned that they had no obligation to pay them, as they had been bought and owned them lock, stock and barrel, body and soul. They provided them with shelter and food and had Sunday off as a day of rest. What more could they want in life. Where would they go. Was it not a better life than from where they came from with all its dangers?

In St Catharine, a small town on the bank of the Welland Canal, Canada, close to the Niagara falls, a clandestine group of Canadians gathered for their monthly meeting. Three generations ago these artisans had fled across from America in 1776 as loyalists to the Crown and then sailed across Lake Erie or Lake Ontario bringing with them their tools and skills. They were a people used to being on the move with a commitment to their close community. Generations before that they had arrived in the New World from Europe fleeing from persecution full of hope for the future.

They had no definitive agenda that evening after work as they gathered in their clap board hall adjacent to the brick built church, with a small bell tower over the west end that tolled only on Sundays. The community of three faiths were of a common mind to help those less fortunate than themselves and they had the money and the desire to achieve their beliefs.

The slow migration of escaping slaves from America had grown into a flood in the past year. The new speaker from the nearby town of Hamilton, and a delegation from Boston were expected to create a buzz not seen for a while in the community, and they were not to be disappointed, arousing them about the continual plight of black Americans trying to escape the conflict in the deep south.

For earlier that year on April 12th 1861 a black cloud swept up the Eastern Seaboard as a force of soldiers and seamen from the Southern States took their positions at the entrance to the Charles river, South Carolina; and waited for the signal to attack, without warning, their countrymen guarding Fort Sumpter on the north bank. Further to the north, a small group of Confederates walked up to the gates of Fort Fisher, at the mouth of the Cape Fear river, fifteen miles away from Wilmington, the largest earthen fortification in America; and known as the Gibraltar of the States, and demanded the keys from the Union sergeant, the sole person who was guarding it.

It was the final act after months of talks and concessions that had resulted in nothing but stalemate and confusion. The secession from the Union in December of 1860 had come to a head when the Confederate of Southern States seized an opportunity to declare war on that fateful morning, a conflict that was not concluded for some four years.

To them in the face of history over enslaved people, from the Egyptians to the Romans and beyond to the modern age, the right of Southerners to continually own and enslave black men and women, and even a new born babe only hours old, was considered sacrosanct—for life, forever.

Chapter 3

Alice May, the younger sister of Nicholas and James Forwood, and daughter of George and Charlotte, acknowledged the courteous salute and goodbye from the doorman as she sallied through the swing doors of Liverpool's latest and largest department store and stepped out into the cool of the early evening. She was one of their most regular customers.

A dusting of snow greeted her and she nearly slipped on the last step, where the flakes were starting to settle, but Alice quickly regained her balance. At twenty three years of age she had long fluid limbs and an easy stride. Her flaxen hair was covered up in a bonnet and a heavy military style long coat with deep slanted pockets that were all the rage.

Delicate fingers snuggled deep into fine kid gloves, and in her right hand she swung a hat box, which was the purpose of today's expedition. Alice adored her collection of fine hats, she loved her wardrobe and indeed her lifestyle which was one continual round of parties and entertainment, but with very little purpose if she was honest with herself. In fact, she was close to be bored with life.

Her education had been at one of Liverpool's most fashionable girls schools, at which she had hardly excelled even though she had an enquiring mind, her form teacher had admitted. A maiden aunt had dragged her off on a European tour at the end of her first term at a finishing school in Nancy, but she protested so much after two weeks of art galleries and ancient sites that she demanded to go home, much to the dismay of her father and the derision of her brothers. Only her mother, Charlotte, who remembered her own rebellious self as a child on her parents plantation, showed any sympathy realising that her daughter's frivolous personality hid a gritty latent determination that was yet to show.

Alice May was trying to find herself. She turned the key letting herself in quietly at the house in West Kirby listening for the usual sounds. Her mother's quiet but authoritative voice, the housekeeper's deep local scouse dialect and the cook's guttural sound, often percolated by a couple of octaves when she was flummoxed by orders coming from different directions. The problem was that although her father had responded to all her wishes, if not demands, being the last in line and a girl at that, she would rather he challenged her demands.

It was her mother, she thought, that really understood her. As for her brothers, she gave them little thought. They were just her brothers after all. Although she loved her father very much he was always giving in, a fact that annoyed her for much of the time. She only had to wag her little finger and what she wanted was hers, when she really wanted him to put up some opposition. She needed a different sought of man for a father, definitely a different sought of man for a lover, not that she had one, and a different life.

"Well my daughter might continue to surprise me but not so my boys," mused Charlotte to herself as she kissed her daughter in the warmth of the kitchen, continuing with her instructions to the cook for the evening meal.

One was in the mould of his father, and the other, in that of his grandfather; and therefore, quite opposites. James, younger by two years, was tall and lithe; all arms and legs, prone to arguments; loved debates and had gone to sea for a brief period around the world, but was still at a loose end. Nicholas, on the one hand, apart from a several months in the Low Countries with his father, had barely left the country and worked exclusively for the firm making his way in the business, as if on a railway track, and was now looking to be accepted as a partner. James, on the other hand, worked for several firms, with whom his father had good connections, but always casting his eye towards his next venture.

Charlotte was expecting them all to be home for supper that night, a rare event as they all seemed to have lives that were far too busy for her liking.

"Sherry, dear," she called out to her husband as he took off his coat and hat and draped them over the cumbersome looking stand in the hall. If it wasn't balanced properly with coats on either side it tended to lean and crash down scattering all before it like some cliff fall.

George looked at his wife and then to his daughter. They could be a mirror image, he thought with only the years between them. And what years they had been. A solid marriage of twenty eight years and three children, helped in part by his wife's share of money in the Emancipation Plantation Act, and his luck with the ageing partners of the firm Harrison and Leech, set up by his father many years before.

Alice kissed him warmly and turned to help her mother, fussing around quite unnecessarily in the dining room, because earlier the housekeeper and the cook had covered every eventuality.

"My day was utterly frustrating," he admitted accepting the drink and taking the nearest chair to the fire. "And yours, were you happy with your shopping, Alice?"

"Well, not really, Father," she teased him showing off her new hat. "It's just that I'm getting bored. My days are so predictable. The boys are always busy. Can't you find me something interesting?"

"And what do you have in mind, Alice?" he said, not for the first time. Usually she scorned his suggestions of finding the right man and bearing children so necessary for the country's future.

"Father, I'll be old before my time," Alice answered with a pout and headed upstairs.

George turned to the fire, gave the coals a shuffle to entice the flame and pondered, or so he thought to himself. "There's a flame smouldering there somewhere."

"I heard that, George," said Charlotte bringing her drink into the room. "Let's hope that its soon. There's no man in the offing that I know about, and at the moment she's on a road to nowhere."

"How was the meeting, Father?" asked Nicholas, the elder of the two, once the table was cleared and the cheese laid out.

George took the nose off the cheese to his wife's chagrin, apologised and then sliced another section to correct his error. At supper once, with the local bishop, he had been vilified at length and had never forgotten it.

"It was more like a conference on how to deal with the cotton diplomacy action taken by Jefferson Davis, the President of the Southern States, as you all know," he replied stabbing again at the cheese platter. "We laid in stocks two years ago on advice of the Board of Trade in anticipation of Davis trying to get us and France into the conflict. Now, nearly a year on those stocks are almost depleted and I heard only today that they have burnt a thousand tons of admittedly the lower grade cotton in Georgia in order to exert pressure on the price."

"Pressure on whom," Charlotte asked.

"Pressure on our government, I guess," George answered.

"That could destroy the industry here sooner than you might expect," suggested Nicholas, who only a couple of days ago had been in the Salt house dock warehouse checking stocks held by the firm.

They all knew that there hadn't been an inward consignment for over a month, and none was expected in the near future. And it wasn't just them. Every cotton trader in the country had similar empty warehouses and mill owners were laying off workers.

"And what did Mr Harrison say about it." James asked shifting his body around trying to get comfortable.

"Fifty years in the business, my lad, and all of it from the Americas, he lectured to me," Nicholas retorted, mimicking the old man's distinctive twang.

They had all heard it many times before, but for all that his opinion had never been rubbished by the three men in the room, such was the esteem they held for the man.

"So what's going to happen now?" the younger brother asked.

James' day had been spent in the Exchange Building, where cargoes were bought and sold; and shippers and Captains met to discuss world trade over numerous cups of coffee.

"As you know, scarcity brings price hikes," George reminded them, "but it's not always good in the long term."

"If the Confederates want war materials and we want cotton, and the only place to get guns and ammunition is right here in the United Kingdom or France, then I think that the question answers itself," Nicholas suggested to his mother's horror.

"Isn't that a bit immoral," she said.

"But the French are sure to fill the gap if we don't," Nicholas answered, not at all abashed by his stance.

"And neither should we encourage Americans to fight amongst themselves," Alice chipped in, having up to now contributed very little to the conversation. "It's an impossible situation for them, when half the country won't accept that slavery, the very thing we abolished years ago is, still an issue for them."

The others looked at her in amazement. Alice had never made such an outspoken statement before. Alice gave a little smirk, all of a sudden quite pleased with herself and disappeared into the kitchen.

George brought the conversation to order. "We have our priorities and they are to ourselves and the rest of the cotton factors, if not the mill owners and workers. Not including Glasgow, we have two thousand mills in Lancashire and half a million workers nationally, many of whom will starve if nothing is done."

"How does the government view it and the Monarch for that matter?" Nicholas asked as the conversation slowly subsided.

"Never mind the official view," George wound up, tiring of the discussion that seemed to have no solution. "Jefferson Davis is banking on cotton and arms winning the day."

"With the lure of the almighty dollar," James added, "and of course the pound note."

"Well, of course the government could bail out the industry in the meantime." Nicholas chipped in.

"I doubt that will happen." James offered to the conversation. "They aren't that smart! They prefer for the market to look after itself."

"At the moment, all we can do is wait and see," the head of the family conceded, "and hope that most of all the cotton still gets past the blockade in the Gulf."

"Don't you know what I am proposing to do, Father?" Alice May piped up. "You've organised everybody else."

"No, dear," he said close to ignoring her. "Just what are you going to do. Some more shopping?"

"No, Father, I've decided I have enough clothes to last a lifetime. Today I met a couple in Dalkey's, you know the latest coffee shop. There was nowhere else to sit. They're Missionaries on leave from Africa and tomorrow I am going to a meeting with them in Rams bottom. They've travelled the world and are so interesting and knowledgeable to talk to." The other four in the family looked up in amazement.

"They were telling me about a lady called Mary Seacole, a black nurse and a contemporary of Florence Nightingale." Alice explained without elaborating too much.

"You're going to meeting in Rams bottom supporting the mill workers?" Nicholas exploded with indignation, whilst George fumed with subdued rage. "You'll be wanting to support liberation of women next."

"Well, for the moment I want to hear what they say," Alice confirmed in a moment of defiance.

"Do you want me to come with you, dear?" Charlotte suggested trying to diffuse the pending argument, "and give you some support."

"I'd rather see for myself," she said, surprising herself at her stand.

28

"It could turn into something dangerous." Charlotte argued, "Why don't you try something else to latch on to?"

"No, Mother," she said, turning to them all. "I too would like to do something useful and I'm going by myself."

Charlotte turned to her husband as Alice flounced out of the room and gave him a reassuring smile. "You must have known it was coming sometime, George. I told you something was brewing but I didn't expect that. Some of these women's groups are quite intimidating I'm told."

"I suppose so," he said in resignation. "But who's this Mary Seacole and you know what I think about women working!"

"It's a fast changing world, dear," Charlotte confirmed to her husband. "I thought you always read the papers from cover to cover."

"For the moment you and I, James," said George, turning to his two sons, "are going on a trip to Glasgow, I've something mulling over in my brain, something we have not bothered with for a number of years, and I need to check out my yacht on Lake Windermere. We haven't been up there for some months and we can do that at the same time."

"I'm interested and game," James said jumping up and walking over to the fireplace to admire the sleek lines in the photograph on the mantelpiece and the smaller sister of the boat kept in Dartmouth for channel passages.

"But what's Glasgow all about?" he questioned before George could continue.

Glasgow was hardly an area of outstanding beauty. It was though the epicentre of the world's shipbuilding industry, and for five miles down the river the skyline was full of cranes and building ways. Not only that, but every facet of industry was being developed there. Railway engines, pumps, mining equipment, steel making powered by coal; and a ready supply of ores combined to make the Clyde valley the most concentrated area of industrial activity in the country.

"We're just not going to sit for things to happen that might just not happen at all," George said, trying to gauge his younger son's reaction. "You and I are going to see first-hand the latest technology at sea. I've an inkling we can turn this war to our advantage."

Nicholas looked at his brother, who in turn looked at his father. "When were you thinking of leaving, Father?"

"Just as soon as I can book the tickets," he said, head down, opening the latest periodical on shipbuilding in Scotland.

"And how was your visit to Rams bottom?" George asked his daughter on their return from Glasgow, hoping that she had not been inspired by all the meetings, which were being held throughout the Manchester area.

"Only by being there could you really understand the strength of support for anti-slavery in America," Alice stated as her father's face took on severe look of hurt.

"And what next?" he asked eventually.

"I'd like to go and see for myself," she said defiantly.

"And then?"

"I'm not sure, but my Missionary friends have colleagues there and offered me accommodation and to show me around," Alice replied "They say New England is a destination not be missed."

"I'll stop your allowance. I'm not having my daughter tour a foreign country and not know where she is." George fumed.

"I have to go. I need to go, and I am going with your blessing or not," Alice said finally, glaring at her father as she had never done before.

She turned and appealed to her mother, then stormed out of the room, leaving her father to wonder at the blow to his pride. Alice had never challenged him so before.

"Have you not forgotten, George," Charlotte said quietly, 'she is shortly due an inheritance from my mother."

Chapter 4

Joseph L Adams and Henrietta, his wife of fifteen years, looked out at the grey morning and stepped off the *S.S. Etna*, the latest steamer of the Inman line; and on to the broad first class gangway and carefully made their way to the shore. The last of the passengers to leave, they took their time savouring the skyline only to be met by the dismal surroundings of Liverpool in the damp morning.

The purser had told them the previous night over dinner that the ship would be berthing at Canada dock, but in the event the ship squeezed into the Queen's dock, a little closer to the city itself. Adams wondered which queen it was named after. He was not much enamoured with British Royalty, his grandfather having been killed by German troops in the pay of George, the Third; but he did have some respect for the Parliamentary system which was doing its best to help President Lincoln. Now he was more than pleased and proud to be representing him as his special envoy.

He sniffed the air and blew his nose, and sneezed twice as his wife busied herself on the quayside around the hand luggage. Passengers from the other classes were pouring on to the quay and already the hatches were open and cargo being pulled out by the spindly cranes, that scored great arcs across the grey sky like a fisherman landing his catch. Joseph and Henrietta looked at each. The noise, the grime, the rubbish that lay about was not what they expected, not to mention the pungent smell of the enclosed dock and the floating debris. They had left the clean air of the Eastern Seaboard, the never ending colours of the autumn and were now pitched straight into industrial England in one quick scoop.

Joseph had travelled extensively within the thirteen states, but apart from a conference trip to Quebec, where he could not understand why the Canadians were reluctant to speak English, had never travelled abroad before. He was on a Mission of great importance to the Union cause, and whilst his wife might well achieve considerable pleasure from the famed Regents Street and the drawing rooms of Mayfair, he expected to be locked into the pressure politics of

Westminster, commuting daily from the financial power house of the city to the intriguing machinations of Parliament.

Trained as a lawyer in Connecticut and a specialist in human rights, he and Lincoln had been colleagues over a number of years and was his man of the moment at short notice to bolster up the be beleaguered Ambassador, who was increasingly bending under pressure.

Diminutive in stature, but with the inner strength of a Democrat honed from many years in the courtroom, where his speciality was releasing former free slaves from trafficking gangs in New York working for plantation owners in the south, he relished the task ahead. He liked nothing more than a fierce debate across the benches and the satisfaction of a judgement that had gone his way.

Joseph mulled over his instructions whilst they waited for their guide to make an appearance. The ship's agent had assured them that the second secretary from the Embassy would be meeting and entertaining them at the Adelphi Hotel; whilst they recovered from their journey.

November was not one of the best months to travel the Atlantic, they had been advised in New York and so it proved to be true. A day of fog off Ambrose light, then several days of continual gales had exhausted them, reducing both of them at times to sickness and confinement to their cabin for much of each day. Although a new ship with comfortable first class accommodation, they were constantly aware of the pounding steam engine powering along in melodic tones, the groans from below them as the iron plates worked in the seaway and the shriek of the rigging as the wind tugged at the sails pitching the bow down.

Over conversation one evening, when the sea had subsided, the navigator had told them the sails enhanced the speed by two knots on a following wind. Anything that brought arrival day closer was music to their ears. Now any dry land, even though it was the drab banks of the Mersey, with Liverpool on one side and Birkenhead on the other, was as welcome as spring after a hard winter.

At two hundred and eighty miles a day, Joseph and Henrietta had plenty of time to go over their plans, read the ship's daily broadsheet and converse with their fellow travellers without saying too much about the reason for their visit, which they disguised as being a social Christmas holiday with family. A shrewd observer gained by observing adversaries in moments of stress Joseph, backed by his wife who was well used to his ways, made sure that he knew more about them than they knew about himself.

Gathering up their trunks and piling them onto a cumbersome trolley, the steward, who had looked after them throughout the trip manipulated the vehicle across railway lines and into the covered dank shed that was the clearing house for the customs. A converted brick single storied warehouse, it was no match for the elegant stone Doric columned building on the waterfront fronting the next dock downstream, where all the documentation for the port was processed. But such was the dramatic increase of passengers to and from America it would have to do until a dedicated reception hall could be built.

"Here we are," the steward announced reaching the desk just ahead of another couple with even more luggage. He had already been well rewarded for his attention during the voyage and hoped now to get a top up.

Adams looked around taking in the apparent dismal squalor.

"Can't go beyond the desk," the steward said, pocketing the loose change of American coin that would come in useful on the return voyage,

The crew had noticed that prices were slowly rising back in New York.

Extra dollars would certainly not go amiss for the runs ashore in Manhattan.

"There'll be plenty of assistance on the other side," he said cheerfully, thanking them profusely and touching his cap.

A shout from a smartly turned out couple on the other side of the barrier holding up a hand written plaque took their attention, as a cab driver heaved up the trunks and piled them haphazardly in the back of the cart, until Adams remonstrated with him, after which he secured them with a strap.

"Where to, mate?" the driver asked Adams in an irritating tone as the couple rushed over to introduce themselves.

"Sorry to be late," the man said as he hailed another cab "We caught the mid-afternoon train to Manchester yesterday and stayed there last night."

"Together." Henrietta interjected rather too quickly she realised, making the mistake of judging them before she had been introduced.

Their guides looked at each hiding a smile that said everything and nothing, and showed them their credentials from a folder that the girl held. Adams looked askance at his wife's indiscretion, but then she never minced her words.

The Adelphi Hotel was but a short ride from the docks and after a more relaxed introduction in the foyer, the programme for the next week was laid out for them starting with the following morning. It was to be a glad handing session briefly with the Mayor and the leading dignitaries of Liverpool, then the train straight to London. Adams looked at the brief. He hoped that it wouldn't take long. Most of the dignitaries seemed to have an undue interest in the southern cause, he noted.

"Just what is the real situation back home?" the young American diplomat asked the elder; whilst the two ladies sat on the other settee and established their common ground.

"Well, to be quite honest, it's going from bad to worse at the moment with the Confederates making some surprising ground," Adams confessed, "and we are having the devil of a job holding them."

"But surly we have all the resources, control the waterways and most of the railway network?" replied the other, rather incredulous to hear the latest news. "And that's without the industrial heartland."

"Yes, that's true but unfortunately they seem to have taken the initiative and caught the north on the hop," Adams outlined to the younger man.

On secondment from a course at West Point, one of his responsibilities in London was to assimilate the military reports and make certain that the Ambassador had every detail to hand. He was looking forward to his return to his regiment, but admitted privately to himself that he had no wish to be pitched into battle with his fellow countrymen.

It would not do to let his fellow officers know that he did not relish conflict of any description and fortunately his present appointment had given him time and respite. Perhaps resigning his commission was the only logical conclusion, but for now his current duties could put any such thoughts to the back of his mind.

"The battle of Manassas was a complete disaster," Adams continued outlining the finer details of the combat. "General McDonnell never expected to lose and General Jackson for the Confederates never expected to win."

"But that was within striking distance of Washington," the young soldier said. "Quite unbelievable. Emily, over there with your wife. Her family has an estate on the banks of the Potomac."

"Thirty miles to be exact. They were almost on the doorstep." Adams confirmed going back to the battle, "It's reckoned that he didn't carry on because his troops were so exhausted and he didn't allow for any reserves. But for now, I think we could do with a rest. What time have you booked dinner?"

"And how come that you are here in England, Emily?" Adams asked the girl, when the foursome met up for dinner that night moving the conversation away from the troubles three thousand miles away.

"Well, I've often wondered that myself," she said after something of a pause, "I always wanted to travel beyond the limitations of America and I never really fancied heading west, too uncivilised for me and dangerous as well. Europe's stormy history did interest me, but I was more drawn to that of the United Kingdom. I wanted to experience how the minority elite have managed to control the majority without the country being torn apart by revolution, and how it was a very small number of that elite managed to persuade Parliament to overturn slavery here."

"I think the British wondered that themselves," Adams replied. "But I'm sure I will find out in due course. We expect to be here at least six weeks."

"I would say that the time will run away with you," Emily replied. She had dressed simply but very effectively for the dinner something that had not gone unnoticed by the other diners. "London will occupy your every day, and if not Birmingham and Manchester certainly will."

"I'm rather interested in Manchester actually," Adams asked. "Have you been there? Lincoln has made an appeal to the city and it seems the mill workers are responding. Goodness knows what the owners make of it."

"I am actually trying to find out," Emily answered, "I'll tell you later."

The conversation swung from American history to Roman history, to British history and then back to the first fifty years of American problems. Coffee came and went; and they were into the second pass of the port and deep into the westward movement across the plains; and the removal of native Indians from their homeland, of which Emily had strong views. In a stimulating conversation that didn't quite come to blows, Adams and Henrietta finally settled on a peace agreement of their own that would have done credit to any politician. Adams was keen to draw Emily back into the world that they were currently living in.

"And how do you view the British public and Parliament on this problem we find ourselves in Emily?" Adams continued, steering the conversation away from the contentious views in his country and the removal of the Indians to settlements. Dealing with the Indian war not that far back in history and not a subject he liked to be reminded of.

"For a start by all accounts," she said, "They say one thing and often do another. Right now the government, on the face of it, is supporting Washington, but many in the House are openly helping the south and that's mainly the industrialists, who see a great opportunity to make money out of America's problems."

Adams nodded, encouraging Emily to carry on.

"Oddly enough the workers here in the north, who stand to lose most, are all for yourself and Lincoln," she said. "And in some cases have refused to process American cotton."

"I wasn't totally aware of that," the envoy said, rather surprised to hear that workers weren't just raising their voices for more wages. Here was a principle he had not bargained for. Workers taking such a stand was completely new to him.

Emily explained her movements for the following day.

"As soon as you are on the train to London," she carried on, "I am to take another northwards to observe such a meeting in Ramsbottom tomorrow night and report back to the Ambassador before his next big meeting with the Prime Minister."

"And where is this Ramsbottom place?" Adams asked reaching for a map of Lancashire on the next table that had just been vacated.

I'm not sure that you'll find it on there," she said pointing at Manchester. "It's quite a small town up a valley, just north of the city. By all accounts, the workers are quite vociferous so it should be an interesting evening."

Adams peered at the map. It showed only the larger towns and the railway system in the north.

"I'll let you know how it goes, when I get back to London," Emily agreed, pointing to where Ramsbottom was situated. "The press will be full of it of course, but the papers depending your view, are bound to reflect the views of the editors so you might have to depend on me to get a balanced opinion."

"But how do I know you will give me such an opinion?" Adams asked.

"I'll make a detailed paper on getting back," she confirmed.

"Are you meeting anyone there?" Henrietta asked out of curiosity and then regretted it immediately. Her personal life was of course nothing to do with her. Her husband would take her to task later she realised.

"No," Emily said quickly, "but I've been introduced to a movement of educated Englishwomen in London recently, and I can tell you that these ladies do not mince their words."

The two Americans looked at each other in silence.

"My remit tomorrow is to say absolutely nothing, particularly with my accent," she continued laughing.

"Maybe we will meet up on your return," Adams suggested, well pleased with this new information. "And what do you intend to do with the results of your evening in Rams bottom."

"File it, submit it and then forget it," she replied.

"Somehow, I just don't believe you, Emily," he countered. "You look more positive than that to me."

Emily smiled at him sideways. First of all she had to throw off her colleague, who was paying far too much attention to her than she wished. Thank goodness they would be going their separate ways in the morning.

"What do you make of those two?" Henrietta asked as they retired to one of the best bedrooms in the hotel. Since he had known her, his wife could not help delving into other people's lives as if it were of national importance.

"The introduction letter from the Embassy described them perfectly," Adams replied, sinking into the nearest chair with a large whisky.

"Yes but what do you really think?" she pressed him.

"I don't actually," he replied wearily not up to an in depth conversation after a very long day. "And certainly not at the moment."

"Yes, you do, Joseph," she continued, "I know you better than that.

"She's made quite an impression I think. What's her name again?"

Adams looked at his notes. "Emily Wollaston." he answered, shifting his position in the arm chair. His wife had a habit of always delving into the inner thoughts of people she had met; whilst he preferred to make his observations and keep them to himself. She just couldn't help herself.

"They must be well thought of to be sent all this way," she persisted. "When we could have just let that new travel agency make all the arrangements. What are they called?"

"Thomas Cook's," he called out over his shoulder as he made for the bathroom.

"Anyhow, the girl?" she continued.

"Bright lady ambitious, but maybe a little pushy and devious," he answered. "Plenty of drive, but I have no idea what her ideals are. Her family home is right in the line of fire. Has all sorts of complications when she gets home."

"And the young officer," Henrietta asked, as he relaxed having turned out the gas light, refusing to give up on discussing their companions for the night.

"Nothing more than a straight forward commissioned officer looking for promotion and an easy life I suspect," came a tired response. "Definitely not a die-hard soldier wishing to end his life in a futile battle.

"Now let's just go to sleep, my dear," he said finally. "I need to be fully alert for tomorrow. Good night."

Emily pushed open the revolving door of the hotel and made her way across the polished wood floor to the counter and pinged the bell until it crackled sharply and waited for the reaction. She had left the other three on the London bound train at Manchester and joined a two coach stopping train up the Irwell valley.

Intrigued by the meandering contours of the landscape, she watched the countryside flash by compelled to look out of the windows on either side as the railway, road, river and canal crossed each other at frequent intervals. At each sweep of the river, where water wheeled driven mills loomed up, white water foamed in the tail races, flushed away to the next waterfall of obstructing rocks.

At every outcrop of rocks, a wooden lead diverted the water to yet another wheel. Away in the distance, she could see plantation woods being cropped by gangs of men and teams of horses; and on the very horizon, hills of gorse merged into the pale afternoon sun. Village after village passed by, station after station came at the next tight bend, at which the train stopped briefly, before it continued in a slow motion between the houses, tied into groups of terraces, dressed in dismal grey stone and hung with slated roofs; all in absolute uniformity marching up the sides of the hills. Emily had shuddered slightly as the temperature dipped. It was so unlike the broad swept valleys of her native land.

She pushed the bell again, harder and firmer.

"Alright, alright, I heard you," came a shrill voice from the back of the office, and the ungainly body of the receptionist came into view.

"Are you booked?" the voice boomed again, as the hawkish lady leaned over the counter adjusting her cardigan and looking at her watch. "We're booked up you know. There's a big meeting in town this evening."

"Yes, I am," Alice countered looking into her handbag and confirming her booking for one night. "Why, is there a problem?"

"Name, then," demanded the lady on the other side of the counter.

"Alice, Alice Wollaston,"

"You're American then by the sound of your accent. North or south?" the receptionist persisted in her interrogation.

"Not that it matters to you," Alice retorted, "But I live near Washington."

"Aren't they fighting down there?" the woman continued, determined to prise more information from the guest."

"I believe they are," Emily said. "Not only that, they are fighting everywhere."

"Just interested, dear," she said handing the key. "First floor, second on the right. Supper is at six. Early for this meeting outside the town hall. I suppose you're a journalist?"

Emily said nothing and looked outside. There was just time for a walk.

I suppose that we ought to be getting back to the hotel, the two Missionaries suggested to Alice as they finished tea and flat cakes in the main square. watching carpenters make the final adjustments to the temporary stage.

"I'll pay," Alice said opening her purse, as the waitress laid the bill on the table. "It's the least I can do. Just how many speakers are there going to be tonight?"

"We're not exactly sure," the lady said. "But my husband here is going to make the first address and there is a lady with some very forceful views from the new Lincoln Society coming from Manchester and I expect there will be others. Apparently, she has a letter from America that she wishes to read out."

"This is all quite new to me," Alice said, "My father would likely be mad as hell if he knew I was attending a rally like this. I suppose it could turn into something quite nasty?"

"It's possible, Alice," the man said. "But I don't think so. It's not an objection to wages or conditions, something that the authorities understand, but in support of the government, who on the face of it are all behind the Union Government of Lincoln."

"Just as well it's going to be a fine evening," the lady announced as they walked across the square arm in arm. "We've time for supper before we are due back for the action."

Emily too, strolled around the mill town, which was hugged on all sides by the hills rising steeply out of the valley; listening to the strains of the town band warming up in the church hall and the faint clattering of the looms in the largest of the mills. Rows of three storied terraced houses faced the sun so that the hand weavers of an earlier generations could get the best of the light from the large windows on the top floor.

If the size of the town hall was anything to go by, she concluded, it was one of the smaller communities in the valley. Another train disgorged a horde of people, some in their finery, but most in drab clothes of the working man and his wife; and in the distance she could hear another locomotive wheezing up the valley.

Emily looked at her watch and wrapped her scarf a little more tightly round her neck. She remembered the advice that she had been given, when her office heard that she was heading north. Not only was it cold, but also damp that could chill one to very marrow. It was getting cold early as it always did in the valleys, and now time to get back to the warm hotel and supper.

"You're a little late," the frosty receptionist announced with a wave of her hand. "The restaurant is full, but I think I can find you a table to share."

"I'm quite happy to share," Emily agreed taking off her hat and coat.

"Edith," the receptionist shouted to the waitress passing by with a canteen of soup. "Show our American lady to the table over there with a space."

The restaurant smelled faintly musty as if need of a spring clean. Heavy draped curtains pulled across the windows swept the bare wood floor at every movement of the draught A flocked wallpaper hung down to the dado rail and the carpet curled at the corners. On the mantelpiece, a grandmother clock clicked away striking sonorously six times as Emily walked in following the waitress.

"I'm Alice, do come and join us, and these are my friends from Manchester," Alice introduced herself, showing Emily the only spare chair in the room and realising the table guest was from across the Atlantic. "We're here for a meeting in the town tonight."

"Pleased to do so, Alice," Emily replied picking up the menu, immediately warming to the introduction. "I'm Emily Wollaston up here on request by my principals to observe the proceedings, and of course I'm interested on my own account. If they are anything like meetings back home, it could be a lively evening, so I will be standing at the back and not saying anything."

"I think that I will be also," agreed Alice, "but my friends here are very used to public speaking and will have something to say I'm certain. They have strong views on slavery in your country and indeed freedom of speech not to mention the emancipation of women generally."

Alice's friends nodded in agreement and continued scanning their notes.

"It's not only America that has its problems Emily," the man said eventually choosing his words carefully. "Progress in the wealth of this new world we are in on both sides of the Atlantic just has to be matched with the expectations of those that provide the labour."

"But surely those that provide the impetus and the vision should not be disadvantaged either and rewarded for their efforts surely," countered Emily, relishing the opportunity to sharpen her wits with this man of principle.

Alice looked on with astonishment as the two, who had only met within the hour, clashed before her with their obviously opposing views. "It is the inevitability of it, Emily," he continued quietly, "These people tonight are not against progress, or wishing to destroy the machines of progress, as they might have done in the past, but they are very much in support of the freeing of all slaves wherever they are, and that is the essence of the meeting tonight."

"I'm here more as an observer than an opinion maker," Emily said to the Presbyterian Missionary standing her ground. "Whatever I might think, my parents back home have a few slaves and a few free ones, I might add. Most of the politicians have as well and, of course, yours did here until quite recently."

"You shouldn't be so intrusive," the Missionaries wife interrupted scolding her husband, "She's not only a guest at our table, but a guest in our country."

The husband grumbled and mumbled an apology, realising that he should save his rhetoric for the evening.

"I think that it's time we were going," Alice said folding up her napkin and standing up. "We don't want to Miss the opening and I can hear the band tuning up."

As soon as they all left the hotel, it was obvious that it was to be a well-attended meeting. Everybody on the streets were going in the same direction; and soon Alice and Emily were having to push in with the crowds, something that Alice had not experienced before, and which came as a bit of a shock. Emily grabbed her hand to prevent them separating in the wake of the two Missionaries, who were clearly quite at home at such meetings.

The noise became deafening as they surged into the square, the revellers shouting in good humour to a clutch of policemen near the stage. In the town hall, the local magistrates waited in a back room gauging the tempo of the meeting, and whether it would be necessary to clear the area with a detachment of mounted troops waiting just out of town. The band struck up, their uniforms a patchwork of reds and blues, and brass tassels on the sleeves and shoulders. Emily could hear the strains of "Lincoln and Liberty" over the noise of the crowd followed by more recognisable "Hearts of Oak."

"Every town has their own band," Alice shouted over the noise of the crowd.

"We have them too," replied Emily tugging at Alice's arm. "Look at those two making for the platform. Are they taking part?"

"He is going to speak first I think," Alice replied. "Don't forget, I hardly know them. I met them in a coffee shop in Liverpool only a week or so ago and they invited me here. They are very passionate about their cause, aren't they?"

True to the expectations of the organisers, the Ramsbottom meeting was without incident and a show of hands resulted in support of the motion that the meeting support the legitimate Lincoln Government in continuing its opposition to the Confederate Government of Jefferson Davis in any way possible.

"I have to say that the man was very impressive on the platform," Emily said, as the two girls linked hands on the way back to the hotel to avoid the pushing and struggling crowds heading towards the station.

"I was going to ask you, Emily," Alice said as they finally pushed opened the door of the hotel and found the two nearest comfortable seats.

"Ask me what?" Emily replied.

"When you go back to the States," Alice blurted, "can I come with you. I'd just love to see it for myself. We have an uncle there in New York and the friends of mine you met tonight have colleagues in Canada and Boston, where I could stay."

"Let's talk about it over a hot chocolate," Emily said. "I'm freezing. I'll write to you when I get back to London. I have put in a request for extended leave home in the States, but whether it will be granted I don't know."

Chapter 5

It had been a long day for the President of the Board of Trade, who had convened a hasty meeting at the Admiralty Buildings by special request of the Foreign Office. They had not even stopped for the usual liquid lunch, such was the long list on the agenda, most of which concerned the looming economic crisis in the Lancashire cotton trade and the civil unrest in America, the root cause of the problem.

He was in a difficult position caught between the crossfire of politicians, the government and the chiefs of industry, all at odds as to solving the problem across the Atlantic. Apart from the Crimea War some ten years earlier, the country had managed to disassociate itself from squabbles around the globe. How could the problem that had been tackled and solved in London some thirty years earlier, when slavery was finally abolished and the carriage of slaves on British ships was outlawed thirty years before that, still be seemly unsolvable in an America that had declared everyone was free in 1776.

It was inconceivable to the Foreign Office, the Board of Trade, the prime minister and Parliament that America threatened its own stability Now the Southern States, who claimed they relied on slave labour and could not survive without it, were opposing any freeing of slaves and challenging the Union of the North, its government and the will of its people.

"It's not our affair," came the cry of many of those attending, at the most difficult time of the meeting.

"It certainly is," was an equally vociferous reply from a smaller, but more active section, most of which were drawn from the valleys north of the Black Country.

"Free trade is being interfered with beyond which is not acceptable in this country," he continued as the tension rose. "Not only is the quality of life here affected, but also the colonies who are dependent on our finished goods."

"And they are burning their own crops we hear," said another voice.

"But if they wish to burn their own crops as they did last night, then surely their own business," replied a foundry owner from Birmingham.

"Can you not import cotton from Egypt or India," offered another member from East Anglia, an area that in the past had suffered from the loss of the wool trade a century before.

The tension in the room grew as members tried to get their word in above the noise. The Chairman frequently tried to keep order, frequently banging his gavel on the table and demanding silence.

"And what they are not burning, they are holding to inflate the price," an exasperated mill owner from Ramsbottom cried out, eventually finding his voice in the crowded room.

"That's all very well getting cotton from the east. Neither country can provide the quantity nor the quality," an expert from the industry reminded the room.

"And the word is that some cotton traders from Liverpool are holding on to stocks to inflate the price. Can't the government force them to release stocks in the Liverpool warehouses so that us mill owners can at least continue some business," another furious miller complained.

"Cotton comes graded as you might imagine," a tall top hatted man speaking for the first time addressed the crowd. "And it is reflected in the price of course."

"Tell us more about this standard then, if you will," queried a new voice.

The earlier speaker continued as the rest of the room listened attentively. "It's known as the Middling Orleans and the price of all other grades is set against its quality."

"More like muddling Orleans," came a voice from the rear of the room, where a man was heading for the exit.

At that the room dissolved into laughter and the President seized the opportunity to look at his watch and declare that he was not going to take a vote at this stage, but would communicate the feelings of the members to the Prime Minister. The Board of Trade's most senior man had decided the day before the meeting, that he need not disclose to his colleagues that President Lincoln's special envoy was at that very moment disembarking from a ship at Liverpool, intent on putting the case from the Union that Britain should refrain from any involvement in the conflict on the other side of the Atlantic.

Already aware from several meetings with Select Committees in the corridors of power in Westminster, some of which were highly sensitive to the warring sides, not to mention the Monarch's opinion, he mulled over his conversations with the Foreign Secretary. The Foreign Secretary was also treading a narrow line on America. The Monarch had made a stance, and it was well known that she considered that America was still part of the Empire. Only a few months earlier at the Opening of Parliament, she had proclaimed with the backing of Prince Albert that, "Her Government should not break a legally constituted blockade."

Now barely six weeks later, her beloved husband had died and the country was still in mourning; whilst still fiercely contesting an issue not only in Westminster, but in debating societies around the country. The surprise to many was the mills of the north, where workers openly supported the Monarch's support for the American President and disdain for his counterpart in the south.

Two days later whilst his wife was enjoying the sights of London, Adams and the Ambassador were welcomed into the Foreign Office in Whitehall and immediately taken into the inner sanctum.

Abraham Lincoln's request was laid out flat on the table after the merest of formalities. It was a short note as Adams well knew and straight to the point. Lincoln did not skirt round the issue as all his close colleagues knew. It was a straight forward plea for help on the one hand and condemnation for those renegades in the south on the other.

"It was inconceivable," he had written, "That the British Government should do anything to damage the relationship with the duly elected American people."

"Quite so, quite so," the Foreign Secretary replied sincerely. "It has been said time and again over here, but there is some opposition from the back benches and the whips have a difficult time on some of the votes.

"So, what happens then?" queried Adams, well aware of the filibustering between the Senate and Congress back home, that often resulted in no action or a fudged issue.

"Well, they keep making amendments so that it gets thrown back and forwards from the Upper House," explained the civil servant. "Only in a national emergency do they seem to act with any haste."

Adams was treated with similar sympathy and cordiality the following day at the Board of Trade, and came away pleased that the first hurdle was over. From one state building in Whitehall to another, Ambassador and envoy presented the case for the American leader, hearing all the right noises on the surface, but concerned about the under-current of opinion from the business world in the city.

Adams conferred with his wife after a long meeting with industrialists in Birmingham that had not gone quite so well as hoped.

"It's going to be a long haul, my dear," he said at last taking her hand and sitting her down over a welcomed cup of tea. "We cannot expect to be home by Christmas."

"Well, you know as well as I do that politics is never straight forward," she answered matter-of-factly. "Don't forget I was your secretary for ten years, and your mistress for five years before that."

Adam's chuckled to himself. It was a good and bad time in his life. He well remembered her sharp brain that surprised him, and the body that ensnared him.

"Ethics, slavery and the almighty dollar are going to take some separating out," she said gently pouring out a second cup of tea and offering him a scone. "And that's without the complication of the British pound."

A week later, an invitation embossed with the Royal Crest arrived at their hotel. Although still in mourning for her husband, the Queen had agreed to host a small party of senior politicians and the American delegation desperately hoping for all out support. Hiding his long held reservations about the Monarchy, Adams spoke eloquently in reply to a toast to the former colonies, and looked to see if he could make anything of the speeches, knowing in advance that the Queen would never make her opinion really known. Two days later, the two Americans were called to Downing Street.

"I can say with complete confidence, Mr Ambassador, that my Government will wholly support your President," Palmerston announced.

The Ambassador acknowledged with a nod, and Adams followed.

"Not only that, but Her Majesty has re-stated her view in no uncertain terms that the action of the Southern States is completely unjustified." Adams nodded in approval.

"And you can tell your President that the Queen is not amused," the Prime Minister confirmed.

"Not amused," the American queried, not exactly certain what Palmerston was getting at.

"Not amused by the pressure that the Confederates are putting on certain sections of British Industry," came the reply. "It can only come to no good."

"That's very good to hear," Adams replied. "With that knowledge do you think that I can book our ship home."

"Well, there's little more that you can do here at the moment," the Ambassador agreed with Adams. "But why don't you a look around the culture here before you go. I have to give it to the Brits. We've got a lot to learn, but I mark you, inside a hundred years they will be looking at us."

Chapter 6

A hundred miles to the north of the border, James Kirk walked briskly through the gates of his shipyard, fifteen miles west of the Glasgow city centre and beneath the towering Dumbarton rock that dwarfed the town at the mouth of the little river Leven. Trained as a draughtsman, man and boy with the North British Railway Company, he was now Yard manager and part owner of one of the most well-known Clydebank shipbuilders. As far back as he could remember his life had been dominated by engines powered by coal and water, and now he was one of the leading exponents in the industry. His knowledge, skill and dogged Viking determination to push out the boundaries had made him a fearsome debater around the country. But he wasn't expecting anyone to doff their cap at him because he usually dressed in the drab working jacket and trousers, heavy boots and a flat hat; and it wasn't his way to expect his staff to bow and scrape. Although he would have been immediately recognised by the worker had they been in the Yard, he was in fact, half an hour earlier than the whistle for the start of the day and was expecting visitors according to the Chairman's brief.

He exchanged words of brief recognition with the night watchman, who was stamping about and keen to go off duty, and walked to the time keeping office, a good place to assess the mood of his staff. Kirk was a man who moved easily amongst his workers and the Board, but he limped when it was damp, and it was always damp in Scotland. A launching had not gone well thirty years previously and he was lucky to get away with a slightly crushed foot.

Kirk and his colleagues in the Glasgow Institute of Marine Engineers, of which he was the current President, had been so successful in developing the reciprocating three stage engine that they had virtually conquered the world market in building ships and particularly small fast paddle wheeled ships. But he couldn't rest on his laurels for one moment such was the pace of innovation. Registering a patent was becoming increasingly difficult and it often made better sense to issue a licence and use the finance to make another improvement.

As far as the eye could see from Bromielaw Quay in the heart of the city, the Clyde river was lined with a forest of building ways. Here the pure waters of the

48

river that rose a hundred miles inland met the muddy waters of the estuary and the deep water began.

Angled across the narrow river the slipways deposited the bare hulls of the ships as soon as they were watertight from where they would be towed to a finishing off berth. The job of fitting out might take another year to complete in the case of passenger ships, but in most cases was expedited inside six months, despite the weather that could be bitterly cold in the winter and gloriously warm in the long summer.

For nearly twenty years, the sound of mechanical saws in the timber yards, the plating and riveting in the iron yards, and the hammering forging and casting in the foundries had spawned steadily all the way to Irvine and beyond to Greenock, until there was hardly a space left on the flatlands. Two miles further on at Gourock the river widened into a Forth with lochs stretching into the distance; and here the ships bound for the oceans would disperse while the small, but commodious, coasters puffed away to the Scottish islands.

Kirk walked from slipway to slipway with his deputy then, when satisfied that every man in the yard was fully occupied, he slipped away to change into his suit for the rest of the day. Today, he was meeting a visitor from the other side of the Atlantic according to his Chairman, who had received the request at quite short notice. A resident of Charleston he was lead to believe.

Now what would an American want to know about paddle steamers, which were designed for river, and general inland waterways work, Kirk thought. It sounded like a long meeting and he was not going to be alone apparently as a Colonel in the Confederate Army was with him and their Glasgow agent.

Kirk smiled to himself. A dour Scot like himself and a hard-nosed Yank on the other side of the discussion. He decided to invite his chief draughtsman, as together they made a team of many years and he was the man that had the latest information at his fingertips.

He glanced at *The Scotsman* lying on his desk. The front page was all about the trouble in the former colonies, a workers meeting in Rochdale that was supporting the cause of black slaves, and the opening of Florence Nightingale's new school for nurses. Of Nightingales contemporary, in the Crimean War there was no mention. What was her name he tried to remember, but then he wasn't surprised, she was hardly ever mentioned? She was after all a black nurse and the daughter of a slave. Neither of the headlines concerned Kirk very much. Politics changed on the shift of the wind and governments came and went. He was more concerned about balancing the books and making a profit, and the weather for the following day when he would launch their latest vessel on the top of the spring tide. It was expected to be the fastest side wheeler they had built and probably the fastest on the Clyde to date.

Of the latest construction, iron hull on iron frames it was a sleek roomy passenger vessel, and all eyes would be on it when it would be taken to the measured mile further down the Forth of Clyde, once the engine was in and the vessel fitted out. The new owners wanted it for service on the Irish Sea between Holy head and Dublin.

So confident was Kirk about his new vessel that he expected a repeat order. The Thames Estuary, the Seven Estuary and the English Channel, as well as Forth of Clyde were crying out for fast paddle steamers and he had the skill and the men to satisfy the need. And now America was looking for paddle steamers. He thumbed through his journals. They had them on the Hudson River in numbers. Why would they be interested in his, when apart from anything else they would need to cross the Atlantic unless they wanted them to be part built and carried over in cargo ships.

"Is this the train to Dumbarton?" John B. Shaw junior asked the nearest porter as they stepped onto the fore course of Queen Street station and looked at the destination boards over the platforms.

"Take the Helens Burgh train. It's the station after Bowling," the man replied genially. "You can't Miss it. The rock is as big as a mountain."

"You winna see some of ours," the American joked. "Over here, yours are nothing but molehills by comparison."

"I had heard," the porter retorted quickly, not in the least fazed by the one one-upmanship of the man's quip. "I have a cousin over there. I'm thinking of joining him."

For half an hour, the train rumbled behind the backs of the houses of Finnis ton, Patrick, Scots hill, Yoker and Clydebank in quick succession; and Shaw and his colleague could see the bows of ships appearing over the roofs of the houses. Baulks of scaffolding reaching into the sky, from which men appeared to be working without support with scant regard for safety. The Americans looked at each other in amazement at the jumble of housing, where washing could be seen on a line, and within feet of the drying clothes a railway track would spur off between the houses.

Carts and wagons drawn by horses and occasionally by men, containing materials of all descriptions criss-crossed the roads then disappeared behind high gates. Almost immediately on passing Clydebank, the houses petered out and the train was in open countryside before stopping at Bowling, where the canal from the Forth river terminated and the river was in full view. In no time at all, the train pulled in to the east station at Dumbarton, where before the skeletons of ships and cranes dominated the skyline. Deposited on the cobbled road outside the yard by the cab, even though they could have easily walked, the Americans surveyed the yard with a critical eye dusting down their coats and reaching for their leather briefcases. How on earth did these people condense everything into such a small site, when in America there was no such premium on land.

Ahead of them solid brick buildings topped with chimneys, some tall and tapered, others squat and square were framed in the arch of a double cast iron ornate gate, inside of which a brazier was throwing off a good heat, and a watchman was rubbing his hands.

Tacked on to the brick warehouse like buildings clung wooden lean to structures heavily creosoted in black waste oil waiting for permanent replacements. Roofed in heavy slate, the offices had large floor to ceiling windows in contrast to the sheds, which had few windows and corrugated roofs that deposited any water straight onto the ground below.

Clearly the yard was bursting at the seams with activity, equipment laying scattered in all corners, neatly piled as if waiting for an invisible conveyor belt to deliver them to the ship when all was ready. Shaw looked towards the slipways which were partially obscured by the buildings. There were three of them, all out in the open surrounded by scaffolding and cranes.

He could see that there was an order of things here despite the works being hemmed in from all sides. It had been the same in every yard the train had passed, acres of human endeavour in yards and factories, whilst above the belching out of black smoke lay in a haze above the river, as if reluctant to take flight and escape into the atmosphere.

The ringing sounds of metal on metal came from all corners as they made towards the open gate. John Shaw junior, a third generation southerner, his family formerly from Wolverhampton, was pleased with what he saw before him.

"We are expected," he said to the man at the gate, who was shuffling some papers.

"I have it here," the gate man said handing him a plan of the shipyard.

"Mr Kirk is waiting for you."

Kirk watched from behind the glass in his elevated office adjacent to the drawing office and the laying out floor, trying to evaluate his visitors and then descended the stairs to meet them entering the reception room. He had little experience with Americans apart from a joint adventure with some promoters the previous year, looking at new vessels for the Hudson river route from New York to Albany, one hundred miles and fifty miles to the north.

That had come to nothing. He wondered about the urgency of their visit. The vastness of the inlets and rivers of the American eastern seaboard was well known, and American seafarers had plenty of experience with early steam vessels. Beyond and around Cape Hatteras was known as an area of dangerous seas in bad weather.

He would be interested in what they had to say, but sensed that he could not provide them with what they wanted, a fast seagoing ship in good and bad weather capable of carrying several hundred tons of cargo. His ships were designed for relatively short voyage across the Irish sea and on estuaries, and in any event the ship coming off the stocks tomorrow was already accounted for.

"So this one, that is ready tomorrow, can do thirteen knots in smooth water you say, Mr Kirk," reckoned the American as his colleagues looked at the ship on the stocks and he reached over and fingered the laid out blueprints.

"Without a doubt," Kirk replied as he rolled up the detailed plan of the engine room. He didn't want his guests to make too close an examination of the plans until they had made a commitment to purchase. "And probably more if the engineer dared to screw down the boiler relief valve after which it might blow up," he chortled.

"What makes you so confident?" one of Shaw's colleagues asked, having said nothing up to now.

"We have conducted several tests at the Institute in the new tank facility and that coupled with the underwater form calculated by Mr Simpson, the eminent mathematician here in the United Kingdom." Kirk's senior draughtsman intervened. "We are convinced that it will be two knots faster than any vessel either side of the Atlantic."

"What are you hoping to achieve?" the Chairman of the Yard asked the two Americans as he came through the door into the meeting, apologising for his late arrival. "Indeed, what do you want with a vessel like the ones we build. If I am not mistaken yours are for inland waters.

The two Americans and the agent closed ranks in the corner of the drawing office; whilst the plans for the latest ship were gathered up by the draughtsman and put away into racks that lined two walls.

"We are not necessarily looking to purchase any of your vessels at the moment nor indeed any of your competitors," Shaw finally confessed as they resumed talks.

"Then what are you looking for then," an irritated Kirk replied, realising that his time had been wasted.

"We are trying to assess the chance of ships like yours being able to make a transatlantic voyage in good weather during the spring." Shaw admitted finally.

"But they can't take cargo of any consequence nor passengers come to that," countered the Chairman, becoming more irritated by the conversation that was developing. "And apart from that they have a limited bunker capacity and fresh water for the boilers."

Shaw was not to be put off, and went into another huddle with his colleagues, deciding that they would have to disclose the real reason for their visit.

"We want to make a base in Bermuda or the Bahamas and run the Union blockade into places like Charleston and Wilmington to get supplies in and cotton out." Shaw continued, "The cotton would be shipped back over here in cargo ships or passenger liners.

"And the outward cargo?" the Chairman queried, becoming more intrigued with the turn of the discussion.

"Military supplies and civilian requirements that are denied the Confederates at the moment," Shaw replied quickly, not wishing to elaborate too much.

"Paddle steamers will need a number of modifications to take on any role like this," Kirk offered as the meeting started to close down. "Now just what would you like us to do for you, Mr Shaw?

"Look at modifications and costs to your next vessel that would fit the requirements to make a venture like this a possibility." Shaw eventually started realising that some progress would have to be made before they left. "At the moment we are not in position to purchase a vessel for ourselves, but we may find backers to make it happen."

"On the face of it and with our experience, this sort of venture is an undertaking without precedence and is fraught with danger," Kirk advised them.

Shaw nodded, "Our naval advice is that in the right conditions of the year, it is possible with experienced seamen."

"And you realise," the Chairman said winding up the meeting, "it is likely that you will have to purchase a vessel. Chartering is an alternative, but with the risks involved insurance premiums are likely to prohibitive."

"I accept that," Shaw conceded, "My principals are prepared to finance a viable operation if conducted by the right men."

"And who are they?" the Chairman asked, wondering whether he already knew the answer.

"Jefferson Davis," came the prompt reply, 'the Southern President."

"Then he may well have to dig deep in his pockets," the Chairman suggested. "I will leave the details with Mr Kirk, but we will need a deposit before proceeding. Good day to you all."

Kirk steered them towards the biggest table in the office laying out a plan of one of their earlier ships. "You'll need a fleet of ships to shift cargo like that. Side wheelers at best can carry only a few hundred tons of cargo, because you'll need to take coal on deck as well."

Shaw looked at the plan. The design, of course, was nothing near like stern wheelers on the Mississippi.

"Stability will be another great problem that must be considered throughout the voyage. Any coal carried on deck must be used first. Have you considered that?" Kirk continued.

The Americans nodded.

"And what about the rivers. Are they deep enough? In the Southern States, I have always thought they are rather shallow," the Scot questioned, hardly taking a breath as the Americans studied the plan.

"New Orleans is by far the deepest, but it's a long way round Florida," the third man in the group offered. "Wilmington and Charleston are the favoured ports and they are guarded by Confederate troops.

"They are the nearest to Bermuda and Wilmington is not far from Richmond, the Confederate headquarters. We prefer them as they are shallow and Wilmington has a particularly well-guarded difficult approach."

Kirk pondered a while and went to the bookcase and pulled out an atlas. "What is the distance," he asked the third quiet speaking man, who was obviously a mariner as well as their agent.

"Seven hundred miles at the most, say three days in favourable weather," he answered. "I assume that your vessels can be fitted with masts and sails. We anticipate a round trip in ten days," he continued in a nasal accent, that slightly offended Kirk.

"I'll make some preliminary drawings and calculations for you to be ready by the end of the month." Kirk concluded. "In the meantime, I'd like you to meet our accountant before we go any further. Up here we like to see deals done in the right order, which in this case means a large deposit. A vessel converted for an order like this is hardly likely to be converted back for use over here, should you default."

"I understand," said the American, who had done most of the talking.

"Where is your next port of call?" Kirk queried when the room was down to himself and the three Americans, expecting the answer to be another yard on the Clyde.

"The Enfield rifle factory near London; Whitworths in Manchester; and Armstrong's of Newcastle. Then Stroud near Bristol for uniforms and leather; and then back to London for medicines," Shaw disclosed without giving away too many details. "We are told they produce the best that money can buy, my colleague here is an expert on guns."

Kirk looked at the man, who had said very little during the meeting, but had obviously taken in a great deal. He looked every inch a soldier.

The Confederate Colonel picked up the ten-year-old design Enfield.702 Minnie 39-inch rifle and hefted it easily from one shoulder to the other, testing its balance and then cupped the walnut butt in his left shoulder before trying the right. It felt comfortable in his experienced hand, and said so to the designer and then placed it down on the green baize table.

"Would you take it apart?" he asked the man.

The engineer expertly reduced the gun to its component parts in a blur and McClure watched intently as he laid the dull metal sections down on the table, then just as quickly pieced it together handing it back to the American.

"May I try?" the Colonel asked when the engineer had finished and while Shaw discussed some financial arrangements with the designer, he soon acquainted himself with the weapon. But it was not really this weapon that they wanted. What they wanted was the later model, the one that the British Army was currently using.

They had travelled from Glasgow the previous day and then taken the train up the Lee Valley to the works, that were straddled between the railway and the canalised Lee Navigation. The canal terminated on the north shore of the Thames, some five miles short of the City. Situated in a score of acres, the brick and wooden buildings were scattered over the site, separated and linked by a series of canals so that gunpowder and ammunition could be moved around in wooden boats pinned together by bronze and brass fittings, minimising the chances of explosions.

The American took the gun from the table to make the first move in dissembling the gun.

"Watch the lever action spring," the engineer cautioned. "It has a vicious movement until you get used to it. Not so on our latest model."

With slow deliberation McClure took it apart, watched intently by his colleagues, and re-assembled it several times, assessing how his men would cope with the weapon in the field and the heat of battle.

"I'd like to test it on the range, if that is possible," he said as he looked down the barrel of the muzzle loading gun.

"You don't sound American to me," the engineer suggested as the rifle was handed back to him and once again laid flat on the table.

"No, I'm Northern Irish, Belfast born, but British Army. Royal Green Jackets for seven years. Fastest marching regiment in the country, but I left for the States after the Crimean war," came a swift reply.

"And he was no Colonel either," interjected Shaw, who had finished walking around the workshop. "He was no more than a sergeant he told me, and now he is a fully paid-up infantry leader and a damn fine one at that."

McClure smiled thinly as his leader slapped him on the back with a chuckle. He didn't really like to be reminded how he took his leave from the British Army; having been seduced one night at the Aldershot Camp, lost his savings and then subsequently engaged by an agent, who signed him up and put him on a steamer for New Orleans.

"Now we'd like to see your latest rifle," he said once his composure had returned and the engineer had replaced the 1851 model back in the rack. 'the model that you have just shown us is well out of date, and we will be in the market for the new short barrel version if we can get a delivery date in time for next year."

Five hours later, after testing the latest version with the smaller bullet and the improved velocity, which McClure was confident would be useful to the cavalry as well as the infantry, they called a halt to the proceedings.

"We'll need an export licence for this order, Mr Shaw," the accountant for the Company reminded Shaw as they left the range and walked to the offices. "We'd rather this order is kept much to ourselves, as it might not be well received in certain government circles. The Chairman may have to circumnavigate some of the usual procedures, but I'm sure that the order will be delivered to your time scale."

The deputy chairman looked down at the list of requirements in front of him. It was no mean order at a time, when government orders were thin on the ground. Three hundred rifles, two hundred of them from obsolete stock which the Board would be delighted to move on, and a hundred thousand rounds and a promise of a further bigger order once they had been delivered.

"I'm sure that a bill of exchange could be worded for South America, we do occasionally sell arms to Chile, and put on a ship that is going via Bermuda," he said quietly to Shaw's team, now breaking up as the meeting came to an end.

Shaw nodded in agreement.

"We'll need cash of course for a transaction of this nature. We can't be seen to be actively working contrary to the Government's wishes," he concluded well pleased with the day's work.

Shaw shook hands with the Enfield director.

"Our banker will have the money with you within forty-eight hours," Shaw confirmed. "Half in dollars, the rest in sterling if that is acceptable?"

The Enfield Chairman winced to himself, but tried not to show it. He was hoping that the payment would be all in sterling notes. But then he had managed to dispose of the oldest weapons, that would otherwise stay on the shelf until some uprising on the other side of the world.

The Board of Ordnance at Woolwich Arsenal would not need much convincing that the consignment of the latest guns were going to some reputable South American country, and that the older weapons were defective, not worth modifying and needing to be destroyed. The Director there was an old University colleague, and a special dinner the next time he was in the City would square the paperwork. After all what was going on three thousand miles away was of little concern to his company, despite the Government's increasing concern about fuelling the conflict.

Two days later, he received a short telegram and immediately sent for his chief engineer and the accountant.

"Look at this, you two," he said as he read the message for the second time. "It's from the Union Army Headquarters in Albany this time. They want at least five hundred of the latest rifles and probably more later."

"Well, I'm damned," replied the engineer turning to the shelves behind him and extracting the latest stock lists. "We have enough of the latest Bessemer steel for the barrels and mechanisms, but not enough walnut for the stocks, although I guess, we could find an alternative."

The Chairman looked over his shoulder running down the ledger with his fingers. "Apart from that can we get the line moving?"

"I suggest that we extend the working day and increase the tooling up," the engineer reckoned after looking at the figures for a second time. "How long do you think this will go on for?"

"The papers say they are having running battles every week and both sides are losing up to a thousand men every time they clash," came the Chairman's response.

"Thank Christ we have avoided a revolution here," the Chairman stated casting his mind back to the Peter-loo riots in Manchester some years earlier, that resulted in troops slaughtering innocent and peaceful protesters.

Two days later, Shaw, McClure and the Confederate Paymaster, who had joined them; and had spent the past week in protracted discussions with some of the most well and respected private banks in the City; were at the workshops of Joseph Whitworth. Encouraged by the War Office and Whitehall, who were still counting the cost of the war in Crimea, his latest invention had an impressive reputation that the Southerners wanted to see.

"Now this is something else," McClure proclaimed, turning round to Shaw with a broad smile on his face.

"It's known as the sharpshooter," Whitworths senior sales engineer explained showing them the finer points of the rifle.

"Yes, I've heard," the Irish American replied, secretly pleased with the fact that whilst he would never been allowed anywhere near the Whitworth factory, had he remained in the British Army as a mere soldier, he was being treated as someone of importance.

"Incredible results last year at Bisley. Even the Queen tried her hand by all accounts," the salesman continued looking forward to a sale. "You could create a lot of panic on the battlefield with one of these."

He passed the rifle to Shaw, who looked down the barrel and saw how it differed from all the other rifles to date, and which gave it the extra accuracy over all its rivals.

"They don't come cheap, Sir," the salesman reminded them looking through his sheaf of papers that had the latest prices clearly marked. "And there will be a delay in any order over twenty according to the factory manager."

"Twenty it will be then for delivery by the end of next month if you will," Shaw confirmed. "We are holding space on a ship leaving Liverpool late February and another from Glasgow a week later. We will pay fifty per cent by the end of the week, the rest payable on loading in your yard, if that's acceptable."

Before the salesman had started to calculate his bonus, McClure asked about the latest field piece that Whitworths had developed. General Stonewall Jackson had raised the question before the three of them had left all of two months ago. The stubborn American had heard that the mobile breech loading twelve pounder had performed well in trials and was known to be accurate at well over two miles.

"It's a great piece of ordnance, Mr Shaw," the salesman confirmed passing the manual to McClure, "but it's in a different workshop and you won't be able to inspect it until I have obtained a special permit, as it's still under trials and that won't be until tomorrow."

McClure thumbed through the manual flicking the pages from the back in the manner of most soldiers. Only half educated, having volunteered for the British Army as soon as the recruiting officer would take him, he was being tutored by an accommodating lady back in Charleston. He couldn't totally comprehend all the literature before him, but understood enough to realise that this was a very powerful machine that could tip the balance in open fighting.

"How many of these are available?" Shaw asked the following day having consulted with McClure as they trooped off the field having seen an impressive display of fire power.

"Two are available right away," the salesman replied having worked out the details with the senior armourer the previous night after the Americans had left for their hotel in Enfield.

Shaw totted up the list of purchases, just enough to make up a small consignment on a ship, but large enough to make a difference on the field of battle. He looked through the list provided by General Lee back home. They were due to head west for Stroud the following day, where numerous streams fed the river there and more than thirty mills made the best military cloth.

Finally they had to visit the leather factories of Northampton where the finest military boots were made. Exhausted from their travels, but elated by success in getting enough equipment to fill a small ship, they surveyed the long list of guns, ammunition and all the sundries required by an army.

"So it's off to Paris then?" McClure asked Shaw on the last day of their visit, which had taken them three weeks.

"Not if I can help it," he assured the Irishman, who was only too pleased to hear that he would be returning to his pretty governess before she tired of his absence.

"I think we are near the five hundred tons of hardware we've promised General Lee for the first ship into Wilmington," he continued.

"And after that?" the soldier asked, already suspecting the answer.

"We'll be back time and time again for weaponry and stores in exchange for cotton and tobacco until we've sent those Yankees five hundred miles beyond the Mason Dixie line." Shaw declared as he sat back and flung a whisky straight down his throat.

"One trip is enough for me," replied McClure. "I'll go for a posting if it's all right with you."

"Well, you've done well enough I must admit," Shaw half congratulated him, aiming a meaty hand to slap him on the back. "Are you sure you weren't a deserter all those years ago?"

McClure laughed. It had been an experience that he was hardly likely to forget.

He drained his whisky, noting with interest that it was Irish and one of the best. He was indeed well pleased with himself having tested numerous weapons, the tools of his trade, talked to experts in the field and increased his knowledge threefold. But his place was in the field of battle, not in some country far from the action. He was not bothered by the politics, the deals, the arguments, the deceits and the fallouts; and wished only to get back to the warmth of his new homeland and the business of a soldier.

"There's one more visit to make," Shaw declared having booked their passage home for the following week. "We need to pay a visit to Armstrong's yard on the Tyne."

McClure looked up from his magazine.

"They make warships and big guns, very big guns; and rumour has it that Lincoln has managed to purchase a battleship that was for the Argentinians," he explained to his colleague.

"Who's carrying on with these purchases when we're back home?" asked McClure as the evening drew to a close having consumed half a bottle of the best malt. "Surely ships are outside our remit?"

"I have two agents working on our behalf and of course maritime purchases need an enormous budget," Shaw confirmed pouring out yet another drink. "But this could be a long war and President Jefferson Davis, I understand, would like to know more."

"How long do you think this war will last?" McClure asked.

Not more than two years came the reply from a tired Shaw. He too was wishing that someone else would take over the job. Thank goodness he was not having to deal with the French. They struck even a harder bargain than the British.

Chapter 7

The eight o'clock fast train from Birmingham, New Street emerged from the deep cutting and tunnel and approached Liverpool terminus station, coming off the summit level; and rumbled in to the platform, brakes squealing to a halt. The train was late but only marginally, due to points icing up and both driver and fireman had worked hard in the last hour to try and make up some lost time.

Second and third-class passengers, most of whom had joined at Manchester jostled shoulder to shoulder in the closed compartments of the carriages, ready to spill out and make a quick exit onto the platform and into the city. The hard slatted seats bolted firmly to the floor and the minimum of springing in the carriage construction encouraged them to stand up well before they needed to; and the northern banter permeated throughout as they removed packages and bags from the overhead racks.

City workers, travellers and salesmen, peddling for their principals in the Industrial revolution that was sweeping the country, made up the bulk of the passengers. And for Victorian Liverpool and Manchester that meant cotton, the heart of the textile industry. Shouting over each other they eased open the doors before the train came to a stop, contrary to the regulations of the Railway Company, and hundreds of mainly young men in tight fitting and well-worn suits made ready for the barrier.

But it was not all men. A scattering of women, less noisy and concentrated in small groups, waited for the melee to subside before emerging onto the platform. They were the new generation of young ladies finding their way into commerce, where dexterity and neatness were in demand.

For to get to Liverpool in 1861 from all points north, east or south of the bog lands of Lancashire, the railway was the fastest means of transport, if not the only means to get into the city.

In the first-class compartments, a more fortunate clientele enjoyed well upholstered seats with arm rests and a toilet shared between compartments. The majority of these passengers were also men, but some had wives with them and they certainly would not be making a rush for the doors. They would wait until the engine had kissed the buffers at Lime Street station, and the mass of passengers had departed, before gathering umbrellas, portmanteau bags and top hats and leisurely making for the hansom cabs lined up in the station fore course that they had booked in advance.

George and Charlotte Forwood stepped awkwardly from the carriage, as the bulk of the passengers disappeared towards the barriers, and beckoned the nearest porter, neatly turned out in livery complete with a tie and stiffened collar, and his badge number freshly polished on his sleeve.

Above them the condensed steam and fine soot from half a dozen engines spiralled slowly upwards to the glass and cast iron roof that spanned the six tracks, finally lodging in the crevasses of the structure. It was just about the busiest time of the day and the station thronged with humanity at its basic level.

Placard walkers strolling silently from platform to platform, advertised the latest eating houses, newspaper vendors screeching the overnight news, pasty faced young men held up display boards, pickpockets waiting for their prey; and flower ladies pressed for a sale their baskets full of spring colours.

Taking their luggage with the ease of a man well used to manual work, the porter deftly steered his trolley through the last of the crowds, nodding as he passed a railway policeman and humming contently to himself.

George was heading off for a meeting with his partners, Messrs Leech and Harrison, a union that started shortly after Napoleon had been beaten at Waterloo, and trading as cotton importers at offices in Dale Street. His news did not make very good reading. In fact it was not good news for anybody in the cotton industry, right the way down to the workers on the shop floor.

Liverpool, Manchester and indeed every small town in Lancashire were reliant on the crop to keep the mills turning, the workers paid, and the profits coming in. He was going to report that in the last six weeks only two cargoes had arrived from the Southern States, when previously it would have been at least two ships a week.

"It's no good Charlotte," he thundered as she blew him a kiss behind his ear just as a jockey would calm a stallion. "This situation in America has to be sorted out soon and quickly too. The government are reluctant to help and factories are closing."

"I fully understand," she soothed. "I was brought up on a plantation as you are fully aware. It was resolved then and it will be again."

She patted his gloved hand with her own, brushed a stray hair away from her forehead and straightened up.

"Now go and explain it all to your colleagues whilst I take a cab home, check the latest with the housekeeper, and discuss supper with the cook," she instructed. "For a change everyone is home for dinner and the weekend."

George looked benevolently at his wife, admiring the sweet lines of her body despite being well into her middle age.

"Now just don't dwell too much on your precious cotton. Give a little thought to the mill owners and the workers and my regards to old Leech and Harrison. But for them, their wisdom and financial help over the years we have to count ourselves lucky." she lectured as a parting shot.

George grunted in general agreement, as he hailed a cab, settled her into her seat for her journey to the west of the city, and then turned away for the short walk into the city.

"And don't be late," she called out as the cab driver flicked his whip at his horse and turned smartly of the pavement. "We've lots to discuss."

It was now late in 1861, but the past few months of the troubles in America and the cotton crisis had taken its toll on George. Charlotte had chided him only the previous day in their Birmingham hotel. He had to admit his step was not quite so sprightly, his back and hips ached at times, his paunch was a little more prominent and his grey hair that was slicked down ever so slightly, was receding and thinning. But at a little over average height, he still looked a commanding and confident figure measured against many of his colleagues, and certainly when compared to his partners, both of whom were well passed retirement age, but reluctant to give up the reins.

George thought that the walk would do him some good, clear his mind from two days of difficult meetings in the Midlands. Five minutes later, he took the steps up to the imposing building with renewed vigour, passed the brass plaque announcing the business of the partnership and ordered a fresh coffee from his clerk.

"Any mail?" he enquired as he pushed open the heavy door into his office, which just overlooked the river and walked towards his desk. The pile stacked up, spilling over the leather surface, answered his question.

"I would go home if I was you," his secretary suggested as he sifted through the most interesting looking packages. "And come back with a fresh mind in the morning."

Nicholas completed unlocking the massive doors of the warehouse in Salthouse dock, pocketing the master key, a substantial piece of ironwork and hung up the chunky lock by the hasp. The foreman and the two brothers pushed open the oak doors which protested and creaked on the curved iron track, as the weight was taken equally between the oiled hinges and the rusty metal set into the cobbled floor. Immediately above the main doors and on each floor of the long building, smaller apertures fitted with folding hatches and equally strong double doors gave the impression of fortress. Opened out as required when the warehouse was being filled or emptied of cargo, it enabled several gangs of men to work at the same time with hindrance.

On the highest floor affixed to the walls of the brick building and tied back to the roof with iron struts a rusty crane, with an equally ancient chain and hook, looked down haughtily onto the quayside at just the right angle to remind one of the birds by which it was named.

Inside, the warehouse opened up into a vast windowless space, the floors above supported by huge pine pillars. It had not been opened up for the best part of six weeks. Like all other cotton warehouses that were almost empty, the ground floor had been cleared of bales, all of which had been removed to the upper floors. Here the air was less dank, and fresh air could circulate. The void space of the main level was scattered with rubbish, wood dunnage, rope and the remains of rats dissected by a family of cats, who survived only by the numerous vermin that roamed the building buried in nests, deep in the foundations.

In the far corner a substantial stairway connected each floor and having pushed aside the debris, which the foreman should have made certain was cleared away in accordance with the dock regulations, the three men made for the first floor.

A sweet smell greeted them as they examined the square bales, covered in burlap and secured by tough string from corner to corner. Stamped in the name of Pym and Kellack, the Company's agents in New Orleans, at least the cotton was in good condition, even though it looked somewhat pathetic stacked three high. The warehouse contained only about three hundred tons. It should have been full with over a thousand tons of cotton, with five hundred tons coming in each week. Nicholas and James cast around at the dismal state. Nicholas kicked at a bale, whilst James looked out of the barred window. The foreman just fumed to himself reading his paper lounging on a dilapidated wooden chair.

They were waiting for four railway wagons to be shunted along the quay, so that they could despatch fifty tons of cotton away to one of their best customers, a mill owner from Rochdale, who was begging them, even prepared to up the price, if necessary, to keep his mill going.

George had worked out a fair means of ensuring the meagre contents of the store could be shared out as fairly as possible up the valleys, and it was taking all his time, which was why he was late. But it was an impossible task as all the other cotton factors were finding, to ensure that the wheels could be kept turning, the raw material spun and the shuttle cocks flying.

Nicholas and James paced up and down the near empty warehouse, resorting in the end to amuse themselves by examining the roof of the building, which they leased from the dock company. They could see daylight in one corner and Nicholas made a note to press for a repair. They had despatched the foreman to find and engage some stevedores to lump the bales to the open doors and load them for their onward journey.

The two hand cranked cranes were oil primed, for action safety catches on, ready to drop the bales twenty feet into the wagons below. Although not a fragile cargo, cotton had to be kept dry, and the bales intact, as any damage would be noted when it reached the mill, and that might incur a measure of compensation. As they peered round the upper floor door, they could see and hear the wagons they clanking up the tracks and across the points, preceded by a dock railwayman, red flag at the ready.

James kicked the last of the dead rats over the lip of the opening and stared across the dock, that should have been full of ships unloading the base goods from America and loading the finished articles from the country's factories to places across the world. Only two ships were tied up and neither was discharging cargo.

There was little evidence of any activity, the few dockers that were around waiting to be called for a job, collected in small groups around the lock pump house, the fires of which would normally be belching out smoke. Today, the fires were cold, the pistons stationary and the great beams that usually oscillated in such majesty were locked like an enormous weighing machine poised to make a calculation.

George arrived in time to see the last half dozen bales squeezed into the wagons, which were then swiftly covered by a dirty tarpaulin and lashed down. They would be marshalled into a train that evening, for a journey up the valley of the River Irwell in the morning. At least the looms of Rochdale would be kept clattering and chattering away for another week or so.

As the wagons banged gratingly together, and the procession moved down the dock, Nicholas slammed one door shut and James the other, slotting the timber strong back into place and wedging it firmly so that it was impossible to open from outside. Dancing down the wooden upper staircase worn in two grooves, where countless dockers had climbed up and down, they glided down on the bannisters of the last section like two teenagers until they reached the ground floor. Here they repeated the exercise on main doors, putting their backs into the last inch or two of the travel, until they were snug enough to slide the bolt into the hasp. Nicholas exerted his privilege as the elder and produced the key just as George called them over.

"Be at the house for supper at seven o'clock sharp," he said, playfully poking them each in the chest. "I've some important news for you to digest over in the next two days."

"But I've a concert ticket for tonight, Father, as you well know," James reminded him. "Can't it wait?"

"They'll be performing tomorrow surely," George protested.

James nodded reluctantly in agreement.

"Cancel it, give it away," George answered, not taking no for an answer. "This is business, family business; not pleasure and I never joke, as you both know."

James knew well that he didn't joke. Years earlier he had been trying to persuade his father to let him go to sea, but George had refused point blank, insisting that he complete his education and settle for a life in the city, making money in the port. It was only after a family walking holiday in the Lake District that it all changed.

They were caught out in a deluge and after struggling back to the house, James had been laid low with a cold that went to his chest. For three months he was confined to bed, worrying his parents to the point that they thought he would not pull through. It was not until the doctors declared that the sickly boy would benefit from continual exposure to the sea air if he were ever going to improve, that George finally relented.

From that day on James had been his own man. A voyage to Australia and back where his sharp mind had conquered the basics of navigation, and with spells on the Liverpool pilot boats and as deputy harbour master at Runcorn he had a good grounding on the ways of the sea.

James shrugged off his father's insistence and made a parting brotherly comment to Nicholas and headed back to the workshops of the chain and block company, which he had recently joined as a buyer of raw materials. The foundry there made every conceivable size of anchor chain and pulleys, capable of making the new wires that were standard requirements for ships and mines. Tomorrow, they were due to take delivery of a machine that could test heavy chain to destruction, and James with his maritime experience was keen to see it in operation.

George waited until they were all relaxed after supper before he tapped the table and attracted their attention. Nicholas and James snapped into attention, Charlotte less so and Alice May not at all.

"How was your visit to Ramsbottom," he asked Alice, "has it answered all your questions?"

"Oh yes, Father, it has indeed," she answered. "I have made up my mind and I want to go the America to see for myself."

"I see, I see," George answered leaving Alice in some doubt that he would sanction it. "For the moment, I have something more important to say."

"I've joined a small group today," he announced casually as they fidgeted in their chairs in anticipation. "We have come to the conclusion that we must do something positive, if not completely daring and I concede somewhat hazardous."

Charlotte and the three children looked at each other, wondering where the conversation was leading to.

"It's not illegal, but is frowned on in Government circles, so it will be somewhat clandestine so as not to draw too much attention," he continued. "We don't want to make the situation any worse than it is already, but doing nothing is not an option. Too many livelihoods are at stake including our own."

"And what exactly is proposed," said Nicholas, somewhat taken by the excitement of it.

"We propose to form a consortium to ship weapons and ammunition to Georgia and the Carolina's in direct exchange for cotton and tobacco."

George continued, "New Orleans is almost completely blocked by the Unionists, but it is thought that small cargoes could be taken up the shallow rivers on the east coast."

The four of them looked aghast at the proposal of such a far-fetched scheme. It didn't seem feasible let alone legal, and this from their father, who had always been a pillar of society and always played a straight bat.

Nicholas and James bombarded him with questions. Charlotte and Alice looked at each other dumbfounded and then disappeared into the kitchen. Whatever would the man of the house come up with next.

George continued at length with the full attention of his two sons.

"The plan is that we acquire a ship, and maybe others later, and run cargoes Bermuda to Charleston and Wilmington on a continuous basis in the spring," he outlined. "Each voyage will be a round trip of two weeks, so that over the spring and summer of next year we should be able to do about ten runs."

Nicholas and James looked at each other.

Having got their attention, he continued, "At say, about two thousand tons of materials in and maybe three thousand tons of cotton out it should keep us in business over the season."

"But they don't produce cotton in that part of Carolina," Nicholas reminded his father. "It's a highly wooded State and they mainly export timber."

"But they do have a rail road connection all the way into Tennessee and Kentucky and intend to ship it out past the Union blockade," George said showing them the letter from Mr Pym.

"Apparently there are a number of ships operating, but they are not fast enough to run the gauntlet. Fortunately, the Union Navy just does not have enough chase ships, even though their base is not far away at Hampton Roads, so a considerable number of ships get through."

"But didn't the Forwood, Leech and Harrison Company own a ship before that went disastrously wrong?" Nicholas reminded his father.

"We aren't necessarily going to own a ship this time, Nicholas," his father answered, adjusting his glasses and pulling yet another sheet of paper from his briefcase. "And it will be a different company in any case."

James pressed his father to elaborate. "What's the exact proposal?" His interest in ships had never waned even though he hadn't been further than the Bar light vessel in five years. Lloyds List was the first paper he read each day before anything else.

"We are going to charter the largest and fastest paddle steamer on the market and run it from Bermuda to those ports that I've just mentioned, and I have a job for both of you." George said pulling out a plan of one of the latest vessels on the market. "It's about time you were both at the sharp end.

"Nicholas, I think that it is time that you looked at the American operation of Pym and Kellack, and I'm arranging for you to go to New York on the next available steamer." George said after they had all relaxed after supper. "Take one of their small ships to New Orleans before Lincoln manages to close down the port completely, and ensure that what is left of the supply chain still functions."

Nicholas, who only the previous day had listened to an impassioned speech at the Manchester Free Trade Hall, and heard for the first time of Lincoln's appeal to the Lancashire mill workers, which was having some effect, spoke up.

"Surely we can do more to encourage Egypt and India to make up the shortfall," he retorted, protesting about the proposal, but realistic to know that he was wasting his time.

"Now James," George said, regaining his composure. "You and I are going to Glasgow just as soon as I can make arrangements. I doubt that you can remember going to the shipbuilding yard of James Kirk?"

"I can, Father, just," James reminded him, "That's when I became fascinated with ships and the sea."

George sat back in his chair and twirled his whiskey glass in his hand. It wasn't one of his finest hours, borrowing money from his family, which resulted in some of them emigrating to Australia.

The skeleton of George's first venture into shipping was still visible in the mud at Birkenhead. It's failure was not so much in the hull or the engine, but in the boiler of all things, Kirk had said in his letter of consolation when the project failed.

"And what about me?" asked Alice, once again put out by not being mentioned."

"Ah, Alice May," he said taking her by the hand, "If you wish you can take the same boat as your brother."

Chapter 8

James Kirk walked down the slipway, ducking beneath the shores that held the *City of Dublin* upright on the solid base of the yard. It was first light on the last day of the month, and a heavy frost lay sprinkled at his feet as he crunched down to the muddy waters of the river Leven. It was low water, the tide was well out and the bank opposite looked no distance at all.

The yard had yet to come to life and the swans looked absolutely majestic gliding around the debris that never seemed to go away, picking up the remains of bread thrown out by the kitchen staff preparing the Chairman's luncheon party. Launching day was a time for celebration, the yard full of excitement, the men cheerful at the thought of a grand meat pie lunch washed down with free beer.

It had been a challenging build, both technically and in construction and as a result she was late in completion. He expected to make the time up in the fitting out berth though, because mechanisation and outsourcing of the passenger accommodation was going to speed up the finishing date.

The owners of the *City of Dublin* needed the ship for the following season and he needed the space for the next ship that was due to be launched in two months. That was destined for the Thames Estuary running between London and the new piers at Southend and Herne Bay.

Fortunately, he had not succumbed to a punishing delivery clause in the contract, although he had been pinned down to a speed and dead weight carrying clause and a fixed price for everything else. The new technology was causing all the shipbuilders to re-consider delivery dates.

Kirk was confident on all counts that the ship would perform on the time trials, if not exceed the expectation of the owners that required the ship to be the fastest on the Wales to Ireland cross channel service. Speed was the all-important factor for the new generation of shipowners.

Kirk walked down the slipway, ducking underneath the shores as he moved from the bow to the water's edge. The tide would be at its highest in four hours or so, and then stand for an hour over the period of launching. It was an ideal day and always looked forward to by the yard workers, who had the day off apart from those directly involved with the launching.

The *City of Dublin* was their largest vessel to date and destined for the Holyhead to Dublin service, although the ship would not go right up the shallow River Liffy, but would terminate at the new port of Kingstown, recently protected by a harbour wall.

The owners had demanded that the ship should be the latest in all technical respects, and today when it settled in the water, although it would not be yet down to its marks, they would realise what a greyhound their *City of Dublin* was going to be.

On reaching the midship section, Kirk looked up at the massive sponson on the starboard side and its connection to the hull. The strains on the securing of the iron work to the hull and through to the other side were continually testing his drawing skills. At this point, the ship was at its widest at fifty feet and almost grazed the sides of the machinery shop on one side and the carpenter's workshop on the other.

Three ships were on the building ways and they couldn't build a bigger vessel with modifying the yard first. Fortunately, the Chairman had responded to his pressure at the last Annual meeting and secured an option on some nearby land at a reasonable price. Kirk and his colleagues at the Institute were convinced that within the next decade ships would double in size, if not treble, such was the demand and pressure on the industry.

The launch would have to be a precise operation with the ship to be totally upright as it travelled down the slipway. He checked the additional supports under the paddle wheels to make sure the launch was true.

Kirk watched his foreman supervising the laying out of the drag cables, the dressing of tallow of the ways, and the wedging of the cradles that would take the weight of the ship and allow the ship to slide on the given word and strolled over to him.

"Your best white overalls and cleanest flat hat, Arthur," he called out to his most experienced man, who was still in his usual blue boiler suit, having made the usual inspection of the bilges from inside the hull as a high-pressure water hose was directed on the ironwork.

The shipwright laughed. "Only when the guests have arrived," he replied balancing his twenty-eight-pound sledge hammer on the nearest keel block. On his command four of his best men would strike home the wedges in unison to send The *City of Dublin* on its way.

With the launch timed for midday, there was still a great deal of tidying up work to complete before the Chairman of the Western and Irish Packet Company arrived along with the dignitary of the town. Kirk was expecting about fifty people for the event and that didn't include the local brass band.

By the time the sun was up, caterers were appearing with tables and benches, spits and roasting trays for the hog and venison and portable ovens for the foul. In a prominent position, an ox that rotated on a spit over a fire tended all night was spitting gently into the embers.

Boxes of plates and utensils were marched in and a hog, already speared and warm from earlier cooking over a fire appeared from behind a shed straddled by two young cooks, who shouted in vain to get the stands made up. At the bow of the ship and within feet of the boardroom, carpenters clamped the last of the handrails of the viewing platform into position, watched by Kirk, who was peering out of the open window, keenly aware of the dangers to the guests. It was not unknown for accidents to happen in the enthusiasm of catapulting a bottle of champagne at the bow of a new ship from a temporary wooden stage some fifteen feet off the ground.

Kirk watched the base of the slipway as the water slowly crept up the yard bringing with it the flotsam and jetsam from the city. Like most rivers it was an obstacle to small boats, the paddles of steamers and the water intakes of all vessels. It swished daily up and down the river, the larger timbers having been retrieved for firewood, until finally being swept out to sea on an ebb tide with the assistance of a rare easterly wind. Half salt water and half fresh it supported everything that floated; the Clyde was a sewer of mud, human excrement, but a life blood; one that a million people depended on.

By mid-morning, the yard was buzzing with workers making the last adjustments, visitors arriving before time and the townspeople gathering at all the best spots for watching the launching. A large boisterous crowd congregated on the far bank, where a local publican had secured just about the best position for those not allowed in the yard. Here the vessel would rush up the bank at breakneck speed pushing up a tremendous wave before the chains brought the ship to a halt. If the wave came over the bank and swamped them in a foaming wave crest it would be considered a bonus, if not good luck.

The band drifted in through the gates in twos and threes with the conductor clutching his music tightly for fear of losing it. If he lost his grip it would surely end up in the murky water, before his colleagues could pluck the sheets from the swirling air. In dark blue uniforms trimmed with gold tassels and brass buttons, the Dumbarton band was one of the smartest on the Clyde and played a wide range of music. For the first time, a lady trombonist was included after much objection from the Masonic elders, who considered it not the done thing.

They were of the opinion that she should be confined to private parties and definitely not to wear trousers. The band had been tuning up in the bandstand close by between Victoria Street and Bruce Street for the past half an hour and the strains of their music could be heard above the general excitement of the workers only yards away. Kirk listened to one of his favourite pieces, smiled to himself. It was going to be a grand day.

Right on cue, the main guests stepped off the special train at Dumbarton East station less than a quarter of a mile from the yard. Kirk had despatched the company secretary to meet them and had ordered cabs for the party, but only the Chairman from the Shipping Company and his wife had taken up the facility. The rest of guests, mainly the younger generation, could see the chimney stacks of the yard, and that it was no distance, and in the warming sun they strolled across the Knox-lands and through the main gate.

It was an hour before launching time, timed to be just before high water in case the tide didn't make. Although there was plenty of water in the river Kirk always liked to have time in hand in case of unforeseen circumstances. The Chairman effused at his guests, his customers of course that were always right, and offered them coffee. Away to one side the ox and hog were turning slowly over glowing embers, barrels of beer were being lifted onto trestles and taps fitted, and the waitresses driven by a dragon of a supervisor were adjusting the tables and benches.

At the precise agreed time, the Chairman of the Packet Company in morning suit, top hat and spats, which he always wore whenever in doubt over rough ground, guided his wife up the dozen steps to the platform, that brought them right out under the bow. The champagne was in a rack ready to guide the bottle right on the prow ensuring that it broke with a clean swipe.

After a short vote of thanks to Kirk and his team he introduced his wife and stepped back a pace. With a clear steady voice, of one used to public speaking, she pronounced the vessel, and with considerable aplomb despatched the bottle, which smashed immediately, scattering glass and champagne onto the ground below. In just a moment, the ship with the yard number of one hundred and twenty-one, a series of riveted metal plates, became the *City of Dublin,* a legal entity.

The band started up, the crowd cheered, the foreman swung his sledgehammer followed by four others in strict unison and the ship started its first short journey with the hiss of wood sliding on wood. After a slight hesitation the ship slowly gathered speed and the crowd gasped and cheered. The blunt stern smacked into the water with a resounding shock wave crescendo, and the drag chains rumbled, muffling the band, who upped the decibels in response.

Within seconds the ship was free off the cradles that held it, and they floated away on the tide to be gaffed by waiting boats. In no time at all, the hull approached the opposite bank at speed, much to delight of the watchers there, and stopped short of grounding. Ropes were thrown to waiting tugs and by the time the dignitaries had left the stage, the ship was secure in the fitting out berth. The launching was finished, but the party had yet to start.

"When do you expect our next vessel to take to trialling?" the Chairman of the Packet company asked as they supped a fine wine and lunch in the boardroom.

"All being well and if we don't get too hard a winter, I am looking at three months' time. Four at the most," Kirk answered. The first instalment had been paid at the laying of the keel, the second at launching of the ship, the third on commissioning, and it yet had to be registered.

"Good," replied the shipowner, "but we may have to change our plans."

"Oh really," the builder responded, thinking back to the contract for the ship that was in the files in the next room. "Why is that?"

"Tell me," the new owner of the *City of Dublin* continued, "can a vessel like this make an Atlantic crossing?"

Kirk looked at the man, slightly incredulous at what he was hearing, although he had heard rumours and that similar conversation with the Americans only a few days previously.

"It's a possibility," he answered moving the man to a corner of the room to keep the conversation to themselves. "A number of modifications would be needed, some permanent and some temporary. And it is unlikely to be cheap."

"I see," answered the other. "Good and bad news then."

Kirk thought about the alterations out of contract clause. It could well be profitable to the company and he rubbed his hands together under the table at the prospect.

"It would need the latest design of feathering paddles, increased bunker space, a refined condensing plant to avoid corrosion of the boiler and a simplification of the cargo space." he announced ticking off the extensive list mentally.

"Could you make some minor alterations to the City of Dublin here?" the man asked. "Like increasing the bunker space and the improved condensing system."

Kirk made a mental note and nodded. "There will be a considerable adjustment to the final cost, you understand?"

The other man nodded beginning to understand the complexity of the request.

"I presume that you would want still want the first-class accommodation arrangement?" Kirk asked.

"Oh, yes," the owner answered. "We just want to keep our options open at this stage, but for the next vessel we want a clear space that could be used for cargo or passengers."

"That sounds like a radical change in your commercial plans," Kirk pressed him.

"Yes, it is," agreed the owner of the newly launched *City of Dublin*, "At the moment we are not just certain about the market and proposals from interested parties are coming in by the minute."

"If you and I are thinking along the same lines then make sure you find the right Captain and that he doesn't drive it too hard." Kirk advised him.

"Are they hard to come by?" the other questioned, "Do you know anybody who'd suit?"

"I'll give it some thought," Kirk replied putting the man at ease. "In the meantime, I have a yard to manage."

The owner of the *City of Dublin* nodded.

"And out of interest just where might this consortium be coming from?" Kirk continued.

"Liverpool," the other said.

"I thought so," Kirk replied, turning away from his guest. "Good day to you."

Despite his earlier assurances, Kirk could not complete the vessel within three months, nor indeed the four months, but a day in from the beginning of April the *City of Dublin* was guided out of the fitting berth paddles thrashing, slowly into astern and then into ahead, until the ship was in midstream. Resplendent in the company's livery of black and white hull and a green funnel topped with a black band and in company with a yard tug, both vessels belched smoke in unison as they took the big sweep of the river towards the junction with the Clyde itself. A crowd, much smaller than that at the launching waved them away, and the yard whistle signalled a message of good luck. On board the owner's choice Captain looked on as the pilot guided the ship between the buoys and the training wall, which had been built up on the south bank to deepen the channel. Down below Kirk and a group of engineers from the yard, the Lloyd's Register inspector and the owner's representative watched on the engine room plates. Slowly the dials crept clockwise as the pressures increased to the red marks on the dials and the main boiler relief valve hinted that it would lift. On the bridge, one of Kirk's best seamen flicked the spokes of the wheel effortlessly from port to starboard as the compass adjuster picked his landmarks, checked bearings and re-arranged the correcting magnets. On passing Port Glasgow and Greenock, Kirk decided that all was well below and took the two flights of stairs to the open bridge that was protected from the elements by nothing more than a canvas screen to appreciate the vista of the mountains which were opening up to the west.

Ahead of them could be seen Helensburgh to the right, Dunoon and Holy Loch ahead. Rounding Cloch Point, they headed towards Largs to continue the work-up, before final testing off the measured mile to complete the trials. With the sun and the breeze over the port quarter, the smoke turned to a haze; and with the little tug left well behind at Greenock, the *City of Dublin* slipped through the placid waters of the Forth like a knife through butter leaving the merest of trails.

Incoming vessels hooted as they passed, crews of fishing boats looked up briefly then resumed their work hauling nets, indifferent to the occasion. Two large yachts, their crews smartly turned out in duck trousers and matching sweaters, moved effortlessly through the Forth; sails billowed out in perfect symmetry. Rounding Little Cum-brae Island, the pilot guided the ship back up the Forth towards the series of painted white poles on the land ahead on the port side. The wind had died away to nothing, the tide was at its weakest. The way was clear for the all-important speed trials. Kirk called the principal members of the crew to the bridge They would begin without delay, and within the hour it was confirmed when the stop watches were consulted. The ship was the fastest that had come out of Dumbarton.

Two days later, when the *City of Dublin* lay on the Brome law Quay, as close to the city as a ship could get, the owners hosted a small party of journalists, ship yard managers and city dignitaries. They were lauding platitudes on Kirk's team and his timed record of thirteen and a half knots on the trial day. Kirk remained nonplussed about the acknowledgements. He was already thinking of the next ship due to be launched in a week, and which he thought would be even faster. His thoughts were taken away by his accountant, who pushed his way through the revellers with the latest copy of Lloyd's List.

"Look at this," he said, bypassing the back page which was exclusively for ship movements, and opened up the centre page.

"Well, I'm buggered," replied Kirk, chuckling to himself.

In bold print, where there were several advertisements for second hand ships and redundant equipment was a block column for as ship, they both knew well.

For sale or charter

A new vessel just launched and trialled on the Clyde. Fitted with first class and second class accommodation. A side winder of 350 tons gross and capable of over 13 knots, the fastest vessel to date. Fitted with a combination of square and fore; and aft sails on two masts additional bunker capacity; and the latest navigational and safety equipment.

Chapter 9

Shaw and McClure looked down the waterfront at Glasgow trying to locate the *S.S. Lettita,* a medium sized cargo ship with a woodbine funnel, two masts and four hatches. Negotiating the cobbled quayside and railway tracks, burnished by the constant movement of wagons they passed taverns spilling out drunks, boarding houses advertising cheap rooms, and ships agents selling tickets on the nightly ferry to Belfast. It was only late afternoon and they watched with interest as an incoming ferry approached stern first at seemingly high speed, its paddles thrashing away in reverse to stem its progress before coming to rest as smoothly as a train in a station.

They had been advised not to walk the Bromielaw and Anderson quay after dark unless in company, and they still hadn't found what they were looking for. Beyond the Irish ferry, which was loading up for the night crossing, they could see the construction of the new Queens dock looming up, and a hundred men moving steadily among the granite blocks making the final cuts and joints before they were lifted and slotted into place.

They wondered whether they had been given the right information; and just as they were about to give up and retrace their steps the *Lettita* appeared at the very end of the quay. At only two and half thousand tons, the ship was already loaded down to the marks, and her decks were below the quay, so that to the casual eye she was almost camouflaged

The two men stood at the top of the gangway and looked around at the dismal surroundings. The ship was streaked with rust, the tall thin single funnel supported by four wires showing only the barest sign of the colours of its owner. They looked down at the wooden decks scored and grimy from the countless passage of men. All the hatches, except number two immediately underneath the bridge, were battened down for sea. The derrick above it swung gently, the guy ropes holding it in place loosely secured so that it described a lazy arc across the skyline before being jerked back whenever a vessel passed by. A black board on the quayside announced that the ship would sail at four o'clock, but there was little sign of activity even though the time was fast approaching. A wisp of smoke appeared from the cigarette thin smokestack and two men slammed open a door to climb the gangway.

"Go aboard," the younger man said pointing to the sleeve on his jacket, explaining, "The Captain's waiting for you. The bosun and I are off to drag the crew out of the nearest bar. They won't see Glasgow again for a good six months and maybe longer and like to savour the last moments."

The ship was bound for Santos, South America, but via Bermuda as the two Americans well knew. It had taken a lot of organising on Shaw's part to secure the deal, and book a passage for them and the shipment. McClure relaxed as the Captain offered them a departure whisky. Within the month they would be back in Virginia; Shaw with General Lee, and McClure with his girlfriend.

"I'm afraid your cargo has yet to arrive, Mr Shaw," the bluff Scottish Captain advised the two no sooner had they had picked up the tumblers.

"But we were given to understand by our agent that it's here in the port," Shaw replied, perplexed and angry that the shipment was delayed.

"Well, yes it's in the port, but not right here," the seafarer confirmed. "The harbour master and the lead agent thought it best to keep the consignment away from prying eyes."

"But it's marked machinery like the rest of your cargo to South America," Shaw complained.

"But that's genuine machinery not like yours," the Captain chuckled. "Don't worry, we are going to pick it up at Bowling on our way down. It's about an hour away. The wagons are already there."

Shaw took out a large handkerchief and wiped his brow with relief. It had been a tortuous journey acquiring and organising the deal, and although it was not the full order that he'd hoped for it was a start. Soon they would be in Bermuda and making the next arrangement with the agents there.

His job of making the purchases, establishing the pick-up places, and the routes would soon be over. He would be able to report a successful Mission to Jefferson Davis and then to bask in his success back on his plantation in Georgia.

"I'm afraid your accommodation won't be up to much," the Scotsman said once he had outlined the procedure at Bowling. "You've a choice of an unused cabin aft amongst the crew or a storeroom just down the alleyway midships. Two mattress' are all we can offer. It's not a ship for passengers, you understand."

On the quayside at Bowling four locked box wagons were being dragged into position by two dray horses. Stacked waist high inside were wooden crates marked machinery for South America via Bermuda. The *Lettita* glided gently alongside as the sun dipped below the horizon, lines were quickly thrown ashore and ropes secured the ship alongside. The steam winch clanked into action, and within the hour the cargo was on board, the hatch secured and the derrick housed and clamped.

The crew took a welcomed tot, the harbour master waved them off and in near darkness the pilot set a course for Gourock, his home town and where he would disembark. The *Lettita* was bound for the island of Bermuda, a port that in the space of a few months had been catapulted into notoriety. The Captain looked at the papers in front of him. It was none of his damn business to comment on the cargo they had just loaded as far away from prying eyes as possible.

Making money for his owners was all that concerned him. The money that they had just rewarded him for the short diversion would help, but hardly likely to buy the Clyde puffer that he was trying to acquire. Tramping the seas for the last thirty years had dampened his enthusiasm for adventure, and now a small coaster on a regular trade to the islands beckoned. If only more business like this was available his ambition might be achieved.

It was some time before the Captain could pick out the skyline of Bermuda in the evening sun. It was not quite new to him, but even so his Chief Officer checked and double checked the chart as the waters shallowed and the buildings came into focus. For winter, it had been a surprisingly trouble free voyage, as could often be the case in February, and the ship would not be delayed long, depending on whether a berth was immediately available. There were rumours of a great deal of activity in the port. It was almost a year since the first attack by the south, a short naval battle at the mouth of Charleston, and the papers in Glasgow were still full of subsequent actions that seemed to go the way of the Southerners.

"There's a space for you," the pilot advised the Captain as he boarded the *Lettita* at the harbour entrance to Bermuda. "But you will have to wait."

"Wait," said the burly seafarer, struggling into his well-worn jacket that was stained with beer and the remains of a boiled egg.

"Well you will have to wait today, Captain." the pilot replied as the ship rounded into the harbour, adding, "I've never seen so many ships here this month. When were you last here? They are coming in from all over the world. Even passenger ships on the Atlantic run are stopping off briefly."

The Captain tapped his pipe on the wooden taffrail emptying out the remains on the deck and grinding them in with the heel of his foot. Like most Captains, he was an impatient man.

"Shouldn't be too long, pilot," he said, "We've only two parcels to discharge, about two hundred tons and coal to discharge for the port I, understand. Five hundred tons in all. Two days is all we need if there is plenty of labour, three at the most otherwise."

"I'll send a boat away to the harbour master for you," the pilot suggested, as the anchor splashed into the blue waters of the inner harbour. "In fact I can drop you off."

"Don't want my crew to get too much of a chance to jump ship," retorted the Captain to the pilot engaged in conversation with a local tug, whose assistance had been turned away.

The pilot laughed as he watched a bumboat being expertly sculled by two striking young women. "They won't be short of distractions here, Captain, I can assure you."

On the deck below, Shaw and McClure paced the deck, as the ship lay at anchor all night in the outer harbour. Being cooped up at sea with little to do but watch was not in the least appealing. They had managed to get a message ashore by boat to their agents, Bone and Watcher, and had arranged a meeting once the ship was berthed the following day.

"Come in, come in," beamed Bone, somewhat of an ambling giant of a man, once the ship had been secured.

They had met in the Globe Hotel in the St George district, out of the way of too many prying eyes. It was a large room, painted white with large windows to take full advantage of the sun. On the walls a few paintings gave the place some appearance of atmosphere, and in the ceiling a large fan turned slowly from an unseen supply of power.

"Norman will be here soon," he effused, guiding them to a low suite of chairs and pouring out a glass of cool lemon.

Shaw sat back relaxed now that his part in the operation was now nearly over. McCluskey sat awkwardly as the conversation drifted around, wishing he was back in some sort of action.

"Tell me about your visit to England?" Bone continued, "It's been some months I guess since you were last here. And a lot has happened, as you might guess."

Shaw nodded, content to swap stories with the agent, who was fast becoming a major player in the trans-shipment of goods heading in all directions, but mainly to the Southern States.

"There's even a liner stopping off tomorrow with five hundred tons of coal bunkers that will be dumped on the quay and snapped up within twenty four hours." Bone continued as Norman Watcher entered and introduced himself.

"And that rust bucket of a ship that brought you here, can't imagine that you enjoyed that passage, especially you, Mr Shaw?" Watcher chipped in, ordering another round of drinks.

"We could have made a better choice," Shaw agreed, wishing to get down to the business of the day. "We're carrying on to New York by steamer once this consignment is on the way."

"Now the cargo," Watcher intervened, "Here's what we have arranged so far. You'll be aware that Bermuda is full of informers and spies, and even now the waterfront knows what is in the hold of the *S.S. Lettita*."

Shaw grimaced at the fact that despite all his clandestine efforts, the contents of his cargo was going to be bandied about on the waterfront grapevine.

"I shouldn't worry," cut in Bone. "This is not the first consignment that has passed through Bermuda. It has been going on for some months, but not a big scale yet. Guns from Europe have been heading for both the North and the South. The problem for you is getting it to the Southern States without the ship being confiscated."

Shaw interjected. "We're well aware of that, of course. In fact whilst in England we went up to Glasgow to look at the possibility of using the latest paddle steamers."

"Well they haven't arrived here yet," Bone confirmed, flipping through his records. "And they couldn't risk a crossing until April at the earliest."

"We weren't actually going to buy one," Shaw intervened. "We were looking at the logistics. It's never been attempted before by all accounts."

"It's the only sure way of breaching the blockade. I've seen them on the Hudson River," Bone assured them.

"So, what can you offer at the moment?" Shaw asked.

"A coastal sailing schooner," the agent confirmed. "Sailing tomorrow."

"Just a sailing schooner," exclaimed Shaw, totally surprised that it was the only option. "A vessel under sail alone would never make it."

"That's something, I suppose." answered Shaw, not quite convinced.

"You'll be surprised maybe to hear that before the war, six hundred ships traded there a year on regular routes and that at any one time a dozen would be lining the quays," Bone said. "And a regular steamer sailed from there to Baltimore every week. Of course, that has stopped now. However, Wilmington has one of the best rail connections on all the east coast which is why it's now so important."

Second Officer Toby Barnes of the steamship *Perthshire* looked intently through his binoculars at the coastline of Bermuda away on the port bow. The skyline was trying hard to burst above the horizon, but at not more than an atoll in the middle of the Atlantic, it was an island that was often Missed by early adventurers.

The ship was trading regularly between Liverpool and New York, and carrying a full load of passengers and cargo, but on this voyage it was stopping at the British island because of the demand that was being placed on the Company. A growing number of passengers who wished to holiday there dictated a diversion. A mixed population of Americans, British and ex-colonised Negroes on the island had resulted in an easy-going life, which was thriving from being on the trade routes between the new world and the old. Well sheltered apart from the worst of the Atlantic storms, which fortunately often passed it by, the naval base had developed into a commercial port where ships met and transactions were made. Along with it spawned the ships agents, the warehouses, the hotels, the boarding houses and brothels that serviced the industry of carrying people and goods across the oceans.

The *Perthshire* was due to disembark a hundred passengers or so from Liverpool and take on fifty or so bound for New York. In the brief stay there, they were due to unload mail for the island, fifty tons of cargo that the island needed, and a parcel of machinery in boxes. Toby had been in charge of loading the boxes and stowing them in the strongroom, a large steel boxed section between deck.

On questioning the bills of lading with the agent and in conversation with the Chief officer and Captain, who weren't really interested as long as it was properly stowed, secured and locked, he put it at the back of his mind. But it didn't stay long there and when he was checking the strong room during the passage he looked more closely at the consignment, that was not one but two.

Although similarly boxed they were both marked 'Machinery' and had different markings and a code as to the destination. The smaller consignment was for Bermuda and the larger for Albany on the Hudson River.

"It's not something we are going to talk about, Toby," said his Captain when he had broached the subject of machinery in the boxes, that really didn't look like machinery.

Having been an apprentice on a store ship for part of the Crimean War, Toby recognised army supplies when he saw them.

"Whatever they want to do with each other is up to them. The bill of lading says that it is milling machinery so just leave it at that," the Captain declared. "And don't discuss with the other junior officers, or you'll all be detained on board in New York."

Toby knew the Captain had the whip hand. He was hoping to meet his aunt Agnatha in South Street Seaport. She had retired from the sea and whilst her husband was on his last voyage, had just started a respite house for apprentices and junior officers, and was immersing herself in the New York social and religious scene.

Not more than three days later, the *Perthshire* was nosed alongside her usual berth at the southern tip of Manhattan and the passengers were streaming ashore to be quizzed by officials. Customs and Immigration officials were getting more and abrasive with nationals and non-nationals alike, as to their reasons for returning and visiting America.

In charge of the mailbags and cargo of specie, Toby was kept busy for most of the day and it was not until the evening that he was able to relax and discover a note from his aunt Agnatha inviting him to lunch the following day. He hadn't seen her since finishing his apprenticeship some five years earlier and couldn't wait to hear of her latest enterprise. Toby had told the two cadet officers on board of his relatives scheme of providing a quiet refuge for young seafarers in the port.

"Can we post mail there?" they asked, "And read the latest papers and periodicals."

"Don't see why not," answered Toby throwing them a map of Manhattan. "But I don't think she will sell beer, just soft drinks and the latest in sweets."

Toby remembered her as a trim lady of medium height, hair tied back in a bun with a severe face as if she was carrying the woes of the world on her back.

But then she would look up from her handiwork and smile from ear to ear, and demand to know what her visitor was thinking. Aunt Agnatha had no children of her, just a couple of nephews and nieces that she never saw, and Toby her favourite. And as such he had a small collection of socks and sweaters, most of which were fortunately on board, but now rather on the small side and well worn.

Agnatha's house was only two blocks away just off the waterfront and aimed at those young sailors on cargo ships in port for days, if not weeks; rather than for those on passenger ships, who would be turning round in a matter of hours. Even so any and all would be welcomed in her house, a fact that hadn't escaped the authorities in the port and some worthies in Manhattan.

Toby sent the two cadets on their way with a warning about the perils of New York and sifted through his drawers for the best choice for tomorrow. It would have to be the rolled necked sweater and the latest pair of socks she had sent him, one red and the other green.

"Oh my dear, Toby," Agnatha gushed at him as he climbed the two steps up from the cobbled street and flung her arms around him. "And you've grown so much. You're even quite handsome now, you've filled out."

Toby winced inwardly and then relaxed, as she took his arm and marched him through the door of the terraced town house of three floors and a basement.

"What do you think?" she asked, sitting him down after a brief tour of the building.

"It's splendid," he answered admiring the paintings and the nautical collection of books and instruments that his uncle had acquired over twenty years of command. "I could spend many an hour just leafing through the books and handling the equipment."

"He's a great diary writer, my husband," Agnatha said producing two slim volumes of his travels.

"Why did you decided to settle here opposed to back home, aunt?" Toby asked. "I'm sure the great ports of London and Liverpool would have welcomed your ideas."

"You're probably right," Agnatha said, leaning over the back of the chair nonchalantly. "But we thought that there are so more opportunities in America and so many challenges to overcome."

"I'm coming to that conclusion that that as well," Toby answered, opening the first of the books and admiring his uncles copper plate handwriting.

"I think your uncle is planning on opening a navigation school when he gets back from his next voyage, "Agnathan announced, as two cadets from a square rigger held up in the port burst in and asked for some advice. "He's had enough of the sea and wants to give something back."

"But that's a big undertaking?" Toby said, remembering his last exam in a freezing cold church hall and his abysmal lodgings. "Nevertheless, I'm sure there's a great demand around the corner. Ships are flying off the stocks back home, and men and boys are being swept off the streets to man them."

"Now lunch. You've a choice. Steak pie or hot pot?" she offered. "After that I want to show you my cellar, where the apprentices can relax. It's full of tables and chairs, books and a couple of bunks should they want to stay over a night."

"Hot pot will be fine." he said. "I eat anything as most sailors do."

"Now tell me how your career is going, Toby?" she asked after lunch as they were sitting down with the sun just managing to filter through the net curtains.

"Fine, just fine," answered with not too much sincerity in his voice. "I'm itching for a chief officer's position, but the list is long; and as for command, it's just out of the question. We call it dead man's shoes out of hearing of the ole' man, which it is if they don't get a superintendent's position, a surveyor's job, ashore a pilot or start up a college like uncle."

"It's surprising how very often the way becomes clear just at the time you think it's never going to happen," Agnatha replied patting him on the hand and offering a desert. "You'd do well to be patient."

"Maybe," Toby answered. He was more than full having tucked into his aunt's cooking.

"They are trying to tempt young ambitious officers over here for this wretched war," she said. "Both the Unionists and the Confederates. You might get an approach whilst you're here in New York. Agents for both are hanging around the docks."

"I've heard that," Toby admitted. "But fortunately we are leaving tomorrow. Do you know we brought two consignments of guns in this trip. One batch we dropped off in Bermuda, presumably for the south. Goodness knows how it will get there. The agent there says that the eastern seaboard is blockaded with government gunboats and the only available vessels at the moment are small sailing vessels. They are trying to acquire fast paddle steamers from Europe. The other guns are going to Albany, which I believe is the main Union Army bases."

Agnatha nodded at her nephew, adding a few comments that made Toby suddenly realise that she knew quite a lot about what was going on in New York regarding the war situation.

"How come you are party to all that information, aunt?" he asked when he could finally get a word in.

"Well, I've become a bit of a clearing house for information situated here as I am," Agnatha said, explaining herself more clearly to Toby. "Comes from the many contacts established by my husband. Word seems to come in with all these young officers and I pass it on to a contact of mine. He has offered financial help when my husband starts up his college here."

"A government official? "asked Toby wondering which side of the line her visitor was.

"Oh, from the North of course," she answered promptly. "On secondment from the Navy, he tells me. This war is turning into a very nasty business and information is becoming a vital part of the operation."

Toby was relieved when he realised which President she was siding with. As a student of history in his spare time, he had formed a strong opinion of the Southern States and their objections to the ideals of the Thirteen States. They had all rightly fled from a similar tyranny in Europe a generation or two ago and set up their own form the new world, but what they were doing now was something that did not sit easily with him.

"And we have other plans," she added probing Toby out of his thoughts.

Toby nodded aware that for a moment his mind was far away, imagining armies of workers slaving away in the cotton fields. A subject of which he had no experience.

"What other plans do you have, then aunt?" he answered keen to find out more about this lady's involvement, so soon after establishing herself in the city.

"It's a movement to get slaves out of the South and re-settled in the north." she said carefully picking her words. "Sort of underground but not of course."

"And how does it work?" Toby asked.

"I'm not certain at the moment, but I believe it involves the railways and the Great Lakes," she answered noncommittally. "Now, hadn't you best get back to your ship. You told me earlier that you were duty officer tonight."

"Duty officer duties don't start until after dinner," Toby reassured her. "And I'm curious about these contacts of yours."

Agnatha laughed at his impetuousness. "And don't forget that I'm due on board for lunch tomorrow. I want to have a look around at this ship of yours and meet your Captain. I'm looking for more support for this young officer's hostel of mine, and I'm told he is quite interested to hear what I have to say."

"You might find him a bit testy," Toby answered. "He got a bit of a grilling yesterday by the Port Authorities according to the Chief Officer. They were asking him about Bermuda."

Chapter 10

Emily looked over the rail of the *S.S. Perthshire* and watched the last of the cargo being lifted aboard. She had been aboard for two days, along with most of the other three hundred passengers and the ship was late leaving Liverpool on the regular run to New York. Cargo had been arriving on the quayside night and day and at every opportunity except when coaling, during which the dust permeated everywhere.

Emily had been on deck watching the fascinating sight of a ship preparing for sea. Alongside a barge disgorged the coal into the ships bunkers, the stokers were stripped down to dungarees and vests. Hair tied back with a bandanna they toiled, swearing non-stop, shovelling the coal into the bowels of the ship in six hour shifts. On the gangways, a crocodile line of stewards passed box after box of stores from one to another until the food disappeared into the very depths of the ship. But most fascinating of all to Emily was the cargo that was being lifted into the ship.

Emily had hoped that Alice would be joining her, but it had not been possible. It had taken time winning over her father, but she had eventually succeeded, she said in her letter; and would be travelling over with her brother in due course and staying with the Kellacks, an associate company; that traded in cargo ships between the North and the Caribbean.

She had not outlined her plans, but expected to move on to friends of the Missionary couple in Ramsbottom, and hoped that they would meet up in the summer. Emily recalled the serious girl, who had come out of her shell in the course of one evening and had been so fired up at the raucous meeting in the mill town. They definitely had similar interests and goals.

By learning over the taffrail she could see the stevedores filling large nets on the quayside with boxes of every shape and size, and the cranes and ships derricks effortlessly lifting them over to the ship's hatch. With hardly a pause the cargo would descend into one of the four cavernous holds, directed by the ganger with a gesture of waves and twirls of his fingers, and then to be dragged away from the hatchway by a system of rollers, ropes and pure brute force, before the next load could be dropped in.

Emily's attention was constantly diverted from one collection of men to another, the seamen dodging the incoming loads as they went about their business of cleaning the ship, the officers casually checking list after list of paper work, the stevedores in their flat hats, collar less shirts, and hob nailed boots; and the stewards in their high necked button up tunic tops and highly pressed trousers.

Since breakfast time she had wandered the boat deck, keeping out of the way, occasionally talking to other passengers and looking through the skylights at the massive engine below. Fortunately the rain from the two previous days had abated, and under a brilliant but cool sky, the only thing that enticed Emily inside was lunch and an early tea.

Even inside the ship the noise was hardly suppressed, until a whistle sounded ashore bringing the whole dock to a standstill as hundreds of men flocked to the gates and the nearest public house, eventually heading off to their homes.

There was something about it that reminded Emily of her life back home, where men worked from dawn to sunset endlessly with few breaks.

One by one the holds were filled, hatch beams and boards slotted into place until only one was left, the one immediately below the bridge and into which bags of mail were being dropped. As the rest of the passengers filtered away in the closing light of the day, she caught the eye of the officer with two stripes on his sleeve, who was obviously in charge and making notes on his clipboard. She gave him a half wave as he licked his pencil to make his last scribe before tucking it behind his ear, then watched him give her a broad wink before disappearing from view.

Within minutes the ship's carpenter had put the final wedges in the hatches; the whistle announced departure, the gangways were dropped ashore, and three tugs appeared from the corner of the dock billowing steam and smoke. Seamen in heavy coats and gloves appeared at both ends of the ship, the windlass and winches clanked into action and the *S.S. Perthshire* was turned towards the open dock gate.

Disappointed at not seeing the officer with the smile, who had so caught her attention, Emily turned towards the warmth of the ship and settled down to the second Atlantic voyage in her career. She hoped it was more interesting than the first one two years previously.

It was a full two days later before she saw the officer again. By then she was on nodding terms with some of her fellow passengers, but still trying to get to grips with the daily routine. All she spied regularly was the Captain, a severe looking man with a trim beard; the Chief officer with his three stripes; and the jovial Purser, and that was mainly at mealtimes. Most of the passengers were of a different era and to make matters worse she was allocated a table of guests a good two generations older.

"You won't even see the Chief Engineer," a well-meaning American lady who usually dominated the conversation at mealtimes offered, when Emily asked casually about the officers on the ship. "He isn't really regarded as an officer according to my husband, who's a steel maker at Bethlehem up the Delaware river, if you know where that is."

Emily nodded. "Yes, I know it," she retorted.

"Mind you, he also says that the ship wouldn't move an inch without the engineers," the lady continued. "And that doesn't go down well with Captains."

"So where do the engineers and all the younger deck officers eat if it's not in the restaurant?" Emily asked, having scoured the decks of the ship until she came to the signs that said 'Crew Only'.

"They all eat and relax in the officers mess room, and the crew themselves have an area entirely to themselves. Called the pig and whistle I am told," the woman continued, obviously pleased as being the font of knowledge on all things nautical. "You certainly won't want to be seen dead down there, that is if you ever got out alive."

"Sounds like the very place to be if you want an entertaining evening," Emily replied with a laugh, trying to keep up with the flow of conversation.

"It is if you want live music and Irish ceilidh," another woman chipped in, explaining the history of Celtic music. "I came over in 43 and I've just been back for the first time. It was not a pleasant experience, but for all that emigrating was worth it."

"But the deck officers and the engineers. I guess that they are kept very busy then?" Emily added nonchalantly as if she had little real interest in the running of the ship.

"I think so. You'll have very little opportunity for meeting them," she suggested. "My, look at the sweet trolley the stewards are bringing in!"

The *Perthshire* was making up time in the surprisingly benign Atlantic rolling in an easy motion when Emily came across the Second Officer, who was pinning up the ship's position on the wall chart of the Atlantic. She watched him for a moment as some of the passengers milled around to see if they had won the daily sweepstake for the number of miles travelled.

The ship had covered nearly five hundred miles since rounding the Isle of Man, and taken the narrow passage between Ireland and Scotland. Finally, when the knot of passengers had left, realising that they had not won, she plucked up enough courage and introduced herself.

"I'm Emily, Emily Wollaston, on my way home," she said demurely, looking at the intent and smart young man and offering her hand as he fumbled with his pencils and notepad. "Do you do this every day?"

"Every day, I'm afraid. It's a ritual," the navigator said, "as soon as the Captain, Chief Officer and myself decide the position of noon. And every other day I go round all the clocks and move them half an hour depending on whether we are westbound or eastbound."

"You must all be very clever making all those calculations," Emily smiled looking him directly in the face.

"I don't know about that," he said. "The real calculations are made each year at Greenwich for the sun and the stars, and without the clocks or chronometers it wouldn't be possible to accurately work out the position. The chronometers have to be wound each day without fail."

"You don't give lectures then," Emily asked brushing aside a stray hair.

"Hadn't thought of that," he answered, "although my uncle is supposed to be starting up a navigation school in New York when he leaves the sea."

"I was wondering whether I might meet you during the voyage," the officer replied affably. "The ship is quite big as you see and quite often, we don't see some of the passengers again until they disembark."

"Well, it's nice to meet someone nearer my age," Emily answered. "I'm sitting at a table that's full of business men and women. Conversation is kind of stilted most of the time."

"Well, it's pretty lively in our mess room," the officer said adding, "unfortunately passengers are not allowed there apart from exceptional circumstances, which is rarely given."

"By the way, I'm Toby Barnes, Second officer; and Navigator for my sins. Pleased to meet you Emily," he continued extending a warm and firm handshake that Emily was reluctant to be released from. "But I have to dash on watch.

There's a bridge visit later this afternoon. Go and book with the Purser. It's limited to fifteen people at a time."

Emily wandered across the wheelhouse fingering the brass engine controls on each side of the bridge, listening to Toby go into great detail of the chart and the instruments with the knot of passengers. Some were intently watching the quartermaster flick over the great wheel, who never took his eyes of the compass and all whilst answering questions. Emily looked astern at the wake as they all looked out to see if there was the slightest deviation in the ship's track. It was as straight as a farmer's farrow.

Emily did not want to monopolise the Second Officer during the tour, nor did she need to, as he had suggested they meet up under the lifeboats after supper, when he was due to make his rounds before turning in for the night watch at midnight.

For dinner, that night she selected a warm suit and slung a coat over her chair, knowing that it would be cold on deck, and waited to be quizzed by those on her table. It was not long before the well-travelled steel maker and his wife asked of her day, and she was just able to suppress a smile as she parried their questions.

Emily was not the only person on the boat deck as Toby stepped out of the officer's accommodation doffed his cap in mock salute and kissed her hand. A full moon had drawn other passengers out to enjoy the last moments of the day, and as the boat deck stretched a good two hundred feet on both sides and was joined across by a balcony the width of the ship, it became a circuit of exercise. Toby wasn't able to dally for long as he had to walk the decks from bow to stern and return to complete the ship's log, all before the third officer took over the watch from the Chief officer.

"I won't be five minutes," he said, showing her a concealed space close to the lifeboats. "Don't go away."

They snuggled up briefly not quite touching on his return from patrolling the decks, wedged in the shadow of a ventilator and the aft funnel as a few moonlighters strolled past completely unaware of their presence.

"I want to ask you so many questions," she asked as he broke away to make for the bridge.

"Fire away, but it'll have to wait until tomorrow," he answered ruffling her nose. "Same time unless I see you in the foyer with my pencils."

"I'll be there," she said quietly and watched him stride away and take the companionway steps two at a time. "After all I've little else to do."

To her annoyance Emily was late, when the ship's position was plotted on the foyer chart the following day, all because she was waylaid by the inquisitive and formidable American lady, who was trying to introduce her to a bland fellow passenger she had met in the library.

But by walking the decks after lunch, she was able to see him at work on the bridge during his afternoon watch. Pretending to look over the side she saw his broad back leaning over an instrument taking a sight line and talking intently to the lookout. They were clearly a team which pleased her. In fact, it pleased her very much that here was a man at ease with her, himself and his fellow seamen.

After dinner, she loitered as planned on the decks for a few minutes acknowledging her fellow passengers, then slid into the shadows caused by the towering red and white ventilators and the base of the funnel. A breathless Toby arrived just as she was about to give up and wrapped his arms around her.

"Sorry I'm late." he gasped. 'the old man buttonholed me after dinner and I had the devil of a job getting away."

"The old man," she said, "Who is he?"

"Short for the Captain," Toby answered, "Standard nomenclature used at sea."

"Are you in trouble?" she answered kissing him lightly on the lips.

"Not really," Toby responded, pulling her a bit closer. "He wanted to know if I had all the chart courses laid out so he could check them."

"Does he trust you to do all that?" Emily asked.

"Yes, he's one of the most popular Captains I've sailed with," Toby agreed. "But best that he doesn't know that I'm seeing a bit too much of a particular passenger."

Emily tilted her head and offered a generous kiss.

"Well, it's frowned on by the company, but most Captains turn a blind eye as long as it's not too obvious," he continued. "And of course, all passengers eventually leave and more come aboard."

"But I might like to see you every time you come to New York," she teased, stretching on tiptoe and putting her arms around his neck.

"I'd like that," Toby said. "Perhaps we could steal away for a weekend."
"Mm," she said having got his full attention. "Toby, why were we late leaving Liverpool? I thought all passenger ships left to schedule."

"I'll tell you tomorrow," he said. "For now, I just have to dash."

Emily tossed and turned in her bunk two decks down from the bridge, tempted to get up, dress and find an excuse to wander the decks; and risk unchaining the barrier that banned passengers from going to the bridge. She knew that Toby would be up between twelve and four pacing the wheelhouse to keep out the cold, regularly examining the chart, and talking to the lookouts to keep them awake.

She liked the thought that he was totally in charge for four hours and sole guardian of a four thousand ton ship, the safety of three hundred passengers and a crew of a hundred, and finally the cargo safely stowed deep in the bowels of the ship, while the Captain was asleep in his cabin immediately below. For some reason her thoughts shifted from Toby to the cargo, which was being talked about in whispers around the ship, and then back to the man on the bridge who had taken her eye.

Emily, wrapped her warmest coat around her, eased the door open so that she could see if she was alone, and passed the wash rooms, then opened the storm door to the decks. The wind whistled as she took two steps, then realised that the decks were on the move and turned back into the warmth of the accommodation, feeling just a little ashamed of her nocturnal venture.

The following day, Toby was besieged by a larger than usual knot of passengers, when Emily sauntered down to the foyer trying to look as if she had only a passing interest in the proceedings. A woman shrieked with delight at having won the pot, and was in the process of being congratulated by her husband and her fellow passengers, which enabled Toby to make eye contact with Emily and confirm their meeting just before eight as usual.

She dressed casually after supper fending off yet another pertinent question as to whether she was enjoying the voyage, and found that another couple had secreted themselves in the very hideaway that she and Toby had found for the past three evenings. It was another cold, but dry night, and she just managed to waylay him as he stepped out of the officer's accommodation.

"Can't we go somewhere else?" she whispered catching him by the collar of his greatcoat, "The cargo decks or the winch houses?"

"Not possible," he answered snatching a kiss. "Out of bounds, and in any case it's where the seamen and stokers gather for their evening smokes."

"Oh damn," she said in frustration. "What then?"

"I've a much better idea," he said, his smile turning into a grin, "I have the keys to open the funnels from the boat deck."

"Is it warm in there then?" she asked as they by passed the life jacket locker and came to the door.

"You bet," he answered, "Warmest part of the ship."

"And how did you get the keys then?" she asked relishing the thought of a few minutes in the warm.

"Well, it was luck really." Toby confessed. "The Second Engineer came to the bridge with a request. They had blown a steam joint in the boiler room and couldn't find a spare gasket joint, so he came to me for an Admiralty chart, which is the next best thing in an emergency."

"And he gave you the spare key, I suppose." she laughed as Toby unlocked the door and a blast of warm air greeted them.

Toby guided her on to a small platform and squeezed in alongside her. There was hardly space for one let alone two.

"I suppose that you've done this before," she said, pushing him gently in the midriff.

"No, I haven't actually," said Toby quite truthfully. "This is only my third voyage on the ship. Look, I've got to go briefly to finish my rounds. Just don't move. I'll be back in five minutes, and I've some other news."

"Can't we go to your cabin, instead," Emily asked, as he opened the door and disappeared into the moonlight.

"Definitely not," he replied, drawing a finger across his throat.

Emily looked around her as she became accustomed to the light. Forty feet below she could see the dull red light of the boiler room and men in sweaty singlets shovelling the coal from the bunkers onto the plates ready to fuel the fires. Ladders descended from the small platform on which she was standing to other platforms in a jumble of metalwork.

Inches away from her the two insulated flues from the boilers spiralled up into the sky, above which she could just see the brightest of the stars describing an arc as they came and went in view. Bracing herself against the rail she undid her coat and let it fall around her shoulders. What other strange places were hidden away on this ship. The door creaked open and Toby stepped inside closing the door firmly and reached for her body.

"You didn't take long," she said, pulling his tie gently until they were nose to nose. "Now give me a kiss, a proper kiss."

Toby put his arms around her waist feeling the slimness of her body as she pulled his face towards hers and swamped him with a long penetrating kiss.

"Now, what kept you?" she asked after she broke away for air.

"I've had to rearrange the watches," Toby said. "Nothing really, The Chief Officer's not well and I have to re-organise the deck officers roster."

He laughed softly as they separated and he put his hands, that were now warm from the heat coming up from below, round her waist realising immediately that he was feeling her bare flesh.

"What does that mean," she asked, teasing him with a moist tongue.

"I shall be on at four in the morning instead of midnight." he answered finding the hem of her sweater and sliding his hands up her ribcage, until they rested against her breasts.

"So, we can have an hour here then instead of five minutes," she asked, moving her hips closer to him and feeling the pressure of his body.

"I don't know about that," Toby replied. "We'll get roasted in here."

"Mm," she murmured in contentment and pleasure as his fingers and thumbs rolled around her aroused nipples.

"I'd still rather we were in your cabin," she said parting his teeth with her tongue.

In his new temporary role, Toby was too busy working with the bosun and the deck crew during the day to even give Emily a passing nod, but at noon she was there by the pursers office milling around with the passengers as Toby's deputy posted the daily position. She could see that they were half way across the ocean and Bermuda could only be two or three days ahead.

On the third night of their funnel meetings, Emily put on her flimsiest of blouses buttoned up the front underneath her coat and daringly left off her shift just to see how long it would take Toby to find out. She slipped off the lock and climbed into the funnel casing making sure that she was seen by not a soul. She could just hear Toby above the whoosh of the exhausts, talking to the couple that walked the decks religiously every night, waiting for them to move on. With a brief rat tat tat on the door the hinge cranked open and Toby was in her arms holding her head still and enveloping her in a kiss that got to her inner soul.

"We're going to be in Bermuda in two days' time," he announced pulling away from a deep kiss and licking her ear.

"Is that good then?" Emily asked pulling at the waistband of his trousers in retaliation and then letting go.

"Well, it's only a short stop. Long enough to drop the mail, unload some of this cargo that everyone is supposing is guns for the south when it's actually only a few guns and mainly uniforms, boots and medical supplies," Toby confirmed.

"How long do you reckon?" Emily asked.

"Oh, and some passengers to discharge and take on." he continued, mentally adding up how long they would be there. "Twelve hours, I should think."

"I was hoping to get ashore and look around," she said. "I'm told it's a holiday destination and quite lively in the old town."

Toby looked deeply into her eyes, his hands lowly moving up her ribcage and then round her back feeling every notch of her spine. "If we get the chance, I know of an ice cream parlour not far from where the ship berthed the last time we were here."

"That will do just fine," she said, first pushing him away and then pulling him closer, so that she could feel the tension inside him against her body.

"But you'll have to lick me all over first," she added probing with her tongue. "Just like this."

Her body shuddered slightly and she gave a low moan pressing her body up to his.

"Toby Barnes," she said slowly hanging her arms around her his neck and slobbering him with wet kisses hoping that the moment would never go away. "It's possible that I love you, but if it can't be your cabin, it will have to be a bed."

"Emily Wollaston," Toby answered, "I shall find a bed, I'm not sure where, but when I do I will throw you on it and you won't get off it all night."

"But you haven't said that you love me," she reminded him putting her hand over his.

"I love you, Emily." He answered, "You just don't know how much."

Toby was bent over the hatch under the bridge supervising the unloading of a cargo net of mail. He knew that she was watching him from the deck. He had been promised a two-hour run ashore by the Captain, as the Chief Officer had recovered from the spell of gout that had obliged him to elevate his leg under the instructions of the ship's doctor, who had little sympathy for him. The junior officers had the deck for the rest of the day. Toby wondered where the consignment marked.

Wilmington was going to be ware housed out of the way of prying eyes.

Now don't think I've not seen you casting your eye at that Miss Wollaston, Toby," the Captain admonished him slightly as he signed the day orders for the ship's stay.

"Yes, Sir, I'll remember that," Toby answered somewhat abashed that his movements had not gone totally unobserved.

"I was young once," the Captain replied with a smile and the hint of a wink. "Incidentally, here is a letter here for you. A New York stamp. Looks like your aunt's handwriting. What's she up to now? The sooner that husband of hers swallows the anchor the better for all of us."

Toby took the letter, felt the contents and put it in his pocket, uttering his apologies and left trying to disguise his haste in distributing the orders, before slipping on a fresh shirt to meet Emily waiting at the bottom of the gangway.

Sipping a cold drink on the quayside they watched the boxes being discharged on the quayside, pleased to be off the ship; Toby even more pleased to be sitting opposite the girl with the doe eyes that fascinated him. They were playing kneesy under the table, Emily occasionally running her toes up his leg and watching his reaction.

"So, was it the cargo that delayed us in Liverpool?" She asked holding her drink in two hands and leaning her elbows on the table. "You know that I went to a mill worker meeting in Ramsbottom, and actually to another one two weeks later on the instructions of that Mr Adams."

"No it was the weather actually," he answered. "There was a gale in the Irish Sea and the Captain asked the Company to delay. One of the very earliest passenger steam ships foundered off Ireland and it took a year to salvage it. The cargo came as a late delivery," he explained drawing a plan of the Isle of man and the North Channel on his napkin.

"You're all very cautious, aren't you?" Emily probed, "And ambitious too."

Toby nodded. "I suppose that I am a man in a hurry, but there's nothing wrong with that."

"I like a man like that, someone who is committed," she said, looking him straight in the eye. "I haven't met many so far, although a few in the Embassy came close, but they were too politicised for my liking."

"At your service, madam," he mocked with a laugh. "I've just remembered, I have a letter in my pocket from my aunt in New York."

"Are you going to open it now?" she said playfully, rubbing fingers and thumb together, waiting for him to lay it on the table. "Come on, open it up."

"She's not going to be there when we get to New York," he announced scanning the one-page letter quickly. "That's a pity. I was hoping to introduce you to her before you leave for Boston."

Emily tried to read the letter upside down, then put her hand over his and slid it sideways, so that she could read it.

"She's off to Niagara Falls, and then Chicago and Cincinnati by all accounts," Toby said, mentally counting up the distances.

"On holiday then?" Emily asked.

"I don't think so by the sound of it," he said thinking about the previous conversation he had with her. "She's a wonderful lady, nursed the sick on ships, taken Missionaries all over the world, helped in a hospital in Africa. She's my mother's youngest sister, never had children of her own."

"And what about your mother, Toby?" she asked gently.

"She was from New Bedford; so I'm half American, I guess," he replied. "My father went there on a ship to pick up whale oil for Bristol and she followed him back to England."

"How romantic. Was he on a whaler then?" Emily asked.

"No, he didn't like the killing of whales nor animals in general and certainly not humans," Toby replied. "And neither do I for that matter."

"And Agnatha, you're her favourite nephew?" Emily said softly as he folded up the letter.

"The only one that she knows well," Toby replied. "And it's only rarely that we've met up."

"What do you think she's doing then, Toby?" Emily asked.

"She was talking of a secret track way. She's loads of contacts, and I think that she has heard of an escape route to the north for fugitive slaves," he answered, aiming to get up and walk back to the ship.

"All the way through the Southern States?" she questioned.

"I guess," Toby confirmed. "Maybe up through Mississippi and Tennessee."

"And what do you think, Toby?" Emily said stopping, and turning him round to face her.

"I cannot get my head around it," he said. "How all these people fled Europe to be free and then think enslaving people to serve them is acceptable."

Emily looked at him pensively deciding that it was best not to let him know that her parents had slaves on their holding, even though they had been told they could leave or stay on a low wage. She had now watched him at work and at play and his view on the world. If this man was anything like his aunt he was worth having.

"Aunt also says that if I want a complete night ashore, I can use her spare room," he said casually. "Apparently her friend and the maid are looking after the place while she's away."

Emily took her opportunity to tease him as she searched into her bag and thumbed the pages, looking for the month of April and the four little crosses in pencil.

"What are you looking for," Toby asked slightly perplexed.

I'm just checking what day I am due at Mr and Mrs Adams' house," she said trying to hide a smile. "Have you ever stayed in your aunt's house?"

"No," Toby answered. "I've actually only been there twice before."

"Then you won't know whether it has a big bed then?" She pressed him.

"Emily, you are the wickedest girl I have ever known," he laughed as she swung her bag at him.

"I forgot to tell you," he said as they strolled hand in hand along the quay, releasing her hand reluctantly as they neared the gangway. Tomorrow is St Georges Day and the Captain has said that the officers mess can have guests for supper. Steak and kidney pie is the menu I believe. Mind you, you'll have to find a chaperone for the evening."

"I dare say I can find one," she said, as they reached the ship. "But what is for afters. Are you sure the food compares to the restaurant?"

"Here's a letter for you, Sir, more of a note really," the seaman addressed them at the foot of the gangway. "You're not the only one to get one. They are all from Bone and Watcher, the agents in Bermuda for all this stuff we keep unloading."

Toby stuffed it in his jacket to look at later.

"It's all around the waterfront, Sir," the man continued, handing over the Missive. "There's three paddle steamers due here next month from Glasgow and they are all looking for crews apparently."

The next day or so was a whirl of land spotting as the ship passed the Ambrose lightship and it's mournful fog signal in the mist, the sandy hook that curled around to the south and finally the Verrazzano Narrows which opened up to the vista of the city. All of which was relatively new to Emily, but quite familiar to Toby, and who like most seafarers would have committed it to memory from the first entry.

Toby and Emily strolled through Battery Park, hand in hand to Agnatha's house several streets away, hanging on to each other over the unforgiving cobbles; cobbles that had come all the way from Southern Ireland as ballast from the emigrant ships. They stopped briefly to admire the terraced house, then skipped up the four steps and pressed the bell. Agnatha's maid a trim Negro with a wide smile, rolling eyes and a mass of curly hair was expecting them, and gushed forth a welcome.

Below in the depths of the house Toby could hear voices. A small knot of apprentices and a newly promoted young officer were in the cellar rest room, reading and joking. Whilst Emily was upstairs in the lounge busily telling Agnatha's friend about the voyage, Toby sat down to talk to them.

They were off the big cargo carrying sailing ship further up the river unloading coal and had just sailed around the Horn. By the time five thousand tons had been discharged and the holds swept out it would be weeks before they were ready to sail to Europe with grain. No wonder that they took advantage of Agnatha's haven for seamen.

Emily's eye was taken by the previous days New York Times that was scattered on the table. The headlines jumped out in bold print.

It read—New Orleans fallen to the Union Troops giving the barest of details. In smaller print it outlined the worst of the battles in the previous year. Fifty-two battles and skirmishes since the war began and an unknown number of deaths and injuries.

It was the first successful outcome for Lincoln's Government in a year of fighting.

Chapter 11

"I was wondering whether you were involved in this Liverpool consortium that I've been hearing about," Kirk said shaking hands with the George and James and taking them round the yard.

Of the three vessels on the slipways, one was having the keel laid down, the second was in frame and the third only a month or two away from launching. In the fitting out basin the *City of Dublin* was swarming with tradesmen completing the final work. The Dumbarton Shipyard had reached its full capacity, there was not an inch of wasted space and little or no room for expansion.

"So, the owners are prepared to charter out the ship for a year?" George asked as the plans were laid out before him. "And its classed A10 with Lloyd's for the summer months on a transatlantic voyage."

"Apparently so," Kirk replied. "Although I would personally be very circumspect of taking it across the Atlantic. These sorts of vessels have to be carefully handled and not stressed by some gung-ho Captain. Also, the Chief Engineers have to be very sympathetic and diligent, often treating the engines with the care as if they were their very own child. Fortunately, we have a great number of experienced men on the Clyde to call on."

"I've already made some enquiries on the Exchange," George confirmed. "I expect it will be a bare boat charter for six months initially, with an option to extend."

"And you have a crew and a cargo?" questioned Kirk, laying out the ship's specification and plans and reminding them of the hidden complications of owning or chartering a ship.

"Not at the moment," replied George, "but James here would go out in some capacity, if we can get an exception on the basis of his previous sea service."

"Well, I can help you with the cargo if you haven't arranged anything on your own account," Kirk continued, "Two Americans, a Mr Shaw and McClure shipped out goods for the South a couple of months ago on a small cargo ship and I have their agents address here in Glasgow."

"Would you be able to recommend a Captain by any chance?" James intervened looking up from the plans.

"At the moment there is a Captain Stewart on board with a surveyor and if you like I'll introduce you to them, whilst I discuss some complicated procedure details with your father," Kirk answered taking George to one side.

"You've got full details on this ship, I suppose? asked George when they were together. "We need to be assured that the vessel will stand up to the rigours of the Atlantic."

"I ought to. I built it remember," Kirk reminded him. "As it happens I have a copy of a charter party for such an adventure from a previous enquiry."

"Of course, I apologise. So, we are not the first to be looking at your vessels, Mr Kirk? George asked, beginning to realise that there were others in the market to speculate in the risky venture.

"Oh, no," said Kirk, "The next one on the stocks is already going to be up for charter to a group here in Glasgow. By the way you will have to rename it."

"Yes. We had thought of that. It will be *Fannie*. A family name," George replied. "And if we acquire any more we've names for those too."

Captain Stewart looked James over with the practised eye of a man used to engaging and sacking men, before introducing himself to the younger man. They were on the fore deck and he was watching workman putting the finishing touches to the bunkers, which would hold the additional coal for any voyage beyond that of the Irish Sea. On the quayside sheets of curved corrugated iron waited to be bolted over the foredeck like a turtles backs, to keep heavy water flooding the decks and wetting the coal.

"Should this charter come off I am certain that we can get you a berth as Second Officer, but you'll almost certainly be sharing a cabin." he said after looking at James credentials. "So you can take sights of the sun and the stars and sail as well?"

"I'm somewhat out of practise and it was half a dozen years ago." James answered.

"I can tell you that navigation sights on the Atlantic are a bit hit and Miss compared to a voyage to Australia, but we shouldn't be too badly off in finding the sun in the spring," the mariner assured him. "What sailing have you done since then?"

"Well, the family have a yacht on Lake Windermere, Sir, and another at Dartmouth, but we don't use it enough," James replied a bit sheepishly.

"Never mind that," Stewart assured him. "Let's go and see what you are letting yourself in for."

The summer solstice had not long passed before a scratch crew of sailors and stokers with the promise of good money boarded the converted side wheeler, and at first light the following day the *Fannie* slipped away for the two and a half thousand mile journey to Bermuda. On board was three hundred tons of material desperately required for the Southern army, two hundred tons of additional coal and a spare suit of sails.

Once clear of the land they would sail for as much of the journey as possible, but they were of course heading into the general eastward movement of the wind and weather, and therefore tacking for most of the way. Stewart estimated a voyage of three weeks nursing the ship for much of the time. The Chief Engineer settled down to caressing his engines all the way on a voyage that the *Fannie* was never designed to do.

Following behind, unknown to them, two other side winders also headed up the North Channel that separated Ireland from Scotland destined for Bermuda and eventually the coast of Carolina. George and his partners were spreading the risk, all three ships registered with different companies.

Stewart's estimate of three weeks was only a day out and after a combination of sailing and steaming the *Fannie* glided through the Heads of Horse Shoe island to a welcoming crowd, who had never seen such a vessel before. Second Officer and supernumerary James Forwood, dapper as a drake in a pond with his new uniform watched in admiration as his Captain approached the berth, deftly giving the orders to the engineers below. Below the bridge the paddle boxes holding the great wheels churned up the water as the silent swish of the steam engines transmitted the power to the blades, gradually slowing and finally reversing, thrashing the water around and hissing the *Fannie* to a stop.

James looked up at the Governor's flag flying straight out as they made their way to the imposing building. Bermuda had been a naval port for some two hundred years and the port was substantially developed for warships with a dry-dock and now for passenger ships as well. He waited outside on the steps of the Harbour masters office, whilst his Captain cleared inwards with the papers. The harbour was alive with activity. Clerks were rushing around clutching bags and papers from ships to offices and back again. Boats glided across the harbour as bronzed backs effortlessly propelled stores and people across the water to ships at anchor. Bronzed young women sculled across the harbour selling their wares and offering their bodies for evening entertainment.

Whereas in Liverpool cargo was shifted from ship to quay with hardly a word of command, here the air was full of orders, counter orders and constant laughter induced by the warmth of the sun. In every spare corner between the squat buildings, stalls selling fruit not seen in England were offered with a beaming smile. Almost to a man Hamilton was a town and port of a happy and contented black population, all of which at one time would have been slaves on the American mainland.

"You will need to take a pilot to get you up the river to Wilmington," Norman Watcher confirmed to Stewart and James as they lounged in the offices of the premier agents working on behalf of the Southern States.

"You have a pilot already here, then? Stewart asked.

"Oh, yes," Bone chipped in. "We have several here waiting. In the main they are basically fishermen with some retired Captains, and all have an intimate knowledge of the waters. They won't be that useful until you get into range, but after that they are invaluable."

James looked at the chart. The Carolinas didn't look a particularly inviting area with its flat coast and shallows, and very few landmarks.

"You will need to shift over to your best steaming coal a day after leaving here and of course douse your lights." Watcher suggested making a mark on the chart. "There are patrol vessels operating off Bermuda here and we are trying to monitor their movements, to ensure that you slip away undetected."

"Presumably they have sailing gunboats offshore and powered vessels patrolling the coast?" Stewart asked, looking at a poster that depicted the current ships of the Union.

"By and large," Bone interjected, "Their sailing navy come in from time to time for stores, but we rarely see their capital ships. Most of the sailing ships are powered too, but often with old and unreliable engines so in general terms you should outrun anything with your speed."

"And of course, they are completely aware that Hamilton here is the pick-up and drop off port for guns; ammunition and outgoing cotton and tobacco," Watcher added, "But they cannot do anything about it in our waters. Quite extraordinary."

"And if we are stopped in American waters?" James asked.

"Well, they will confiscate everything of course, take the ship into port and auction it off," Bone continued, "The Union want the guns as much as the south and the cotton they sell on to Europe for Lincoln's coffers."

"What a state of affairs," Stewart said. "How did we as civilised people get into this position."

"We're not into the business of moralising, Captain," Watcher said. "That's for others. Now let's get on with planning this voyage. It's the first one using a side winder here, although I understand they have them around Florida from several other nationalities."

"Your mean the French, surely," Stewart questioned.

"Oh, no. Not just the French," Watcher replied. "The Portuguese, the Mexicans and the Brazilians are all operating in the Gulf."

Stewart picked up his notebook and James looked out of the window. The future of the family business was resting on his shoulders unless Nicholas could conjure something out of the Mississippi and Alabama.

"There'll be no moon and you should time your arrival off the banks one and a half hours before high water," Watcher explained.

Stewart looked at the tide book and the Nautical almanac.

"If a gunboat is in the vicinity it will be more than likely hiding here," Watcher continued, pointing to a bay north of Cape Fear. "Just out of range of the guns at the fort. There's a constant stand-off."

"With your draft," Bone said, "you should have no problem over the banks and the pilot will select the best channel. A Confederate marker vessel will be inside and the river is safe from Union guns once inside the shallow water."

"Do they light the channel?" James asked.

"The port has floating beacons that they take down the river when a ship is expected, and flare them if necessary, but if they are too far out the Union Navy dismantle them," Bone explained, "So your pilot is absolutely essential."

"The main floating beacon ironically enough is called *The Frying Pan,*" he continued showing them the banks that shallowed, braking into heavy seas horrendously on an easterly gale that could overcome a ship in no time at all. "Fortunately, it's rare in these parts and never in the spring."

"And the Navy will try and sink us," asked James realising for the first time that it was a venture with more risk than they had first thought.

"They don't want to sink you as far as we understand, but you will be fired on," Watcher advised. "They want boats as well as the guns, and are looking for crews to man them, so don't be surprised that, if and when you are captured, you'll be sent home after a fine. It's not unknown for the crew to be induced to change sides."

"All things considered, they will have you discharged and loaded within two days and provided the tides are right you should be back within ten days," Watcher confirmed.

"And one other suggestion," Bone said as they departed and walked down the quayside, "We'll going to give you half a bale of cotton to take back."

"What's the significance of that?" asked James. "I thought the whole idea was to bring cotton out, not take it in."

"Apparently if you soak it in turpentine and throw it into the boiler it will give you a quarter of a knot more."

"Mm," said Stewart, "I'll see what my engineer says. More likely a clean bottom would have a greater effect."

"It can only but help," said Watcher, "Before you go you had better meet the two Americans, who have spent the last three months procuring all these arms. They are not coming with you but are joining tomorrow's passenger ship home."

By the time they reached the *Fannie* the ship was barely recognisable. The topmasts were down and lashed on deck, the hull and the paddle sponsons had taken on a light grey hue, all distinguishable marks had been removed and the crew were relaxing on deck. At the stern the engineers were setting up the emergency steering gear just in case the main control chains carried away or was damaged by a lucky shot. It hardly looked the same ship and certainly not one only six months old.

"Good work," Stewart congratulated his Chief Officer, the bosun and engineer. "All hands still here, no deserters?"

"Not when they heard the danger money that's being offered," the Mate replied.

"We'll sail at dusk then," the Captain confirmed. "And tell the cook right away."

Later that day, the side winders, *Scotia* and *Sunbeam,* curved their way into Hamilton, and two days later they departed in line astern carrying with them an arsenal of weapons, clothing, boots and medicines.

As three separate enterprises, but all controlled from the same base they were out to ensure that money continued to flow into the coffers of the company, which was to be a considerable part of the Liverpool shipping scene for the next fifty years.

About the time that the *Fannie* was approaching North Carolina for the first time, the Royal Mail contracted liner *S.S. Perthshire* was securing alongside her regular berth in New York; Shaw and McClure prepared themselves to face the scrutiny of the port officials. On the bridge, Toby looked out across the quay for any sign of Emily, who had promised to meet the ship on arrival. Taking their time and trying to appear as causal as possible.

Shaw and McClure were ready with a plausible story. With his recent passport, Shaw was confident in convincing the immigration officials that he was in the business of exporting sewing machines to Europe and importing paper for bank notes. Tucked into his pocket was the address of a sympathetic New Yorker to speed them on their way; and a receipt from Del la Rue, who had been most helpful in providing documentary evidence.

The immigration officer looked intently at Shaw, "Papers in order. Carry on," he said, directing him to the customs official at the back of the hall.

"You, Sir," the same official addressed McClure. "You have an address to go too."

"Yes, Sir," McClure answered dreading the next question, quickly pulling a scrap of paper with the name and address of the priest, who had looked after him when he first arrived from Ireland.

"And when did you last see you Mother, back in Kerry?" the official pressed not quite convinced.

"Just got to her before she died, so I did," McClure said, crossing himself and uttering a short prayer.

"Carry on then, Mr McClure," the official said, giving the Irishman the benefit of the doubt.

McClure pocketed his substantial bonus and with the briefest of goodbyes, parted with Shaw at the safe house in upper New York. He checked his few documents and Shaw's letter to General Lee outlining the outstanding work he had undertaken on behalf of the Confederacy; and made his way to the oldest part of Manhattan and the ferry to Albany.

Unlike Shaw, who had one of the first passports to be issued before he switched sides, and could, therefore, travel with impunity, he had to be careful in the north avoiding questions on his business which could result in detention and expulsion until he got to the safety of Richmond.

He could well have taken the quicker train route up the east side of the Hudson stopping at places such as Poughkeepsie, but decided that it would be safer to take the ferry and then a canal boat all the way to Buffalo. A boat trip from there on to Erie before heading south cross country for General Lee's headquarters; and his report to the Confederates quartermaster at Richmond, would give him time to think about his career as a mercenary.

It was for others to consider the morals of this war.

Without having notes to remind him, he calculated that he and Shaw had acquired enough weapons and ammunition for at least two infantry regiments; purchased enough uniforms for two thousand men and in addition had bought four pieces of heavy artillery. But he knew that the Southern Generals would need more, much more, to sustain their assault on the democracy of the north. It had taken three side wheeler blockade runners to get his cargo across the Atlantic, but it would take a hundred more to make any difference.

McClure knew that Shaw would be going back with James Bollack, one of the many agents now engaged by the Confederates in getting more of the munitions that he had tested and approved. His companion for the past three months had been introduced to bankers, Messrs Fazy and Trueform whilst in England, and they were going to buy not only any future weapons, but also place orders for fighting ships.

Chapter 12

"Have you seen your girlfriend?" the Chief officer teased Toby as he locked up the wheelhouse and they walked down the deck to the bar.

"Not yet, I'm expecting her to arrive from Boston. She has a three day leave from Mr Adams in Boston, so hopefully she won't be far away." Toby replied shuffling the keys in his pocket.

"I'm sure that I saw her in the welcoming crowd," the senior man confirmed. "You'll know soon enough when the gangways are down."

Pushing past the stewards taking passengers light baggage down the crew gangway, Toby swept Emily up in his arms to the sounds of jeering and catcalls from the crew.

"Oh, how I've missed you. Have you missed me?" she said as they walked the decks towards the accommodation continuing to tease him. "I thought that cabins were out of bounds for passengers,"

"Ah, but you're not a passenger any more, just a guest." Toby laughed opening the door and showing her his cabin for the first time.

Once his duties were completed, they slipped off ashore and melted into the Manhattan crowds, counting off the streets as they walked hand in hand through the gates of Bowling Green Park to spread themselves out on one of the few seats. It was a perfect afternoon Emily thought, away from the politics of her employer.

"We didn't get much chance to explore before," laughed Toby as he remembered the brief visit on her return north, when they didn't get much further than his aunts spare room.

"Do you know the Broadway?" she said pointing to the gate on the north side of the green.

"Never been further than that this street here," he answered, startling the birds as he stood up pulling Emily to her feet.

"Well, it's the only road that reminds me of London," she said dragging him by the hand. "Let's go and explore. It's going to be a lovely weekend."

Emily looked at the letter from her mother in the office of Mr Adams, in one of the smartest districts of Boston. The date was some six weeks earlier and it had clearly taken far too long to get out of Virginia. It had been opened, and marked by the censors stamp, but was fortunately not blacked out. She was waiting to get some leave which was not proving to be easy. Mr Adams was a tough, but understanding employer; and had promised her a month off at the earliest opportunity, but he relied on Emily to process much of his work, and Emily knew that she would be missed.

The urgency in the letter demanded that she get south without delay, and she waited to get Adams in the right mood.

"Of course," he said to Emily, when she showed him the letter. "I should have given it more thought before."

"I'd like to go tomorrow, and I shall need a month away," she pleaded. "I can get a train to New York without a problem of course, but beyond Baltimore the timetables are somewhat spasmodic as you know. Hasn't Lincoln moved out of Washington yet?"

"No, it's well defended, but movement south is not easy; and for you to get home it will be a problem if not impossible," Adams said consulting his atlas and the railway system that was open.

"I have to try," she said. "I must know what is going on."

Emily stood on the empty Washington platform well out of the city, the end of the line from New York and pondered on her next move. She still had the best part of a hundred miles to go.

"The only way to get there, Miss, is to get across the river where there is a goods depot to the south," a friendly porter explained taking care of her two leather bound trunks,

"Thank you," Emily replied finding a couple of coins from her purse.

"But if you manage to get a train, you'll get no further than Alexandria. The line from there is taken up," he continued putting her trunks on a barrow.

"And from there, what do you think?" she asked with a note of alarm in her voice.

"There are troops all over Virginia. And the naval battle off Newport was only last week," he continued. "Not a nice place to be, Missy."

"I have to see my parents," she answered glumly.

"Folks say best to take a boat down the river from Alexandria," he said finally, hailing a cab to take her across the city.

Emily sat uneasily in the stern of the noisy little steamboat, which she had part chartered for the day and searched the horizon on the right hand side of the boat, where she knew were outposts of activity. There was nothing apparently wrong, yet it didn't look quite as she remembered it either. The trees still marched down the hillsides as usual, the little wooden jetty's and quays that they passed were all there with the occasional boat tied up, and the waterfowl skittered across the placid sound as they always did, but there was an underlying silence. She opened up her lunch and the boatman made a pot of coffee on the top of the boiler which refreshed and relaxed her, but Emily knew that something was not quite right. She questioned the boatman, his crew and the other passengers but they said very little. Finally, after dropping off everyone else and they were nearing the little cove which she knew so well the boatman turned to her, dreading the news that he was about to impart.

"Miss," he said quietly, "I have some bad news for you. I think that I had better go up to the house with you. You stay here, Joseph, with the boat. I think I shall be a little while with Miss Wollaston. We'll stay alongside here the night."

Emily could just see the house between the avenue of trees, but it wasn't all there. It appeared that one side of it was Missing. She sank to her knees in anger, realising something was desperately wrong, her upended cabin trunk supporting her, and sobbed buckets of tears.

"What has happened, Jeb," she cried out. "Tell me."

"The house was right in the way of a battle last week, Miss," he said gently lifting her up and sitting down in the covered way shelter at the end of the jetty. "A Union troop commandeered it, but the Confederates brushed them aside and sent them packing. Your mother died of a heart attack remonstrating with them, and your father was hurt trying to stop them. Don't know about your workers. The last I heard they were cowering in the barn not knowing what to do."

Emily stood in amazement, shocked but defiant at the devastation before her very eyes, then drying her tears marched up the hill.

Half way up she stopped abruptly her despair turning into fury. How dare the military desecrate her family home.

"Bring up my bags," she cried over her shoulder. "Three generations of struggling gone in a flash for what." She railed at Jeb, who could do no more than just stand there trying to commiserate.

"The bastards. All of them. And for what."

Emily sat on the veranda and surveyed the devastation, the wanton damage so totally unnecessary, looking at Jeb wandering around as well.

"Why was her brother not here at her time of need," she cried to herself, as she went from room to room surveying the damage.

But it wasn't quite as bad as she feared, when running up the drive from the jetty The house was damaged but not destroyed. The furniture was scratched, defiled, marked and re-arranged; but basically intact apart from the beds and bedrooms, which would have to be replaced. Hardly a pane of glass had survived though, and outside the stonework was peppered with bullet marks.

Damn those Yankees and damn Jefferson Davis and his followers. Between them they were ruining the country, destroying her family, her livelihood, and her life. She must find her brother, he would know what to do. Her kid sibling always had the answers when they were growing up, loved to tinker with machinery on the estate, and was always there to tease her when she returned from the University at Richmond.

She read the letter he had left for her in the study. It was six months old. He had been persuaded to join General Lee's army, it said in simple terms.

Goodness knows where, she thought. Was he alive; was he injured or was he dead? She would get him back as long has he hadn't been skewered by a Union bayonet, but where to start, she had no idea. And her best slaves, where are they; the estates skilled workers, the ones that her father had promised to free; whatever came of the conflict.

She wandered into the garden, the boatman following behind, looking for any sign of life from the plantation workers, all of whom looked motionless underneath the largest tree to the east of the house. The eldest and oldest of the workers struggled to his feet and shuffled over to Emily.

"Miss, your mother," he said, not wanting to look her in the face, "she is here." Guiding her back towards the house and into her parents favourite part of the garden.

Emily knelt there, looking at the low mound of earth and the little cross facing north, and the childish writing.

"Who did the writing?" she asked, standing up and brushing down her dress.

"I did it myself, Miss," the old man said, bursting into tears.

"And my father?" Emily asked, holding him by the shoulders.

"He was taken to hospital," he said, as the rest of the workers shambled over in threes and fours wailing a low chant. "He's hurt real bad."

"But not everyone's here? Where are the rest, our strongest workers?" she asked the old man.

"They have gone," he said, "The soldiers have taken them away."

Chapter 13

A somewhat dejected Toby Barnes left the *S.S. Perthshire* after breakfast, the day following the ship's arrival in Liverpool, and walked along the waterfront to the Shipping Offices, a government establishment adjacent to the ornate Custom House building with the imposing Doric columns. It was the centre point of all the business for the port and where the government collected all the dues that they demanded from cargoes coming in and leaving the port.

He was expecting a letter from Emily, but it had not arrived, and he wondered whether she had actually written one as promised. It was a dismal and grey morning reminiscent of the latest Atkinson Grimshaw painting, which he knew hung in the foyer of the Custom House and depicted Liverpool in the days of sail, when forests of masts and yards dominated the port, stretching as far as the eye could see.

The crew had been paid off on arrival, many of them disappearing to the doss houses and the underground world of prostitutes and pimps. The more sensible ones registered in the sailors homes, which had been set up by some of the more responsible shipowners, bowing to pressure by the government and the local council, where they could find a bed and a meal at reasonable prices before signing on for their next trip.

In tune with the other shipowners, the owners of the *Perthshire* were not inclined to supplement the crew, even the regulars, by directly keeping them on-board whilst in port. Many, particularly the younger ones, having emptied themselves of body and money with the local harlots would take a ship heading for the warmer climates of Australia and South America.

Toby, like the rest of the officers was in regular employment, in as much as they could expect to make voyage after voyage without a break, provided cargoes were there to be loaded and passengers transhipped. Fortunately, the *Perthshire* was on a regular advertised passenger service, and passengers there was in plenty on the Atlantic run to New York. But Toby was a young man in a hurry, with a newly granted Master's certificate in his pocket and a background of sailing around the world as his life experience.

He trudged past the tally houses, skirted the railway tracks that fed every quayside, skeins of metal set in cobblestones avoided the weigh bridges that would trap an unwary foot until he came to the dock gate. Nodding to the gate-man, who was stamping up and down to keep his circulation moving, he looked up at the clock tower, turned up the collar of his great coat and headed down Dock Street to the city.

The Captain had despatched him to the Shipping Office with a list of crew required for the following voyage back to New York. It was his job, guided by the Shipping Master, a retired seafarer himself working out his last days, to find the various grades of seamen required, check their suitably and experience. Toby scoured the extensive list of men looking for work, some of whom he recognised, and compared it with his Captain's list.

The heavily bound register book held by the government official was a permanent record, which would match ship's names to the thousands of seafarers in the port. The Captain would not want to engage any trouble makers, if there were alternatives, but he also knew that the Shipping Master would want him to be not too discriminating, often giving the man the benefit of the doubt after a searching interview.

The Merchant Navy was still full of overbearing and uncompromising captains and bully mates capable of taking the men to the limit. A successful voyage though was a team effort of leaders and followers born out of hundreds of years and countless voyages.

After two hours of constant leafing through the ledgers Toby came away with a list of crew, which he thought his Captain would approve of. He knew that the list of stewards, who were essential to keeping the first class passengers likely to return time and time again, would receive the closest of scrutiny. If he didn't linger too long at the naval outfitters he reckoned to be back on board for lunch.

"Excuse me," called out a voice, as he tripped down the steps and surveyed the sky which had cleared, somewhat much to his surprise as the clouds had looked set for the day. "Are you Toby Barnes of ship that arrived yesterday?"

Toby turned to see a well-dressed man striding towards him. "Yes, but what of it," he answered brusquely, not pleased in seeing his thoughts interrupted.

"You might be interested in this and what I have to say," the man answered, waving a broadsheet in front of him.

Toby ran his eyes down the page. The message was short and to the point and couched in nautical terms. But, he didn't dismiss it out of hand. Instead, he folded it up and tucked it into his inside pocket and carried on.

"May I suggest we go somewhere quiet?" the man insisted quietly in an accent that Toby recognised from his voyages state side. "A pub or a café?"

"There's a place just around the corner that's handy."

Intrigued by the accent, Toby followed the American and was soon ushered through the doors of a small hotel.

"I'll come straight to the point." the man said as Toby wriggled out of his coat, slung it over a nearby chair and placed his cap on the table.

Toby sipped the offered cup of coffee and looked at his watch.

"We're looking for young British Merchant Navy officers with a knowledge of the eastern seaboard to help us," the man said. "It's probably on a short commission of six months or a year, but could be longer if things don't go to plan. The pay, conditions and prospects would be more than you get at present."

"And who is 'we'?" Toby asked thinking quickly of the conversation he had on the waterfront in Bermuda a month earlier, and which had caused him to think that 'we' could easily be one of two sides of a tossed coin.

"The Union Navy," the man continued flatly and at that Toby relaxed. He had been brought up in a god-fearing family and was somewhat abhorred about the stories from the south, even though the rewards might be higher. "But you don't have to give me your answer right now."

Toby smiled for the first time in the interview. "I wouldn't have done in any case," he replied.

"Here's my contact address and that of my colleagues in Bermuda and New York." the American said, handing over three cards. "And thanks for listening."

"How did you know my name?" Toby queried as they parted.

"Don't you have an aunt in New York, Toby?" The other replied as they made for the door that opened out into brilliant sunshine. The rain, the wind and the depression had obviously passed over.

A thoughtful Toby headed back to the ship. He had Missed lunch, Missed the meeting with the Marine Superintendent that all the junior officers were expected to attend, and he had a pile of navigation charts to correct.

"Here's the list of potential crew replacements, Sir." Toby said knocking on his Captain's door, unfortunately interrupting his afternoon doze.

"Leave it on my desk and go and get your lunch," the elder man said gruffly, spreading out the list; and then immediately subsiding into his easy chair. "I suppose we have the dregs of Liverpool again."

Hanging on to good crew and resisting the engagement of men with dubious backgrounds was a constant problem for all Merchant Navy captains. It was less of an issue with the regular ships across the Atlantic, where continuity was a blessing to the likes of the operators of the *Perthshire,* but even then they could be surprised.

"The Shipping Master says that some the best stokers and seamen are being enticed away with the offer of good wages in America." Toby added as he went to close the door.

"And I suppose that you too have been approached. According to the agent it's common knowledge that Americans on both sides are seeking quality seafarers," replied the *Perthshire's* Captain, settling back onto his day settee.

Toby said nothing. He knew that he was well thought off by the Captain, who was also Commodore of the Company and a lasting colleague of his father, still on the other side of the world as far as he knew.

"Well, my lad. Just make the right choice if you're tempted and give me plenty of notice and certainly not at the end of this coming voyage," he added.

Toby nodded.

"And that girlfriend of yours, Emily, isn't it? Off to Boston you seemed to think. Don't bank on seeing her on this voyage. I'm afraid our turnaround times are getting shorter and shorter."

"I'll find a way somehow, Sir," Toby chuckled, "even if it busts a gut."

Toby scuttled off to the galley picked up his lunch, which had fortunately been kept warm by the chef, on which he was on good terms; and sat down with the purser, who appeared from his office with a smile as wide as the Mersey River.

"Is this what you have been waiting for?" he eventually came out with, handing over the letter with a smudged American stamp on it.

The *Perthshire* carried huge amounts of mail and Toby being the officer in charge of the mail lockers was well versed in the postal system and immediately realised the letter had been on a tortuous journey with the over stamping. He thought that she was in Boston, with the American couple she had met in London not in Washington.

What was she doing in the battle zone? He carefully slit the envelope. A slight hint of perfume came off the letter. That she still loved him as obvious. Tucking the letter back into its pouch to be devoured later, he headed for the chartroom remembering he had forgotten to wind the chronometers, a duty that was precisely carried out at nine o'clock each day.

"It's all right, Toby," the senior third officer assured him as he made for the lockers set in the chart table that housed the instruments. "I realised that you had your head in the clouds this morning, so I checked with the Chief and wound them for you."

"Thanks, that's worth at least a beer after supper," Toby said, thanking him profusely, screwing up the reminder note and sending it spinning expertly into the waste paper basket.

"The Captain says I have to understudy you, just in case you take off to the States," the single ringed officer laughed.

"And what rumours have you heard," Toby replied cuffing him round the head and laughing with the infectious smile that came so naturally.

"No more than you," came the retort.

"Bollocks."

"Not bollocks, Toby," came an immediate reply. "And I've just heard we have another consignment for Bermuda coming tonight, but no coal this time, thank Christ."

It was bad enough coaling up for the ship, murder for the stokers working extra to bunker the side wheelers in Bermuda, and it played havoc with the laundry bill. Toby sat down and carefully opened the letter. He had known her only a couple of months and it was only the second letter he had received in exchange for his three, but then he did have plenty of spare time at sea. The three pages of neat handwriting spilled across his desk as he excitedly relaxed in his chair. Within seconds he was in despair of its contents.

Dearest Toby,

I am at my parent's home, which is south of Washington as I have told you several times. I barely have the energy to put pen to paper as when I arrived on leave from Mr Adams I found nothing but desolation and my life has changed for ever. Our house has been all but destroyed in a battle when Union troops tried to take the peninsular most of which is our land. My mother, who was not well, died whilst remonstrating with them and my father is in hospital in Alexandria after being roughly treated. I didn't tell you before but my brother, who should have been looking after our small plantation, joined the Confederates whilst I was living in London; leaving our trusted overseer in charge under my father. He along with our youngest and three strongest men has been taken to join Lee's troops. It is nothing short of madness, forcing slaves from the south to fight freed slaves from the north and I can't bear the thought of what it is doing to my country. Death is all around here; fields are trampled; crops ruined and our workers traumatised. All I know is that I have to stay here, look after my father when I can and help my people harvest what little there is left; and do my best to keep them alive and safe.

I honestly really do not know which way to turn, but until this war is over it is doubtful that I will be able to see you, hold you and enjoy your love. Please give my regards to your kind aunt.

Your dearest Emily.

Toby read the letter again, and again and then walked out on deck.

Bugger and damnation. He had seen the side wheelers the last time in Bermuda lying in the coal berth, hidden away like skunks delivering the implements of death to a legitimate government and kicked the steel scupper way viciously. He thought of Emily in her distress trying to hold her possessions together and felt for the letter in his pocket. He would resign as soon as possible and do his best for the new world, but it couldn't be until after the next voyage.

On passage to New York two days later, Toby brooked the subject with his Captain.

"I wondered why you were so down in the dumps," he said as Toby took him in the noon day position. The sun had been out of view since they had taken a departure position off Ireland, and they had to rely on dead reckoning ever since. The weather matched Toby's lack of enthusiasm, something that was soon picked up by his fellow officers.

"You'll be able to get down to see her surely," his closest colleague argued. "Washington's still possible by train."

"But after that it's disputed territory as she says in her letter," Toby pointed out, looking at the map spread out on the table.

"Well, I can't see this conflict going on that much longer," the Chief Officer said, coming into the chartroom and pinning up the orders for the day.

"I'm not so sure about that," Toby answered resignedly. "My aunt who seems to be extraordinary close to what is going on seems to think otherwise."

"Well, whatever you decide, Toby," his Captain advised after a long discussion on the wing of the bridge. "I shall need your resignation by the time we arrive in New York. And don't think that the Company will necessarily release you immediately. It may take a month or two. Head office aren't impressed with what's going on."

"I can wait," Toby said, realising that leaving was not going to be easy after all.

"Where will you base yourself then, Toby?" the Captain put to him.

"What about your mother's family in Massachusetts?"

"My aunt has said that I can have her spare room whilst I go through the process of joining up," answered Toby, wishing that the interview would come to an end.

"You'd best be absolutely certain that you will be engaged before going any further," the Captain of *Perthshire* advised. "The Union Navy may change their mind, so I would get a formal invitation in writing before we leave New York this time."

"I agree that with the United Kingdom supplying weapons to both sides is not exactly helping the situation," Toby agreed, "but it is also an opportunity for me to push my career into another direction."

"I'm not sure about that," his mentor commented, terminating the conversation and dismissing his officer with a sigh. "You'd be better off with your kitbag in a bunk here."

Chapter 14

James leaned over the canvas dodger which protected the wing of the bridge, and gave the tiny wooden wheelhouse some shelter from the elements. Inside, the pilot and the Captain whispered instructions to the helmsman, who was concentrating on the oil lamp above the compass.

They were approaching Cape Fear from the north and nearing the area regularly patrolled by the government's gunboats. A widespread layer of cloud blanketed out the sky. It was the ideal situation for running the blockade of Wilmington. There was not a man jack asleep as the *Fannie* crept towards the shore at a steady ten knots, well below her maximum speed, but ready to accelerate if needed.

"Douse that light," came a gruff instruction from the Captain, who looking over the rail had noticed a stoker lighting up and trying to hide the flame.

"Go round the decks, James, and tell all hands that anyone smoking will forfeit his bonus," the Captain continued.

"Yes, Sir. Anything else?"

"Tell the cook, coffee for all hands. We are getting to the critical stage."

Within minutes a seaman had sidled up to James and offered a steaming cup and a cheese roll. It was two o'clock in the morning and none of them had eaten since supper, some eight hours earlier. "Coffee, Sir," the seaman whispered, then turned to the wheelhouse with three more mugs on a tray. "Sorry, it not cocoa."

James looked over the side watching with almost hypnotic fascination, as the paddles bit into the water leaving a perfect wake of silver and green florescence displaced plankton, dancing away in the night. The only sound was the steady thump of the engine and the occasional scrape of a shovel against metal as a stoker topped up the boiler, before slamming the door shut with a resounding clang.

The Captain had signalled to James that they would soon be reducing the revolutions and he checked the taut line that stretched from the lookout's position and connected to a small bell. In an attempt to keep excited voices down to a minimum, he would ping it to alert the bridge if he heard or saw anything ahead.

"How many Union boats can we expect?" Stewart asked the pilot peering into the darkness.

"Last boat into Hamilton reckoned two, but they all seem to be deep drafted at about twelve feet, so they are wary about coming in too close," the pilot explained stabbing a finger at the chart. "They seem to stay in this bay here to the north and keep well away from the *Frying Pan* shoals."

"I see, tucked well out of the tide," Stewart said. "I'd probably do the same."

"Rumours have it that the Union now have more than a hundred vessels patrolling the coast from Cape Cod to Florida," the pilot intervened, "and they would have many more if they had captains and crew to man them."

"So they roam about, more or less at will," James whispered, poking his head into the wheelhouse.

"They have some opposition, but the Confederate ships are smaller with dubious weapons, so they don't tend to engage unless they have to," the pilot replied. "But I hear that on the Mersey, a heavily gunned warship is being completed for them."

"Where does all this information come, Pilot?" Stewart asked.

"Bone and Watcher in Hamilton. They know everything that is going on," the fisherman chided Stewart. "And you say that your government has no plans to help us."

"Which channel are you taking, Pilot?" Stewart asked his guide, reminding him that they were still covering a mile every six minutes.

"I was thinking of the New Inlet, but that takes us north of Bald Island and a run rather close to the beach off Cape Fear," the pilot explained. "But it is closer to Wilmington."

"And the fort. The one they call Fort Fisher?" Stewart asked. "Is that manned?"

Stewart looked at the channel not unlike the approach to the River Humber with its hooked sand spit.

"Like I said," the pilot answered, "by the time the Union Army realised the importance of Wilmington, the local militia marched in and persuaded the caretaker sergeant to join them, and General Grant has never bothered to recapture it since. Mind you, they will one day when they realise that Wilmington is so important and then there will be an almighty battle. It was built fifty years ago and the largest bastion on the east coast."

"And Fort Caswell. What about that one?" James asked, listening in on the conversation whilst looking at the chart. "Is that a stone fort or earthen?"

"That is very definitely stone. The militia control that as well," the local man confirmed. "And there's more forts up the river. All down to your Navy I'm told"

"Now this is the main the channel, but it has a dog leg approaching Fort Caswell on the west side," the pilot replied, "see here."

"It looks extremely complicated. How do we gauge the turn?" Stewart questioned.

"We will be met by a boat just inside the *Frying Pan* shoal." the pilot answered. "There's a schedule known only to us."

"All understood," Stewart replied feeling the hairs on the back of his neck bristle in anticipation of a port entry in the dark, that he had never experienced before. "My crew is ready."

"Then stop the engine and be ready with the lead," the pilot suggested.

James felt the ship slow down and finally stop. The control of the engines, usually by a clanging bell and the movement of a big brass lever, had been abandoned in favour of a series of hand signals all the way down to the engine room plates. He moved to the stern to see the chain clanking across the deck and around the blocks to the rudder head, with the crew desperately trying to deaden the noise with pots of grease.

The most experienced of the seamen stepped out from the shadows on deck and gently swung the weight into the water.

"Four fathoms," he whispered to James, who passed it silently to the captain.

All movement on the *Fannie* stopped as it glided on through the water.

"Another sounding," whispered the pilot.

"Three and half fathoms and sand," replied the seaman turning over the lead weight and feeling the tallow trapped in the base.

"What can we expect to find past the bar," the Captain whispered to the fisherman pilot, who was guiding them in.

"Two and half fathoms, when we've passed the *Frying Pan,* which should be coming up soon," he confirmed. "That is if it's still there. The Union navy occasionally attacks it with boats and sink it, but we have replacements in the port if required."

"Lookouts reported something in the water," James whispered to the pilot, resetting the trip line.

"Reckon it's a boat crew leading us in, Captain," the fisherman confirmed straining his eyes in the dark. "They've probably decided not to flare the float."

James could just distinguish a boat with four men resting on the oars.

"Take another sounding then dead slow ahead, Captain," came another quiet order."

"Dead slow it is, Pilot," Stewart replied. "All the way?"

"No, we will get inside the forts, which we control of course," the pilot replied. "Then we will anchor until first light."

"From now on withy sticks will be marking the channel so we need some light," the pilot confirmed. "The river passage is due north, but the channel twists this way and that."

"I'll sure be pleased about that," Stewart replied downing the dregs of his coffee. "Say, how many trips have you done up this river?"

"This is my first one as a pilot," the man replied with a broad smile creasing his black face. "But I've known it since childhood."

"How come?" asked Stewart.

"I've been a fisherman for most of my life on an estate that we'll pass shortly," he answered, just as a blinding flash followed by a dull explosion split the air.

"Bloody hell, where did that come?" shouted James in shock, as the splash of a falling shell was seen astern.

"Shall we stop?" a concerned Stewart said, turning to the local man.

"No, full ahead," the pilot responded, adding quickly "He's out of range and can't follow. They usually only have old Parrott guns with a maximum range of 2,000 yards and if they don't get you with the first shot they give up. It takes them five minutes to reload. Steer south-west, a quarter west. But best to get the hell out of it. I'll tell you when we have to swing north."

"What about the other two boats behind us?" James reminded them. They had both caught up and the three were in convoy.

"They will lay off until tomorrow or head down to Georgetown or Charleston, but that's over a day away," the pilot assured the pair.

"How long now?" asked a weary Stewart, as he gave the order to drop the anchor.

"Two hours unless we run aground," came the reply from an equally relieved pilot. "I'll let you know when to heave up."

"Tell me," Stewart said when they were in clear water with the sun climbing out of the sea behind them and the *Fannie* was proceeding up the river. "If you're enslaved why didn't you just stay in Hamilton?"

"Well, first of all they'd find me and take me back in chains, and second I have a wife and kids on the plantation," the pilot answered chewing on a piece of tobacco. "And lastly, I'm a free man, as are most of the skilled men in Wilmington. I can sell my fish on the open market as long as the owner has what he requires. You'd be surprised how many freed slaves there are hereabouts. My house is up Town creek, four miles away."

"And what do you think about this war then?" Stewart pressed for an answer.

The Negro thought hard and shook his head.

"Ah, don't at all. I just believe in no one but God, and he's an awful lot to do!"

James looked down the dock at Wilmington. The railway line showed signs of rusting, where it should have been shiny from the constant contact with the covered box cars bringing in bales of cotton and timber. Beyond the *Fannie* was a damaged sailing vessel, mounting a single cannon in the bow set on a crude carriage running on a circular rail track.

It had been displaced to one side by a direct hit and a group of men had assembled a tripod from the spars in a vain attempt to repair it. Dressed in an assortment of uniforms, they were a mixture of seamen and locals under the direction of an elderly Confederate lieutenant, who was also trying to coax the engineer into bringing the steam deck winch back into life.

"You the Captain of that side winder?" he grunted, as Stewart stopped to talk at the very moment the cannon slid off its slings and toppled down the deck, scattering the engineers.

Stewart nodded as a barrage of expletives blasted the air.

"You got some decent hardware on board then?" the old timer asked. "Cos if so we'll have it right here. That General Lee keeps all the best equipment for his troops and we just have to manage with what we can salvage."

Stewart cast an experienced eye over the vessel and reckoned that it wouldn't be sailing within the week, and probably longer than that.

Beyond the warship several two masted sailing schooners were loading and discharging local cargoes of food and timber for trade up and down the coast. The pilot, who had caught them up and was about to climb down to his own gaff rigged fishing cutter further up the quay, waved and told them that ships would ply up and down the creeks and rivers without any hindrance at all.

"Between Wilmington to Cape Hatteras and beyond, the inlets and canals provide a haven of travel for shallow draught vessels," he confirmed. "The Union boats just can't penetrate without being blown out of the water. All the entrances have small forts with Confederate guns at the ready."

James walked up the quayside, leaving his Captain still in deep conversation with those working on the Confederate warship. In the distance, a good half a mile away he could see the shipyard, that the pilot had talked about, and he pressed on until he came to a crude gateway.

For years and covering several acres, the yard had been building trading ships and now vessels were emerging for the Confederate navy. Wooden ships, fitted with any gun that they could find and a metal ram bow, or a torpedo rocket. Anything that could take on the iron clads of the north.

Seeing his senior back down the quay, James retraced his steps to find Stewart being hailed by a lieutenant in the grey uniform of a Confederate officer. Behind him a detachment of soldiers drew up with a train of wagons.

Further on a plantation owners' representative and a slave were unlocking a warehouse opposite the ship. James looked inside to see hundreds of tightly packed bales stacked floor to ceiling.

"Who the hell are you?" a loud voice greeted him as he stepped inside the cool of the building.

"Well, that's not much of a welcome," James replied equally as terse, "when we've run the blockade with your guns and supplies."

"Ah, hell," the man answered. "Sorry about that. Welcome to Wilmington such as it is."

James smiled. He had made his mark.

"As you can see, Limey," the man questioned, realising the stranger before him was not a local. "Half of the town have gone to the hills where they hide away with their wives and children. Wilmington is a ghost town with the militia in control. Most of them are pensioners from the Indian wars or snotty nosed teenagers, who can hardly wipe their arses. And as for the town. Prices are so high, folks are eating the soles of their shoes."

"How long has this warehouse been full?" James questioned mentally calculating it to one in Liverpool.

"A good six months," the man replied. "And there are others on the line out of town. There must be thousands of tons here in Wilmington, and all we managed to shift was a few bales on sailing ships to Bermuda, until they were hunted down."

"Well, we can take about four hundred tons we reckon until we get to a free board measure that the Captain can live with," James said, adding, "and to my satisfaction as well."

"Well, do your best then, my man," the agent said as the trusty locked the door. "We never knew what cotton looked like round here until the Mississippi was blocked. It's all timber, rice and oils round these parts.

"Mind you, these guns will be welcomed in Richmond, General Lee's base. It's no distance at all by our standards as long as the railway is running, and that ain't often."

"And what about the town here?" asked James, looking back up the quayside.

"It's a quaint place. Not unlike New England in places, not that you ever know, I guess. Even got an opera house. But it's all shut, the whole place I mean. There's a few bars, and the girls will come out at night. You'll be wanting to get away as soon as possible. It's a rough place at the best of time, but when the blockade runners are here over the new moon time, it's not a place to be at night.

"Thanks," James said turning round to see the first of the boxes being lifted ashore, and a wheezing steam engine trundling three box cars down the line. "I might just take the time to find out for myself."

The following morning, whilst the first of the cotton bales were being manhandled on trolleys towards the *Fannie;* James passed the wharves again, full of the activity of a busy port. He strolled into the town, found that the newspaper was still being printed, and carried on only to find it deserted just as he had been told.

But it was the theatre that had taken his attention, and plastered on the walls were posters of the most recent and popular events. A well weathered and faded advertisement for the Barnum circus caught his eye; but what really attracted his attention was one for Jenny Lind, the very lady that had enthralled him with her singing in Liverpool.

He stepped back to look at the building in all its magnificence, despite the ivy that was now taking over, when the main door opened and a young lady emerged, tripping over the step and nearly tumbling into his arms.

"Oh, I am so sorry," she gushed, extricating herself from his arms and regaining her composure. "I'm so clumsy at times."

"Well, you're lucky that I was here," James said. "I was just walking around and amazed to find an opera house in so small a town."

"It's more of a theatre than an opera house," the girl said. 'there's been a society here ever since General Cornwallis used Wilmington as his base," she said. "By the way I'm Carolyn Jones, family have been here for generations. And you? You're English by the sound of it. What brings someone like you to a place like this?"

James had to confess that he was on business, business that not everyone approved of.

"Well, you're not a soldier by the look of it so you must be a seaman," Carolyn said, looking him up and down. "An officer by the look of it. Can't be anything else, but if you are interested in opera. Would you like a look around?"

"I can't think of anything better to do on a day like this," James answered, his day already lifted by a notch.

"Then let's go," she said lightly, leading him into the darkness of the auditorium.

"Is there an ice cream parlour here?" James asked when they emerged five minutes later, squinting into the daylight. "Surely the whole town is not deserted. What were you doing in the theatre before I came along?"

"One question at a time if you don't mind," she said scolding him on the one hand and encouraging on the other.

"Well, my father is the mayor and he wanted the place opened and aired," Carolyn explained. "There are usually several productions a year, including Shakespeare, but for the past eighteen months it has been closed down. It's a total disaster."

"Where has everybody gone too then? James asked

"Unless they have business in the town, they take to the hills and just come back for storing up. Since the war prices of just about everything have rocketed in Wilmington," she explained, as they turned a corner in the street and found the only parlour in town.

They had been talking non-stop for the best part of an hour, with the ease of a couple far more acquainted; discussing the arts, history and education; before the subject of the civil war came up. Meanwhile, the Negro waitress, not daring to speak up, had been waiting patiently for them to go and close up for the day.

"I must get back to the ship," James said looking at his watch.

"Would you like to come for supper tonight?" she asked, thanking him for his company and picking up the pile of theatre programmes that had been rescued from the theatre.

"But we've only just met," James protested lamely.

"Don't worry about that," she assured him. "I'm sure my parents won't mind. They are used to entertaining. These are going to the library for safekeeping," she added wrapping them together with string. "You can take one if you wish."

"I'm sure I can get away," James answered, selecting one of the tattered copies. "They've started loading the bales, but it certainly won't be finished tomorrow at the earliest."

"My father will send a trap for you," she said unrolling her parasol. "He's a bit fierce but don't worry. My mother is a dear."

"Not unlike my home," James said with a laugh. "What time can I expect the carriage?"

"Six o'clock sharp," she answered. "We Southerners eat early, go to bed before ten and rise with the sun."

"So what brings you to Virginia, young man?" the town mayor asked his guest as soon as James had alighted from the trap and surveyed the brick and clap board house a mile out of town. "My daughter tells me you're from Liverpool?"

James opened his mouth, but the man continued before he could get a word in.

"Of course," he continued clapping James on the shoulder. "You're our saviour at the moment, but I doubt that it will make much difference in the end. Risking your life for a few bales of cotton to keep the mills turning and your workers off the breadline.

"Well, we are all under a bit of pressure, Sir, as you might imagine," James explained, as the girl looked on and he detailed his role in the cotton industry back home.

"Anyhow," Carolyn's father continued, "enough of that for the moment. Come on in and meet my wife. Supper is on the table. Jane has probably told you. We eat well before sunset, particularly in the summer."

"So you're well-travelled then, James?" Mrs Jones asked as they all relaxed on the veranda and watched the sun go down.

"As it turned out," James replied, "but I have no real desire to have a career at sea. I suppose I will continue with a life dealing in cargoes rather than transporting them."

"The sea's best left to those to those who really have salt in their veins," the mayor interjected. "Look at me. I own a couple of forests, three factories and we produce turpentine, oils from the ground and even gas for the town. That's enough for anybody to deal with. I'm a local politician, with no high political views, just trying to keep the place on an even keel."

"But I thought everybody here was staunch Confederate," James asked. "Ready to face down Lincoln."

"It's more complicated than that James," the mayor continued. A third of the population here, that is when they are at home, are blacks and one in ten are artisans and free men. Our lifeblood is industry, commerce, import and export and at the moment we are being strangled. The sooner this war is resolved the better for all."

"I'm not certain that is totally understood back home," said James, looking at Carolyn who gave him a resigned smile, having heard it so many times before.

"Now why don't you let Carolyn show you round the gardens. We don't have water on tap here." he said with a smile. It mainly comes from wells and neither to we have proper toilets. Everybody in town has outside privies,"

"When are you going to be back?" Carolyn asked on the quayside the following day as the gangway was being pulled in.

"In about two to three weeks," James said, taking the opportunity to kiss her on the cheek.

"Be safe on your journey then, James. Watch out for those Yankees," she said. "I'll be waiting for your return."

By the time the side winder *Fannie* had enough steam in the boilers for Captain Stewart to cast off the ropes, two more blockade runners had appeared around the last bend of the river, and with much assistance from the river boats, full of oarsmen, had secured further up the quay. All of a sudden the port was full of shouting and activity again as bottles of wine were opened, hatch covers were released and another train of wagons could be heard rumbling down the tracks.

With the merest assistance from the rudder and the engines, the *Fannie* skewed herself off the quay, helped by the ebb tide and turned smartly in the mid-stream. James gave a frantic wave to Carolyn, as she climbed aboard her trap, and then walked down the deck checking the lashings on the bales. The ship was as full as Stewart and the Chief officer dared.

They might have the weather behind them, but it was imprudent seaman that succumbed to the risk of overloading his ship on any voyage, particularly the North Atlantic ocean. It was just as well that the second officer, effectively the owner of the ship on behalf of his father was also not keen to risk his life, nor that of his fellow colleagues and sailors. It was a balance between risk, balance, chance and reward.

"Will we be taking the same channel, Pilot?" asked Stewart, as Wilmington faded into the distance.

It was a different pilot that they had for trip downstream, and with him he had three colleagues to make up a quad ready for an influx of side winders waiting in Bermuda now that they were well into the summer. The warehouses in Wilmington were overflowing with cotton, the shipyards boasted that they could build a ship within three months and there was rice enough for the population to withstand a siege at the same time should it be necessary.

"Yes, Captain," came the raw reply. "We'll coast down to sugar loaf point and wait for the signal from ashore, that will tell us if there are any Union patrol boats hanging around the corner of Fort Fisher ready to pounce.

Stewart looked at the complicated chart with so many fortifications as the pilot continued, "The fort guns will keep them at bay, so be ready for full power as we pass Fort Anderson on the starboard side. The last reports indicated that there were two in waiting, but they are only two converted sailing vessels. They won't aim to do anything but wing you, so when we are past the Buchanan Battery all should be well, unless there is a third gunboat off the shoals.

"So I hear that you were fraternising with the mayor's daughter, James," Stewart teased the young officer, once they were clear of the *Frying Pan* and on course for Bermuda.

Well, not quite, but I admit she is rather tasty," James said, not really wishing to elaborate on his run ashore.

"Richest family in the district, I heard," Stewart continued, "How did you manage that?"

"Are you interested in opera, Sir?" James retorted to his superior.

"Not at all, music hall is about the limit of my interest," Stewart replied.

James laughed, "You always meet the best girls at the opera house," he said, as Stewart looked on slightly baffled at the turn of the conversation.

"Don't tell me," he said, "a place like Wilmington has an opera house."

"Oh yes, Sir," James replied as he turned to watch the helmsman alter the wheel to the next course. "It may not be London or Milan, but Wilmington has an opera house, oh yes indeed it has."

"We have a big load for you, Captain," said Mr Watcher, of Bone and Watcher, the shipping agents, no sooner had Stewart slapped the *Fannie* alongside without the use of the tug which was looking for business and was loitering in the background. "The big liners seem to have almost stopped calling in, to be replaced solely by the cargo ships which can ship in and out a thousand tons of arms, cotton and coal in one go."

"Let me see," said Stewart, "it's midsummer of...where are we...64, and a couple more trips and we'll have to lay up for the winter. Can't risk a boat like this in the hurricane season. And after that the bergs come rolling in, although they are just about melted by the time they reach Bermuda."

"You could always run out of the Bahamas." Watcher suggested.

"Nassau has yellow fever," Stewart reminded him. "Causes all sorts of problems. The port authority at Wilmington insist on quarantine for incoming ships and the military try to overrule them."

"Of course, of course," replied Watcher.

"Now what are we taking on board this time?" Stewart asked, keen to get back to the business in hand.

"We'll do our best as always," Watcher smoothed the *Fannies* Captain. "This time it's all uniforms, boots and medical supplies. And of course a hundred tons of coal."

"What are the latest rumours from Washington?" asked James as they sat down later with both partners in the best St Georges hotel. "In Wilmington, they seem to think that Jefferson Davies is losing the edge."

"Well, the early successes of 61" and 62" do seem to be deserting him, but Lincoln doesn't think he has them on the run yet," Watcher outlined; doodling on a piece of paper. "Vicksburg fell last month, but in Louisiana and Mississippi General Lee still has the high ground."

"What about at sea though?" asked James. "Have we still the advantage there?"

"At the moment, yes by all accounts, but Lincoln is gathering ships of all sorts and sizes," Watcher confirmed. "Tomorrow the *USS Bangor* is calling in on her way back from a tour of the Mediterranean. Apparently, it's the last warship to be pulled back from the overseas, so now every bit of iron that the navy owns is back on home turf."

Threading through the scores of dock workers and the strollers taking in the warmth of the evening sun, Stewart steered James towards a cafe that spread itself beyond the cantilevered blinds onto the quayside, and found a table that was free.

"Have you ever handled a paddle steamer, James?" he said having ordered two iced coffees.

"No, but I've watched you like a hawk and I was given a chance or two on the Liverpool pilot boats," he replied, stirring his spoon to the bottom of the glass.

"Well, it's about time you did," Stewart said, "I'm giving the Chief officer a drive when we leave, and a transit up the river on arrival and all things equal you'll you can take charge on the trip back. I'll be heading home when the hurricane season starts, and that can only be after two more voyages. *Fannie* can winter here or in Wilmington. What do you think?"

"I guess that Wilmington will be the cheapest to lay up," James said.

"Somehow I thought that you might say that," Stewart answered, a sly smile spreading across his ruddy face.

"The cargo and coal should be loaded by the time we get back," James confirmed. "Best that we are not around when that warship docks, I guess."

"Well, he can't touch us inside the twelve mile limit," Stewart said smiling. "And I'm sure that you haven't forgotten. You represent the owners and the cargo, whereas my responsibility is to the crew and all on board."

Within the week, the *Fannie* had passed the *Frying Pan shoals;* had slipped past Fort Caswell, the Buchanan battery and the mighty earthworks of Fort Fisher, without the hint of any opposition; and was resting against the wooden piles just a few yards from the main warehouse.

Ahead were a string of sailing ships and paddle steamers, and at the inner most part of the harbour, a newly launched warship with a piercing bow ram menaced the yard from which it had emerged. Rows of boxcars waited, doors open to receive a thousand tons of military equipment from the newly arrived side winders; and a detachment of soldiers in the grey uniform of the Confederate army lounged around waiting for the dockers to commence unloading the ships.

James settled down to the paperwork for which he was responsible, knowing that Carolyn would not appear until the day's work on the dockyard had finished, and that wouldn't be until late afternoon. Least that was what he thought, but then it was almost a month since they had parted on the quayside with a lingering kiss.

"You're early," he teased her towards the end of the day as she appeared round the last of the wagons, lifting her skirt as she negotiated the iron rails and stepped on to the gangway.

"Can I come aboard then?" she retorted folding her parasol and hanging onto his arm. "I've only been on one of these on the Chesapeake and they go awfully fast I recall."

"That's why they are in such demand here and in Charleston." James answered taking her hand. "Like greased lightening we call it."

"But you aren't going to Charleston?" she questioned.

"Not if I can help it, when I get a reception like this here," James said, accepting a kiss on the cheek. "And after all, when I have the responsibility on behalf of my father, I have quite a lot of influence on where we trade."

"Now show me properly around this vessel of yours then, James," Carolyn instructed, "and then with luck, supper will be waiting."

James walked her through the decks strewn with straw and debris that was used to protect the cargo and into the lounge which was once fitted out to the highest standards, but had been stripped out to make way for the most vulnerable items of the cargo. The wide windows had been blocked off with timber bolted to the frames and then strong backed with more baulks of wood.

At the forward end, the galley windows were protected inside and out for fear of a sweeping wave down the decks, the only ventilation being for the massive cast iron range concreted in to the steel deck. With only fifteen crew on board instead of up to a crew of thirty and five hundred passengers, the dining facilities were reduced to two long hardwood tables and four benches.

James opened the temporary door that led to the grand staircase and the upper lounge, and guided Carolyn to the curved rail on the side and the wide shallow steps. The upper deck was boxed into small cabins for the Captain and officers, and a large space with hammocks suspended on hooks for the steward and the rest of the crew. With no natural light, the only recognisable part of the ship was a bank of toilets on each side that exited straight to sea via a system of valves, and which were locked when not in use. A swill room, the remnants of a baby changing room was tucked away at the end of the corridor.

"And you live here?" Carolyn expressed, horrified at the way the once beautiful vessel had been turned into nothing more than a cattle boat.

"Ah, but it's much better on the bridge," James bridled, as they took to the staircase which lead directly to the wheelhouse without needing to venture on deck. "We've got two temporary bunks up there in case we don't want to go below."

Carolyn wandered round the wooden framed wheelhouse perched high over the decks, going from one instrument to another and stroking the brass levers with her gloved hand.

"But there are two steering wheels," she explained, spinning one and then trying the other one that was locked solid. "What's this one for?"

"That's for when we go stern first in the long rivers back home," James explained. "The first thing we had to do before leaving Glasgow was to completely plate up the bow rudder."

"And you're putting up with this existence just to help us out?" Carolyn questioned pulling him across the engine room control lever and planting a substantial kiss on his lips.

"But it's not without its rewards," James replied, drawing breath and leaning over the obstacle to hold her around the waist.

"So you've shown my daughter over your ship, James," asked Dan Jones, the mayor of Wilmington as he poured out a cool glass of lemon on the veranda. "I bet that was a surprise. She's a game girl and her young sister is even more sparky but she usually shies away from the business end of industry."

"Well, I have to admit that she was taken aback to start with but she rallied round in the end," James agreed.

"You wouldn't believe it but she has challenged the local Colonel here more than once on the way he treats the locals," the mayor said, "She's fearless at times. Carolyn and her mother make a strong team."

James looked through the doors into the lounge to see Carolyn talking to her mother wondering just how that could be.

"Tomorrow, if you have time, I'll take you to the mucky side of my factories," Jones suggested. "I presume that you can ride?"

"Well enough, but not as well as my sister," James said, wondering just where she was at that very moment.

"Come on into the house for supper, James," the mayor said, taking him by the arm. "And tell me more about your family."

"Well, it's all quite simple," James explained. "My father and grandfather have both been involved in shipping in a small way, but now my father just concentrates on importing cotton."

"Daddy was most impressed to hear that your brother and sister were journeying up the Mississippi," Carolyn said on the way back to the ship, snuggling up to him.

"Well, my father pushed Nicholas into it," James answered. "Alice just went for the experience."

"I'm not sure that my father would have agreed to an adventure like that," Carolyn replied as he stepped down to the quay.

"I don't think she told father her full intentions before she left," James laughed.

"Are you sure about that," Carolyn teased.

"Well, I think so, but as I haven't heard from them since they left New York, I can't be too certain," James said giving her one lasting kiss.

"Be ready for eight o'clock in the morning," Carolyn instructed James as the mayor's driver pulled up alongside the ship; and the two separated themselves from the plush seating and James made for the gangway.

James picked his way across the cluttered deck. Most of the cargo had been discharged and only three box cars waited for their bellies to be filled. Tomorrow the warehouse doors would be flung open and the half ton bales would be jammed into every corner of the ship. Enough to fill the company's order book back home for a week. Not a great deal, but at least it was something.

"Another good evening ashore, James," teased Stewart ably abetted by the Chief officer as they called him in for a nightcap.

James grinned and accepted the drink. Never one for taking too much alcohol in the day, he nevertheless liked a shot of rum to retire with.

"We were just debating what to do with the ship over the hurricane season," Stewart said. "It's fast coming and we need to confirm whether to lay up here or back in Bermuda."

"I suppose that to a degree that depends on what is being shipped out from England," James said. "I'll get a message back to the Chairman on our return, but it will only be by letter so when I get a reply goodness knows."

"One of the problems will be the crew," said Stewart twiddling with his pencil on the table. "Even though you might pay them a retainer for the six to eight weeks they will get restless. The engineers will be fine. They will have the boiler to overhaul pumps to clean and the bearings to check, but for the fireman and seamen there is a good chance they will defect.

"What's your opinion, Mr Mate," James asked the Chief Officer, who was almost as experienced as Stewart.

"In my opinion," he said after some deliberation, "if we lay up in Bermuda they are more likely to get absorbed into the activities of the port which is growing all the time and then enticed out on another ship. On the other hand, if we hide up here until the hurricane season is finished we might be able to find employment locally," he continued. "They are all good men. I know that they would be welcomed in the shipyard as riggers and the local militia are looking for men to improve the earthen works at Fort Fisher."

"It's something to give serious thought too then," said James.

"By the way, gentlemen," said Stewart, rising and making his way to the largest of the temporary cabins. "I shall be leaving the next time in Bermuda. I've been called back to Scotland to prepare the latest steamer for next season."

"We're going to the lakes at the head of the river," called out Carolyn the following morning as a two horse carriage and a chuck wagon pulled up on the quayside, and she jumped down dressed in sweater and slacks. "Have you have got some suitable clothes?"

" Give me a minute," James replied, disappearing into the accommodation and returning in no time at all in his only pair of casual trousers.

The mayor had taken the opportunity to take his whole family up the valley and to inspect his lumber yards and oil factories, something that he often did and particularly on Independence Day, when he laid on celebrations for all his staff. It would be a six mile drive, he explained to James, where the Cape Fear river opened up into a series of lakes and islands.

"And where do you get the power from to drive the machinery?" James asked as the team headed north out of the town, past the shipyard and the railway marshalling yard, the carriage rolling easily from side to side over the dirt road.

"A combination really of skeleton windmills completely different to yours back home, and watermills where the gradient drop is sufficient.

That's not really until you get way the valley, and of course steam power," the mayor replied calling a halt, and instructing one of his staff on the chuck wagon to clear a fallen tree on the track.

James stepped down to help drag away the branch so that they could proceed, much to the amazement of the mayor, who looked at his wife equally surprised.

"There's such an abundance of wood here we mill it down for building ships and houses," the mayor explained afterwards. "It's all pine in these places and we distillate the bark for turpentine."

"And iron ore deposits," questioned James as Carolyn tapped him on the knee, a signal that they should stop talking about business and concentrate on the landscape.

"None that we know about but we're hopeful and there are plans for drilling down for oil," Carolyn's father confirmed, spreading out his free arm to show James the extent of his land. "It's not all owned by just one or two families, James. Most of it is individual plots granted in the last century."

"Now what do we have for lunch in that great hamper, ladies?" he asked, turning round with a large grin and smiling at his wife and two daughters.

"All your usual favourites, Father," the younger daughter piped up for the first time in the journey. "Can we go for a swim at the lodge by the lake?"

"Sure we can," the father confirmed, flicking the reins as they came to a slight incline in the track. "That is if your mother agrees. But first we've got to drop off the stores in the wagon and I have to make an inspection of the machinery. I won't be long," he added.

"You always are, Daddy," she complained. "I want to see if James can stay underwater as long as I can."

"Well, it will have to be before lunch for sure then," stated Carolyn looking firmly at her sister with the look of keep quiet until you're asked. "Wouldn't you agree, James?"

"Absolutely," agreed James. "I'm entirely in your hands and at your disposal."

"Don't forget that lunch is within the hour," Mrs Jones shouted out to her husband, who had parked the carriage and was walking down the track to the distillation plant which was billowing out smoke and polluting the surroundings valley.

James and Carolyn were at the water's edge skimming stones across the mirror finish of her lake whilst lunch was being spread out. A squirrel approached, hesitated and then scampered away to be followed by another, bolder, who approached a tantalising basket that was laid out on the rug and then had second thoughts.

"Your sister doesn't miss a trick, does she?" James said as he skimmed another stone that bounced four times before sinking.

"She's watching us like a hawk," Carolyn agreed, her stone sinking after one bounce.

"Then perhaps we ought to reward her," James said taking the opportunity to steal a kiss while unobserved. "Can she really stay underwater for longer than a minute?"

"Oh, yes," came the immediate reply. "She swims like a seal. Now, are you going to kiss me again."

They were driving back slowly down the valley, full and content from the contents of the hamper, the ladies dozing close together in the fold of the carriage cushions. The big sweep of the horizon was taking James' attention, hills and trees as far as he could see, and the curling smoke of fires from furnaces on either side of the lake spiralling upwards, trying hard to escape into the atmosphere.

Only the constant and unremitting thud of the drop hammers, the occasional shrill of a whistle as a steam valve released under pressure, and the constant chatter of the crows that followed behind them, spoilt the serenity of the scenery.

"What do you think of our countryside then, James?" said his host, as James shifted position, and looked over his shoulder at the three women, lolled together; lulled into sleep by the clip of the horses and the steady crunch of iron on the gravel.

"It is a fine sight, Sir, and so endless," James had to agree.

"As are the opportunities my lad," the American continued. "Once this war is over."

James sat silent for moment, thinking of home, the factories like cathedrals, but without the grandeur of towers and spires; the countless rows of houses squashed together by some gigantic hand; the valleys of grey people eking out a living to see them through the next week.

"I'm lucky that I cannot deny," James said, "as are you with space that seems to go on for ever and a conflict that matches it."

"I agree to a point, James. This war can't go on for much longer and although I'm a politician, I'm well down the scale with no ambition other than to serve my people," the American stated. "But tell me, James, what are you likely to do when it's all over?"

James pondered for a while. "I could go back to Liverpool and take over the business, but that is really my brother's destiny. There is an opening if I want it in my uncles shipping company in New York. They trade fruit from the West Indies. For certain, I don't want to be transporting contraband for much longer It's excitement I could do without."

"But it is making you money, and plenty of it by all accounts," the mayor responded.

"Yes, I must agree. It is extremely remunerative, but that is a function of wealth, the challenge and the excitement," James stated, not wanting to get too involved with the stakes in the venture.

The mayor nodded casting his eye back to his eldest daughter, who was coming too and dabbing her eyes with a perfumed hanky. "You've an option or two then?"

"Fortunately, yes," James answered.

"You know," the mayor continued, "We could with fresh blood like you in this county, if not this country. Good business experience, well-educated and keen on the arts. You know we've had a theatrical society here for the last fifty years and it's been dormant ever since 61."

"Yes, Carolyn was telling me about it. You've had touring world stars, I believe?" James agreed.

"When are you due back, James?" mayor continued probing again gently into James plans.

"Three weeks or so, and the trip after that *Fannie* will probably lay over here during the hurricane season," James suggested. "It's too risky and we can't get insurance cover."

"Good," the other said, lightly whipping the horses into a trot as they came to a rise in the land. "Just don't let my daughter down, will you. My wife says she has eyes for no other, and having watched her today I am of the same mind."

"Now you've observed me several times now, James," said Stewart as the last of the bales were stowed. "I want you to take the *Fannie* away. Let the tide do the work. You can't work one paddle against the other. To many ships have sunk that way by turning the paddles violently in opposition and the Board of Trade and Lloyd's won't allow it. Kirk has had to modify all his latest vessels."

James walked from one sponson to the other looking down into the paddles to ensure that no baulks of timber had lodged in during the stay in port. A guard gave some protection, but a damaged paddle would cause a delay of at least a day and much consternation on board. The spare elm boards kept in the racks were an essential part of the safety system, and although they were pre drilled and shaped to fit, the shipwright carpenter would not thank him for Missing a rogue obstruction.

Stewart was nowhere to be seen, probably checking the manifest, James thought, so he had to go through the pre sailing check list with the Chief Officer. Two decks down, the Chief Engineer looked at the dials climbing slowly clockwise to the red marks, mopping a sweaty forehead with a red rag and shouting instructions to the pair of stokers firing up the best anthracite coal.

With luck, he thought, they would be able to sail once clear of the shoals. He'd just heard that they would be laying up in Wilmington for the hurricane season. It would give him time to overhaul the boiler, already getting salted more than he wished, and re-establish the deep relationship he was having with one of the girls in town, who liked men that got their hands dirty.

James remembered just in time to wave to Carolyn, who stood on the quayside with her sister, as the headlines were slipped and the stern pushed back against a spring line, until the ironwork of the paddle sponson and the stern rested on the quay. With a touch of ahead power and the merest of rudder adjustment, the *Fannie* turned almost in her own length and within five minutes was nothing more than a smudge on the horizon.

Carolyn looked down at her sister, who was still waving energetically as the *Fannie* gave a last toot on the whistle.

"You like that man, Carolyn, don't you?" she said.

"Yes, I like him a lot," Carolyn answered, wiping away the hint of a tear.

Chapter 15

Six weeks later, Toby waited patiently with several hundred passengers in the Liverpool Customs Hall, waiting to board the sister ship of the liner that he had been Second officer on for the previous eighteen months. His release had been a tussle with the Company's Marine Superintendent, who had made him do another voyage in an attempt to retain him, but to no avail.

With his certifications, letter of introduction and ticket furnished by the Union agent in Liverpool safe in his pockets, Toby waited patiently in line with the second class passengers. His uniform and nautical instruments were buried deep with his other personal possessions in the two trunks ready to be loaded into the hold, leaving him with a small case for the voyage. Instead of his own cabin with a hand basin, he would be sharing a space with a dozen or so fellow travellers. Almost without exception his companions, immigrants in the main, would not have planned destinations in America, but he was heading for Boston, one of the training bases for the Union Navy.

He looked around the customs hall, expecting to see people that he had worked with, but none appeared to recognise him. He wondered what his mother would have thought of him. From New Bedford, his father had found her, when he was shipping whale oil destined for England and brought her back only for her to die, while he was still at school. Still at sea on passage from India, Toby had left a message for his father at the family house in Goole, and hoped that he would approve. Only his close friends and of course his aunt were aware of his plans. And of course, Emily. That is if his letter ever got to her.

"Hey, Limey, welcome aboard," the training officer for the Union Navy in Boston, called out to Toby as he looked up at the once pride of the American Fleet. Now over fifty years old the *U.S.S. Constitution* was well past its heyday, but it looked smart enough to the casual eye, having been recently pressed into service in the corner of the dockyard for inducting new officers. Toby was well used to seeing such ships on the Clyde, the Thames and the Mersey, where they were decommissioned; wooden walls with the mast and rigging removed; and usually roofed with a corrugated iron. Here though, was a ship in full splendour as if it had just finished a commission on active service.

Toby nodded, gave a half salute shook hands and reached for his trunk that had been deposited unceremoniously on the quay, by the indifferent driver of the cab, and delved deep into his pockets for a dime.

"Looks a fine ship," he said to the Lieutenant Commander who, he noticed, had a crisp gold star newly sewn on to the sleeve of his jacket. "All my sailing vessels like this were store carriers for the Navy and we had to beg for equipment to keep them going."

"At the moment, no expense spared," the American offered. "By the way you are the third Limey to join us this week. What's wrong with your leaders. Don't they pay you enough or isn't there enough action for you guys."

Toby had to agree that it was all of that, particularly for naval officers, where promotion was dire and the only way up the ladder was to volunteer for expeditions.

"Don't worry about your baggage. Leave it there. I'll find a rating to move it," the newly promoted officer assured Toby. "You'll sleep aboard tonight until we can find you a berth ashore in the barracks. All classes are here on-board. Now come and meet the Captain."

"Now, you're not from the real navy, I guess," the Commandant of the *Constitution* greeted Toby with a laugh promptly sitting him down in a high-backed colonial chair and calling his steward for tea. "As you know we don't allow alcohol at sea, but we make up for it ashore."

"Well, we're limited on passenger ships for sure as junior officers, but I wouldn't say it applies too much to the Captains," Toby replied brightly. "Nor to the senior engineers, who run a show pretty well to themselves on the basis that the engine room is a rum place to work, and few go down there to find out otherwise."

"Anyhow, we are damned pleased to see you chaps come aboard from which ever navy you come from," the Captain continued. "We just do not have enough experienced men to draw on."

Toby relaxed in the others company as the man scanned through his documents and notes.

"So, your mother is American and you have an aunt in New York and a girlfriend over here," he said looking up and over his glasses.

"My mother died some years ago and my girlfriend was working here in Boston, but had to go back to her family home," Toby replied flatly. "As you can see my aunt has a business helping with seafarers."

"Very commendable by the look of it," the Captain said. "It would appear she is not unknown here either."

"I find that hard to believe," Toby answered.

"Well, she is I can assure you," the Captain added, "She seems to be making contacts here in Boston as well and much above my level. We need ladies of her calibre in these difficult times as well as men."

"You'll have no problem getting to Manhattan to see your aunt. But as far as getting beyond Washington to your girlfriend, that might be a little difficult," the Captain said trying to be jovial. "But then you never know. America is the land of opportunity they keep telling us."

"Now, as far as your commission is concerned," he continued, "It will be for one year in the rank of lieutenant with a possible extension. After a two months course, you will be designated a ship. We are short of uniforms, so you will wear your own with our flash until the outfitters here get some more supplies of cloth."

Toby noted it down in his mind as the Captain brought the interview to a close.

"Supper is in the mess ashore," he said sweeping his papers across his desk and rising to his feet. "Report on board for 0900 in the morning and thank you for joining us."

It was not until he was halfway through his induction course, that he remembered that Emily had told him where the Adams' family lived in Boston. He had a few days leave due him and New York beckoned now that his aunt was back from her excursion out west, but perhaps Mr and Mrs Adams, who he had never met of course, might just be able to tell him more about Emily. Her letter was still buried in his heart.

"I shall find Mrs Adams," the maid said closing the door and leaving Toby admiring one of the finest houses in the city, "Mr Adams is away and my lady doesn't usually accept visitors, unless he is here, but I will ask."

Just as he was about to turn on his heel and walk back to the dockyard, the maid returned, curtsied and invited him in to a large ante-room.

"Now you must be that nice passenger ship officer, but by the looks of it you're now in our Navy," Mrs Adams said looking at the flash on his shoulder. "But where is the rest of your uniform?"

Toby explained that he was wearing the less ostentatious Merchant Navy uniform for the time being.

"Now," Mrs Adams said bringing out a fine tea set and teasing him about the Boston incident. "Emily said that you were debating between your career, your conscience and your prospects."

"Well, everything was tugging at me," Toby said feeling slightly uncomfortable, although Henrietta was doing her best to relax him.

"We are living in difficult times for sure," Mrs Adams agreed.

"It makes one wonder if a sensible decision can be made on anything," Toby replied thoughtfully.

"Now tell me. Have you been posted to a ship yet?" she asked as the maid arrived with a plate of cookies.

"No that will come soon enough," Toby replied. "I've just been informed that my course is shortened and I can have a few days off."

"You'll be wanting to get south I guess?" Henrietta questioned him.

"But don't expect it to be easy."

"I've been told it's almost impossible, but I have this letter of nearly three months ago," he said. "Do you know how she is?"

"Yes I do," she said turning round and taking a letter off her table. "I doubt that you'll ever be able to see her. Certainly not in the short term. She blames the Union for her mother's death; and now her father has died too she is at her wits end and without her brother. It will take her a long time."

"A long time, for what?" he asked.

"She is determined to run the plantation, find her brother and restore the house. As you know she has plenty of grit and won't give up even, I suspect, for you," Mrs Adams said after a while.

Toby sat dumbfounded at the latest news.

"I'm so sorry, Toby, I know she was so in love with you," she added. "She told us so on many an occasion."

He nodded, taking it all in, trying to suppress a tear.

"What will you do?" The lady asked eventually, trying to gauge Toby's thoughts.

"I don't really know, but I'm pledged at the moment," he said. "I'm committed to help now that I've signed up and see it through whatever that is."

"I'm sure that you're doing the right thing," Henrietta confirmed to Toby excusing herself. "Now I'm about to meet a lady here in Boston with the most extraordinary life experience and she is definitely doing the right thing."

It wasn't until an afternoon lecture on artillery that the question of how many British officers were signed up in the Union Navy arose. Until then all the students had been concentrating on the course with little chance for small talk. Toby had established a good working relationship with two British Lieutenants, who had taken a sabbatical and were destined for one of the monitors under construction on Staten Island.

"We have currently less than a hundred ships to patrol Lincoln's anaconda ring," the training Captain and lecturer for the day explained to the group.

"The anaconda ring," asked one of the student officers, "What is that?"

"For this war to be brought to a close, Lincoln has to have a stranglehold on the commerce of the south, that is crops—cotton and tobacco; so none of it can be exported," he explained to the fifty or so young men on the course. "And that, in essence, means blockading all means of transport out of the south, a difficult task when you consider the size of the country."

Toby's attention was drawn to the map that was unrolled on the wall.

"The Navy intends to strangle them by patrolling the whole coastline from New York down to Florida, around to New Orleans and up the Mississippi, a distance of over three thousand five hundred miles and that can't be done with one hundred ships. And we are relying on the Army to actually patrol the rivers, mainly the Mississippi, the Ohio and the Tennessee."

Toby looked at the thick line superimposed in a big swirl just like a snake.

"We need five hundred more ships and thousands of men from wherever we can get them," the Captain explained. "Now you can see why you are so important."

"And you can built them all here in the North?" asked Toby when the noise finally subsided.

"Good point, Lieutenant Barnes," the lecturer answered. "The straight answer is no. We are buying them from all over the world, but not yet from Britain. Lincoln is more concerned about thwarting the sale of warships from the United Kingdom to the Confederates."

A low buzz of questions came the way of the small cluster of British officers of which only Toby had some experience of a war zone.

"Now, let's look in detail at the Armstrong gun," the instructor said changing over the map for a drawing.

"If we can't have a British battleship," he said with a twinkle in his eye, "at least we have a British naval gun."

They were lined up on the deck of the old warship flanked by their instructors. It was the last day of the course and they were to be appointed to their first seagoing positions. The course, hurriedly contrived by the Navy Board to supplement the main naval college near Washington, was boosting the officer complement by five hundred officers a year, and yet more were required.

"Ensign Alderman, step forward," the Commanding officer of the *Constitution*, the Navy's most revered vessel barked out.

"Yes, Sir. Thank you, Sir," the fresh faced twenty year old, saluted nervously and crunched the deck as he took one pace forward.

"You've nothing to thank me for yet, Alderman."

"Sorry, Sir."

"Appointed to *USS Sceptre*, sailing frigate, based here in Boston."

"Thank you, Sir."

"Lieutenant Anderson, step forward," the Captain called out looking at the sheet held by his secretary, as the first newly appointed officer stepped back into the line.

"Yes, Sir."

"Appointed to *USS Dictator*, monitor, currently in Providence."

"Thank you, Sir, thank you."

The fifty or so officers were paraded in one line on the upper deck of the ship in full view of their families on the quayside waiting for their first ship to be announced. The appointments that would decide whether they would become a hero in the annuals of the Navy, or a household name spread across the nations paper or, more likely, just another name on the roll call of a hurriedly constructed ship or a captured and confiscated confederate paddle steamer. doing no more than holding the blockade line.

The only officers not surrounded by admiring families were those of the volunteered British navy officers, with the exception of Toby. His beaming aunt had made the five-hour detour journey from New York on her way back to Cincinnati.

"Lieutenant Barnes," the sonorous voice boomed out, and Toby made the one step forward.

"Yes, Sir," replied Toby, saluting the long way up and the short way down he had learned from his two British colleagues.

"Appointed Second in Command of the armed sloop *Audacious*, currently under repairs in New York."

"Thank you, Sir," Toby replied, thankful that it wasn't a lumbering monitor, that stayed in port for most of the time, rolled like a pig in anything but a flat calm and were uncomfortable to live in.

"I suppose that you will all be away celebrating tonight?" Agnatha asked, as they were all being dispersed.

"I don't have to," replied her nephew. "I actually find some of them rather juvenile."

"Then we'll have supper at my hotel. I'm booked out on a train in the morning," she suggested. "Make it for six."

During the course he had thought regularly of Emily, but it was six months since they parted at the Grand Union Station and he had not heard any more from her, his last letter having gone unanswered. He had tried once wiring her, imagining her house set in a clearing with the land down to the water's edge, but her image was dimming in the concentration of his duties and there were plenty of diversions in Boston to take his attention. One thing he did know, was that whilst he was happy to relax in the company of the younger officers, most of which were six or seven years younger than him, for an hour or two; an extended evening ashore with them was just not for him.

"Now exactly what are you doing in Canada and Cincinnati, Aunt? "He asked as they made their way to a table.

"Making contacts," she answered quite truthfully.

"That has to be a two-day train voyage at the very least?" Toby queried. "And how long do you expect to be away?"

"Until the job's done, that's all I can say," Agnatha answered, keeping it brief. "I thought I told you before," she added, "In fact I know I did."

"No, you didn't, Aunt," Toby retorted. "You're so secretive these days."

"I'm glad they wanted you to keep your uniform," she said changing the subject quickly. "Their Navy caps are so over the top with braid."

Toby laughed and hugged his aunt. "Don't let the captain hear you say that. And in any case the outfitters have just taken a delivery of cloth and I have to get fitted up."

"Stop changing the subject, Aunt," Toby said, "and answer the questions."

"Well, like you," she explained, "I wanted to do my bit and my friends back in Manhattan persuaded me that I could move around without drawing too much attention, and smooth the passage for people wanting to escape from the south."

"Can't they make their own arrangements, and who are they in any case," Toby asked trying to fathom exactly what she was doing.

"They have no money and no help," Agnatha explained, "and they are not like you and I. They are fleeing slaves."

"Ah, I see it now," Toby responded, smacking his forehead with the palm of his hand. "How stupid of me not to realise."

"So, I was asked to set up a clearing house in the last city that they would need to pass through on the way to Canada," Agnatha continued. "A sort of boarding house come hostel, so in the end I opened up a travel agency ostensibly for the wealthy as a front."

"Now it all makes sense," Toby said, "Just how long are your tentacles?"

Agnatha smiled. "It's a long story and even now I'm not sure how I got involved. So now uncle is back and busy, I'm off again for a few months to try and find an assistant. This war is coming up for two years of misery and is unlikely to finish in the coming year according to my information."

"The Navy certainly haven't managed to strangle the trade at sea," Toby agreed, pressing for some detailed clarification on his aunt's work. "So escaping slaves are moved up country by teams of sympathisers working undercover, staying in all manner of places?"

"That's it, they're moved around by carts, boats and sometimes short distances by train; always travelling by night," his aunt explained.

"And you arrange to hold them and move them under cover of your agency?" Toby asked. "Extremely devious if I might say so."

"It has to be," Agnatha continued, "Once past Cincinnati, and into the wilderness of Ohio to their destination on Lake Erie and a boat to Canada they are relatively safe. Unfortunately, many of them die from the cold as Ohio is bitter in the winter, but we have to keep moving them along for their own safety. Some stay at the farms where they have been quartered and go no further. Instead of carrying on they help the farmers and sympathisers organise the safe houses in the country. It's too dangerous to wander in the towns, gangs roam as bounty hunters, tracking them down for reward. And at three hundred miles to the Lake, the ground is full of rivers, swamps and forests with little cover."

Toby doodled on the napkin as Agnatha got up from the table.

"I've an early start and you have to get back to your ship," she announced kissing him on the forehead disappearing out of the restaurant.

Travelling south in his new uniform two days later, Toby found the *USS Audacious* in the corner of a repair yard in Staten island. At first glance and to all intents and purposes, it wouldn't be sailing until the fall, although Toby knew that chaos on a ship in dock could soon be rectified with commitment from a willing workforce.

"Come aboard, come aboard," a booming voice welcomed him. "Duck your head. I'm Commander Evans, Captain here for the foreseeable future. Been here two months trying to sought out this mess without a number one and only a skeleton crew."

Unlike most naval ships, where the Captain enjoyed the full width of the stern as his quarters, the *Audacious* was a cargo ship and the space was a jumble of stores and equipment.

"Come into my cabin," the commander beckoned. "Yours is on the other side, smaller of course."

Toby ducked under the next lintel. It wasn't quite what he was used too.

The great cabin is going to be converted sometime, but there's plenty to do in the meantime as you'll see," the captain continued, "Take a seat and make yourself comfortable as best you can."

Toby squeezed his frame into the spare folding chair and stretched himself out.

"Looks like you and I are the only ones with any experience," David Evans declared looking at Toby's papers. "I was an ensign at the siege of Veracruz, but the ensigns here are straight out of Annapolis. Fortunately, they are willing and look good material, but time will tell."

Toby looked down the crew list and the wide variation of names.

"The engineers are a mixed lot, some out our Merchant Navy and the Hudson tugs and the gunner; well, he has been borrowed from the Army. He was taken at the surrender of Fort Sumpter and exchanged earlier this year in a deal with General Lee." Evans continued, "Oh, the cook and his assistant are Chinese and out of a railway under construction in the west which is on hold for lack of materials. Can't release the steel to carry on building. So, we couldn't be more cosmopolitan. Sometimes it works quite well though."

"You know my background," Toby said, keen to find out more about his senior before they got too deep into conversation of the *Audacious,* "What was your previous command?"

"This is my first command," Evans explained. "I was first Lieutenant on a monitor warship for my sins. Lethal they are and look like a submarine that doesn't dive underwater. Several of them have done just that and not come up."

"Certainly, don't look stable enough for me," Toby agreed. "We went on board one during my induction course."

"Now back to this rust bucket," Evans said. "If we can keep this floating for six months we'll be doing well."

"Audacious was a three masted cargo ship with an underpowered engine," he explained, as they walked through the dockyard to the Admirals building. "Captured and confiscated in the Bay of Mexico for gun running, it was considered too good to be auctioned off so the Navy requisitioned it on the Admirals advice."

"So what do you think, Toby, having seen it in its raw state?" Evans said, as they negotiated a tortuous route, looking back to see the ship in the distance, framed between two cranes like a picture.

"It looks a tall order," Toby answered. "I'm no engineer, but fitting guns and fixing recalcitrant engines are usually more in months than weeks."

"In ordinary times, yes, Toby," Evans said evenly "But these are no ordinary times. Let's go and see the Admiral. He's got a lot of respect for you limeys, and wants to tap your brains about these paddle steamers from Glasgow that can outrun anything afloat."

"Now this is where this Parrot gun is going to be mounted," the grizzly gunner addressed Toby and the two young ensigns the following day, marking out the deck with chalk.

"It can't be swivelled easily see, on a ship like this, least not for the moment, and as we want to fire it without bringing the rigging down, we have to mount it ere' or between the masts over there," he explained.

The three officers looked over the rail at the massive gun on the quayside covered up against the elements whilst the gunner found some more chalk.

"The Captain wants this one to fire straight ahead, but we can't do that, cos we'd bring down the fore stay and everything would collapse about our ears," he continued enjoying his lecture. "So it's offset just ere' in front of the mast so the recoil doesn't bring down the foremast either.

"And the other one, that's ready to come aboard, Sir?" the youngest of the ensigns asked. "The Dahlgren cannon under the tarpaulin."

"Ah, now that one was designed by a naval officer of the same name years ago," the gunner growled, looking over the side as two ordnance artificers were taking the cover off. "See the shape. They call it the soda bottle."

"Where's that going, Chief?" one of the youngsters asked.

"That'll be here, midships where the hatch is right now, but not until the shipwrights have blocked it up," he continued chewing a plug of tobacco. "And as for the popgun that'll go aft, but we won't use that much, will we, sonny?" he continued looking the lad straight in the eye. "That's for people who run away."

"These are rather out of date, aren't they?" Toby asked the gunner, when the others had moved away in a corner to study the firing procedures, the team lists and the ammunition.

"Yes, Sir," the gunner agreed with a smile. "Guns like these were used when your Navy sacked Washington."

"And how long to they take to reload," Toby asked.

"I shouldn't worry about that, Sir, several minutes for a muzzle loader and they only have a range of a mile or so," the gunner said, patting the gun as if it was his own. "If we don't stop them on the first shot that's it. They turn up the wick and that's the last we see of them, particularly those side winders of yours. It needs a squadron of patrol boats like this to box them in."

"I guess I'd better have a word with the Chief Engineer then," Toby said as the lecture came to an end, and the gunner sauntered down the deck to show the ensigns where the powder locker could be found.

"I think the bosun would like you to check the rigging and sails with him before too long," the gunner called out over his shoulder as he disappeared out of view. "He's not that happy with his lot either!"

"So you're the new number one," an oiled stained boiler suited man said, emerging from the open crankcase and shaking Toby's hand with a very firm grip. "Pleased to meet you. Not many of you limeys around here, but you're most welcome. Now what do you want to know?"

"I suppose mainly that it's going to hold up for a six month tour. The Captain tells me that it's pretty beaten up?" Toby asked.

"Well, we're having trouble re-aligning the shaft with the flywheel, but once that's done it should hold out, but one can never be certain with old engines like this," the engineer explained patting the main steam valve. "It's had a rough life and at other times it would have been put on the scrap list. And it will never push the hull along faster than six knots so our chances of making a catch are somewhat slim."

"The gunner told me that also," Toby said, somewhat dismayed about the chances of some successful action.

"I'd go and talk to the bosun and sail maker," the engineer suggested disappearing into the depths of the sick engine. "They were part of the run crew when it was captured."

"So what do you think?" Evans asked Toby at the end of the day as they relaxed amongst the many boxes that needed to be sorted.

"I've often found that the happiest ships are those that pose the greatest challenge." Toby said. "Now I must write to my aunt, she's the only rock in my life at the moment."

Six weeks later, the one hundred foot and eighty-foot-long *USS Audacious*, formerly the *Pedro of Bristol*, slid out of the dock without ceremony, full to the brim with bunkers and ammunition. Short by twenty of her full complement of over a hundred men, the ship made for the Ambrose light vessel and clear water and a work up, a two-day, session before turning south. Their Mission was patrolling between Cape Hatteras and southern Florida between ten and fifty miles off the coast. To relieve the expected boredom the Captain, Commander Evans had managed to acquire a sorted array of brass instruments, and the purser had assured him that there was more than a handful of musicians. Their orders were quite simple. Stop and search everything that floated.

Such was the urgency to get *Audacious* on patrol joining the fleet the shakedown work up was compacted into two days from the usual week and the ship headed south under full sail. Training would be a daily event.

"Now here are our specific orders," Evans addressed the officers the following day, laying out the charts. "We will be working ten mile square boxes on these marked days so that base always knows where we are. In effect, we will be beating our way south off the coast and coming back with the gulf stream in an anti-clockwise direction. At fifty miles a day we should do two circuits within the six months before returning to Hampton roads."

"What about water and food and indeed bunkers?" the victualling officer asked.

"There are no available ports between here and the Bahamas," Toby reminded the assembled officers. "The Confederates hold them all."

"We're just about on our own then," the Senior engineer questioned.

"That's the usual nature of blockading, I'm afraid," Evans answered.

Audacious had been at sea for two months, stopping only a brief rendezvous with a store ship to take on food and water and very little action to show for the intensive daily training.

"It's almost as if they can predict where we are," Evans agreed going back through the log sheets and double checking the accepted trade routes.

"The inshore boats may be more successful ambushing them, Sir, but according to the report we got yesterday from the *Sceptre,* we still don't have enough ships to stop them," Toby suggested.

Evans nodded in agreement. "Any suggestions?"

"Not really but the men are getting restless, Sir," Toby said thinking of all the Missed opportunities. "Can I suggest we have gun drill this afternoon and a concert this evening. They love bangs and music."

In all the monotony of patrolling, the *Audacious* had scoured the coastline from Florida all the way back to Cape Hatteras, but had only apprehended two blockade runners heading into Charleston, and they were small sailing ships of no great significance and with only a few tons of guns and ammunition.

"Take off the cargo, Toby, and put a small run crew of ours on it under the command of the most competent ensign," the Captain had instructed. "We will keep the Master on here in chains and land the crew ashore in a boat unless any of them wish to sign up on board. We're short of good men."

"Yes, Sir," Toby replied. 'should only take the rest of the day. Do you want to instruct the ensign I've selected?"

"I guess so," agreed Evans, "send him in."

Time slipped by from days to weeks and on to months, without finding a paddle side wheeler in view let alone within firing range. Toby and the victualling officer went through the stores. They would soon need to store up again.

"We can only get at them," Evans said on the pop deck looking at the almanac. "If we get in close to the ports and stay there just out of range of the guns."

"What about our instructions, Sir?" Toby asked running his fingers down the hundred fathom contour.

"Let's just look again and see if we can re-interpret them," Evans said with a twinkle. "It wouldn't be the first time that that has happened, eh."

"We will need water soon, Sir," reported Toby, when the ship was heading south for the second time, some twenty miles off the southern port of Savannah and right on the direct trade route. "Not sure that it will last until we get back to Hampton Roads. We seem to have galloped through the water despite rationing."

Evans checked his orders. They were permitted to make for Nassau or Freeport in an emergency and in fact the Bahamas channel was a favourite choke spot for encountering blockade runners. They were spotting three or four vessels a day, most of them liners well off the land, and only the previous day had stopped yet another on its way to the West Indies.

But the monotonous hailing of a suspect and then launching of the boat to find that everything was in order was telling on the crew. Apart from the need for more water, the crew would have given a day's wage for the opportunity for a day ashore. Even band practice for the musical crew was waning.

"We won't be stopping longer than it takes to water up, take some more coal and stock up on fresh fruit," Evans announced to the crew just before they entered Freeport.

The crew groaned, but knew there be no change to the orders.

"But, we will, Toby," he said afterwards. "Take advantage to inspect these blockade runners that reports indicate are in some numbers preparing for runs up to Jacksonville and Savannah. The last message I had when we rendezvoused with the *USS Serenia* was that Lincoln was getting impatient at the number of blockade runners getting through."

"It's just a game of cat and mouse, and at the moment the mouse is winning," Evans said, wrapping up his orders and putting them to one side. "At least we can go ashore and have a beer."

"It's quite unbelievable the shipping activity," Toby observed as the two men weaved their way through the quayside three days later, and surveyed not less than six deep sea cargo ships, with side winders tied up outside them, exchanging military supplies for cotton.

"And there's nothing we can do about it until they hit the high seas," Evans said as they found an empty table and two chairs. "Our consul says that from here they can head for any of the small ports up the coast, but prefer Jacksonville, Savannah or Pensacola in the Gulf."

Audacious received fresh instructions before leaving the Bahamas. They were to track back north and lay in waiting off Charleston on information that a small convoy was to arrive on the night of the next new moon.

"How are your crews, gunner," asked Evans as the ship made slow passage doggedly up the Florida coast, at ten miles off and under easy sail.

"Ready as they will ever be, Sir, just raring to go now the ship's full of provisions," answered the gunner, hopeful that they might at last see some action.

"Don't forget you get one shot, and one shot only," Toby reminded him. "And it has to be either the paddle box or the rudder."

"Aye, aye, Sir," he replied. "Just get me within range and we'll do the rest."

"Up funnel, Chief," called out the captain to the senior engineer, "and give me five knots of speed. We are closing the port now."

"Stow all sails, Bosun," Toby whispered to the bosun, his leading seaman. "Where's the Master's mate? Stand him by with the lead line."

"Nothing ahead yet," came the call from the lookout half way up the rigging.

"All primed and ready with that gun," Toby checked with the veteran. "Aim for the paddle if you can see it."

"Yes, Sir, but we don't want to sink it, do we?" came the reply.

"No, we just want to disable it and use it ourselves," affirmed the First Lieutenant.

"Any sign yet lookout?" came a call from the right up in the bow of the ship.

The sky was inky black and where it met the horizon, there was the barest of lines. It was as if they were in the middle of a dark void, instead of five miles off the port.

"I see a light now," the lookout coughed out in excitement, trying to stifle the volume of his voice, "Port side about four points."

"How far?"

"Can't see, Sir."

"Steer ten degrees to starboard, helmsmen," the Captain of the *Audacious* whispered.

"Aye, aye, Sir," came the reply.

"Can't see it now," the lookout called out quietly.

"Damn," said the captain, "and bugger."

"It's getting light, I can see some horizon. You know how there is little twilight in these waters," observed Toby, closing up his telescope. "We might just get a shot yet."

"How far off is Charleston now, Navigator?" asked the Captain in frustration at the prospect of losing his quarry.

"Three miles. At this speed twenty minutes," came the reply.

"What's the range of the forts guns?" Evans asked.

"They have the new Whitworth guns, Sir, according to reports," whispered a reply. "At least a mile and a half."

"O.k. When do you reckon you'll get a clean shot, Toby? Don't think she's seen us," Evans pressed for confirmation.

"Five minutes, and we'll have to turn away. I can just see her outline coming in," Toby reminded the Captain.

The gunner tapped the barrel, looked at his crew. They had not fired a shot in anger for months. He poured in the powder, lit the linstock and stepped back.

"Fire and re-load, Gunner."

They watched the ball disappear into the darkness and then a flash of light.

"She's away, damn her," thundered Evans in disappointment. "She's escaping!"

"But we've winged her," shouted the gunner as Evans ordered the helmsman to follow the blaze of light on the paddle steamers deck.

"Mile and a half off the harbour entrance," reminded Toby, "suggest slewing off. We'll be within range of the forts gun."

"Hard a starboard then, and lay off damn ship, has obviously got away." Evans stormed and turned away in disgust.

"Don't think so," said Toby as the gunner rushed up for fresh orders. 'she grounded in the shallows and is laying over. Looks like the gunner hit the steering gear."

"Stand by to drop the hook," bellowed the captain.

For the next six hours, as the sun came up, they watched just out of range of Fort Sumpter's cannons whilst a posse of boats unloaded the cargo, and the crew of a tug repaired the damage, before towing it away into the shelter of the port. Evans finished his report and filed away the fair copy, congratulated his crew and set course back for Hampton Roads. The engineer had told him over breakfast that the boiler tubes had to be replaced and soon.

"We're turning round and going straight out," the Captain announced to Toby and the crew as soon as a gang of platers and boilermakers trundled up the gangway at the base, with armfuls of tubes and equipment. "The good news is that the Navy have more and more ships coming on line and after this tour we'll be having a proper refit and you'll all be on leave."

Six months later, the *Audacious* sailed back into the Portsmouth yard with two scalps, a pair of French side winders from the Loire River, that had been trading from St Nazaire to Nante with half an arsenal on board. A letter was waiting from his aunt Agnatha. Toby opened it eagerly. It was brief, but then he knew it would be.

Dear Toby,

I understand that you have had a successful tour. Hope you are in good spirits. Uncle's college is doing well and full with students and he hopes that you might lecture sometime. I am home from Cincinnati and have left a young English lady in charge for a while. Both the travel businesses are doing well if you know what I mean.

Your loving aunt, Agnatha

"How easy is it to get to that peninsular on the Potomac river that I've talked about?" Toby asked his Captain once they had relaxed after supper and were deep into a game of chess.

"Are you thinking about that girl again?" Evans asked kindly.

"Well, I was half thinking of it. It's a good eighteen months since I saw her." Toby replied, "rather too long I suppose."

"Has she written to you?"

"Well, she might have, but I haven't received it," Toby admitted.

"Well, we couldn't let you go in any case. The Staff Admiral wants to see you. The Navy have doubled the ships in the past year. I'm to take command of a monitor warship and they want you to take command here," Evans said extending an arm to shake his hand. "You always wanted a command and now you have it."

Toby looked slightly astounded at the news.

"You do want command, don't you?" Evans asked.

"Oh, yes I certainly do. It was just so unexpected," was all Toby could say.

Toby walked across the same yard, in the same state as he had done the previous year when he had first joined the *Audacious.* But it was even busier than he remembered. A floating dock dominated the scene with a monitor warship high and dry on the floor plates peculiarly perched as if it was about to dive into the sea, the two guns poking out of a round turret.

Ahead of it alongside the quay another monitor was having an angled protection structure removed having been damaged by a shell that had clearly ripped through the timber structure. Away to his left. Toby saw the French side winder, that they had captured some weeks under repair. Shipwrights had the iron framed sponson in pieces, exposing the paddle wheel and the cranked feathering mechanism.

He passed between the plate shop and the rigging loft feeling the warmth of the forges shaping half melted iron. Ahead the administration offices loomed, a building that had been hurriedly constructed three years earlier and hardly changed since. The sentry saluted him smartly and he walked in announcing himself to the clerk.

"Ah, Lieutenant," he said, "The Admiral has had to leave for a pressing engagement cancelling your appointment, but your arrangements are all here."

"My arrangements?" said Toby.

"Oh yes," the clerk said, "You're to attend a command course of one month in the Navy college at Annapolis.

"Annapolis," said Toby, his heart suddenly missing a beat. "That's close to Washington, isn't it, on the Chesapeake?"

"Yes," the clerk said, passing over his instructions. "But you won't get anywhere near the Capitol. It's all army controlled. You'll catch the train to Baltimore and change there for the steamboat. Here's your warrant. You are to travel on Friday and be billeted overnight at the navy base there on Fells Point."

"Thank you," Toby replied, snapping to attention.

"Any questions?"

"No."

"Then good day to you," the clerk concluded. "*Audacious* should be ready to sail on your return if the refit goes to plan. You ought to know that it's a compressed course. There will be little time off."

"My, you have changed, Toby," his aunt said, six weeks later as Toby hammered on the door looking forward to an entertaining evening with his aunt.

Toby had taken to short ferry trip across the Hudson river for an evening with his relatives and a freshly made up bed for the night. He didn't expect that his quarters at Annapolis would be any more comfortable than those in Boston.

"And you've filled out a touch and brown from all that Southern Sea air," Agnatha continued hardly stopping for breath. "Come and meet your Uncle that you haven't seen for how many years is it, fifteen at the least. And you on your way to a top course at Annapolis. Are you getting promoted?"

Toby nodded in agreement.

"And that girl marooned looking after her parents estate. Are you going to see her? Agnatha queried looking for her nephew's reaction.

"One question at a time, Aunt," Toby said, finishing her hug with a kiss.

"Of course, of course, so stupid of me. Uncle is lecturing up to a dozen students now and we've had to rent the next house. I'll see if he's free."

"I've got all day," Toby confirmed. "But have to get to Baltimore by tomorrow evening."

"So you'll stay the night then," Agnatha said, giving instructions to her maid to check the spare bedroom.

"All evening for Uncle to tell me about his last voyage and how he came to start up the college," Toby said, settling down into the most comfortable settee, "and for you to tell me just what you have been getting up too?"

"I thought you would want to quiz me on that," she said. "At the moment. I've left my business in charge of a very capable lady from England. She has been out there with her brother."

"I would have thought that Uncle would have wanted you back here permanently," Toby asked as they walked through to his small lecture room, where they found him discussing the finer details and merits of the cylinder micrometre sextant with four students.

"If you had the time, I'd like you to spend some time here backing me up here," Reginald Turner said over dinner that evening laying out the basics of the curriculum on the table. "They're pretty sharp, these lads, at all the latest aids of course, but I have to bring in help with practical boat work and sailing."

Toby looked at the rigged models on the shelf. He thought that he could easily slot into lecturing.

"There is so much opportunity here in New York let alone anyway else."

Toby's uncle continued. "Mind you, what will happen when Jefferson Davis finally gives in is anyone's guess."

"Well, the Navy will certainly be cut down to its gills," Toby suggested. "They may be dragging out boats from every creek, but most wouldn't pass muster to sail beyond the Narrows. Last week they towed a flotilla up to Albany to go through the Erie Canal to the Lakes and down the Ohio canal to Cincinnati and the Mississippi rather than take the sea route. I somehow doubt my commission will extend beyond my next tour."

"Go on," his aunt said, encouraging him to expand on the day to day problems of the Navy.

"I can tell you that there is nothing more boring than days and weeks of box patrolling, and endless drilling without ammunition." Toby explained, outlining the daily routine.

"So, you regret signing up then," Reginald Turner asked, having listened to the details of blockade management.

"No, not really," Toby continued. "Basically, it was a good move and I think there are some advantages to be gained. In our Navy back home as you know, they have little regard for commercial seafarers, but here they have a more relaxed view.

"With the world opening up faster than ever before, there are so many opportunities. We still know so little about the poles, not that I want to go there, and even Australia is not fully explored. I suppose I came here out of some sense of duty and I haven't regretted it yet."

"You'll go back into the Mercantile Marine then," asked Agnatha gathering up the plates and calling for assistance from the kitchen.

"I think so, Aunt, or maybe pilotage. It's anyone's guess at the moment," Toby suggested, "What about your plans?"

"I'll be back tying up some loose ends soon," she said giving her husband a well-deserved kiss on the forehead. "After I've raised some more funds here. Uncle complains that he's retired and still doesn't see enough of me."

"Are you for Baltimore?" the ticket collector called out as Toby struggled onto the ferry for New Jersey, trailing a kitbag of clothes ready to take the train south.

"Yes, certainly am," Toby confirmed taking the combined ticket from his pocket and handing it to be punched.

"You should be just in time then, Sir," the ferryman said. "Turn right at the landing stage and it's just a stroll."

Toby looked around the decks of the ferry that would get him across the Hudson in ten minutes. One of his colleagues was about to take command of a similar requisitioned ferry, which was in the same yard as *Audacious,* and being converted for military use. He walked around the decks looking intently at its construction, wondering how it would survive a couple of shells, or one of the newly developed torpedoes which the Confederates were supposed to be using.

Twenty minutes later, he boarded a train full of sailors and soldiers heading for what was the front, not much more than two hundred miles away. Fortress Washington and Annapolis might be ringed with water and steel, but on land the two opposing forces skirmished regularly on a weekly basis, often followed by a monthly all-out battle, when the result often caused a surprise victory or was in some cases inconclusive.

At the head of the Chesapeake, Baltimore was a transit city thronged with military and civilian activity; and Toby noticed as he alighted that the train continued west to Cincinnati. That's how aunt got there then.

Fells Point to Annapolis, Toby was informed, was not much more than a morning's journey on the crowded steam ferry and no sooner had the ship left, then the bay opened up, inlets and creeks on either side, the Atlantic many miles away. Full of keen naval officers and cadets exchanging experiences, smoking and downing drinks at the bar, it was just one of many boats on the water, taking goods and personnel in both directions.

Toby waited for the inevitable limey comment, concentrating on the beauty of the river, which stretched out in all directions. Stands of deciduous trees just coming into life in the warmth of the spring morning, marched in columns to the water's edge, and the occasional fisherman waited for a catch. A more peaceful scene he couldn't imagine.

He cast his mind back to the *Perthshire,* it was nearly two years ago and he was now close to his first command. They passed a monitor battleship at anchor, clad in sloping wooden sides, looking like a grotesque tortoise, and armed with a single menacing gun. Then another came in view, squat and ungainly, as if it were barely afloat. A compact version of a clipper, but higher in the water painted with black and white stripes came in view, two decks of ugly guns stabbing out from the bulwarks, and the crew aloft in the rigging setting sails.

Widening out into a vast inland sea, the ferry passed the elongated Kent Island on the port side, and then in a big sweep to starboard rounded the wooded promontory of Sandy Point, and headed for the Maryland State House the highest and most recognisable building. Below the domed building, the low structure of the college sprawled out across extensive grounds which was to be his home for the next month. Here and in the adjacent Seven river, he would be drilled and lectured in the management of a lower ranked warship.

"How was your course then, Toby," asked his former Captain on returning to the yard, where the *Audacious* was nearing completion. "Don't expect that you managed a visit to your girlfriend. As the crow flies she would only have been about fifty miles away, but in reality it could have been five hundred."

"Not a chance, too busy on the course, not a day off let alone a weekend. Emily's just a past memory now unfortunately," Toby answered not quite truthfully. "I just cut my cloth accordingly, and wholeheartedly joined in with the rest and the social life."

"Good for you. Did you get yourself a girlfriend then?" the outgoing Captain asked. "The town is full of girls, I'm told."

"Not quite, but had a good time for sure," Toby confirmed.

"That's the style. I'll hand over in the morning," his colleague replied, slapping him on the back. "Ready for that beer?"

Chapter 16

Isabel Nugent brushed a stray hair aside and turned the page of her diary. She was sitting at her husband's desk, the design where two people could sit opposite each and work. It was usually strewn with documents and medical periodicals, but now was covered with empty boxes on either side of her.

She had finally managed to clear off fifty years' worth of his work over a career, which had established him as one of the most respected doctors in Boston. In that time they had moved houses four times from a boarding house in the swamp area and the most deprived part of the city to Boston Common, where they had lived for the past twenty years in complete harmony with their fellow Bostonians and as one of the pillars of society.

Looking across the harbour it was just possible to see the masts of naval ships of all sizes, tied up to the or anchored in the vast harbour where the three rivers came together. Crews jostled in the bars waiting for orders to take their ships out on patrol down to New York and beyond to Florida, looking for Confederate warships and blockade runners.

But it not this activity that interested Isabel. In her experience, and it was a lifetime away, a memory that had almost faded completely apart from the mark on a left shoulder, ships were places of misery, hardship and death. Isabel had suffered a frightening journey as a slave from Africa, but by the slimmest of good fortunes had been rescued from a lifetime of mistreatment to be bought and loved by a man she had adored through five decades. Even her closest friends had not realised her background, although some wondered how this dignified elegant lady of colour and position had blended in so well.

But for Isabel, who long harboured a desire to redress the wrongs of her country it was her time to repay society for her good fortune where possible, and today she was going to a gathering in the Old South Meeting House.

"Welcome, Mrs Nugent," the chairman of the small group said brightly, ushering her in to the smallest of the rooms.

"Please call me Isabel," she said, taking one of the hard seats.

"Of course, and thank you for coming," he continued. "You're early, but never mind. The rest are coming shortly. Now may I introduce my wife."

Before long, five other couples had quietly let themselves into the building and the door was locked from the inside. Not that they didn't want the public to know of the meeting, because it was a subject that was reverberating throughout the city, but it was best interest that the finer details were kept to just a few.

"Now perhaps we might like to let our fellow guests have some idea how we came to this meeting," the chairman announced, when they had all made themselves comfortable.

One by one they stood up and introduced themselves as puritans, abolitionists, evangelists, Missionaries on leave from Africa, doctors and nurses all interested in helping slaves escaping to the north and safety.

"And you, Isabel," the chairman asked, sensing that she would be the most reticent in the group. "Can you tell us something of your history."

"Well," Isabel said, standing up and holding the chair so tightly that the veins in the back of her hand showed through.

"Take your time," one of the ladies sitting next to her counselled.

"I'm not certain how I can contribute," she said searching for her words. "I'm not sure how I can help. You might have to tell me?"

"But did you not realise Isabel, that for some years your husband was financially helping escaped slaves flee from the South," the leader said softly.

"I suppose I was," she replied thinking back over the years. "But he never discussed it outright with me for fear, I think, of bringing back memories of his arrival here, and mine as well. It was as if he was ashamed of his early life. We did go to Ontario for a holiday, when the railway was opened and he met a group there whilst I looked over the Niagara Falls"

"And now you would like to continue with his good work then?" one of the ladies asked.

"Very definitely," Isabel answered, twiddling her fingers around her scarf. "However, I can."

"I'm sure that we can find you a rewarding role," the deputy chairman who had up to then had said very little. "But it would probably involve a journey if you feel up to it."

"I was thinking of possibly set up a trust for a small hospital," Isabel answered. "It was I'm sure at the back of his mind. I am still trying to sort out his financial affairs. And at the moment, this looks possible according to my solicitor, who was also his best friend."

"I'm sure we can help you in the fullness of time, but for now the immediate need is to help the flood of slaves seeking assistance into Canada and the Northern provinces," the chairman reminded her and the other visitors.

"You're older than most of us," the deputy said kindly, interrupting the chairman, who was about to speak again. "But we would like to know what is really driving you, Isabel, when you could be just enjoying your autumn years?"

Isabel, hesitated, picking her words carefully.

"I've never ever told anybody how it happened," Isabel said in a faltering voice. "In fact I can hardly remember it. Because I was a slave once, a very long time ago, but I was never actually enslaved and my husband, saved my life!"

The room looked aghast as Isabel sat down heavily on the chair.

The chairman turned to his wife. "I think Mrs Nugent could well do with another cup of tea," he said looking at the astonished gathering around him.

"Molly," Isabel said, on getting help back to her house with one of the couples, who then said they would be touch shortly. "Have you ever been out of Boston?"

"Not really, Mam, I was brought up in Boston as you know. My father was a carpenter and given his freedom to come north and build a mansion on Rhode Island."

"What do you know of Canada then?" Isabel asked.

"Nothing, Mam. Never been beyond Suffolk County," Molly answered, rather flustered at the tone of the conversation. "Is it cold there?"

"I'm told that it can be quite cold at times," Isabel replied. "But then it is here in the winter."

"Are you going away then?" she continued gathering herself together, but still worrying about the way the conversation was going.

"Yes," Isabel answered in the voice that Molly recognised as not to be argued with. "And you are coming as well. That is if you want to. We are going together and you as my companion and no longer my maid."

"What about the house?" Molly answered, "Who will look after it?"

"I'm going to rent out the dispensary to one of the doctors, and an agency will do the rest of the looking after," Isabel stated, immediately relaxing Molly, who was starting to become agitated at the thought of her home being used by somebody else.

"How long will we be away do you think?" Molly asked mentally thinking about the luggage they would need to take.

"Six weeks I think, maybe longer. But it's late summer, so we won't be too cold," Isabel confirmed.

"But, Mam. If it's not a holiday and you haven't said that it is, why are we going?" the maid persisted.

"We are going to help a slave ship," Isabel replied.

"But I thought that there were no more slave ships," Molly cried in disbelief remembering the parchment sheet she had been shown.

"Neither did I until this afternoon," Isabel confirmed, taking the faded parchment document from her desk and showing again to her maid. It had laid in her desk a full six months since she had first shown it to Molly.

"But this is different," Isabel continued. "We are going to be rescuing slaves that have fled north after escaping from all the fighting, or those that have just been abandoned by their owners."

"Oh, my god," Molly cried and fled the room in tears.

"Here are your contact details, Isabel, and the people that you will be staying with at St Catharine's," the Chairman of the Boston rescue committee said, a week later on the forecourt of Boston's station to the west. "And the money that we have collected for your journey."

"But I don't need any money," she said handing it back. "I am funding myself and you must put it back into the account. I've waited all these years to pay something back to society, all those years when our Good Fathers only played with being a Free Country."

"We'll mail it to them for their funds then. They are good people, very good people. I've not met them, but they are the final link, and they need money to charter other ships as well as yours."

"Where do they go from St Catharine's?" asked Isabel, still only vaguely aware of the big picture.

"All over Canada in the main," he confirmed.

"And how do they get to St Catharine's in the first place?" she asked.

"Usually by boat from the small ports on Lake Erie," the chairman confirmed, "they arrive there by the so-called underground railway route."

"An underground railway?" Isabel asked.

"It's not really a railway," he explained. "They are helped by many helpful people, taken by road from one safe house to another, often by boats up rivers and canals, sometimes by the railways, although not often. It has been going on for years, since your arrival from Africa actually, but the pace has accelerated in the past year or two."

"Don't they get tracked down and taken back?" Isabel replied, mentally taking in her kinsfolk being beaten, dragged and drugged by thugs with little interference by the authorities.

"Every big town and city in America have such gangs," he continued, "but fortunately there is an equal number of concerned people from all walks of life determined to help them make a new life. As for the slaves many have skills learnt on the plantations, that will earn them money, wherever they settle."

"You mean carpenters, metalworkers, engineers, bricklayers," Molly interrupted, "Just like my father."

Molly was keen not to be left outside the conversation.

"Oh yes," came an immediate reply. "It's not unknown for some to be nurses and even doctors."

"And how will I be able to help, my mistress, Isabel." Molly continued not yet used to her new role.

"I'm sure that you will be so occupied, Molly," the leader of the group continued. "Before many weeks you will be part of the community as if you were a local."

"And my role?" Isabel asked. "Surely I'm too old for any real role apart from some financial help."

"We think not, Mam," he said. "You are living proof that once these poor people have made the short voyage across the lake they will survive to make something of the rest of their lives. Canada is a country of opportunity just as much as America is."

"And you're sure that our contribution will make a real difference?" Isabel pressed, still somewhat concerned.

"Absolutely," he answered. "Although Ohio is considered a safe state once out of Cincinnati, there are many slave hunters in Buffalo ready to catch the unwary and collect the bounty money."

"It's not advisable for those escaping to go directly to Buffalo," he continued sensing Isabel's reticence.

"I see," answered Isabel.

"Your passage across the Falls is but a short journey, and you will be met on the other side." The chairman continued, handing Isabel an itinerary. "I wired our contacts earlier and they have made all the arrangements, including your accommodation. There is a great deal of building going on in the town in anticipation of next year's influx."

"And the boat I am chartering, or rather the boat that my husband would have been organising had he lived?" Isabel asked. "I am very keen to see it."

"It's in dock by the side of the canal," he confirmed. "It will be frozen in during the winter, but will be ready as soon as the ice thaws."

"So we have about three months to make it ready," she asked, looking up at the clock marking down the time for the trains departure.

"Yes," he said with a smile, chivvying her along as passengers started to gather in numbers on her platform. "I'm told that your ship will be one of three setting off as soon as the weather allows."

Molly fidgeted with her coat, hopping from one foot to the other, and gazing up at the station clock every minute ticking away to departure time, while Isabel ticked off the last of her questions She couldn't remember ever going beyond the parks and the shops and a pleasure boat in the harbour, and here she was on the very first adventure of her life.

Molly stamped her feet on the ground to keep out the cold, wondering just how warm the train would be. She was not yet twenty five years of age, had never enjoyed a man's caress, and could only ever remember working for Isabel and here she was going abroad. Molly looked at her mistress, saying goodbye to the ladies grouped around her, and gazed affectionately at the lady, who was everything to her. Wrapped up for the journey ahead, she had never seen Isabel more animated in all her life.

"Good bye, my dears," the leader said with a kiss for Isabel and a hug for Molly, before disappearing into the crowd with the good ladies of Boston.

A porter wheeled away their luggage and they walked slowly up the platform, Molly hanging on to Isabel half in anticipation and half in fear of the future as they headed towards their allotted coach.

"All aboard for Buffalo," a man called out waving a flag, and within minutes they were away; heading for the towns of Worcester, Albany, Syracuse and finally, Lake Erie.

Chapter 17

It was only after her Presbyterian Missionary friends had suggested that by visiting the South and travelling the Mississippi northwards would she experience the real hardship of slavery for herself, that Alice relented.

"It might be a very good way of really bonding with your brother," the couple suggested to Alice as the three of them strolled around Castle Clinton park whilst Nicholas was in the offices of the Atlas Company on 25 State Street. "And of course it will be much safer for you."

"But I really came to find for myself," Alice protested slightly, "and how this great country sees itself in the eyes of the world. From what I hear it's not how it likes to project itself."

"You have to understand that it's a young country, barely two hundred years old populated by the old world," the lady explained as they came to the castle walls. "You know Europeans don't always have the same ideals."

"All I know," Alice interjected, "is that the indigenous Indians have been decimated and the imported Africans are not treated like humans. That's not freedom as I see it."

"That's not totally true, Alice," the man countered, trying to ignore the subject of the native Indians. "Although you have a very good point. Look at New York, the blacks are nearly all free here. But I agree, it has to change. We have to make it change, along with people like you. Go and join your brother and come back in a year's time when Lincoln will have won the country over."

"I was also hoping to meet up with my American friend after our evening with the mill workers in Lancashire," Alice reminded her friends. "But she had to leave her job in Boston and go back to her home."

"Where's her home?" They asked, almost in unison.

"Well below Washington, in Virginia," Alice said, "Just here," pulling out her address book and a small plan.

"You'll never get there, Alice," the man said checking on the area. "It's under martial law. Best to go with your brother and come back when things are more settled."

It wasn't Alice's first choice to take another passenger voyage, when she had only been in America no time at all, but she conceded that it was a reasonable option to accompany her brother, in the family quest to keep the cotton flowing, and it would be in the sun.

"I'll come with you to New Orleans," she heard herself say to Nicholas. "But I really don't want to see plantation after plantation of slaves in pitiful conditions."

"Let's just take it as it comes," answered Nicholas, producing two tickets in first class. "We're booked for tomorrow."

"There'll be a bridge over the sea, just here in a hundred years' time," Alice suggested to her brother, as they stood underneath the wheelhouse of the Atlas steamer *Athos*.

The New York skyline was fast disappearing and the ship was approaching the Narrows heading for the open sea.

"If Telford and Stephenson can build those great bridges across the Menai Straits," Alice declared, "then the Americans can do the same here."

"I didn't know that you had been there, Alice?" Nicholas questioned.

"Oh yes," she answered, looking down at the wake bubbling away in the distance with just the merest of water disturbance. "We stayed at Bangor for the weekend. The bridges are so graceful particularly the suspension one."

Nicholas nodded in partial agreement. No longer was his sister just a nuisance around the place, she was positively blooming since leaving Liverpool.

"Let's go in, it's getting cold?" he said, pulling at her scarf in brotherly love.

"No, I want to stay a while," she answered as the *Athos* gathered speed. "There's something about bridges. They're always so majestic, so graceful and meant to join people together, not pull them apart."

"I'm afraid that it's almost impossible to get cotton out of the Mississippi," their host said over dinner, "as for getting guns in that's equally difficult."

Nicholas wiped his brow with a large coloured handkerchief and stepped back into the shade of the veranda and made for the large glass of lime juice, which had been left for him. They were more than one hundred miles from the sea and the Mississippi was still a mile wide at the point, where the gardens of the estate dipped gradually to the water's edge. He and Alice May were guests of the Chairman of the Importing and Exporting Company of Louisiana, agents for a number of French blockade runners and also for the Atlas Company of New York, the company that had been incorporated by their mother's brother.

Trading between the West Indies and the Gulf of Mexico American ports, they owned several ships and carried mainly fruit northwards and machinery southwards. The *Athos* was fitted with limited passenger accommodation for those wanting to escape the winter, exchanging the cold northern states for the sun of Florida and beyond.

They were not the only guests on the estate for the weekend. Away on the shaded firing range at the rear of the house, a French arms dealer was demonstrating the latest weaponry from the armouries of Nante, to the Confederate Colonel in charge of the district, watched by a gathering of plantation owners.

A hundred miles upriver of New Orleans, they were at Baton Rouge and due to the blockade, and the capture of the city by the Union Navy, their journey had involved three ships. The *S.S. Athos* had stopped at the Bahamas on the way, where Nicholas had taken the opportunity to write to his brother in Bermuda and his father back home with the latest situation in the Gulf.

The Bahamas, he said in his letter, was full of steamers trying to ship arms into the Southern ports of Mobile and Pensacola, and export cotton out of course, but not without great difficulty.

The Atlas liner, itself, was denied docking in New Orleans on account of its cargo of milling machinery, which the Union blockade considered was likely to be destined for a cotton plantation.

The Captain deviated to Cuba and turned round at Jamaica leaving the machinery on the quayside. Nicholas and Alice had transferred to a local steamer to complete their journey to the be-leagued New Orleans city and then transferred to a stern wheeler up the Mississippi river to Baton Rouge.

It was only two months earlier, when they had left together on a direct passage from Liverpool to New York, that George had reluctantly agreed to let Alice make the passage. It was much too late for Alice to sail with her new American friend, Emily, to her disgust; but at least Nicholas was agreeable company.

The spasmodic shots from the firing range ceased and shortly afterwards the guests filtered back into the house.

"What are the alternatives?" the Frenchman asked, complimenting his host on the choice of wine and pressing for the latest route of getting his guns into the interior.

"There are two railheads on the Alabama coast to the east, still controlled by Jefferson Davis," the chairman confirmed showing the two the latest survey. "But they are frequently sabotaged and the locomotives and stock are under constant repair."

"What's the feasibility a running from the Bahamas. We saw a considerable number of ships in the port?" Nicholas asked as he and the Frenchman marked off the ports that could be available. "My brother is organising ships to the Eastern seaboard."

"There are a number of vessels running the gauntlet and they tend to be vessels of two thousand tons and they get protection from the Confederate warships in and out," the exporter explained, "But it is a risky business."

"And what happens if they get stopped," Nicholas asked.

"The cargo and the ship is confiscated. If the ship is useful it is taken by the Union Navy," the host explained. "The crew are taken off and imprisoned; and any foreign crew, and there are many, are either imprisoned or sent to New York and despatched to their home country."

"And the chances," the Frenchman asked before Nicholas could get his question in, "of getting through?"

"Less than fifty percent now. And the odds are getting worse," the American explained.

The Frenchman shrugged, Nicholas thought of what he would write in his next letter home, whenever that would be.

"So you have an ongoing operation in Bermuda I understand, managed by your brother?" the American confirmed.

Nicholas nodded. "I'm not sure how it is going. Of course we are only dealing in small quantities. A few hundred tons at a time, when we are used to shipping thousands of tons a month."

"Can't you wire him when he gets to Wilmington?" the estate manager suggested.

"I've tried that several times," Nicholas answered. "Left a message for him in New Orleans, but it never got through. Least I never heard back."

"The lines are often cut and if not are frequently tapped," the local man replied. "What are your plans now, Nicholas?"

"Whilst I am here, I must at least find some more agents to appoint," Nicholas said. "I can't go home completely empty handed with nothing to show for it."

"And you?" the estate manager asked the Frenchman.

"I shall go back down to New Orleans and fulfil the order that you have made," he answered, pocketing the contract. "We have a shipment ready in Martinique, that was just waiting for a purchaser."

"It'll have to be Mobile then, or even Houston," the Confederate Colonel suggested.

"And what would you like to ship out. Anything in particular?" the chairman asked the Frenchman, "tobacco, cotton, fine timber?"

"Whatever pays the most. Just like you Americans," the Frenchman answered with a wry smile. "Dollars, Sir, just dollars!"

"And you, Nicholas What are you going to do?" the Southerner probed for the second time.

"I'll talk to my sister, I guess that we will press on provided we don't have too much of a problem with the Union Government," Nicholas replied. "I understand that it is the Army and not the Navy that control the rivers."

"I'd carry on up the Mississippi, then turn up into the Tennessee river, and find your way back down to Mobile by rail. A man like you could have a fine time before returning home," chairman chuckled. "Let's go and join the ladies."

"We'll leave the Frenchman and the Colonel to you in morning," Nicholas announced as supper came to a close and they were all relaxing on the lawns watching a patrol vessel make its way downstream. "We're going to take your advice and make for Vicksburg, is it."

"I shouldn't rush it," the host said, "there are several stops on the way and the stern wheelers are searched at regular intervals for contraband. Lincoln is really trying to maintain tight control on the rivers. It'll take a good three days."

"We're in no real hurry and I am going to take the opportunity of establishing some more agents," Nicholas underlined, as his host passed over a serviette with a rough outline of the river upstream.

"I can certainly put you in touch at several big plantations," the chairman offered, marking the spread out cloth. "The wire communications should still be operating at least as far as Vicksburg unless the Union saboteurs have been busy At the moment, the Union warships don't get much beyond Cincinnati and General Lee has tight control at Vicksburg itself. Say, when is this transatlantic cable going to be laid? It can't come soon enough for us?"

"Another ten years, they reckon," Nicholas answered. "Before it's reliable.

"You've not said a great deal Alice?" said the chairman's wife, speaking for the first time since the meal was finished. "What are your expectations, if not your plans?"

"Well," she answered, planting her elbows on the table and taking her time before she spoke. "First of all I would like to thank you for your hospitality. I am still soaking in my knowledge of this country and I fear that I have a long way to go before I fully understand it, and maybe I never will. It's so vast, so diverse, so complicated, but listening to you all, I think I will leave my brother to his commercial dealings, here in the south and carry on to Canada."

"By yourself." the host questioned. "It's a tough country."

"But I won't be the first," Alice retorted, "And I doubt that I will be the last."

"And when you get to Canada, what then?" the hosts wife asked.

"I shall make my way to New York and hopefully meet up with Nicholas there, or even my other brother James," she answered, defiantly.

"And what do you say about that, Nicholas?" asked the lady host, looking across the table at his reaction.

"Well, it wasn't quite what I expected to hear," he said, looking at Alice with admiration. "But then she never stops surprising me these days. She has her own money, and when you think that her other brother set off around the world at seventeen, what can I say."

Alice smiled realising that with no effort at all she had won round her brother.

"Mind you," Nicholas said after a pause. "I might have some words to say to her later!"

"We were wondering," the woman said turning to her husband, who was engrossed with the Frenchman and the Confederate Colonel on the likelihood of the war going on four years. "We were wondering if you might like to call in on some business associates of ours in Natchez?"

"By all means," answered Nicholas. "Are they cotton growers?"

"Not really. They import machinery and repair stern wheelers. They'd be interested in hearing about the latest mill machinery in England I'm sure." she answered. "I'll check with my husband, when he's finished talking."

"What's that, my dear?" the host said, breaking off the conversation with the two men on hearing his name.

"Oh yes, I'm sure the Allington's would be pleased to meet them." he said. "Old English name, came out here a good hundred years ago. I'll see if we can get a message to them."

They were walking down the jetty about to negotiate the broad gangway onto the next ship towering above the wooden jetty. The stern wheeler was ready to depart. Behind them a retainer followed with the luggage.

Are you really intending to go all the way north on the Mississippi by yourself Alice?" Nicholas said as they parted company with the American family, promising to maintain contact and extend the business opportunities.

"Why not," Alice answered. "I've no intention of Missing the opportunity as I've told you before. It's the most comfortable way if this ship is anything to go by."

"They'll get smaller and less comfortable I'm sure as the river gets narrower," Nicholas told her.

Alice gave him a pout. "That doesn't bother me. And I understand that these stern wheelers are the same size all the way into Ohio."

They were exploring the decks of the two funnelled stern wheeler *Cairo,* as the last of the local cargo was carried aboard, and the gangway was removed. Three decks high, with a central lounge overlooked by a gallery, from which the rabbit hutched cabins were situated on either side with outside windows.

Big enough only for a single bed and a chair, the *Cairo* had one hundred cabin passengers, and an unlimited number of day passengers. Every ten miles or so the ship would cruise up to a jetty either on the Louisiana or the Alabama side to the same volume of noise and hullabaloo at each stop whilst making its slow passage upriver.

Alice hugged her brother as the whistles blew, the bells clanged and the engine awoke with a cloud of smoke driving the paddle wheel at the stern in a flurry of foam. To Alice it was reminiscent of a liner leaving Liverpool, as a passage of a thousand miles on the Mississippi could easily be considered an adventure.

"How far were you intending to go before you turn east into the real plantation country, where they have thousands of acres and hundreds of slaves?" she asked as they leaned over the rail admiring not only the view, but the number of different types of craft either fishing or just plying the waters.

"I was thinking of Vicksburg and striking off there to Jackson on the railway," Nicholas said. "I am told that the growers there are in despair of selling their crops and if we could rail bales to Mobile it's not too difficult at the moment to get ships in."

Alice reminded him of the conversation the previous evening, "I don't think that will happen whist this war is on, Nicholas. You've got to be realistic."

"I suppose so," he said in complete resignation.

"I was hoping that you would go as far as Memphis?" Alice said trying to gauge her moment.

"Why? Are you changing mind?" Nicholas said, turning round and facing his sister. "Having second thoughts now that you dashed my plans?"

"Not at all," she answered, "but our hosts told me that the most dangerous part for ladies on the Mississippi is the stretch from here to Memphis."

"I'll tell you what I'll do then," Nicholas said after consulting his map of the river. "I'll go as far as Osceola, just up from Memphis, where I am told there are some big plantations growing best quality cotton, and then ship out east from there."

"That would be a much better idea. Look at that steamer. It just Missed us," she said, startled at the closeness of another vessel heading straight for them. "How come when the river is so wide?"

"It is rather, but looking at the buoys it's obviously quite narrow here." Nicholas answered, watching it pass at no more than a hundred feet. "And sometimes they don't make it."

"Hopefully not with us on board," she commented, as the ship moved back into the deep-water channel.

"Have you seen this, Alice?" Nicholas called out to Alice looking at an information board in the foyer as they were nearing the jetty at Natchez.

"This place is named after a tribe of Indians and not only that but the Spanish and the French have been here in the past."

"Well, by the look of what I have seen in the past week, America is large enough to accommodate everybody, without fighting over it," she answered briskly.

"Doesn't quite work like that," Nicholas answered softly.

"I know," she said, "that's the worst of us humans."

"I think I can see the Allington's," Nicholas stated, acknowledging the waves from a couple of the quayside as the *Cairo* approached the jetty. "Let's just enjoy the American welcomes and forget about the morality of it. After all it could be said that it's nothing to do with us."

"I suppose so," Alice accepted, "But the smaller the world gets, the bigger the problems that appear."

"So you are in cotton, James?" Mr Allington asked after a short ride to the lower slopes of the town, from which their house had a commanding vista over the river with its own jetty.

"Well, yes, and a bit of interest in shipping. My brother is running a side wheeler into Wilmington from Bermuda; but we've been told that if we want to run the blockade throughout the year, it's better to use the Bahamas as a transit port.

"Well, we could do with a few in this part of the world, but I'm sure you've been told that New Orleans is the end of the line; and we fear that soon Lincoln will close the trap all the way. We're fine here at the moment with the Confederates overlooking the river from the hill forts, but it won't be long before the Union capture the stronghold at Vicksburg, the next town upstream."

"And can you rail out there?" Nicholas asked.

"No, we would have to take our exports a hundred miles up where the railhead is," Mr Allington answered. "And then the line to Mobile is so unreliable, it turns a simple operation into an impossible Mission."

"Lincoln's got a stranglehold then," agreed Nicholas.

"Slowly but surely," agreed Allington.

"What brought you here then, Mr Allington?" asked Alice, intrigued at the serenity of the surroundings that seemed far away from any conflict.

"Well, my grandfather came out to install some sugar refining machinery and never went back," Allington replied. "It went from there. We have a small plantation here and my works in the port. I import and repair machinery and maintain some of the river steamers. Not just the big packet boats like the one you came in on, but all the smaller sizes of craft as well."

"And your workers?" she asked, "where do they come from?"

"All over," Allington replied. "A mixture of races; a few of French origin some black, but all with some skills and many are quite intelligent and all of them earn a wage."

"How does that work?" Alice asked.

"Well, some slaves buy their freedom on account of their scarcity value, and others are given it when they get too old for manual work," the host explained. "Usually slave tradesmen, that are freed, have to leave the county and find work outside the area. On our plantation I have freed two men not strong enough to work, but they have stayed around and just do odd jobs."

"It's all very complicated," Alice agreed.

"Everything in America is at the moment, my dear," Mrs Allington said in an effort to bring the subject to a close, and turned to Nicholas engrossed with her husband on the subject of sugar.

"You hadn't thought of importing sugar then, Nicholas," he continued, "There's as much sugar as cotton in these parts, and we are hoping that sugar and molasses will not attract as much attention as cotton."

"Not really, Glasgow and London are where our refineries are," Nicholas pointed out. "It's a bit outside our operation."

"Now that's enough of business," interrupted the host rather taken by the direct questions of Alice, who was looking at some early photographs of the family.

"Do you have children?" she asked the hostess.

"Unfortunately not, Alice," the lady of the house replied. "But we haven't given up trying."

"Let me show you around," the host suggested, attempting to change the subject. "Our workers on the estate may not have the best of lives here, but they are warm, relatively healthy and probably have a better standard of housing than those in your slums."

Nicholas and Alice looked at each other, as they came across the huts and sheds, and found the workers squatting on the ground or lounging in home-made chairs cooking on an open fire.

"One thing we were going to ask you about if you make a stop at Vicksburg?" Allington asked. "We have distant relatives there; the mother has recently died and the husband is desperate to get his young teenage daughter to safety in Canada."

"To Canada," said Alice, "Where? I know little of Canada and Nicholas is leaving at Memphis and staying here in the south for a while."

"I'm sure that you can help him, my dear," replied Mrs Allington. "You look very capable to us and it will give you something to focus on, when your brother has gone."

"Now why not stay another day and catch the next steamer?" Allington suggested, "I'd like to show you our factory tomorrow and some of the area."

"What do you think of taking this girl with me?" Alice asked her brother as soon as they boarded the *Queen,* a sister ship, and the vessel was stirring up the muddy waters, heading for one of the most difficult sections of the river.

"I don't see why not," her brother replied. "I shall be with you both for the four day trip to Memphis, and she will give you some company."

"If she is anything like the young ladies that we've come across recently, she could be quite a handful," Alice suggested.

"Well, it will keep you on your toes then," Nicholas laughed. "Do you know, apart from the cities, how small these towns are which we are passing. More like small communities. It's just another example of how vast this country is."

Apart from an inspection visit from a Union warship, which came alongside and then struggled to maintain contact, such was the inadequacy of the engines, the passage upstream was uneventful. The skipper of the patrol vessel, not much more than a teenager, had lined up the passengers and inspected the steamer's papers on the pretext of looking for escaped slaves.

Alongside at the small port of St Joseph for the night, brother and sister walked ashore as the sun folded behind the tree line, listening to the crickets and their mating call, and the faint strains the of a banjo being strummed in the distance.

"How have they managed to cultivate this enormous acreage of land?" Alice asked her brother as they sipped a cold lime juice in the cafe shack at the end of the jetty.

"I heard that, madam," the jovial lady in a brightly coloured print dress on the other side of the counter thundered. "By two hundred years or more of our cheap labour, and I mean free labour, that's what!"

"By why don't you leave, escape, run off?" asked Alice as the lady burst into a laugh, the rolls of fat on her arms quivering in unison with her creased up face.

"Cos, mam, you're English, aren't you? You don't understand lady," she said, once she stopped guffawing. "We've nowhere to go, nothing to look forward to, and we might as well stick with what we know, as opposed to what we don't know."

Nicholas and Alice looked at each other somewhat abashed.

"Don't worry," the lady apologised. "You're forgiven."

Late the following afternoon the promontory hill of Vicksburg loomed up and Alice spied a tall upright middle-aged man with a large sun hat, holding the hand of a girl in a gingham dress and a long plait of dark hair, anxiously scanning the decks of the steamer.

"I'm Jonathan Merryweather, and this is my daughter, Jane, and we're very pleased to meet you," he said in a slight southern drawl as they stepped off the boat. "I'm very pleased that you have decided to stop off. Can I assume that you will be staying the night, if not a few days? Life is getting extremely difficult here unless you are committed to the politics, which I am not."

"We're not bound by any schedules," Nicholas answered, as the girl curtseyed and offered Alice a small bunch of flowers.

"I've arranged supper for ourselves and some friends," Jonathan said, steering them towards a fine trap and an immaculately dressed horse, munching the grass and tossing its head Alice admired the horse holding it firmly by the bridle and immediately gaining its confidence."

"Do you ride, Miss Forwood?" he asked.

"Of course," she answered, "from childhood."

"You'll enjoy it here hopefully," Jonathan said, helping her up into the trap. "Amongst other things I breed horses for racing."

It was not until the following day, when Jonathan suggested that he and Nicholas go and look at the towns fortifications and the two girls went riding, that the subject of taking Jane with them cropped up.

Nicholas was amazed to see how the Confederate Army had fortified the town with masonry and earthen works, which culminated in a massive citadel five hundred feet above the river.

"You can see that this is almost impregnable, Nicholas," Jonathan explained pointing out the somewhat ancient guns that commanded the land below.

"How long have they taken to construct all this?" Nicholas asked taking in the complexity of the fort, even though he had no military experience at all.

"I believe the French had a small fort here, when they owned Louisiana, but most of this has been constructed in the last two years," Jonathan told him.

"And who were the builders?" Nicholas asked mentally counting up not only the cost but the manpower.

"The engineers were of course from the Army, but most of the labourers came from miles around," the American outlined. "No need to tell you in great detail, but we all had to make a contribution from the fittest on our plantations."

"But the Union Army control the river as far as I can see, why didn't they attack it whilst it was being built?" Nicholas asked.

"The Army control the river mainly because the Navy don't have enough men to control the sea and the rivers," Jonathan explained. "The Confederates confront them from time to time from the land, but haven't had enough fire-power to make any impact."

"It's stalemate then," suggested Nicholas. "Lincoln controls the traffic on the river but little else."

"At the moment, yes," Jonathan answered. "The Union just can't get enough men in the region, but before long they will have an army of a hundred thousand men, and then, and only then will they make an assault on the town and control the whole region."

"And you don't want Jane here when it happens," Nicholas realised. "How many months do you reckon you have got to get her away to Canada?"

"Six months, I would say," Jonathan replied. "Do you think your sister will take up my request? I will of course pay all the expenses."

"You'll have to ask her yourself," Nicholas insisted. "I don't know for certain. We did talk it over on the way up, but she may take a few days to consider it. In any event, your daughter will need to agree. She's more than a mere child. And you know, as it stands, I will be leaving at Memphis and heading for Alabama."

"You're right, of course," Jonathan conceded.

"And you've not found an alternative solution yet Jonathan?" Nicholas asked.

"Not yet, and I am not the only parent with the problem," Jonathan continued, "There are others here wishing to relocate loved ones."

"Tell me, that is if you are happy to discuss it," Nicholas pressed, not quite sure of the response from the man, who clearly had considerable wealth from his hundreds of acres of cotton and a large stable of quality horses.

He took a breath before ploughing in with his difficult question. "How many workers do you have here?" he said eventually.

"I was wondering when the subject would be raised," Jonathan answered. "You British are always so sensitive on the subject. But you are right to ask."

"If I hadn't asked it, I know Alice would have done," Nicholas replied.

"Well, I have over a hundred slaves, shall we call them, on the plantation and another fifteen in the stables," Jonathan explained, as they came off the hills to the flatland of the river bank. "With the horses that fail on the track we bring them up for sale on the market, and that can take up to six months."

"That's a considerable undertaking," Nicholas suggested.

"Actually, I have a young man assisting the saddler, whom I pay and three seamstresses, who make up silks for the jockeys. We sell them all over the south. Horse racing is extremely popular here," Jonathan explained as they approached the house. "I've freed the girls as they make so much money for me and will do the same for the saddler in due course."

"But the rest," Nicholas, asked in the mildest of manners.

"I need them to stay solvent," was the reply. "It's as simple as that. And they need me as much as I need them."

"But you think Lincoln will win," Nicholas said, skirting round the subject as much as he could.

"I think so," the host conceded. "And when that occurs anything can happen. Maybe for the good in the long term. Now let's go and find the girls. It looks from here that they are getting on fine. I'd like to show you my stables and the new barn, where we can train the horses under cover."

"I've not had such an exhilarating ride for a long side," Alice announced as she alighted from her steed for the afternoon.

The four were relaxing having inspected the stalls in the barn reserved for the finest of the animals and the exercise pool at the far end where horses with ailments could be treated.

Jane looked through the glass of her drink, surveying the adults as Alice enquired how the trip into town went.

"Who taught your Jane here to ride, Mr Merryweather?" Alice asked.

"She's very accomplished."

"Well, my wife to start with, but then my best stock man took over for cross country riding and she's never looked back," Jonathan replied giving his daughter an admiring smile.

"What would you like to do with horses, Jane?" Nicholas questioned as the girl broke into a wide smile. "Sometime in the future I mean."

"I don't really want to be a jockey," Jane answered with a shy grin, "I'd really like to train them to win on the track or breed."

"Is that possible out here?" Alice asked Jonathan, twiddling her drink, taking a long sip and waiting for an answer.

"Oh yes, and not only that the girls don't ride side saddle here," he replied. "Let's go in, I do believe lunch is served."

"Do you think Jane will come with us?" Nicholas asked his sister as they lay stretched out on the loungers whilst Jonathan was away with his foreman and Jane had disappeared into her room. "More to the point, do you want to be burdened with her for maybe three weeks or more?"

"I'm not certain at the moment. It's early days not that we want to delay for too long," Alice outlined. "Her governess wants her to stay, but two of her friends have already been shipped out north, which may be the deciding factor. Let's see what she thinks tomorrow. I think that she would be good company and I could hone my teaching skills."

"But you've never taught in your life, Alice May," her brother teased, flicking a half empty glass of water in her direction.

"Maybe not but I'll do a better job than you any day," she retorted, chucking a cushion towards him.

The question was resolved two days later, when Jane came down at breakfast time much earlier than usual. The previous day, Jonathan had taken the four of them out in his steam launch, and they had trailed up the river against the stream, anchoring over lunch just below the Eagle bend so severe that boats appeared to sail across the mud. They had fished under one of the sugar maple trees and watched the Union gunboats sail up and down past the redoubts of the town unmolested, neither side wanting to fire.

"Why are they not firing at each other, Father?" Jane asked finally.

"The forts big guns are mainly facing inland for a land attack, my child," Merryweather answered, as yet another armoured tug swished past.

"And the gunboats only have small guns to stop and search ships."

"So they're are just waiting, getting angry at each?" she asked.

"Yes, I guess so," her father answered.

"And lots of people will get killed then?" Jane asked.

"Yes, I'm afraid so, Jane," Merryweather confirmed. "It won't be nice when it happens."

"Can I come back when it's all finished?" she asked, pulling in the smallest of fish fighting for its life on the end of her hook.

"Of course, Jane, of course," he answered as she threw the squirming fish back into the muddy river.

"Then I think I will go with Alice," she said, laying the rod down across the seats of the boat. "Can we go home now?"

"I know of a hotel in Memphis, where you will be able to stay," Merryweather instructed Nicholas on the morning of the departure. "I will try and wire them, but there was a naval battle there earlier when both sides used ships with rams to sink each other. Now the Unionists control the city.

"From there I am sure the big steamers get to Cairo where the Missouri meets the Ohio, but you may have to take a smaller river craft. Certainly you will get up the Ohio river and from Cincinnati the railways are working all the way to Buffalo and the Canadian border. I know nothing of the state of Ohio, so try and contact me when you get to Cincinnati."

"I have all that," said Nicholas taking the notes down in his diary.

"Where are the two girls, still getting ready I suppose?"

"Now as regards money," Merryweather said, reaching for the bag on the table. "There should be plenty of dollars here and I've booked you on the steamer already. You can draw money on my account at Memphis and Cincinnati. After that I guess that you can get Canadian dollars at the border. I will ask my sister to meet you either at St Catharine's on the border, or at Hamilton. They have a daughter of Jane's age."

Nicholas counted the money, checked the cheques sliding it all into a pouch around his waist.

"You need to be careful for the next few days," Merryweather added, "there are an awful lot of sharp characters between here and Memphis in particular, so I've organised two adjacent cabins on the top deck underneath the Captain's bridge away from the riff raff. They're internally connected, and well secured according to the travel agent in town and I'm told there should be a state marshal for most of the way."

"Alice is my big sister now," Jane announced to the housekeeper and the cook as the luggage was piled aboard the wagon to be trailed behind the trap for the short journey to the quay.

"You keep safe now," Jane's governess requested, giving the girl the merest of kisses on the cheek and taking out the tiniest hankie to wipe a single tear. "Your books are in the smaller trunk and I've given Alice a timetable to follow."

"Are you sure you won't be lonely in that big house of yours, Jonathan?" Alice asked her host, as they stood around saying their goodbyes.

"I'll be fine, I'll be just fine and in a couple of years when Jane is back, I'll have the place ready for her to stamp her mark," he said, looking at her straight in the eye and then at her daughter, laughing with Nicholas over something it appeared she had forgotten.

"It's going to be an adventure for sure," Alice answered. "A year ago I was in Liverpool not knowing which way to turn, when a chance meeting with complete strangers has brought me here. And I'm happy, pleased to be doing something useful and worthwhile, with a future that's beckoning."

"You'll have to go, Alice," Jonathan said giving her a hug and shaking hands with Nicholas, before smothering his daughter with kisses and tears. "I can hear the engineers stoking up in readiness for the off."

It was not until the steamer was round the sweep in the river and well past the fort did Jonathan give up looking in the distance at the disappearing ship. He reluctantly had to accept that Alice was right. He would indeed be lonely.

"Looks like I've drawn the short straw," Alice said as they surveyed the two small cabins which contained a single bed, a wash basin stand a chair, but not much else. "You can have the trunks, Nicholas, one of us is sleeping on the deck and I guess that's going to be me."

"The purser told me coming up the stairs that they didn't have a double next to a single with an adjoining door, so they are going to find an additional mattress," Nicholas replied at his sister's possible discomfiture.

"So we can just manage then," Jane queried. "At least there is a fresh water pump in the alleyway and a sluice."

"But have you seen the toilet arrangements at the end of the corridor." Nicholas reminded them both. "A small closet with a pipe all the way to the water."

"Don't take any change in your pocket then," laughed Jane, joining in the merriment over their new home.

"We might as well make ourselves comfortable, with four days ahead of us," suggested Alice, kicking off her shoes and flopping onto the bed. "And we've only been on board an hour. Perhaps we ought to take a turn around the decks."

The vessel that they had boarded was the *Helena,* named after the small town just south of Memphis and it would stop each night during the hours of darkness as the river became more and more torturous. With a shallow draft of only a few feet it could save time by taking some of the side channels out of the main stream and avoiding the full strength of the current.

At every other stop on the river bank a cord of timber for the boilers would be waiting on the quay, ready for the crew to sweat over. They would be rewarded by a tankard of brew, before the gangway was hauled aboard, the whistle blown and the big paddle aft thrashed away at the murky waters driving them northwards.

"Your father was quite right, Jane," Alice remarked to her charge as they left the dinner table and saw a couple of small green baize folding tables being set up in the smoking lounge. "Do you understand cards?"

"No," she answered. "But my father used to play bridge I think."

"Me neither," replied Alice as she steered the pair of them away to the door leading on deck. "You'll have to ask Nicholas. I have an idea he tried his hand

188

at gambling, but never won anything and fortunately gave it up as a dead loss. He's much better on the markets."

"You mean the stock markets?" Jane surprised Alice. "My father makes money on the markets as long as the wires allow him to communicate."

"I suppose we ought to look at your books," Alice suggested the following day, when they had tired of looking at the same endless scenery and she had persuaded Jane to open up her trunks.

Jane picked up the books and one by one laid them aside, until she came to the last one entitled *Equine Science*.

"What are you really interested in?" Alice asked looking at the book.

"This is the one I'm really interested in. I'd like to be the first lady to have a winner in a derby," Jane replied without hesitating. "Father says that you have one in England and soon they will have them here in America. The Indians have raced horses here for as long as anyone can remember."

"You might have different ideas in two years' time," Alice suggested, delving into the stack of books.

"I don't think so," Jane said confidently.

"Well, for now," Alice suggested. "Let's have a look at this one on geography."

By the second day of the voyage, Jane had snuggled up to Alice, as she read from a small book of poetry and passages from Jane Eyre, as if they were from the same family.

"Do you think I could make you my adopted sister?" she said in all seriousness.

"Mm, I'll have to think about that," Alice said with a smile. "I might just like that, as I've only two brothers. Where did your father get this book from, it's only just been published in England?"

"He had it sent from New York. See here, Harper's got the rights and my mother ordered it," Jane said. "Can you carry on reading, Alice, it's so romantic."

"There seems to be a lot more gunboats on the river," Alice observed to her brother, as they leaned over the rail watching the birds rise up out of the water and fly away as the steamer surged on disturbing the water.

"Well, we are coming up to Memphis and the Separatists control most of the land to the east," Nicholas answered taking the map out of his pocket gazetteer and spreading it out. "Though not of course the river."

"So you think that the life is slowly being squeezed out of the Confederates then?" she asked, as they watched yet another boat pass by at speed in the opposite direction.

"Jonathan back in Vicksburg was convinced that it was having the desired effect," Nicholas assured his sister. "Not that I can tell."

"I don't know about you, but I couldn't work out where his beliefs lay," Alice asked, watching yet another heron standing stock still on the bank.

"Me neither, and I suspect that even when this war is concluded the problems will not be totally resolved. But for us all that matters is we get our cotton out before business at home completely collapses," Nicholas concluded. "Where's Jane, still running round the decks?"

"There's a gunboat on the other side," Jane said, cannoning into both of them with the news. "The two Captains are shouting at each other and our boat has to come alongside at the next jetty for some inspection or other."

"Well, I suppose they have to keep the crews on their toes," suggested Alice as the engines slowed, and the steamer's sailors prepared the ropes for the unscheduled stop.

"What do you think they are looking for?" Jane questioned as two officers stepped off the gunboat and confronted the angry steamer skipper.

"Just a routine inspection, Sir," Alice heard the one ringed ensign insist with an army flash on his sleeve. "Can you line up your crew and get your papers? Shouldn't take long."

The passengers lined themselves up along the deck showing their tickets as the Union officer went down the deck introducing himself briefly. "Sorry about this folk," he said. "We won't be long, but it's going to be routine now."

"Captain," he said out of earshot of the passengers. "We believe that two of your stokers are escaped slaves. You are to stop at the government quay and not the usual steamer station arrival at Memphis, for a full inspection. Good day to you."

"What happened back there," Alice asked Nicholas as the steamer raced away trying to make up time.

"I'm not sure," he replied, "but they are obviously getting concerned about the movement of people."

"I heard," said Jane, butting in on the conversation, "that two of the crew were not crew at all, but were being helped to escape. We had two at home that escaped. One we never heard of again and the other was caught still in the County and brought back. He couldn't work for a long time after that and nobody else tried after that."

"I think that the only passengers getting off in Memphis will be those leaving for good," Nicholas said. "No going off for a stroll while they take on fuel and water. Probably just as well I'm staying on until the next port."

"I've just read that more cotton is shipped out of Memphis than any other river port. Did you know that?" remarked Alice as the city came into sight.

"No, I didn't actually," said Nicholas with a smile, "but thank you for telling me."

"I think it might be a good idea to stop off at Memphis for the night and look at the travel options," Alice said, as the passengers lined the decks watching the ship glide slowly alongside the Army base. "Jonathan has given us the name of a hotel. After all I can't really see much point in you carrying on and then doubling back just for the sake of a day or two."

"Daddy thought that there was a newly opened railway from here to Louisville," Jane interrupted, showing them an old newspaper that she had found in the dining room.

"Well, it would certainly cut a day or two off the journey. I've almost had enough of endless bends, forests of trees and plantations," Nicholas interjected as the others read the article on the railway opening just a year or two earlier and then being closed.

"I'm sorry, Sir," the clerk at the station informed the three as they looked around the cathedral like building close to the river. "The line is finished all the way to Louisville it's true, where you could take another steamer to Cincinnati, but the Confederates keep blowing it up. This is Tennessee as you know and most of it is bandit country. You'd only get to Clarksville, and then you would need to take to the roads. I'm afraid that you'll just have to carry on up river."

"Can I send a message back to my father from here?" the girl asked looking at the mechanism behind the glass window.

"Yes, Miss, just write it down on this form," he said passing over the blank form.

"Well, we didn't expect it to be easy," Alice said, turning to her brother whilst Jane looked at the assorted magazines in a rack wondering whether she might get a reply before they left the next day. "You won't find any newspapers, Miss," the railwayman called out to Jane. "The authorities keep closing down the press and as for you, Sir, you could carry on to Cairo, where the Ohio river joins and take the Tennessee river back south if you didn't want to stay with the ladies."

"Not too many options then," suggested Nicholas, resigning himself to another change of plans.

"No, Sir," the man said. "You're not chosen a good time to travel. And you'll find travel to the east not easy. Unless your definite plans I would carry on."

"I might just have to continue on by the sound of it," Nicholas announced as they left the station for the hotel. "What do you think about that, sis?"

"I was hoping to have my new sister all to myself," Jane said, announced as the two siblings stood open mouthed at her statement.

"Don't you want my brother looking after us," Alice scolded Jane, who was getting bolder by the day, and was now standing there pouting.

"I'll tell you what, Jane," Nicholas said, having given his answer some more thought. "At Cairo, the Ohio river joins the Mississippi. If you like I could carry on to St Louis and do some business there and train to Cincinnati to meet you. What do you think?"

Jane looked at Nicholas summing up the situation. "Can I tell you tomorrow?" she said, as if she was in charge.

"It's more than two hundred miles to Cairo," the travel agent said, laughing as they queued for the tickets. "A three-day voyage at the most as the river is not running fast this month. Nothing by comparison to what you done so far."

If anything, the bends in the river got tighter and tighter, and the trees crept closer and closer as the *Cairo*, now with a full load of passengers headed north, first bordering on Arkansas and then Missouri, stopping at regular intervals to drop off and pick up passengers. A gunboat again challenged, although didn't force them to land for an inspection.

"Best to keep the passengers off the decks for the next twenty miles," the young skipper advised, "in case Confederate skirmishers try pot shots.

"Fort Pillow ahead," the Captain informed the passengers, shouting down the deck, as they neared a high rock overlooking the river, "You might like to know was built by General Lee, but is currently occupied by the Union Army so you have nothing to fear. They won't fire on us."

Nicholas and Alice looked at each other in amazement at the structure, and Jane stood stock still looking at the fort on the hill. It was a miniature of her home town.

"That is," the Captain continued, puffing at his pipe, "until next month. The Confederates are threatening to sack it and all the black Union soldiers guarding it."

"Are you going to leave us at port Cairo?" Alice asked her brother eventually, when the shock of the captain's statement had passed and they had a quiet moment away from their charge.

"Yes, I think so," answered Nicholas. "She's probably quite right, you can look after her perfectly well without me, and she's growing up fast in this environment. I've probably done all I can in the delta, massive though it is and St Louis has a new stock market, which I ought to investigate.

"I'm sure the trains are working through to New York from there, and possibly I could find you in Cincinnati on the way. Either way things are safer in Ohio. Maybe I can track down James. Have you written home recently?"

"Oh yes," Alice said, "Have you?"

Sheepishly, Nicholas had to admit that he hadn't been as assiduous as his sister.

"Shame on you, Nicholas," she chided. "Here's some writing paper. Do it right away."

"And what about you, Jane. Have you written?" Alice asked, almost certain of the reply.

Jane nodded in agreement, "Twice," she said without hesitation.

"We'll be fine, won't we, Jane?" Alice assured her charge as ahead, Nicholas pointed out where the two great rivers merged.

"All change, all change," the steamer Captain called out as soon as the ropes were ashore. "This boat is going no further. For St Louis go left and for Cincinnati go right. All change. All change."

They were waiting in the tearooms, luggage at their feet, sipping hot chocolate freshly made and piping hot. Alice had noted a marked change in the temperature. It was getting cooler and they needed a hotel for the night. Fortunately, there was plenty of choice within distance, all touting for business displaying large painted wooden signboards. Nicholas scrutinised the timetables. The boats would leave in the morning, sharp at eight.

"I've got an address here of a hotel in Cincinnati. I'll wire them from St Louis and meet you there," Nicholas said, coming back with another round of hot drinks. "The river trip for you is several days, and a short canal and locks takes you past the rapids at Louisville. I have some more dollars for you and Jane's father has booked your passage. They tell me it's the most beautiful of all the American rivers, so you'll find plenty to look at when not teaching Jane."

"Jane's beginning to teach me, well on some things," Alice answered, briskly, "particularly American history."

"Is that so, Jane," said Nicholas putting his hands on her shoulders. He was sure she had grown an inch. "Then you'd better look after my sister, hadn't you?"

"So you are the two ladies that have travelled all the way from Baton Rouge," the Captain of the Ohio river steamer asked Alice and Jane, having noticed them loitering behind the wheelhouse and invited them in. "That's some adventure, already over a thousand miles by my reckoning."

They were on the fourth steamer of the voyage heading east with Ohio to the north and Kentucky to the south, lush countryside in all directions. The waters of the Tennessee river had emptied at a fast flowing junction and the ship had bypassed the rapids at Louisville. Cincinnati was not far away.

Jane wandered around fingering the instruments in turn watching the helmsman delicately turn the wheel one spoke at a time, not taking his eyes off the trees in the background.

"Well, I have," Alice corrected the man, who was watching closely the marks on the bank ready for the turn in the river ahead. "Jane here is from Vicksburg and I'm taking her to Canada."

"Taking her to Canada indeed. And what about yourself?" the Captain asked. "You're a good many miles from home in my reckoning."

"Haven't decided. I'm going to meet up with my brother somewhere between here and New York," Alice replied, trying to guard her answer.

"Well, you'll be pleased to hear that the rail road from Cincinnati is open all the way to Buffalo and Baltimore then. Otherwise the only way is the canal to Cleveland and another steamer on the lake. That's a two week trip I would say."

Alice turned to go, but Jane continued to investigate her surroundings looking ahead from the best position on the ship, until she turned round and faced the Captain square in the eye.

"I've heard that slaves flee across the river and when they are in Ohio they are safe," she stated turning to the Captain as if she owned the vessel.

"That's not really your concern, young lady," the Captain replied, taken aback by the directness of the girl. "But, you're right they do, and not far from here either."

194

"Well, we have slaves on our plantation and at least one has escaped, but we don't know where he has made for," Jane stated simply.

"All I can tell you, Miss is that they cross the river where the river is at its narrowest. We'll be coming up to it shortly. Some try to swim, and others try and cross when the river is iced up, but most are rescued by people on the north side, who come over in boats."

"My father says that most of our plantation workers are happy and content," Jane said to the Captain, who was concentrating on the navigation ahead, filling his pipe and tamping the tobacco down with his forefinger.

"That maybe, Miss Jane, but are they paid and have they chosen to be there," the old seafarer grunted and walked away.

"Well, Jane, it had to said by somebody sometime," Alice muttered dragging Jane away and apologising to the steamer Captain.

"We shouldn't have come up here," she said to the Captain, leading Jane to the steps off the bridge to the deck below.

"Not at all," the Captain answered gently. "I've a granddaughter who's equally confused. It's a challenging world we live in, but it will change.

"Another hour or so and you'll be getting off."

Alice fumbled in her bag for the address of the hotel and Jane sat down on their trunks and looked around for Nicholas. It was the end of the line. The stern wheeler would go no further and they were at Cincinnati on the quayside, and expecting him to come bursting through the knot of passengers who were gradually disbursing.

Behind them the crew were unloading the deck cargo and they could hear the sound of the boilers cooling down, something they had heard so many times before on the fifteen-hundred-mile journey. Ducks gathered around the stern as the cook threw the days trash overboard, and a boy in a smart tight fitting uniform stood patiently by his bicycle with a sheaf of messages for the Captain.

Nicholas was not there to meet them, that was clear. Resigned to finding a cab into the town by herself Alice realised that they had already departed except one, who kept looking in her direction, knowing that in likelihood he would eventually get there business.

"You wouldn't be Alice Forwood and Jane Merryweather by chance?" a well-dressed middle-aged lady said, hurrying onto the landing stage.

"Yes, we are," Alice said with some relief. "Who are you?"

"I'm Agnatha Turner. The hotel called me earlier," she announced slightly out of breath. "Sorry I'm late. Your brother has carried on to New York. He found my name in the local directory and asked me to look after you for the next part of your journey. I manage a travel agency here."

"Well, that's a relief," Alice relaxed after they had shaken hands.

"I'll get you to the hotel for the night and come see me in the morning." Agnatha suggested, as she lead them to her cab. "You'll be needing a break of several days, I'm sure."

"You've had quite a journey by all accounts," Agnatha asked the two of them the following morning, having walked them around the city centre, "And you, Jane, what an adventure?"

"Well, it wasn't planned," Alice explained, it just happened. "We were invited from one estate to another, finally ending up with this request to get Jane north away from all the problems."

"And just how bad is it, Jane, to persuade your father and his friends to get their children away?" Agnatha pressed the teenager.

"Well, it's all the uncertainty of it, Mrs Turner," Jane answered in a very adult sort of way. "Farmers don't want to sow crops, plantation owners don't want to spend money on growing cotton that won't get sold, and my father is training horses for races that don't happen, least not as much as they did.

"And my father doesn't very much like selling his horses to the government in any case. They don't exactly pay the true value."

"Wow, that explains a lot all in one breathe," Agnatha replied, recoiling from the statement. "And you, Alice, how did you come to be in this part of the world in these times of stress."

"It's a long story," she answered.

"They usually are," Agnatha answered. "When I think of my travels around the world, I often wonder how it all happened."

"Well, Agnatha," Alice pitched in with a full story. "My father's business is cotton importing and he's an impatient man as you might imagine, and I really just came to keep my brother company and find out about the new world."

"Well, that explains most of it," Agnatha said smiling at the confident young Alice opposite her. "And now that you've found this great country with all its warts, what next?"

"Well, I don't really want to return home until I've made a useful contribution," Alice admitted. "Not that I know how to start."

"Sounds good enough to me and a great service to Jane and her father, that's obvious," Agnatha made the point. "I'm sure that you can do more, if you're in no hurry to return."

"When I've got Jane to her relatives in Canada, I'll have some time to think about it," Alice considered. "Now can you show us more of the city and its virtuous forefathers."

"We're right on the border here with Kentucky," Agnatha explained as they walked through the market, "Cincinnati became a bastion of the North, and only a year ago repelled a Confederate attack from across the river. As you can see it's still heavily fortified with a big military presence."

"Was there was a bridge across the river here?" Alice asked, "I saw some foundations near the steamer terminal."

"The army stopped the completion of it when the war started," Agnatha explained, as they completed the boardwalk. "What made you ask?"

"Oh, I've always been fascinated by bridges. Bridges are so graceful," Alice explained, "and so connecting."

"Well, this one won't be finished until this war is over," Agnatha told her friend. "You'll have to come back one day."

"Tell me, how were you able to set up a travel agency?" Alice asked

"Surely there are plenty of business people here. The army just take all people of working age either as labourers or soldiers, and indeed all available women are pressed into service in one way or another. Warehouses were turned into barracks, and houses requisitioned," Agnatha explained.

"So, when I was asked to come out it sounded a promising way of helping. You see the railway is linked right across to Chicago, and the river as you can see, is full of traffic. A year ago, though, the Army stopped all commercial traffic on the river when the Confederates threatened to attack."

Agnatha turned to Alice as they stopped to admire the view. "Tell me more about Jane and indeed more about yourself. She must be finding this all very strange?"

"Yes, at times. A young lady with definite ideas, but not yet an adult," Alice answered. "She clings to me sometimes and at other times is deep into her own thoughts. She likes to call me her sister and I'm beginning to wonder how she will take to her new home."

"Where is she at the moment?" Agnatha asked.

"Buried into her books at the hotel. I guess that we ought to work out how we get to Buffalo," Alice said. "I haven't heard from Nicholas, although the hotel said he was going to wire a message. Can you look at getting us on a train in a couple of days' time. just as soon as Jane's family reply to my message?"

"I'd like to tell you more about Cincinnati before you leave," Agnatha said looking Alice straight in the eye. "We might just be able to help each other. You see, I could be looking for an assistant for a while."

"I've never really had a proper job," Alice confessed. "But I guess that it's about time I honed whatever skills I have."

"Good," said Agnatha, "It" never too late to start. Let me show you around the office, which is part of the house."

"Message for you, Miss," the hotel clerk waved as they strolled back across town, avoiding a small group of black workers cleaning the roads.

"Detained escapees," Agnatha explained. "Unlucky enough to be caught in the town. The army re-distributed them, the fit ones are encouraged to join up and the less fit work on the fortifications around town. They get paid and are provided with accommodation.

"Nicholas says that he is going to join my uncle's firm in New York for a while before returning home, and wondered whether I could stay with you." Alice disclosed, reading the message for the second time. "Did you actually meet him here?"

"Only briefly," Agnatha replied. "He left the following day. But it was long enough for him to establish that my husband is a seafarer and me to discover your brother is running arms into Wilmington from Bermuda."

"Oh, I've mixed feelings about that," admitted Alice, not having mentioned it before.

"I was wondering that myself," Agnatha said. "Which is why I would like to tell you the real reason I am here. It might take a little explaining but I'll give you an outline."

"It's all about helping slaves find a new life, isn't it?" Alice suddenly said, having realised that Agnatha had skirted round the subject all afternoon.

"Yes, but I think it best that Jane isn't aware, don't you?" Agnatha suggested.

Alice nodded and Agnatha continued, "They flee in great numbers across Tennessee and Kentucky helped by many sympathisers, but crossing the Ohio river is a tremendous obstacle and without assistance by communities on this side is extremely dangerous."

"We did hear something like that from the riverboat captain," Alice confirmed, "Jane was quite taken aback."

"Some continue without stopping, but many come here to rest up in safe houses, being moved around on moonless nights, according to a series of signals," Agnatha explained. "I take on those who are too sick to continue and nurse them back to health, before organising their onward travel."

"And who helps you financially," the girl asked.

"Although there are many people with Republican views here, there are even more willing to help and I have a very good supporter, well up in the Army, prepared to help with food and medicines and turn a blind eye," Agnatha outlined.

Alice nodded staggered at the complexity of the operation.

"The Army only want the fittest here in the city," she continued, "and certainly not anyone with as fever. They dread an outbreak, such as happened in the southern cities, where yellow fever has been a problem."

"And how many safe houses are there in Cincinnati?" Alice asked, intrigued at her description of the web of safety.

"I don't know exactly and I am not sure that any one person knows," Agnatha explained. "As I said before, I mainly arrange onward travel, and that is usually up the Miami and Erie canal, from here to Toledo and very occasionally on the railroads up to Cleveland. I only have one contact there on the Lake. From there they travel by sea to Canada."

"A canal from here to the lake," Alice asked, mentally looking sat the vastness of the country. "That has to be a good three hundred miles?"

"Best part of a week's travel, but fortunately as the canal is much wider than those that you see at home, the boats are bigger and we can conceal half a dozen at a time, with the owners co-operation of course," Agnatha outlined.

"And you get a date to take a delivery?" asked Alice.

"Yes, I shine a light in the attic window on agreed dates," Agnatha replied. "They arrive with me sometime after midnight, but no more than three at a time."

"And in due course you go to the canal basin to rendezvous with a canal boat skipper?" a curious Alice asked.

"Yes."

"I'm exhausted," Alice said finally. "Shall we go and have a cup of tea, no let's have a pot. A very big one."

"Now when you get to Buffalo," Agnatha explained the following day as she waved Alice and Jane away, "there's a short coach trip to the Niagara Falls and the bridge there takes you to St Catharine's. From there you will need to take the steamer to Hamilton, unless Jane's relatives meet you there. There is no train and the road is almost non-existent."

Alice listened intently making notes in her diary.

"Here is a list of people to make contact with once over the border. I only met them briefly on my way here, must have been the best part of a year now," Agnatha continued to explain. "There is a lovely lady that you might come across. She is from Boston and her late doctor husband has financed part of the Canadian operation. I've spoken to her but not met her, but she is highly thought of. Oh and she's coloured."

Alice nodded calling over to Jane, who was leafing through the local newspaper. It was not much more than a broadsheet and had only just been allowed by the authorities, who had closed it down for a year.

"I'll wire you when we get to Buffalo and I've had time to digest your proposal," Alice said hugging the lady who had been most helpful. "A twelve hour journey being bumped over iron tracks will give me plenty of time to mull it over."

Agnatha went over to Jane, wrapped up well in some warm clothes purchased the day before, as the girl stood shyly on the platform.

"These are for you," Jane said, giving a slight curtsy and offering a bunch of flowers that she had selected in the foyer.

"You've been very lucky, my girl," Agnatha said, accepting the gift, "To have Alice here. Another three days and you'll be with your relatives and I'm sure that you'll never forget the journey."

"I'd like to go to England someday," the girl explained. "Alice says I could stay with her. In her city, they race horses over hedges and I'd like to see it."

"Yes, I know," replied Agnatha kindly. "I'm sure you will sometime. And you might come and see me in New York before you go."

"Your luggage is aboard, Miss," shouted out the guard, sporting a crisp navy blue uniform with brass buttons and a flamboyant cap and braid. "Best get aboard, train is ready to depart."

"Did you get a letter off to your father before we left, Jane?"

"Yes, I did, but Agnatha reckoned that it would be lucky to get through," Jane answered, opening one of her favourite books.

Ahead of them the rolling hills of the central lowlands offered little resistance to the bluff lines of the locomotive and the six carriages, as it made its ponderous steady journey, the great cow catcher at the front ready to scatter any critter that failed to move off the track in time.

Numerous small lakes, still frozen even though spring was fast approaching appeared right and left of the train as it sped past rivers and streams emptying their waters towards the south and the Ohio river. Occasionally it wheezed to a stop at an outpost station, where no more than a small number of passengers would step down or climb aboard.

"Have you been on a train before?" Alice asked her charge, who had spent most of the journey staring out of the window from one side of the carriage to the other.

They were approaching the major city of Columbus, half way across the State and which, according to Agnatha, was another network centre for the work that she was doing and supported there by a large Irish community.

"We once took the train out to Jackson and down to New Orleans on a business trip which we turned into a holiday," Jane answered. "I couldn't have been more than about ten. Just after my kid brother died."

"Do you know, Jane," Alice said quietly. "You've never talked much about you mother. What was she like?"

"She was always very loving, read me books, told me stories; but after my brother died she hardly said anything from one day to the next, until in the end she would sit in the garden in the swinging chair, staring into space for hours on end," Jane said matter-of-factly. "She wouldn't eat and faded away."

"And the doctors couldn't do anything for her?" Alice said softly.

"My father had several in attendance, but she just never responded and then one day my father came back from work to find her slumped in her favourite chair," Jane said. "Can we talk about something else please?"

"Of course. Look we're crossing the Sciota river and coming into the station at Columbus. Its stops for a while here. We might be able to get off," announced Alice brightly. "Next big city is Cleveland on the Lake that goes all the way to Niagara Falls."

"Have we got any fruit left?" Jane asked as the train slowed, the brakes squealed and the train came to a stop in the very middle of the state of Ohio. Not many people alighted, but a good number climbed aboard. Columbus was a crossroads and on the direct route to Baltimore, Albany, and the Eastern seaboard.

The light was fading fast as the Buffalo Express ran down the Appalachian plains to Cleveland, endless flatland with hardly a feature. Alice looked at Jane, who was curled up asleep in the crook of the plush seat and the window, an opened book on her lap and a half-eaten apple in her hand.

Her usually plaited hair that snaked around her neck had been abandoned for the day and now curled round her shoulders which gave her a softer look, instead of the focused penetrative stare that made Alice wonder if she was of native Indian stock. Not that it mattered.

There was something appealing about the girl who continued to surprise her. Another day and a night would see the girl in the safety of her relatives. For the best part of a month, they had been travelling together, from the warmth of the lower reaches of the Mississippi early in the third year of the war, to the banks of the Lakes, which would still be frozen, she was sure.

"Where are we?" the girl said coming too, as the book fell to the floor splitting open the cotton backed pages.

"Cleveland," Alice answered showing Jane the railway map that came with the tickets, as the train clattered over the turnouts, hissing and wheezing with more noise than usual; finally braking to a halt violently as if the driver had Missed his reference position. Within five minutes the platform had cleared and the Buffalo Express, freshly charged with water and a new crew steamed out along the shoreline, the frozen sea to the left shimmering in the light of dusk.

"Orders for dinner, dinner in half an hour," exclaimed the steward opening the carriage door beaming delightfully to Alice and Jane, as the train gathered speed heading due east.

"We're coming," confirmed Alice as the steward ticked off their names.

"Which side of the restaurant, Miss. Right or left," he asked.

"What would you suggest," Alice replied picking up her bag and coat.

"Definitely left-hand side, Miss," he replied. "The view of the lake in the moonlight is something you'll never forget."

As the door closed and they got up to gather their belongings Jane turned to her sister and exclaimed, "Why are there so many black people working on the railways, and appear to be so cheerful all the time?"

"I really don't know, Jane," Alice said, wondering how to field yet another of her charge's observations. "For the moment, let's just leave it that both of us are in more privileged surroundings, but it shouldn't stop us treating everybody as equals in this world."

"I think I know why you are going back to help Agnatha?" Jane asked over dinner as empty stations flashed by and the moonlight danced across the ice.

"You do?" said Alice scooping the last of her pudding onto her spoon.

"Yes," she said flashing her dark eyes straight at Alice. "You see whilst you were talking to Agnatha, I walked around her backyard and saw a young black man emptying a pan. He looked so frightened when he saw me and then scurried back into the cellar."

"And what do you think about it, Jane," Alice said, sponging her face with a napkin.

"That I've got a lot to learn," Jane said at last, and then changing the subject. "You will let me stay with you in England, won't you?"

"Yes, of course," came the reply. "I'd love to take you to the Grand National. After all we are nearly sisters, aren't we!"

The Canadian bound stage coach approached the centre of the bridge and stopped right in the middle for the dozen or so occupants to climb down and watch the fresh water thunder down the vertical drop of nearly two hundred feet. Below and upstream a hundred yards away a maelstrom of white foam cascaded under their feet into the gorge.

They all stood for a full minute and would have stayed longer had not the driver chivvied them back into the coach. It would terminate the journey in the tiny square of St Catharine's, the community that was receiving so many escaped slaves. Once on the Canadian soil, the coach passed through neat rows of single storied clap board buildings which opened out into the canal two miles later, bypassing the falls. Completely frozen in it would take another two months, before the ice could be sawn to allow the steam icebreaker to make a passage in either direction and free up movement between the two lakes.

The driver brought the coach to a halt, well clear of the lock gates and instructed them all to climb down.

"You walk across the lock gates," he announced as they all carefully stepped out onto solid frozen ground discoloured by sand, scattered to secure a footing. "It's not unknown for the horses to try and bolt before, now so please be careful and follow the coach."

"How far to go now?" said one passenger, as they climbed aboard on the other side of the lock.

Someone threw a flat stone into the lock that skated across the ice at the speed of a bullet.

"Ten minutes, or you could walk if you like," joked the driver nuzzling his horses and checking the rig.

"We're here, Jane," Alice announced, as the driver heaved on the handbrake of the coach, climbed down, whispered to the two horses and clipped on their nose bags. Most of the passengers were immediately reunited with a small crowd of family members and soon disbursed, leaving Alice and Jane outside the hotel and opposite the church by themselves.

It was soon evident that they weren't being met. The town was abuzz with activity, shops were open, the tills ringing and buildings were springing up in every spare space. People, white and black mingled together, were laughing and joking in the cold, wrapped up against the fresh wind that swept across the frozen lake and lowered the temperature by several degrees.

Alice was pleased that they were both well prepared, but not quite to the style of the ladies of the town, who all wore trousers. Alice looked up at the three storied hotel which looked warm and inviting. Leaving their trunks on the veranda, Alice pushed open the doors to be welcomed by a roaring fire and strode over to the desk.

"Ah, Miss Forwood," the lady behind the counter said, "I have a message for you, two messages actually. Is this young Jane Merryweather? Well her relatives are picking her up tomorrow."

"And the other message?" asked Alice.

"That's from Isabel Nugent," the hotelier said. "She's been living here with her companion on and off throughout the winter, though goodness knows why, when she could be in Boston. But I can tell she is well respected for the work she is doing."

"What does it say?" Alice asked, never having heard of the lady, although she did recall Agatha mentioning someone of that name.

"Well, read it for yourself," she said not unkindly. "Basically she had to go back to Boston for a couple of weeks, but that her Molly will entertain you."

Alice scanned the letter which was an invitation to meet her at her house on canal street.

"How did she get to hear of us," she asked the hotelier, who had in front of her a copy of the *Hamilton Observer*.

"It says here," the lady said, showing Alice the page.

A Miss Alice Forwood from Liverpool England is expected soon to arrive in St Catharine's with her charge, Miss Jane Merryweather having travelled over two thousand miles up the Mississippi, where Jane will be staying with relatives for the foreseeable future.

Alice looked at the short article again which was in the column containing port news, and turned over the page of the broadsheet to read the remainder of the news, that confirmed her observations that this part of Canada was brimming with expansion.

"You could take the tramway out of town all the way to the two lakes and beyond whilst you're here waiting," the lady suggested as the porter brought in the trunks from the avenue which was lined with trees coming into blossom. "It's lovely journey particularly on a fine day."

"We have a town hall, a hostel, a number of churches here of different denominations, but all preaching the same gospels and even a library," the woman continued.

"Have you got a printed map?" Alice asked. I'd like to see the Falls from close up whilst I'm here. The bridge we crossed doesn't give you the best of views."

"You can get the tram there too," the hotelier explained giving Alice the key to the room. "Jane's relatives are coming in tomorrow on the coach. The ferry doesn't start running until next month and it's not guaranteed until the ice finally melts."

"We'll take a tram ride first thing in the morning, and I'll find Mrs Nugent when Jane has left with her relatives," Alice confirmed with Jane, who was wandering around the main room looking at pictures of early settlers.

"What are you going to do when I'm gone?" questioned Jane as they waited outside the hotel at midday, for the Hamilton coach to arrive. They were both well wrapped up with scarves, hats and boots, bought as soon as they had arrived in Canada, and were pacing up and down to keep warm. "I'm going to really miss you."

"Well," said Alice picking her words carefully. "I'm going to have another tram ride and then go skating, which I've never done before, and then I guess I shall be going back to Agnatha's at Cincinnati."

"And what about the lady who desperately wants to see you? Jane queried.

"Oh yes, I must see her I guess. She did write the warmest letter, but why she wants to see me, I have no idea," Alice said. "Now you've got my address back home and Agnatha's in New York, haven't you?"

Jane looked glum, her single plait laying over her shoulder down to her waist.

"Yes," Jane said after some reflection. "But do I really have to go? We've had so much fun and I know you better than I do my cousin. And we're sisters, aren't we?"

"Yes," confirmed Alice giving her a hug, "cross my heart. We're sisters for life. Now I can hear that coach coming. It's only going to stay for half an hour to change horses and will be heading back to Hamilton in no time. Let's go and meet your relatives."

Alice put off going to Isabel Nugent's house for a full twenty hours, before plucking up courage to find Molly tucked away on the long road out to the canal basin.

Picking her way down the side walk only partially cleared of snow, she could see the masts of several three masted ships and the tall slim funnel of a steamship framed between the houses, until she came to the picket gate that had to be the house she was looking for. Taking the newspaper cutting from her bag, Alice rapped the knocker smartly and stepped back not knowing what to expect.

"Are you Alice Forwood by chance," the beaming face of Molly greeted her immediately inviting her in out of the chill morning and just managing to stall a curtsy. "I've been expecting you, and Isabel is so sorry to have missed you. She had to go back to Boston to sort out some financial matters over the ship she is chartering down in the harbour, just as soon as the ice breaks up."

Alice was not unfamiliar with the term chartering of ships.

"She charters a ship," said Alice, "but what for?"

"Well, I don't know too much about it," Molly answered. "But she hires the first ship that sails back across Lake Erie in the spring with escaped slaves, as a contribution and thanksgiving for her life."

"Thanksgiving for her life?" asked Alice. "I'm not sure I know what you are talking about."

"I think that you had better take a seat, Miss Alice," Molly said, "whilst I make a pot of tea with some cookies. I see that you have the article in the newspaper?"

Alice spread out the crumbled broadsheet. "The lady at the hotel gave it to me."

"You see, Alice," Molly said, choosing her words carefully, "Isabel thinks that somehow or other, her life might be connected to yours."

"I don't understand, Molly," Alice protested. "I've never been to America before. Shouldn't it be for Isabel to do the explaining."

"I think that she thought it might be too painful," Molly replied knowing that once started she had to go on. "You see Isabel has the remains of a scar on her shoulder. It just visible as *Eva,* the ship she was brought over from Africa all those years ago. She has an indentured parchment sheet that was her husband's. He was the surgeon on the ship and he bought her in the slave market in Savannah, and they lived together in Boston until he died two years ago."

"But that is awful," said Alice rigid with tension. "But so romantic in the end. But what has it got to do with me?"

"Well," said the former servant and now confident, pulling out the faded parchment record and pointing out the details. "You see, the Captain of the *Eva* was a Richard Forwood. Isabel thinks that he may be a relative."

Alice stared at the paper before her and the signature. It was not unlike that of her father. In fact it was almost identical.

"Oh, my god, oh my god," she cried, tears streaming down her face. "Surely it can't be. I am so sorry. It's so long ago, a lifetime before I was born."

Alice tried to remember the grandfather she hardly knew, the man who had whittled out a ship for her brothers, but who never talked about the sea beyond his sailing ship which took slaves from Wales all over England.

Chapter 18

Molly threw open the heavy curtains in Isabel's house, and looked down at Alice curled up in a ball and fast asleep in the spare room. It was mid-morning, the sun was streaming in and the birds were fussing around the garden, devouring the scraps from her breakfast. She laid down the fresh cup of tea and stole out, leaving Alice to wake in her own good time. An hour went by and, with still no movement in the bedroom Molly, somewhat concerned returned the kettle to the stove, until it whistled and a head appeared.

"What time is it?" Alice asked shaking her mop of blonde hair and attempted to tie her dressing gown belt. "I had an almighty scary nightmare."

"Now, don't you worry about it, Alice," Molly comforted her, sitting her down in the wheel backed hard chair at the kitchen table. "Now get that mug of tea down you and we'll talk about it."

"But, it's so surreal," Alice said, gulping down the hot liquid.

"Maybe," answered Molly "On the other hand, it's probably a coincidence and nothing to do with your family. You know what my Isabel would say?"

"No."

"Go back to this Agnatha friend of yours, and work your cotton socks off until it no longer hurts," Molly said, "and now eat this pancake and maple syrup breakfast I'm cooking you."

It took two full days of comforting by Molly before Alice summoned up the confidence to get a message to Agnatha, confirming that she would go back to Cincinnati, at least until the end of the summer and help in any way that she could.

She wrote to her mother saying all was well, which was only partially true of course. Alice had no doubt that it was her grandfather who had transported Isabel across the Atlantic, and that someday in the near future she should meet her to apologise. It was the very least that she could do, but for now she must play her part in helping others, the ones that had been used and abused for the sake of the almighty dollar. For now it had to be a secret, something between herself, Molly and Isabel.

"You look a bit strained, Alice, I must say," greeted Agnatha on the station fore course at the end of another twelve hour journey.

Alice nodded, "It's all been a bit of an ordeal."

Even the jovial staff on the train failed to revive her spirits, as she either slept soundly propped up in the corner of the carriage, or just stared out into space as the locomotive hurried across the plains. Comments like "Gee whiz, you're English; what a quaint accent," hardly raised a smile and she had heaved a sigh of relief when the train ground to a halt and she was able to escape into the fresh air.

Alice allowed herself to be bundled into Agnatha's transport. "All I need," she uttered, "is a cup of tea and a long sleep."

"Tomorrow will be early enough to delve into invoices, statements, bills and brochures and the running of a travel agency," Agnatha said, but Alice was already fast asleep.

"Just how do you arrange transport for all these poor people?" Alice asked, after recovering from her ordeal, tucking into a hearty breakfast.

"We move them around in a variety of ways," Agnatha explained. "The grocery van has a secret compartment under the driver's seat so we distribute like that, I have something similar in my trap and when boxes are taken to the canal boats, they often conceal a stowaway which I have organised through the local shipping agents.

"As I do a lot of business with the railway and the canal, I am free to move around without incurring too many questions. It can't be done without some money changing hands of course, but many here in town are remarkably generous."

"And they all come through your hands?" Alice queried, trying to imagine the operation.

"Oh, goodness me, no," Agnatha exclaimed, with a smile. "There are Sisters of Mercy in the city and several churches, where they are hidden in the vestries and vaults. My role is to ensure that their onward travel is as secure as possible until they reach the coast, that is."

"And that's where Isabel Nugent's operation takes over?" Alice questioned in wonderment at the scale of the exodus. "And do they all get through?"

"Unfortunately, not," said Agnatha. "If they strike across country by themselves, particularly in the winter they will be lucky to survive. Many give up, throw themselves at the mercy of understanding farmers, and stay helping others on the journey for a pitiful wage."

"I think that I've heard enough for the day," Alice said, flopping into an easy chair as yet another message for Agnatha fell on the doormat.

"You seem to have a good understanding of the booking system, Alice," Agnatha announced at the end of a month of intensive training.

Alice nodded in approval. It was the first time that anyone had recognised and commented on her organisational and bookkeeping skills.

"We'll go off to the bank this afternoon," Agnatha announced. "Tomorrow I'm expecting to arrange a transhipment on the canal, which you might find interesting."

Alice nodded, continuing with the task of processing the tickets, which was taking all of her time. They were well into the third year of the war and traffic from New York to St Louis and onto Chicago, she had noticed was increasing week on week.

"I've just had a letter from Isabel Nugent," Agnatha announced quietly over breakfast. "Now I understand why you have been so withdrawn these past few weeks. Would you like to tell me something about it?"

Alice looked up wondering what to say, so in the end said nothing.

"You can't blame yourself," Agnatha said fetching out the letter. "Isabel is totally understanding and there might be a mistake. It was a long time ago, you know. There are good men at sea as well as bad, just as in every strand of society whether they be lawyers and landowners, priests or politicians.

"My husband and I have met them all over the years. It might sound blasé but many Captains, more than you might imagine would have cared for their cargo, whatever the contents. After all it was in their own interest, being the most profitable part of the triangle, to deliver as many in the best possible health."

Alice nodded in agreement, still finding it difficult to comprehend.

"You may just have to keep it to yourself. Least for a while. Victorian businessmen have tended to draw a line over the activities of their fathers and grandfathers," Agnatha said trying to comfort her assistant. "Now, we're going to the canal this morning. I've to arrange a cargo for one of the tug skippers leaving tonight. But first can you pull the trap into the yard right up to the back door."

"The back door, Agnatha?" Alice checked.

"Right up close, Alice," she said. "And I'll show you how we can squeeze in one small person under the seat."

"But that's only one surely?" Alice asked.

"Yes, but the grocery van will be delivering tonight to the tug and the barges and it will be a big order for three weeks, which will take a couple of runs." Agnatha assured her. "Now can you warn them that they should be moving soon."

In the shadow of the yard, Alice helped Agnatha bundle the young man in the secure hollow over the axle, and they drove out of town to the canal basin. Weak when he arrived in the city, Agnatha and her friends had fed him back to health ready for his onward journey.

He had explained that he and two others had crossed the river at a community called Ripley, and they had climbed a wooden staircase to a resting house nearby, before being moved into the city. Agnatha clipped the horse along at a good pace, heading up Culvert street to the Cheapside basin, squashed between several single storied warehouses, finally coming alongside a squat paddle tug tucked in a corner close to the last lock into the river.

Almost camouflaged into the drab surroundings of the canal the grey and black painted vessel was emitting a fine wisp of smoke, that tried to curl skywards. The smell of bacon on a stove wafted out from the galley across the dock. At the stern a crewman was stacking a cord of timber, and on the tiny bridge another flicked his rod out across the water. Seeing Agnatha and Alice, he tied it off to the rail and jumped ashore to greet the two women.

"What have you got here," he asked kindly as they stepped down and Agnatha exposed the dickey seat. "Will he be able to help us? I'm one crew short and it's a heavy tow of barges, and three hundred miles as you know."

"I'm sure he will," Agnatha assured the tugboat man. "He's recovered quite well. I'm bringing two more this evening and more are coming from the Sisters. There's at least one girl, well a woman, with them. Can you get them on the barges and hide them in the stern along with the machinery boxes?"

"Yes, it's all planned, but they will need food and water with them and plenty of warm clothing," the tug skipper advised, "I don't want to be dealing with any corpses. It'll be damned cold at night."

Alice shivered at the thought of it. The lad that they were hurrying down the ladder seemed fit enough, but for those not so well in a cramped space, it might be a different matter. The papers back home were always reporting canal deaths on the Liverpool and Leeds canal.

"We've provided well for them this time," Agnatha replied. "I've scoured around my friends for extra clothes."

"Who's this lady with you then," the tug skipper asked pulling out his pipe and tapping the remains onto the deck. "Doesn't sound like she's from these parts."

"She isn't," Agnatha answered. "Her name's Alice and she is my new assistant and may well take over for a while, when I go back to New York to raise some more money."

"Pleased to meet you, Miss," he said, extending a rough calloused hand. "This sort of thing new to you?"

"Yes, very much so," Alice replied, warming to the man.

"Well, if you're as good as Agnatha here you won't go far wrong," he said with a broad smile, "She a real pearl."

"How do know when you might be asked to house some more refugees, Aunt?" Alice asked as they drove across town.

A city for only forty years, Cincinnati had grid laid roads; a railway station with a brick structure and overhanging wood canopy; a new four storied medical college; an imposing court house with a high domed roof and a horse drawn tram system and it was a focal point for fleeing slates.

"There'll be a message on the doorstep," Agnatha confirmed, "or something whispered at church."

"As simple as that."

"Yes, we'll drive back past the Zion Baptist church, the Union Baptist church and the Allen Temple, all of which I am associated with," Agnatha said, with a smile turning her trap into Elm Street.

"It's obviously an extraordinary organisation, Agnatha," Alice stated in wonderment. "Who makes it all happen?"

"No one's really sure," Agnatha replied. "It just seems to happen by word of mouth. They say it actually started long before this dreadful war, but over the years the trickle has become a flood."

"How many in a year then?" Alice asked. "Hundreds?"

"Several thousand by our calculations," Agnatha replied.

"All through Cincinnati," Alice queried, staggered at the volume of people.

"Largely, but many carry on through having crossed the river, without stopping," Agnatha explained. "Tomorrow I'll take you to Indian Hills, about ten miles north. I've business, legitimate and otherwise, with the Quakers up there. Their station is a major clearing house and they have considerable influence in these parts."

As they drove into the yard the postman came up the steps from the cellar.

"Message for you, mam," he cheerfully smiled.

Agnatha opened the unstamped letter recognising the handwriting of one of her friends in town. There was to be a meeting in the Zionist chapel that evening.

"Do you think you might cope with all of this, Alice?" she asked as they took off their capes later that evening. "Whilst I go back to New York for funds and appease my husband."

Alice nodded. "I'll do my best. I'm well happy dealing with rail and steamer tickets, but as for the rest of it I'm not sure."

"I'll leave plenty of provisions in and make sure that you only have women and children." Agnatha confirmed. "And my maid will help you. You'll be fine."

The engineer on the grimy tug *Napoleon* piled on the logs into the boiler and watched the needles on the gauges slowly climb up to the red mark. He blew into the voice pipe to the wheelhouse, but there was no answer so he climbed the two sets of iron ladders to find the skipper resting his eyes, sprawled out on an old chair.

It was first light and they had connected up the three tows and all was well. The barges were only half full with manufactured goods heading north, but they had arrived full of grain a week earlier. By the time the train of barges reached the Lake they would be full of cargo picked up on the way.

"All ready to go," the engineer advised as the skipper came to life, with the movement of the secured barges.

"Tell them to let go everything on your way down then," the skipper instructed, walking over and spinning the wheel. "How many crew have we got?"

"My regular stoker, plus those two runaways and our usual deck man. Should be enough," he answered. "And three more hidden away on the first barge."

"Make sure you work those two then. At least they'll be warm. Did Agnatha provision them?" the skipper asked, peering down the quay.

"Enough for a week, but she said they are running out of funds," the engineer answered."

"Stand by for action," the skipper reminded his colleagues. "We've two sharp turns remember, before we turn parallel with the Miami river."

The little convoy was heading for Toledo on Lake Erie, and at the stops on the way which would not be much more than villages, they would be off loading farming equipment and finished goods and taking on grain produce, and even barrels of mined oil.

"What happens to our charges when they get to the Lake?" Alice asked Agnatha the following morning whilst they were riding on the latest horse drawn tram that circled the main streets of the city.

"Well, I've not been there even though you can catch a train," Agnatha explained. "I shall wire a contact set up by Isabel where there's another safe house, until there is a sufficient number to make a shipload or indeed several during the spring and summer."

"Does Isabel organise all the fleeing slaves on the Lake?" Alice asked.

"I don't think so," Agnatha answered. "In fact I'm sure that she hasn't even been there. She told me in her last message that just travelling from Boston to Canada is quite enough. She must be about seventy by now, I would think. She probably uses runners working on her behalf, and don't forget she only finances one vessel each year."

"What a remarkable lady. Perhaps, I should meet her after all," Alice agreed, now more relaxed over the recent revelations.

"But for now," Agnatha instructed as they climbed down from the tram. "We'll call in at this haberdashery shop. I've some details to sort out with the manager."

Spring turned into summer and then into autumn, the leaves started to fall as Agnatha and Alice continued to despatch growing numbers from Cincinnati to the western ports on Lake Erie and on to St Catharine's.

In the city itself, army patrols eased and soldiers dispersed to other fronts as within each month more and more reports came in of Union victories on land and at sea. Alice heard from her older brother and parents regularly, but of James she heard little, other than he was safe.

"I really need to go back to New York," announced Agnatha, "eventually and move on my operation. Sell it actually, because my husband needs my help also. Are you sure that you can manage?"

Alice smiled. "You go ahead, Agnatha, I'm fine here. But I will need to go to New York soon, as well. I've just heard from James. His ship was run aground and he is on parole with my uncle awaiting trial confined to his house in Upper State."

"I've advertised the business here and have some interested parties," Agnatha admitted. "I'll let you know when they want to look at the books. But I must get back to my husband soon, or he'll think that I've gone for ever."

Alice looked at her boss, and friend. "I can hold the fort," she said confidentially, "long as you want, and then I would like to stay with you in a less hectic world for a while."

"You know, Alice," Agnatha said hugging her tightly. "You're the daughter I never had."

Chapter 19

"Can you take some extra cargo this trip?" Bone and Watcher asked the three officers as they sat in his office sweltering under the August sun.

"This is going to be the last voyage for a while," Bone explained. "The hurricane season is early this year and we are trying to clear the stock that is here. General Lee is desperate for these new cannons which have a range almost twice as much as the muzzle loading antiques at his disposal. We have four on the quayside ready to ship out."

"And I suppose that Lincoln is getting them also," the Chief Officer asked.

"Probably so, but then that's not our business," Watcher interrupted.

"Well, it's between these two," said Stewart. "I'm returning home on the next available ship. The Chief officer is taking over, with James here second in command.

"How many are there and what is the weight?" James asked, mentally trying to place where they would be located.

"About a ton and a half with the gun carriages," Bone said, checking his papers. "We'll provide you with extra tarpaulins ropes and chocks."
The new Captain looked at James and nodded. "We'll need extra coal too for the lay-up. There's none readily available in Wilmington. The Union saboteurs have been cutting the line. All the food for Wilmington is coming up the coast inland creeks in sailing ships or overland by cart."

"Are we the only blockade runner," asked James, wondering what to report in his letter to his father, before they sailed.

"The *Senia* will be right behind you, but the *Sunbeam* in the Liverpool fleet was stranded and captured during your last voyage," Bone reminded them. "There are others of course from here. You are not the only ones. Reports say that the Union gunboat fleet now numbers several hundred vessels."

"And those running out of the Bahamas?" James asked, scanning the shipping news in the *St George Herald*.

"They're fearing quite badly by all accounts," Bone reported.

Privately he and Watcher were getting concerned at the success of the Navy to corner and capture the contraband runners. They had been running a spasmodic operation since the start of the war, now almost three and a half years old, but were getting more and more successful as the months passed.

Bone explained in greater detail as James listened on. "The channel at Jacksonville was blocked and the approach to Charleston was getting risky. With no protection from shoals the patrol vessels just wait in numbers outside the range of the Confederate guns at the fort."

"Not only that but yellow fever is rife there," Watcher added, "and the towns people in Carolina, Georgia and Florida are insisting on ships being quarantined, effectively making the ports unusable. Wilmington as you know has the coastal railway and that is making the place even more important than before."

James nodded, taking in the warning and advice and making a note to add to the letter home. Bone handed a letter to Stewart's successor, addressed to Jefferson Davis and marked Urgent.

"We'll have you loaded by the day after tomorrow so that you'll be ready to go on the next moonless night," Watcher said. "And we have some engine spares for you, courtesy of Mr Kirk, from Glasgow. He's concerned about your running hours. And get that Scot of an engineer you have on board to write to him. He's preparing another paper to the Institute, so make it's finished so that Captain Stewart can take it back with him."

"Anything else?" asked James shuffling his papers and preparing to leave.

"Yes," Bone said delving into his bag "I've just remembered. Here's a letter for you with a New York stamp."

James tore open the letter preserving the stamp. His father collected stamps. It was not more than a short note, two months old. Typical Nicholas.

New York
June 1864
Dear James,
I hope that this finds you in good health and without too much delay. Alice and I took steamers up the Mississippi earlier this summer. I registered the Company to trade with the new St Louis Union Merchants Exchange. Alice is taking a girl to safety in Canada. Expect to sail for home soon. They say here in New York that the transatlantic cable will be completed within five years.
Yours Nicholas

"Are you sure we can find employment for the crew when we are laid up ship that was covered in fresh coal dust."

"Oh yes," he answered, "I'm quite confident. I had supper with the local commandant of the militia whilst you were away with your girlfriend. They're desperate for manpower, are happy to pay and the girls will flock back to town to help them spend it."

It was a very relieved crew of the gunrunner *Fannie,* which raced up to the *Frying Pan* shoals to pick out the waiting marker boats in the agreed sequence that signalled the all clear. Dropping down to half speed the ship cleaved a wake of bubbling water, swinging past the island forts to the left and acknowledging a welcoming shot from the ramparts of Fort Fisher. They had brought home the deadliest cargo yet. The latest Whitworth cannon that was only matched in power by the Tyneside built Armstrong guns fitted to the ironclads. Upstream the pilot pointed out the remains of the stranded Confederate Navy ship, *Rayleigh.*

"It was sunk last month, Captain," he said. "Trying to sneak out at the dead of night to drive off a couple of Union Navy gunboats before a couple of runners were due to leave, but got the worst of the duel and was forced back with a hole in its side."

Already rust was forming around the upper works, the decks slimy with the constant washing of the tide. The main gun leaned drunkenly to one side, the two masts broken off at the hounds, the top half of the propeller green with algae. A boat was alongside, the crew of two scrambling around the sloping decks looking for anything removable.

James looked again at the forlorn wreck as the *Fannie* swept passed, the wake pushing gently against the wood and iron remains making it rock slightly, and causing the beachcombers to hang on to the railings.

Concentrating on the river the pilot expressed glumly, "The Union Navy just have too many prowling gunboats at their disposal now. It's slowly getting more and more critical in the port. Food is short at the expense of cotton being railed in and commandeering the few available wagons," he complained. "Even the military trains can't cope and yellow fever is in town."

James pondered as Captain and pilot strained for the dangers ahead. It was getting close to pulling back the operation. He would write home immediately, on arrival, then realised it would be impossible to post it.

The Colonel slapped the Captain on the back, gave James a bone crushing handshake and poured out flagons of beer to the crew as soon as the *Fannie* cruised gently alongside and the gangway was pushed out. Having damped the boilers down for the last time, the Chief Engineer noted with pleasure that the ship had done so much sailing in the past two voyages, that the coal stock on board would take them well through the enforced period of inactivity and joined the celebrations.

He left his two right hand men to complete the cooling down and with instructions not to miss the party that he knew would go on into the night, until most of them would collapse into a stupor of liquor and downright tiredness. Whisky was more to his liking and he had a small cache on board.

James looked for Carolyn, but all he saw was one of the mayor's workers who handed him a note. Carolyn and her father had gone to Fayetteville to see her brother in hospital and would be away for several days. Damn, he thought, how can I keep myself busy. He sauntered over to the engineer and offered his assistance whilst the *Fannie* was under maintenance.

Stripped off to his oldest clothes the following day, topped off with a borrowed pair of overalls he became an engineer in the making, climbing into the boiler and testing the tubes, overhauling the feed water pump and dropping the big end bearings in the flat engine, specifically designed to slide into the shallow drafted hull. By the time Carolyn returned with her father, he was hardly distinguishable from the rest of the black hand gang.

"You'll be ready for a close inspection of my works soon," the mayor had said over dinner that night.

The first of the gales passed over the following night, rain lashing down on the quayside in torrents, sweeping all the debris into the dock leaving the rails shining a rusty hue, the two track ways merging together as one in the distance. The boxcars had gone, the huge doors of the warehouses were bolted.

The quayside was empty, even the rats had gone to ground. James turned the collar of his waterproof up and walked forward to check the moorings and then aft pausing to adjust the stern line and checked that all were aboard, then raised the gangway on its block and tackle and strung off the mast. There was no point in risking damage to the ship's only means of access.

He looked at his fingers. The nails were ingrained, had been for days, the tips smooth and sore from relining the fire bricks at the back of the boiler. Before he was invited up to the house again his hands would need several days of cleaning. He would offer his help to the harbour master, who was taking the opportunity of the season to survey the river.

"My brother is due home from hospital," Carolyn announced on meeting James at the steps of the Harbour Master's office, taking his hands in hers and examining the improved state of his hands. "He's much improved. You can kiss me now."

James stretched his arms around her waist and linked his fingers together without touching her body to enjoy the succulent taste of her lips and tongue.

"Have you missed me?" she said, disengaging herself by ducking inside his embrace.

"A lot," he said, truthfully. "It's been over a month and seems like a year."

"Only a lot," she said, 'that's not much, try again."

"A very lot, a very, very lot," James replied drawing her towards him again.

"That's more like it," Carolyn said allowing him to enclose her, "Now kiss me again, but harder."

"Your parents haven't said a great deal about you brother?" James asked, as they walked towards the horse and trap, hitched to a rail at the back of the office.

"I know they haven't, but he's done his best and father is bitterly disappointed, that my brother has no interest in the family business, which is probably why he likes your open approach," Carolyn explained.

"He's really an academic in the making. He was at Richmond University before the war studying arts and theology and then reluctantly signed up for the university regiment. He's no soldier and hated it. Anyhow he took a bullet in the shoulder that has left him permanently weak on that side and is now permanently discharged. I'm sure you'll like him, although he is very quiet and subdued since his injury."

"Was that why you were away in Fayetteville then?" asked James taking her hand and squeezing it.

"Yes, you see it's also left him badly disorientated and the doctors weren't sure that it was safe to release him," she said. "So it's up to us to get him back on the road to recovery."

"You know," James said, "I just wonder at times why I'm here contributing to all this misery."

"If you weren't, James, then somebody else would be," she said in sympathy.

"I suppose so," he replied in resignation. "But it's not much of an excuse."

"Don't go away, James," Carolyn said with a sigh. "Just don't go way until this beastly war is over. I can't bear it. My mother is fearful for everybody. Surely it can't go on for much longer."

"The Harbour master has said that I can borrow his launch when we have finished surveying the harbour," James said, trying to brighten her up, as he took the reins and headed out of the docks. "We can take your brother and sister up the river for a day out. Do you think they'd like that?"

"Why do you think of so many lovely things to do," she said cheering up.

"Probably because I love you," James said in all seriousness, astounded by his admission.

Carolyn looked up at him and tweaked his hand. "Thank you. You don't know how happy you've made me."

"When did you say your brother was coming home?" he said tilting her chin with his free hand.

"Tomorrow. There's a military train coming in with fifty wounded," she answered dully. "And more coming next moth I'm told. Father is opening up the theatre as a recuperation centre and my Mother is going to organise it. They're as much shell shocked as physically wounded."

James thought for a moment, went to say something but couldn't find the words. Instead he flicked the reins and turned the trap round the last corner towards the house.

Carolyn wanted to continue, "The ladies in town sent them off with extra knitted socks and those balaclavas that you British had in the Crimea war, and all that's happened is they've come back damaged, needing to be nursed, many with no homes to go to."

"And you'll will be helping them?" James said, "Between assisting your mother with your brother."

"Yes," she confirmed. "I think I'm going to be terribly busy, but not too busy that I can't have a day out, and an evening off."

James had to wait a full week before taking the three siblings beyond the town in the steam launch, usually employed as an additional tug and occasional day boat for the council. With a striped canopy in the stern protecting the slatted seats from the weather, James coaxed the fire into a blazing temperature, helped by Carolyn's brother Harold, who's somewhat blanked face turned into a smile as soon as the lines were slipped and the boat silently gathered speed.

It was one of the quieter days of the autumn, the barometer on the *Fannie* had steadied and the sky had cleared leaving just a trail of cumulus clouds away to the east. James left the small steering wheel to Carolyn and Harold and went forward to check the dials and top up the oil pots.

Carolyn's sister was busy delving into the hamper that contained enough food for the day and more besides. James looked at Carolyn, in animated conversation with her brother amazed at the way she was encouraging him to engage in the surroundings. He left them to their world and turned to look upstream.

Here the river was wide and running slowly with only the occasional fisherman casting from the bank. Overhanging willows touched and caressed the wake as they passed by, and a heron preceded them stopping every two hundred yards ahead to scan the waters for any movement before flying on as they approached. Was he really in a war, he mused when there was so much beauty around them?

"I know where we can stop," Carolyn's young sister shouted out as they made a slow turn to the west. "We've been here before. There's a jetty, a beach and a meadow."

"Shall I make you in charge then?" James said, taking off his soft peaked cap and handing it to her.

Carolyn looked at her brother and then at her sister, by this time struggling on the jetty with the wicker basket. "I told you she could be bossy," she said with a laugh. "She knows what she wants even more than I do."

"You do?" he questioned.

Carolyn skipped two paces ahead of him and turned extending her arm and slowly crooked her forefinger from him to her. "Yes. You," she said.

With only a week or so left before it was deemed safe to continue running arms and cotton, the *Fannie* was on the drying out grid, the barnacles were being scraped off the hull, the intakes cleaned of debris, the rudder checked for wear and the great paddle boards were re-bolted. The ship was required to be in near perfect condition for the coming season, the demand for guns being greater than ever.

James even had to decline an offer to help out in the mayor's steam plant in favour of his own work aboard. Apart from an invitation to dinner and a stolen cuddle in the garden James found little time to think of Carolyn and she for him as the sanatorium took all of her attention.

"Can you get time off for a ride out?" She asked him over what looked the last supper that they would enjoy. "Harold is improving and I can leave him for an afternoon as it's my day off at the theatre."

"I'm sure I can, and I could certainly do with a day in the country," James replied. "That is, if it's acceptable with your parents. Tomorrow is expected to be fine and warm."

"Go and enjoy your day out, James," said the *Fannie's* new Captain, as they sat on the deck enjoying breakfast of rolls and coffee. "I'm doing an inspection with the Chief Engineer later and we'll start loading up the bales tomorrow. The rest of the crew have been recalled, no doubt in need of the bonus awaiting them."

They ambled side by side, Carolyn sitting comfortably on her own gelded stallion and James more awkwardly on a borrowed broad backed mare, trotting alongside the river heading for nowhere in particular. The sun was out, the air was warm and the trees were beginning to shed the leaves that were turning to fantastic shades of reds and yellows.

"We've got some lunch I believe," said James, as they came to a clearing right alongside the river. "What is it?"

"Something delicious," she said, sliding gracefully off her horse and offering an apple to her steed.

"Have you got a blanket?" he asked, clambering down less gracefully, almost leaving a foot in the stirrup and ending up sprawled on the ground.

"Did I hear right the other day when you said you loved me?" Carolyn asked coyly as she brushed away the crumbs off the blanket after lunch, and James had found yet another apple for the horses tethered securely to a tree stump.

"Yes," James said, "and I meant it."

"Come here then," she said pulling him to the ground, trapping him so that he couldn't get up, her blonde hair spilling over her shoulders, and her face framed in sensuality that he had not seen before.

She rolled over onto her back, taking him with her, and then took his face in her hands offering a generous mouth and an inviting tongue.

He was propped up on his elbows angled across her body, tonguing her ear lobes and kissing her neck.

"You can take my jacket off," she said, undoing the first button and then the second. "It's hot and I like the warmth on my shoulders."

James fingered the label of her jacket, the smooth serge cut to precision down the side to her tapered waist, allowing for the swell of her breasts. His hand reached for the third button and the jacket fell slowly away and then he stopped to bury his head in her neck, straightening the blanket that had rucked up underneath her.

Stretching her arms above her head, Carolyn wriggled out of jacket, folded it neatly and placed it behind her head. Shaking her curls free she pulled James slowly downwards onto her body. He could feel the perfume of her body and felt the slight heaving of her breasts as she invited him to nibble at her.

"You'll have to take that coat off?" She said pulling at the cloth as he sat up allowing her to feed the sleeves down his arms and toss the jacket to one side.

Carolyn walked her fingers up his arm plucking at the hairs as she went. James felt them stand up in his excitement, not quite sure what to do next, until she took his hand and laid it gently on her bust that was ever so gently pulsating.

"Kiss me there," she instructed her companion as she pushed his hand slowly underneath her blouse and exposed first one, and then the other nipple bursting with tension. Her breasts, small and firm with an areolae disc of the darkest colour, were within a finger and thumb.

"Oh, that's so lovely, James," she sighed squirming underneath the weight of his body.

"And now suck me, James," she uttered, holding him tight against her, one arm around his neck, the other playing with his ear lobe.

James rolled his tongue in obedience and then laid his head on her body searching for an ear to suck, a nose to kiss, a mouth to smother, and a neck to caress. Carolyn looked at the sky squinting in the sun between the trees and reached for a drink, feeding first James with the liquid and then herself with a giggle. In such a short time, it seemed the sun had moved a million miles.

"Are you going to kiss me again," she asked in a manner, that was almost an order.

"I shall kiss you until you can take no more," James answered making a pretence at doing up her blouse.

"I want you to kiss me for ever," Carolyn demanded, pulling him down again and after a while pushing him up so that his weight was taken on his straightened arms.

James wondered what to do next when she reached down to her breeches tight across her flat stomach and held with a fine leather belt. Bare to the waist down she slowly released the belt and undid the buttons one by one.

"Undo the last one, James," she said. "It's just a little tight."

Carolyn wriggled out of the trousers, exposing the neatest of belly buttons until they were just over her buttocks and showing the briefest of silk underwear. James felt the excitement in his body growing as she reached up to him securing a deep kiss then falling back slowly onto her pillow.

"Kiss me, James. Kiss me and suck me," she whispered, "until I cry out for you."

James leaned down towards her shifting his body weight as she twisted and arched her body up towards him.

"And again, my love, I love you," she called out in short cries as he held her, kissed her and sucked her with his tongue, until she fell back in exhaustion in their lovemaking.

"Can you do that again," she said as her panting subsided and she regained her breath, reaching for his body and changing her position again. "We Southern girls like to know the size of what we are letting ourselves in for."

James floated on air as she held him tightly, pulling the blanket over them and burying herself into his body.

"Why is it," she said, looking him straight in the eye, "that English men are so gentle?"

James grinned, "I have absolutely no idea."

"What do you think you'll do after the war," she asked earnestly as they walked the horses back in the fading light. "I can't let you leave with little more than the exploring of our bodies and a declaration of love."

"I just can't say at the moment, Carolyn," James replied. "I want you more than any other girl I know. God willing, I shall be back to continue loving you. We've lost one of our ships, no one died fortunately, but I'm not certain what the future holds. You've work, good work, to do here in the meantime."

"But you will be back, promise," she said more in hope than anything else.

"Yes, I will be back, I promise," he said, as they rode into the yard and stabled the horses.

Carolyn wasn't on the quayside when the *Fannie* pulled off the quayside. James knew she wouldn't be there. He didn't think that she believed him, and in any case he knew that she was on duty nursing the remaining sick, who had nowhere to go, probably no one to go with and with an uncertain future. He counted himself lucky. He had the love of a girl and a good life ahead.

The *Fannie* surged down the channel, past the wreck and another which was of a Union gunboat trying to slip past the fort in a daring raid and shell the town.

The crew were happy and relaxed. They had been paid well as a retainer for the past two months, and they had earned good extra money during the stay, found girlfriends of a sought and looked forward to the excitement of a sea voyage.

The lookouts on Fort Fisher had not reported any Union Navy activity, although it was misty bordering on fog. The soundings increased, and the revolutions were upped as they passed Fort Caswell. They were almost in clear water and the open sea.

"Vessel to starboard," sung out the lookout, "It's a Navy boat, Captain, heading this way, about a mile off."

A gun boomed in the distance and a spout of water fifty yards off the bow rose in the air, astonishing the crew on the bridge who thought they had a clear run. The Captain and the pilot looked at each other, trying to gauge the confidence of their counterparts experience.

"It'll take them two minutes to reload, Captain," the pilot said. "We'll be out of range by then."

"Port twenty, full ahead," suggested the Captain, walking over to the brass engine control and winding it up. The pilot nodded in agreement.

"Another vessel just off the port side," shouted the other lookout in horror. "Dead ahead now. Jesus Christ, bloody hell. He's just fired."

All that James heard was a rushing noise and an explosion that took him off his feet. All around was utter confusion. He got to his feet, then collapsed again, his ears drumming, blood dripping down his cheeks. He couldn't feel his left leg and clung to the rail, slowly bringing himself upright.

He could feel blood streaming down his leg but nothing else. The tiny wheelhouse was no more, two bodies lay lifeless on the deck, shards of jagged timber embedded at ridiculous angles. The big paddle on his side of the ship was turning round smashing everything in its way. The ship was going in a slow circle out of control.

He looked towards the big control lever in the full head position, staggered over to it unable to take the weight of his body on one leg, clung to the lever and somehow heaved it into the stop position and collapsed again. Seconds later the *Fannie*, out of control glided up the bank, reared slightly and settled down. It was fast on the *Frying Pan* shoal, but James knew little about it.

James was aware that he was on a ship, a moving ship, but he couldn't hear the usual silent swish of the paddles, which he was so used too. He turned his head. He wasn't in a bunk, but an iron bed. He could hear voices around him, voices that he half recognised. A Scots accent, a Liverpool accent and that of the ship's cook, a Negro that they had taken on weeks earlier with the singsong twang.

"Oh, so you've come too, I see," said a not unfriendly voice walking over to him.

He could feel himself oddly bound, and tried to move his legs.

"Don't worry about that," the voice said. "That's just to stop you falling out. Your leg is badly damaged."

"Where am I?" asked James as his head cleared.

"You're in the custody of the Union Navy," the voice said pulling back the bedclothes and looking at James leg, "I'm the ship's surgeon. The Captain will be along to see you shortly."

James lolled back onto the pillow, disoriented and dog tired, and within minutes was asleep with exhaustion.

"I see from the ship's papers that you are the Chief officer and also the owner?" an English voice at the end of the bed awoke him.

James thought hard, trying to clear his head of the pain. "No not quite," he said after a while. "My father is the Chairman of the Company."

"But you're on the Board, aren't you?" The Captain of the gunboat said.

"Yes, what's happened to my crew?" James demanded trying to sit up.

"I'm afraid that your Captain, the pilot and one crew member are dead." came the reply. "The crew member was found with a cigarette still in his mouth. It was probably the act of lighting it that gave you away. You know you should have stopped when challenged."

James let his head flop back on the pillow. He vaguely remembered rushing back to the bridge at the first shot.

"And the rest of the crew?" James asked.

"Three wounded here in the sick bay. The rest are fine. They helped my crew jettison the cotton enough to get the ship afloat on the high tide. We're towing her back to Newport dockyard." the voice that seemed to fading away explained.

"And what then?" asked James fearing the answer.

"You'll be taken to hospital in New York and then paroled pending charge," came the immediate answer. "Running contraband goods is a criminal offence in America. You will certainly be fined and as the owner you may be imprisoned. Without doubt you will not be allowed back into the United States for at least five years. Does that answer your question?"

"But I've a girlfriend in Wilmington," James protested.

"They all say that," the captain said, turning to leave.

"She's the daughter of the mayor and I'm hoping to marry her," James groaned, sinking back into the bed.

"Then she'll have to join you in Liverpool, Sir," he said, moving over to the next bed. "It's a place that I know well."

Daybreak had revealed the *Fannie* upright, but forlorn, hard and fast on the notorious bank, just out of protection of the forts guns. A flotilla of ships pulling boats were gathered around, men swarming around on board; the paddler levering bales of cotton over the side and shifting coal into the largest of the tenders.

The two gunboats lay a little further off at anchor, gently wallowing in the low swell. The garrison fired a single ranging shot out of frustration, but there was little they could do in any case. The guns were only short by a matter of yards and they had no hope of driving off the warships. All the garrison commander could do was watch the ship being lightened. Already a floating tow line was being deployed. Before nightfall, unless there was a mishap, there would be little evidence of the stranding.

"It looks like they are sending off a boat this way, Sir," a gunner on the ramparts shouted out. "Flying a white flag. Three bodies are laid out on the thwarts."

"Get a messenger to town, Lieutenant," the Commandant of Fort Fisher barked having watched enough. "And tell General Bragg at headquarters that the *Fannie* is lost, three men dead, a few injured, and the rest have been taken prisoner. And ask him again why we can't have the latest long range cannons. He knows damn well that all will be finished down here within six months."

"Prepare a detail on the landing stage and take them in at the sally port," the Commandant continued, "We'll bury them at sunset."

"Sorry to report this, Sir," the ensign said, dismounting from his horse handing the slip of paper to the mayor. "The Harbour master said I ought to tell you before I continued to headquarters."

Carolyn's father folded the piece of paper and went to find his wife. It was a simple statement on headed notepaper from the Commandant of Fort Fisher. The *Fannie* had been disabled and was being towed away. Three dead and several injured, but with no details.

"When is she home?" he asked, disclosing the news.

"Very soon," Mrs Jones answered, "I'll get you a drink."

"I think we will both need a drink," he said. "She's going to be heartbroken for sure."

"I've had a good day," she announced, breezing in from hospital duty on entering the house and finding the building unusually quiet. "Where is everyone?"

Mrs Jones had made certain that the servants were at the back of the house, and that Harold was with their other daughter in the stables.

"I have some bad news, Carolyn," he said, bringing out the letter and trying to make his words as softly as possible.

"It's the *Fannie*, isn't it? It's James, isn't it? I knew something would go wrong," she cried out. "Tell me, what's happened?"

"Well, it was captured on the shoals and is being taken away," Mr Rogers replied glumly holding Carolyn in her arms.

"He's dead, isn't he. I told him to be careful," she cried, trying to break away.

"Whoa, my girl, calm down. He's not one of the dead," Dan Rogers comforted her unsuccessfully, as she beat his chest with her clenched fists, trying to minimise the blows by holding her tightly around the shoulders. "Least we don't think so according to the Lieutenant, who brought the news. He saw the bodies."

"I love him and he's probably dying from his wounds and it's all your fault, you and your friends," she cried, freeing herself from his clasp. "I'm working with soldiers, who'll never be the same again, and I've lost the only man I've ever loved."

"You don't understand, Carolyn, it's not as simple as that. I'm working hard to convince the Army of the way ahead too," he said, as she broke away sobbing towards the stairs. "Tomorrow the council are going to petition Jefferson Davis."

"It's too late," she cried, turning on the first step and collapsing on the balustrade. "It's too late and I hate you all."

"All you men are interested in is making money and yet more of it, when ordinary lives are at stake, just cannon fodder," she wailed sitting on the step with floods of tears.

"But James was doing much the same," her father said lamely.

"But he was risking his life, not just sitting on the side lines," she protested climbing up the stairs to the upper hallway. "And now I'll never see him again."

The mayor looked at the letter again, convincing himself that James had survived.

"We'll have to do something," he said hugging his wife as their other two children came, in wondering what the noise was about. "I don't know what. They'll all be taken to New York no doubt, but we must try."

"You know, she right, Dan," Mrs Jones said with a sigh. "You might have made a small fortune in the past three years, but the cost is high, far too high."

"James talked about an uncle that had offices at pier 25 on the North River, Manhattan," the mayor reminded his wife. "Somehow we'll have to get a letter to him. How we get it out, I don't know with the postal system and censorship."

"I'll talk to the wife of the Commandant at the Fort," she suggested. "Mrs Lamb looks after the injured soldiers there and the enforced black workers. She comes from Providence, in fact they both come from there, so why he is working with the Confederates, goodness knows. She'll know how to get a letter out."

"It's just another example of how senseless this war is," he answered.

"Let's try and be positive," she replied. "Fetch her down for supper. We can't have two lame ducks in the family."

But Carolyn refused and stayed put for twenty hours.

"You don't think she, you know, gave herself, do you?" the father said later that evening when all was quiet.

"You mean, well, she did say she loved him, and they did spend some together of late," the mother agreed. "I don't think so, she's quite sensible."

They expected to wait months for news, but in the end didn't have to wait long for a letter. A franked letter, over stamped with that of the censor came from Newport Mews. Mrs Jones fingered the letter before handing it to her daughter. It felt like only one page and a one page love letter could only mean one thing.

Carolyn took it to her room and lay down on her bed daring to tear it open, and then in one quick moment slit it open with trembling fingers. She noticed the date. It was less than a week than when the *Fannie* went down.

My Dear lovely Carolyn,

I am here in hospital at .... awaiting to be transferred to .... for a second operation on my leg that was badly damaged when the ship was hit. They say I lost a lot of blood and that it was a close call to pull through. I was obviously very lucky not to be on the bridge at the time as all the others were killed. All I remember was rushing to the bridge from checking the cargo when the first shot came. I'm not sure what is in store as I was not only the Chief Officer of course but part owner too. They say that my body is strong enough for my survival but that probably my leg will cause me problems for the rest of my life. I doubt that you would want to be saddled with me for ever.

All my love James

The envelope was over stamped and had clearly been opened then resealed. Carolyn could neither see where he was nor where he was heading to. Her mother quietly mounted the stairs on hearing her daughter stirring.

"Is the news encouraging?" she called out not wishing to intrude too much.

"He's recovering, but I don't know where he is," she called out coming out onto the landing. "The doctors say he may never ride again."

"But it could be worse," the mother consoled.

"I suppose so," Carolyn answered drily falling into her mother's arms and weeping profusely. "He never was any good on a horse."

It was another month before Carolyn heard from him again. It came from Up State New York, just before Christmas and surprisingly had escaped the censor. James explained he was on parole, pending his trial and that if he absconded he would be severely fined and banned from returning to America for two years. She could contact him only via the consul in New York. He loved her in the hope that she would understand.

James' uncle opened the letter from Manhattan, wishing that it was from Wilmington. It was Christmas 64" and cold, extremely cold, even for a house on the banks of the Hudson River, which often fared well in mid-winter. James had been with his uncle for six weeks on written parole, and there was still no word from the Federal Court in New York on the court case of the captured *Fannie*. Now the Court wished to parole him nearer to the city, and proposed transferring him to a school for boys without homes in New Jersey. Would he be agreeable the letter asked.

"What do you think, Uncle?" James asked on reading the letter.

"Well, you're better and you're bored, and there's little here to keep you busy," James's relative confirmed. "And you've only had one letter from that girl in Wilmington, so you could do with something else to concentrate the mind. And of course, as soon as it's all finished, and it will be within months, you'll be free to see her."

"That's unless they deport me," James answered somewhat fed up with the prospect.

"I doubt that," the uncle replied. 'so, I'll write back to the Court and tell them you agree to be transferred."

"Yes."

"Good," he said clapping him on the shoulder. "I'm sure it's for the best."

With some trepidation James relaxed in his uncles' office on 25th, State Street and signed his new parole papers. There was still no news of his Court appearance, and until that was resolved he could not join the Atlas West India Company, or make plans to go home and he had no wish to return home in any case.

The headmaster of the school met him at the ferry steps with a cheery greeting. He was a seafarer of a previous generation, grizzled with side jobs, wasn't particularly interested in James recent exploits, and explained that keeping the boys interested and focused was the main objective.

Education would come later and only after months of getting their confidence. It wasn't far to walk. James looked at the map of sprawled out buildings. The school was close to the terminus station of the Baltimore and Ohio railway. Baltimore had a weekly ferry connection to Wilmington, well before the war he had been told, and it would be reinstated as soon as hostilities were over.

James had as much of his eye on the news as he had on his charges. In the past eighteen months of trading to Wilmington he had absorbed the terrain, knew all the channels and the protecting forts, and fully appreciated the strategic value of the port to both sides of the combat. Fort Fisher would be under a combined sea and land attack, the New York papers announced early in the New year.

James wrote again to Carolyn in the forlorn hope that his letter would get through knowing that it was highly unlikely. Even reports in the media had ceased, he noticed, although it was well known that the Navy controlled the approaches. James concentrated on teaching and controlling fifty boys during the daytime, and keeping warm in his small apartment during the nights. And had heard, via his head teacher and his uncle, that he was due to appear in court in mid-March. His parole, his internment, his punishment would soon be a thing of the past.

Carolyn watched from the doorway of the theatre, and occasional opera house, and surveyed the steady procession of soldiers in the grey uniforms that the town had got so accustomed too. There was none of the usual laughing and joking, catcalling and obscene gestures, just hundreds of men heads down, heading for General Bragg's headquarters on the edge of town.

By some good fortune, a letter from James had got through to her father's factory, and she had clutched it to her breast as if it was her only possession. She could hear the guns booming in the direction of the sea. It was early February, bulbs were beginning to push through the ground and flower, the birds were gathering material for nests and her father was sure that Wilmington would be relieved within the week.

The town was desperate for food, the inhabitants close to starving, and the railway lines were completely severed. The only good news was that it was rumoured that the regular weekly ferry service to Baltimore would be renewed within weeks.

"James is in New Jersey teaching as part of his parole," Carolyn confided in her father, in a rare moment that he away from dealing with the State Governor and the military. "But goodness knows when we can meet up."

"Well, if you're that desperate to meet up," the mayor said, trying to sound positive, "you'll have to get him because I'm certain he won't be allowed to come here, at least not for some time."

"It's the best part of six months now," Carolyn agreed, "I can't bear it if he gives up and goes back to England."

"I'm sure he won't," he said comforting her. "Your mother and I both agree. Somehow we'll get you there. I can pull a few strings. Now let's see if we can get a message to him that you'll be on the first sailing to Baltimore. Your mother has a friend in New York. I'm sure that you can stay there."

The vessel that steamed into Wilmington in early March three weeks after the town had been relieved, was nothing like the pre-war passenger ferry which had been requisitioned by the Confederates, converted and then finally sunk in the battle of Roanoke island. But it did bring vital supplies, and a few passengers from the Government keen to stabilise the area, and was to return and establish a weekly service.

Carolyn was one of a hundred passengers in the cramped and basic accommodation. In two days, she would be in Baltimore and in a few hours after that with the man she could not forget, the man she loved and had still not given herself to him.

"The ferry will be due in well before the last train leaves," the stationmaster confirmed to James as he read the letter from Carolyn confirming that she would be on the first passage. "Come back tomorrow and I'll give you some idea when the service is starting."

"I guess there's no point in waiting if they haven't got an actual date of departure," James said, trying to make some sense of the proposed service.

"Don't worry, Sir," the railwayman said. "I know where to find you at the school. We've taken on some of the boys in the past and they're good workers. You're a credit to the place."

For the first time in months, James felt that his life was moving in the right direction.

"We've word that the ship leaves tomorrow," the stationmaster confirmed at the end of the week. "The connecting train should here by eight o'clock in the evening on the day that it arrives at Baltimore."

James stood underneath the great clock, dressed up against the chill of the evening. He massaged his leg that still troubled him when it was cold and paced up and down, waiting for the daily late afternoon train from Baltimore to arrive. It was close to eight o'clock.

The passengers streamed passed him in a cacophony of welcomes, kisses and hugs from waiting relatives. James looked intently down the platform searching for the familiar swish of her body and the shriek of delight that she would issue on seeing him, but the concourse was almost empty.

"Did you come on the Wilmington ferry?" he asked a man who seemed as lost as himself.

"No," the man answered looking at his watch, before moving away to the last cab in the line. "I don't think the ferry arrived."

"I shouldn't worry, Sir," the ticket collector said, as James looked for an explanation. "It was probably delayed. The weather down there hasn't been too good. They've no doubt sheltered somewhere. Come back tomorrow night."

James waited the following evening for the Baltimore train and the night after that as well, with still no information on the ferry. He was having his breakfast and all the news from the south was confined to the problem of prisoners from the war.

Perhaps the ship never sailed in the end, perhaps it broke down in the river and was towed back, he considered. One of the boys brought in the New York Times, which he ordered every day of the week. The right hand column on the front page took his attention. It was a bald statement edged in black.

The maiden voyage of the Wilmington to Baltimore ferry was lost in Chesapeake Bay two days ago with many feared dead. Witnesses said they saw an explosion. The survivors had been taken ashore at Newport News. The Navy are still searching the area.

Chapter 20

"Pleased to see you back, Sir," the *Audacious* gunnery officer greeted him, when Toby stepped on the quarter deck with his newly sewn stripe on his sleeve.

Toby smiled and relaxed at the welcome, which he knew, was often a taxing time on taking a new command. Accepting the congratulations from the junior officers, who gathered around him, he noticed that they were a completely new sweep of young men.

How things change in no time at all, he thought. He just managed to smile on hearing the whisper of a more acceptable limey comment than usual taking it as a badge of office. He would be addressing the whole crew later.

"I think we ought to show you our latest baby," the gunner said, throwing back the cover and exposing the business end of the weapon. "cos if nothing else, it's travelled across the water, the latest hexagonal rifled Whitworth 2.75 inch and a present from your majesty to frighten those southerners."

Toby ran his hand down the smooth metal to the breech, and then peered down the inside of the barrel that spiralled away mesmerising his vision like a rabbit trapped in a light. He swung open the loading mechanism to accept a shell and then clamped it shut for firing in one easy motion, and then wondered what it would be like to be on the receiving end.

"And we've two more of these to be mounted in the waist," the gunner continued. "We can traverse those a good thirty degrees. How about we christen it right now before we get commissioned and the whole lot of booze goes ashore."

Toby decided not to tell him the good news that the Admirals were going to relent on the grog issue for the coming commission. It was something he was keeping under his hat.

He looked down the deck at his new command. They were ready to sail from the dismal grey dockyard, even though it was a bright spring morning. Ships and come and gone in rapid succession in the final days of preparations of the *Audacious,* such was the frenzy to get the northern fleet up to full strength for the final onslaught against the Confederate Navy and the blockade runners feeding the fire of war.

He had virtually a new crew apart from his time served warrant officers, who would spend the next few days at sea driving the new men into a team capable of reacting quickly into any situation. A smattering of men were 'turners', those who had been persuaded to change sides after a brief detention in one of the several isolation centres. Alongside him his first lieutenant awaited to repeat his orders, and three new young ensigns waited eagerly at their stations, one checking the flags with the yeoman, the other two marking the actions of the gunner and the boatswain.

"Are you ready, Pilot?" checked Toby, as a crane loomed over to take the heavy dockyard gangway ashore.

High above in the rigging, the top men cream of the sailors, were losing the gaskets in the topsails and topgallants. But there was no one looking on from ashore as the scampered across yards freeing the buntings, right out and many feet above the waters of the murky Hudson.

In the shipyard, every man had his head down concentrating on the next challenge of turning round as many vessels as possible back to sea, in the shortest possible time. It might not have been the same on land, but at sea the Navy had the southerners on the run and intended to keep it that way.

"Tugs just on the way, Captain," the pilot confirmed. "They've been held up recovering an ironclad that broke down in the fairway. It's been in the yard far too long and they still haven't got its engine sorted by the look of it. The engineers here in New Jersey are dead on their feet trying to keep up repairing the ships, let alone completing new ones."

"We'll all be pleased to get to sea, that's for sure," Toby confirmed looking over the side to see the two launches come alongside and hook up.

"See you in six months then," the pilot called out as he dropped into the waiting boat as *Audacious* passed through the Narrows. "Just don't forget to turn right."

Toby looked astern at the skyline of Manhattan, quite sure that it was growing upwards by the day, and then briefly considered his aunt making her small, but significant contribution, wondering what the next six months for him would bring.

He walked over to the shelter that protected the helmsman and the navigation table and stepped inside The youngest of the ensigns on board was ready with the engine control lever. The job of following the Captains instructions with the engines was nicknamed 'toby' following the tradition of the Merchant Navy, something that always amused him.

"Half ahead," he said, to hear the clanging of the bell and the change in beat of the engine as the screw bit deeper into the water and *Audacious* headed out into open water. Above his head, the topsails billowed gently in the following breeze, not quite doing enough of the work of propelling the ship. Once clear of the dangers, the engine would be doused and all sail set.

Handing over the navigation to his second in command, he went to his cabin to digest his wad of documents which would dictate their life for the next six months. He noticed with some little satisfaction, that the Navy Board had consented to allowing limited grog on board on account of realising the monotonous role of blockading ships such as *Audacious,* provided it was marked as medical stores.

Toby thought it should make his job a little easier. His duties had already been spelt out in general by the Admiral before leaving, but the squadron they were joining was already at sea being assembled in the James river beneath the protection of Fort Monroe, and that was his immediate destination. Toby opened the thick leather folder and laid out the papers.

Signal procedures, ship formations, coded cyphers, issue of medical supplements, limitations on the use of live ammunition, and sealed letters to be opened in date sequence. He set aside the packages for the gunnery officer and the provisions officer and checked the weighted bag in the corner of his cabin to be used in extreme circumstances.

He leaned back into the leather chair and rested his eyes. This was the responsibility he had been waiting for ever since he went to sea as a fourteen year old.

A sharp knock on the cabin door brought him too. "First Lieutenant here, Sir. Hands have finished lunch. Permission to stand them down till seven bells."

"Permission granted, Lieutenant." Toby answered.

"Anything else, Sir?"

"Yes, Lieutenant," Toby answered. "Evolutions at 1600 till supper time."

For the next six months, it would be the same routine each day. Swab the decks at first light, clean ship and gun drill before noon, quiet time after lunch and sail drill before supper. On each Sunday, a morning service and an impromptu concert in the afternoon. Only an occasional issue of medical comforts, agreed by the Admiral in command of the blockading fleet would ease the monotony of the routine.

Spring turned into summer, and summer into autumn as the squadron of eight ships, headed by an iron and steel gunship, the latest design without masts and sails newly off the stocks in New Jersey, ploughed up and down the eastern seaboard fifty miles north and south of Cape Hatteras, occasionally venturing as far as Charleston.

Here they would rendezvous with the southern blockade group, exchange mail, pass over new orders and code signals before trekking north and returning for water and stores under the protection of the great forts at the entrance to the Chesapeake. Toby looked at the charts and maps time and time again and wondered at the stalemate.

Richmond, the headquarters of the Confederate cause was only sixty miles away from where they were watering and storing up, the Union army was in control of the forts and ports in Pimlico Sound to the south, and still supplies were getting through. As everyone in the fleet knew the porous port was Wilmington, the graveyard of earlier Union gunboats, the home of marauding Confederate raiders and the blockade runners, those sleek paddlers that could outstrip anything afloat risking all for guns, dollars, cotton and sterling.

Toby opened up the last of the sealed letters. Earlier that day, he had been summoned to the squadron's flagship anchored in the Neuse River, south of the small town of New Bern, where four ships of the small fleet had gathered sheltering from an expected hurricane.

The Commodore was waiting for the remaining vessels to pass through the widest of the narrow gaps between the cays at first light the following day. The crew of the *Audacious,* as were those of the other ships, were using the time ferrying barrels ashore for fresh water. Anchored away from the fleet, were two transports loaded with ammunition, tinned meat, medical stores and holds full of equipment to keep the thousand men in the ships supplied with all the needs of a small town.

"How are the men faring, Lieutenant?" Toby asked his second in command, as the senior officers were gathered in the small ward room.

The glum response summed up the situation without a word said.

Throughout the summer the fleet had stopped no more than a dozen vessels, trying to slip through the defences and into the canals behind the dunes supplying the contingents of Confederates holding the hinterland.

"Not even your attempts at amusing them with chess competitions, band concerts and plays are having an impact, Captain," his senior officer had to report.

"Well," Toby announced to his officers, who crowded together, realising that he might have some encouraging news. "The Commodore has heard that General Burnside plans an assault on Wilmington this winter, and within days the fleet will be ringing Wilmington all the way from Onslow Bay in the north to Long Bay in the south. It is a good hundred miles of water to concentrate on."

"Are you going to tell the men, Captain?" the gunnery officer asked.

"Just before weighing anchor tomorrow," Toby answered. "Not that you can keep a secret on a ship."

The *USS Audacious*, just one of the small fleets of Union ships was heading south in company with its sister ship, *Britannia*. Toby smiled to himself at the name of the ship that had all the hallmarks of an imperial vessel, and wondered who had launched it.

"See anything ahead?" questioned the young ensign, as he peered over the futtock shrouds to shout at the lookout standing with his back to the mast, his teeth chattering in the damp cold of the late evening.

"What are you doing up here?" he asked as the young officer heaved his way onto the platform.

"Captain sent me up here just in case you'd fallen asleep," the young officer said.

"Not a cat's chance in hell that happening," the man answered. "When is my relief due? Two hours up here in this fog is more than enough."

"I'll send one up," the young officer answered taking to the back stay, the short way down to the deck.

"The fog's thicker up above than down here, Sir," the ensign reported on reaching the deck.

"Double up the lookouts, Lieutenant," Toby ordered, "And close up the Whitworth. I can smell the shoals. Just like the Mersey."

"The Mersey, Sir," asked the navigator engrossed in the chart.

"Where's that?"

"Somewhere I'd like to be right now," Toby answered with a soft chuckle.

"Watches changed, Sir," the ships number one reported. "All bells muffled. Gun crews standing by, sails in stops, engine on slow ahead and ready with the lead."

The *Audacious* was running down the soundings of the bank that stretched for miles.

"Where is the *Britannia*?" asked Toby leaning over the binnacle.

"Way out to starboard before the murk closed," the next most senior Lieutenant answered, reaching for the telescope.

"And you can't see a thing then?" Toby questioned.

"Not even the proverbial," came the immediate reply.

"Stop engine then and just listen. Not a word on deck now."

"Aye, aye, Sir."

The *Audacious* glided to a halt, the rigging and the decks perspiring with condensation, the men frozen in anticipation, the horizon coming and going with annoying regularity. In the distance the beat of paddles projected across the sea and mist, hiding the profile of a runner. which could have been anywhere in an arc of fifty degrees.

A man stirred, and then another, throwing off the stiffness in the tension of cold bodies in the dead of night. Away out on the starboard beam came a dull thud, the signature tune of a muzzle loading gun and a faint splash.

"There she is, just off the starboard beam," shouted an excited gunner.

"Half ahead, and fire at will," instructed Toby down the deck in the coolest voice that he could muster, moving over to the helmsman.

The Whitworth barked once, then again in short order as the mist cleared and a flash of light exploded around the sleek ship. They could see a clear mile and the side winder winged amidships, turning in a broad circle to grind up on the bank.

"Ceased firing, Sir," called out the gunner, realising that just one good shot had achieved the object of stopping the ship.

The whole crew looked on in silence as they watched the paddle steamer heel slightly, right itself and then come to a halt.

"Find me some deep water for anchoring, Navigator," Toby instructed. "It's high water. Stand-by to lower the boats. Signal to the *Britannia*. Are we outside the range of the fort guns?"

"Yes, Sir."

"Good, we got about eight hours to salvage it." Toby replied. "Tell the cook prepare for a celebratory breakfast."

The *Audacious* was moving slowly northwards, towing the disabled blockade runner towards Portsmouth dockyard giving Cape Hatteras a wide berth. They had four wounded in the sick bay and twenty more sitting dejected on deck wondering on their fate.

Toby moved through them, talking quietly to themselves and drinking welcomed cups of tea and made his way to the sick bay. He soon established that he was talking to the cook, the senior engineer and a seaman all with minor wounds.

In the corner, the ships surgeon had confirmed was a young man hanging onto life with a serious leg wound and considerable loss of blood. The man came too as he approached.

"You're the Chief officer and also the Owner I understand from the ships papers?" Toby said.

The man in the bed nodded. "Yes, I am, but I'm not the actual owner."

"Well, you'll live apparently as long as you don't get gangrene," Toby said. "We'll have you in hospital by tomorrow, but don't expect the Courts to be so accommodating."

"So you've resigned your commission, Toby," Agnatha asked her nephew sometime after the fall of Wilmington. The *Audacious* was in reserve and the last of the blockade runners were being scrapped or abandoned where they fell, or in some cases were being returned to commercial use.

"Well, it went on far longer than I expected, two and a half years altogether," he answered. 'the Navy have plenty of fresh officers all scrambling for promotion, and *Audacious* had played a good enough part.

They were sitting in her garden that just grabbed the last of the afternoon sun, before disappearing behind the buildings, which were beginning to extend skywards. The Navy had asked if he would like to lecture for another six months, but Toby had declined.

He had made a number of friends, but no real buddy and the pace of change dictated that he move on. Of Emily he had heard no more, and he shied away from writing again, even though the postal service was much improved. It was, after all, many months since their trysts on board and in New York. He thought that he might help out with his uncle's nautical college, but knew that eventually he would take passage back to England.

"Why don't you stay here over the summer then, Toby," Agnatha pressed. "Uncle needs help from time to time and you could travel right up to Canada. There's no better coast for sailing in protected waters and winding down generally whilst you work out the way ahead."

"Talking of Canada, Aunt," Toby said, "You never really elaborated on what you were doing at Niagara Falls and in Cincinnati."

"I was coming to that," she answered, "now that the war is over."

"It's a long story then," Toby suggested.

"Well, it's still going on but not with quite the same intensity," she said, "I was invited to several meetings here in New York and in Massachusetts. and there was a lady in Boston who organised the onward travel from the State of Ohio and onto Canada. I never met the lady, but her late husband was a wealthy doctor and each season she organised a ship to get these people to safety.

"I set up the travel agency, which had two purposes of course. Oddly enough it did tremendous legitimate business a well. I now have an English lady running it for me, but as the business is being passed on to somebody local shortly she will soon be staying here on her way home. You'll like her I think."

"That's a lot to take in, Aunt," Toby said. "You must deserve a medal."

"Like you, Toby," she said, taking in the chairs as the sun dipped leaving a shadow. "It was just something that needed to be done."

Chapter 21

"All stand in Court for the Judge," the attendant shouted as the door opened, and a solemn middled aged man made his way to the highest position in the room.

There were only a dozen people in the room. James was in attendance with his uncle, having said goodbye to his charges over breakfast and not expecting to see them again.

"Hope it all goes well, James," his headmaster said the previous evening over a last drink. "You're welcome here any time. It's been an excellent furlough for you at a difficult time. But it shouldn't have gone on so long."

"Mr Forwood, Mr James Forwood," the Judge called out as James got to his feet, leaving the rest in the courtroom listening and writing.

"Yes, Sir."

"What have you got to say to us about running your ship into our country for the past eighteen months, contrary to our navigation rules and providing support to those wishing to usurp our constitution."

"Nothing, Sir."

"Not to mention providing the means to slaughter innocent people going about their own business."

"I apologise, Sir."

"And what would say if I deport you here and now with an instruction not to return for two years."

"Nothing, Sir, apart from hoping that you do not take that line of action." James replied.

The Judge looked down at his papers and then up, his eyes behind his steel rimmed glasses giving away no hint of his decision. He nodded to the clerk and passed over a piece of paper.

"Fined 500 hundred dollars and two hundred for costs," the Judge thundered. "For breach of Federal Laws. Case dismissed."

"Thank you, Sir," a relieved James stammered.

"Lucky that you weren't deported in the end," uncle declared as they headed for the nearest bar, "You know that you can join the Atlas Line if you wish. We've room for a junior partner."

"Maybe I'll go home first," James said, "It's been a long while and I've memories here that are so mixed."

"I understand that, James," the elder replied "Incidentally a letter arrived yesterday, from Wilmington. It could be good news of course, but if nothing else it will give you closure."

James looked at the letter, turned it over and back again, not daring to open it. Clearly it had passed the censor without being tampered with, but then he had heard that the two post office services were now one. He looked intently at the handwriting, which he didn't recognise, but it was clearly a woman's hand.

He put it down on the table and then carefully took his uncles letter knife and slowly slid the letter out, never taking his eyes off the folded sheet, until he laid it flat down with trembling hands It was only a week old and he noticed that the signature was that of her mother He scanned it as quickly as a lawyer would a brief.

Dear James,

It has taken me a little time to compose this letter and I am sure that you would have hoped that it was in Carolyn's hand. You see she was seriously burned on the hands and arms whilst escaping from the ship and it will be some time before she fully recovers and is able to write herself. She is still in hospital and will be for a few more weeks. She is desperate to see you, speak to you and hold you and hopes upon hope that you are not deported and will visit her soon.

Yours on behalf of my daughter

Doreen Rogers

"Are you alright, James," came the voice of the elder man, as he heard his nephew slump into the nearest chair.

"Yes," James said heaving a sigh of relief, "I won't be going home just yet. Can I take up your offer?"

"So you left your sister in the wilds of America with some pipsqueak stray youngster whilst you just carried on," George questioned his elder son. "Was that a good idea, Nicholas?"

They were sitting in the offices in Dale street, where Nicholas was spreading out details of the contacts he had made in the Mississippi delta, for when the conflict ended.

"There's absolutely no chance getting cotton out down the river as we discovered and the Union has the Gulf of Mexico bottled up," Nicholas answered. "So it made good sense just to carry on."

"But what about Alice?" George argued. "You should have insisted they carry on with you."

"Alice was determined to continue and once she met up with the Mrs Turner in Cincinnati, it appears she found the cause that she was looking for." Nicholas outlined. "She's now helping the lady in her travel agency and intends to stay sometime, according to the letter I received in New York just before leaving."

"And what sort of travel agency is that," George pressed sarcastically. "Hardly likely for tours on the north west passage."

"Actually, helping fleeing slaves escape to Canada," said Nicholas, standing up for his sister in her absence.

"Well, I have something to say to her in due course," George retorted. "That is unless she marries some damn Yankee."

"Have you heard from James?" Nicholas asked his father when he had calmed down. "I tried a couple of times to make contact, but it just wasn't possible."

"He's done a number of successful trips, but is expecting to lay up during the autumn for six weeks or so." George confirmed. "We've lost one of our other boats, stranded at Charleston, but so far it's been worthwhile."

"So we lost the cargo and the ship then," Nicholas questioned.

"Well, some losses were to be expected," George had to agree. "At least all of the crew survived. The ship was put up for auction, but I decided against bidding for it. The captain was fined and the Authorities offered the crew to switch sides and bugger me they did en bloc."

"So much for loyalty then," Nicholas stated, and then realised the stupidity of the statement and continued. "Why should the common seaman not accept an opportunity to benefit from a situation where money was to be made."

George huffed, poured a whisky out from the cabinet and sat down. After all wasn't he, his family and the Company doing just that.

"But we are in profit, Father?" Nicholas continued.

"Oh, yes," confirmed George, "but it's time to withdraw whilst the going is good. I'm proposing to the Board that we look at transhipping fresh fruit from the Canary Islands. There's good trade in both directions and passengers as well."

Nicholas nodded. For all his bluffness his father worked ahead of most people that he knew.

"Now, you'd better look at this letter from James," he said, passing over the bulky contents of a letter from America. "He's waiting on parole in New York on a charge of violating their laws and may well come home a different man. I'm not quite certain how your mother will take it."

"So the *Fannie* was stranded in the end," Nicholas asked.

"Unfortunately, yes. They were surprised coming out of Wilmington on probably the last voyage," George confirmed.

"So we lost two out of three ships in two years then, Father?" Nicholas asked.

"Yes, but that was a better record than most apparently," George answered.

"And it was still worth it, Father?" Nicholas questioned.

"I'm checking with the accountants, but it would appear that it was very worthwhile," George replied looking at the quarterly results.

"I'm not so sure that any war is worthwhile," Nicholas stated, "And I'm sure James and Alice would agree."

Chapter 22

"Toby, come and meet Alice, the girl who has been so helpful to me the past nine months, well almost a year I suppose if you think about it," Agnatha said. "She's staying with me for a while before she goes home. I've suggested that she looks at New England before she returns to Old England."

Toby had taken a break from teaching navigation and they were sitting in Agnatha's lounge keeping warm from a chilly February day. General Bragg's army had fled Wilmington and were on the run back to Richmond and the Union Navy had secured all of the eastern seaboard.

"Did you get round to meeting Isabel Nugent?" Agnatha asked Alice, throwing another log on the fire. "It wouldn't have been too much of a deviation on your way here."

"No, I decided against it," Alice replied, "It's something I ought to try and forget."

"Maybe, but I think she'd be delighted in meeting you," Agnatha assured the other, "I guess she'll be back in Boston as soon as the ice beaks and her ship comes home. If you take the train that way you'll find it a delightful city."

"I'd agree with that," Toby said, "I spent my initial training there."

"What sort of training?" Alice asked immediately interested in the man opposite her with a military bearing, but displaying the more relaxed casual attitude of a civilian sailor.

"I'd be delighted to tell you more," Toby replied leaning forward, slightly tense at the thought of spending some time alone with the girl that was firing his imagination. "But you'll have to tell me about this Isabel Nugent I've heard so much about."

Agnatha smiled to herself, trying to hide her relief at the animated conversation between them, and concluded that with a bit of help neither of them would be travelling back to England in the short term.

"I've a weekend free," Toby announced to his aunt bounding in from the college and his bedsit a couple of days later. "Have you any idea where Alice is?"

"I believe that she has gone to see her uncle at the Atlas Line offices," Agnatha answered. "Didn't she tell you that her brother had an accident on a ship, and she is trying to find which hospital he is in."

"No, she's hardly told me anything apart from her Mississippi voyage and meeting you." James replied.

"She will, I'm sure, but give her time," Agnatha soothed. "Like you this war has had an effect that only time will unravel."

"My brother is fine, improving, but not free to move about," Alice announced to Agnatha and Toby on her return. "He's about to spend some time teaching in New Jersey."

"What was he doing over here, Alice?" asked Toby still rather perplexed at not getting the full story.

"Much the same as my other brother," Alice replied, as both Agnatha and Toby looked on. "Looking after the family business. Which reminds me I must write home to my parents and tell them how he is."

"I think it is time that I booked my passage home," Toby said to his aunt on hearing that Jefferson Davis had finally admitted defeat. "I don't expect that I will get my old job back, but then I'm not sure I would accept even if it was offered."

"Why don't you talk to Uncle over supper," she replied. "He's always full of good ideas."

"I'll see what he comes up with," Toby agreed.

"It's not a good thing to go over old ground in any case," Agnatha replied. "Find a new venture, something to enthuse over, and how about finding a girlfriend or wife. Why, you're nearly thirty if my arithmetic is right."

"I'll give it some thought," he answered, realising that Agnatha was probably right.

"Then do," Agnatha said, "before you miss the pick of the bunch."

Alice returned from yet another visit to her brother without saying a great deal to either Agnatha or Toby, other than that his ordeal would soon be over.

"I've booked my ticket home," Toby announced very matter-of-factly as the four sat around, the men playing chess; Agnatha sewing and Alice writing a letter to Jane in Hamilton.

Alice looked up having finished her letter. "Toby, could we have a day out then? Tomorrow should be nice. I want to show you something at the top end of

Manhattan. It's only two stops from Grand Central station and we could take lunch and maybe have tea out."

"You are full of secrets, Alice," Toby said, "but yes I will come with you. I've never been beyond the park."

Agnatha looked at her husband and nodded, with the slightest movement of her head and getting the merest of responses.

"Check mate, Toby, I believe," he said moving his queen into an unassailable position, at which Toby toppled his king and accepted a nightcap to take his leave back to the bedsit room.

Toby looked back to Alice, who was sealing the letter. "It's an early start then Alice. The American way."

Alice took Toby by the hand and steered him through the crowds onto the right platform. "It's only ten minutes or so away and then a bit of a walk. I've been there before and it's so enchanting."

"What is it then," Toby asked, with no idea where she was leading him.

"It's a bridge," she said arching her fingers together. "I love them and it's the only one in New York would you believe. Come on or we'll miss the next train."

"Why do you love bridges, Alice?" He called out as they raced out of the station to see the magnificent arch rising across the Harlem River.

"It's because they join people together, linking and not severing, and this one carries water, which is the lifeblood for all of us," Alice said, facing him desperate for a kiss, but realising that he was going to be hard work.

"Can we walk across it?" Toby asked as they mounted the cast iron stairway bolted to the stonework of the abutments.

"Well, I did before," Alice answered. "It links up with the Bronx."

They were in the middle of the great cast iron arch, looking a hundred feet down at miniature boats in the river and people scurrying around on the shores, the water of the canal bubbling along gently by their feet.

"Apart from a lovely day out, Alice, why did you really bring me out here?" Toby asked looking at the horizon.

Alice faltered and then rushed out with the words. "Well, your aunt told me of your love for a girl that you met on your ship and that you've never seen since, and how you joined the Union navy in an effort to forget her."

"Yes, I suppose I did," Toby agreed, turning to see an Alice at her most seriousness, as she turned to look down at the water. "It was probably the thing to do. I couldn't get to her and realised it was an impossible situation, and unlike your brothers I wanted to help the side I believed in."

"And I didn't really like what they were doing either, and it was a blessing in disguise that I found Jane and then your aunt." Alice admitted. "It will probably cause the most endless of rows when I get home."

"And when you get home, will you leave here thinking that it was all worthwhile," Toby asked leaning on the balustrade a good stride away from his companion.

"Yes, apart from a burning secret that will live with me for the rest of my life, and that I can share with no one except Agnatha," Alice blurted.

"And you can't tell anyone?" he asked.

"No," she said, wiping away a tear.

For some reason, Toby found that she had taken a step towards him and thrown her arms around his waist.

"Did you love that girl?" she asked burying her head in his shoulder. "I mean a love like no other?"

"Yes, I would have gone to the ends of the earth. I tried actually," he said, his voice tailing away, "and I failed of course, but not for the want of effort. It was an impossible situation."

"But what if she came around the corner right now?" Alice asked, almost demanding a reply.

"I don't know," Toby protested. "It was almost three years ago and I was told that she ended up ill and sick."

Alice put up her hood and stepped away crestfallen with disappointment. It was not what she wanted to hear, but she refused to give up. They had been on the bridge for a good hour.

"Do you think that you could love again?" she pleaded almost in desperation.

"I suppose I could," he said. "I'm sure, thinking about it."

"And could that person be me?" Alice asked placing her hands on his cheeks and pulling him towards her, willing him to give the right answer. "Cos I've loved you ever since I cast eyes on you."

"Yes," Toby said, smothering her in a deep kiss and cuddle that seemed to last for ever. "But I can't go down on one knee. I might fall in the water."

Alice laughed, the tension in her body released, swinging him round and whacking him playfully with her parasol. "Can we go back on a boat? It would be so much fun."

"But you realise I have no prospects," Toby said soberly as they walked back to dry land. "I've no job and I share a house with my father and I haven't seen him for nearly four years."

"But he's still at sea, isn't he?" Alice asked.

"I'm not sure," Toby answered. "The last letter I had from him indicated that he was looking for a career ashore, like most seafarers having been tossed around the oceans for goodness knows how many years."

"And you, Toby," she said stopping and offering herself for a kiss. "You've had command for a good year and that's luckier than most at your age, Agnatha tells me."

"You'll have to work hard at that, Alice," Toby suggested with a twinkle in his eye.

"How about this for a start," she replied pulling him closer.

They marched arm in arm to the station and waited for the next train, huddled on the nearest seat drinking hot chocolate, then noticed a sign for the ferry to lower Manhattan. A porter slotted in a departure board. The next boat was leaving shortly.

"Come on," Alice suggested dragging Toby by the arm, "It'll save us a cab for those forty streets and we could even stop off at Blackwell's island."

"You certainly know your way around, Alice," he said as the boat moved away from the quay.

"That's all down to Agnatha," she replied. "But I don't want to live here all the same."

"Neither do I," Toby said, "although I do like the expanse of the country."

"I just wonder," Alice mused. "But you'll have to tell me again that you could love me."

"What's that? he whispered, looking deep into her blue eyes and confirming his devotion.

"Well, In my father's last letter he wants to set up a new company trading fresh fruit from the Canaries." Alice said. "They've already leased a warehouse in the London docks."

"But what if he doesn't approve of me," Toby protested.

"But I'm sure that he will," she said, nibbling his ear and biting the lobe. "And I know my mother will welcome you with open arms.

"How is that?" he asked.

"You see," she admitted. "I've knowledge of a family secret that has lay dormant for far too long. I might just have to blackmail him a little. I'll tell you when we have our first son."

Toby thought for a moment. "Our first son, I'm not so sure about any of that." he said as Alice looked up in alarm.

"Why?" she said.

"Well," Toby said, as she searched him for a reason. "Not long into my last tour on *Audacious,* I captured a blockade runner off Wilmington. We ran it up on the sandbank. I can't remember the name of the owner, who was aboard. It's months ago now, but something has been bugging me, because I'm sure that he said that he had a girlfriend in the port, and that he had a sister that was travelling the Mississippi."

"And," she said.

"Could that sister be you?" Toby asked, looking right into her eyes.

Alice smiled then kissed him. "Agnatha always wondered, but never said anything. But there's one more thing I have to do, and I want you to do it with me. It will square the circle."

"What's that," he asked.

"Come with me to meet Isabel Nugent."

Chapter 23

Isabel reclined on the wicker chair that swung lazily from the tree above her head. The leaves were unfolding by the day and shielding her from the spring sun, which was percolating through with increasing warmth. She rose slightly unsteadily, and wandered around the quayside of the Welland canal waiting for a ship to arrive, her ship, the one that she had paid for to bring a cargo of escaped slaves from across the border.

Thirty of them, she had been told, were hidden in the hold of the ship, squeezed in between the general cargo of foodstuffs from the little port of Sandusky at the far end of Lake Erie. The snow and ice of the hard winter had gone and it was the first trip of the season for the little steamer which throughout the winter had been laid up at the end of the canal, the crew employed in logging and the building of the town just a few miles away.

The ship had left St Catharine's two weeks earlier, as soon as the ice had broken. In the past few months, Isabel and Molly had become part of the community, frozen in between the two lakes, the canal and the mighty Falls, attending the numerous meetings and church services where they raised funds, and made plans for sending on the many escapees they expected in 1865. They would spread out across the isthmus into Ontario and beyond.

Isabel watched as Molly in her new position as companion, had developed in confidence from a reticent servant to a talkative, vibrant individual and felt somewhat a little ashamed that she had not seen her potential back in Boston. Whilst Isabel was often deep in discussions with the two shipowners in the town, the mayor and the council, Molly was drawn to the men that were making a new hospital in the outskirts and a hostel for the new arrivals. Every afternoon she would come back wrapped up against the cold, full of their talk, their skills and the tools that they were using.

"Isabel," she said shyly, one afternoon after trying her hand at skating.

They were sitting on the veranda of the small house on the edge of the town, which Isabel had rented during the winter, drinking hot chocolate, watching the clouds scud across the sky.

"Yes, Molly," she answered knowing that she was about to be surprised yet again by the girls growing confidence.

"I was wondering," she said, stirring her drink for the third time before she spoke. "I was talking to one of the crew of the first ship out this spring."

"And why not, Molly," Isabel said. "St Catharine's is a very friendly place and I have made good friends too."

"Well," Molly said finally plucking up courage. "I'd like to go on the first voyage this year, the one that you are paying for. To help the cook."

Isabel turned away, a tear in her eye, as she realised that she could be losing her companion, not for just two weeks, but maybe for ever.

"I was wondering when that request was coming," she said rising to her feet and fleeing indoors to be by herself. "Of course, of course. Go and enjoy yourself."

Isabel was not there when the steamer fired up and left the quay, pushing its way through the last of the sheet ice, into the waters of the lake. Some of the townsfolk had gathered on the quay, but she preferred to stay with her friends, knowing that when the ship returned there would be much rejoicing in two weeks' time, when she could join in.

She felt tired, but relieved that at last her journey life was having a real purpose. Having said goodbye from the clapboard cottage, somewhat disappointed that Isabel did not want to wave her off on the quayside. Molly contented herself, busying herself on board and waving to her new found friends From the bridge of the three hatch steamer, well-wishers gathered to wish the crew a safe voyage, before streaming ashore just as the gangway was lifted.

Lazy smoke from the thin cigarette shaped funnel developed into clouds of smut bursting into the chill air, and the shrill whistle indicated all was ready. Around the dock and into the canal, men smashed the last of the thinning sheets of ice with long poles and a thick rope snaked across the dock ready to pull the *S.S. Saviour* clear. Within minutes the propeller was biting into the mush of ice and water as it turned westwards, the whistle sounding a final goodbye.

Molly cheered at the crowds, some who were intent on trailing down the canal towpath as the coaster gradually disappeared in to the distance. In no time at all, a wired message reached the council chambers that the ship had reached America safely, and that the cargo was being loaded for the homeward voyage. The Captain expected that the Lake steamer *Saviour* would be back in Canada with a full load of goods, passengers and an unknown number of relieved slaves, just happy to rest their bodies on any part of the ship.

From her vantage point on a small rise of land, Isabel watched the ship close the port becoming ever bigger from a tiny speck to almost filling her vision. Flags were streaming from two masts and on the quayside the harbour master was flying the flags of the two countries.

An armada of small boats was escorting the ship in and the whistle was sounded with unerring regularity, scattering the gulls that were searching for the scraps. Crowds were gathering to greet the vessel to all intends and purposes just another cargo ship. The mayor and chairman of the welcoming Canadian Government committee had invited Isabel over to the quayside.

"I will join you in the Town Hall later," she said. "I prefer to watch from a distance."

On deck there seemed to be much laughter as the crew laid out the gangway and the passengers hugged each other. Isabel took off her glasses and laid them down alongside her book and shielded her eyes from the sun. Everything seemed to be in slow motion.

Her heart skipped a beat as a flash of memory seared across her befuddled mind of a previous disembarkation, when people, slaves of course she recalled, were pushed, manhandled or dragged off the ship before falling on the ground and weeping continuously, before being finally marched away. It also wasn't like the orderly disembarkation she had seen of passenger ships in Boston harbour, when immigrants from Europe had filed off the gangways and also got down on their knees and prayed.

The passengers of the *Saviour* were both laughing and crying; hollering and dancing; kissing and cuddling as they danced down the gangway, some of them just jumping over the rail in sheer joy, The former slaves fell to the ground weeping and kissing the soil and tearing at the grass with both hands.

Isabel looked again through the mist of her vision. It wasn't quite as she recalled. She shook her head, pushed her fingers through her greying hair and tried to focus.

Towards her was coming Molly, hanging on to the arm of a young man and looking up into his eyes. He was carrying a leather case, the sort that her husband was never seen without. Molly was laughing, her hair flicking in the breeze, her body swaying in an easy motion as they came across the lawn towards her.

Screwing up her eyes again, Isabel felt chilly although the sun was warm on her back. She rose unsteadily from the chair and then sat back.

"This is Doctor Smeaton," Molly said in excitement, looking at Isabel, and expecting a cheerful response. "He has to examine every new entry before they leave America for Canada on behalf of the government."

"Did you hear, Mam?" Molly said, dropping to her knees realising that something was just not right. "Mam, Isabel speaks to me."

Isabel gurgled deep in her throat, coughed and fell back into the arms of the chair as if she was a rag doll.

"Molly," the doctor said, gripping the now sobbing girl by the shoulders, immediately realising the situation. "It's time, I think, to say goodbye to her," he continued throwing off his coat, wrapping it around Isabel and kneeling beside the girl. "And I so wanted to ask permission from her to look after you."

Molly lifted the bottom corner of his great coat and buried her head into the hem, then sobbed until she could cry no more. She hadn't known it just then, but Isabel had ensured that she was safe, safe forever.

From Isabel's right hand dangled the little talisman pennywhistle that she had treasured all her life.